Praise for the novels of *New York Times* bestselling author
Erica Spindler

THE FIRST WIFE

"[A] heated romantic thriller . . . strong personalities make for some wonderfully tense revelations."

—*Publishers Weekly*

"Spindler hooks readers into her latest . . . the mystery is engaging." —*RT Book Reviews*

"This one had me stumped. You think one thing but then it takes a turn you never saw coming. Erica Spindler is a master, her stories will always take you for a ride and never do they disappoint. If you are ever looking for a good-to-honest thriller, look no further than this one or any of Erica Spindler's novels." —*A Southern Girl's Bookshelf*

JUSTICE FOR SARA

"As Kat's investigation deepens, risks multiply; knotted threads, inevitably about money, gradually untangle; and Spindler suspensefully strips away layers of deceit and guilt, revealing years of secrets and silences. Diverting and entertaining." —*Booklist*

"A twenty-seven-year-old woman's quest to uncover the truth behind her sister's murder propels this spine-tingling romantic thriller . . . With red herrings aplenty, Spindler keeps the reader guessing until the last page."

—*Publishers Weekly*

"Spindler's chilling novels explore our deepest fear—that danger is closer than we think. She is a master of addictive suspense."

—Lisa Gardner, #1 *New York Times* bestselling author

"Not only a chilling, close-to-home suspense filled with riveting flashbacks, it's also the story of a complex and compelling relationship between sisters. The emotions and revelations drew me right in and kept me hooked."

—Andrea Kane, *New York Times* bestselling author
of *The Line Between Here and Gone*

"Justice for Sara is a tour-de-force novel of suspense—a small-town murder with a big city twist. Spindler's pitch-perfect characters and elegant plotting propel the story, and you'll stay up all night reading and beg for more. This is Spindler at her very best: deep, dark, and daring."

—J.T. Ellison, bestselling author of *Edge of Black*

"Spindler's latest does a fantastic job of switching viewpoints and time periods, unraveling the mystery and revealing long-held secrets. The cast of suspects is unique and entertaining, and the small-town setting has an atmospheric quality that ramps up the tension."

—*RT Book Reviews* (4½ stars / Top Pick)

BLOOD VINES

"A pulse-pounding, page-turning, absolutely can't-put-it-down roller-coaster ride of a read! Get ready to stay up all night."

—#1 *New York Times* bestselling author Lisa Gardner

"Blood Vines is as mysterious and delicious as a fine cabernet . . . TOP-NOTCH SUSPENSE."

—Linda Castillo, *New York Times*
bestselling author of *Sworn to Silence*

"A fast-paced, intense story that's hard to put down."

—*RT Book Reviews* (4 stars)

BREAKNECK

"SPINE-TINGLING."   *—Star Magazine*

"A GRIPPING STORY that unfolds with breakneck speed, heart-quickening suspense, and characters you can't help but root for."   *—Bookreporter.com*

"TOP PICK! Filled with well-developed, multidimensional characters, Spindler's latest boasts fast-paced action and emotional tension . . . The intricately woven plot makes this novel a sure winner for readers who like to keep guessing all the way to the end."   *—RT Book Reviews*

"A MUST-READ. In this gripping new thriller, we are introduced to a tough, new detective duo set to take the crime fiction world by storm . . . a great read."
           —Evening Telegraph (UK)

"BREAKNECK SUSPENSE . . . *Breakneck* is a taut thriller, which proves Erica Spindler is still a master of suspense. With adrenaline-fused prose, you will find yourself sitting up into the wee hours unable to put the book down until you reach the very last page."
           —Ulster Tatler (Ireland)

"A FIRST-CLASS THRILLING READ . . . *Breakneck* grabs the interest immediately and never lets go. This is a timely and enthralling piece of work, and has a message for all computer users."   *—Fresh Fiction Review*

"Erica Spindler never disappoints . . . *Breakneck* literally moves at breakneck speed."   *—ReadertoReader.com*

Also by Erica Spindler

THE FIRST WIFE

ERICA SPINDLER

St. Martin's Paperbacks

This is a work of fiction. All of the characters, organizations, and events portrayed in this novel are either products of the author's imagination or are used fictitiously.

THE FIRST WIFE

Copyright © 2015 by Erica Spindler.

All rights reserved.

For information address St. Martin's Press, 175 Fifth Avenue, New York, NY 10010.

Library of Congress Catalog Card Number: 2014033634

ISBN: 978-1-250-06975-7

Our books may be purchased in bulk for promotional, educational, or business use. Please contact your local bookseller or the Macmillan Corporate and Premium Sales Department at 1-800-221-7945, ext. 5442, or by e-mail at MacmillanSpecialMarkets@macmillan.com.

Printed in the United States of America

St. Martin's Press hardcover edition / February 2015
St. Martin's Paperbacks edition / August 2016

St. Martin's Paperbacks are published by St. Martin's Press, 175 Fifth Avenue, New York, NY 10010.

10 9 8 7 6 5 4 3 2 1

To my family: the one I was born into and the one I've acquired.
Love you.

ACKNOWLEDGMENTS

Horses. Horse country. Showing, riding, training. Barns, tack, horsespeak. All completely foreign to me. Thanks to the many who opened their farms and stables, sharing not only their knowledge, but their love of these magnificent animals and the unique lifestyle of the horseman/woman. My eyes and heart have been opened.

Francie Stirling, owner, trainer and barn manager, Stirling Farm: Thanks for your time, sharing your stories and my introduction to dressage. Your beautiful farm and training facility inspired much of *The First Wife*'s fictional Abbott Farm.

Richard Freeman, owner and stable manager, Oak Hill Ranch. Thanks to you and Sara for allowing me access to your world class breeding facility and champion warmbloods. It was an experience I'll never forget.

Regina Milliken, assistant stable manager/trainer, Oak Hill Ranch. You were amazing—and amazingly patient. Thank you for all the time, your stories and allowing me a glimpse into the life of a true horsewoman.

Brooke Posey, young horsewoman extraordinaire, for letting me experience a show day through your eyes. Thanks also to Marie Rudd, for setting it up, and

Kathleen Posey, owner, Serenity Farm, for allowing me to spend the day in the barn soaking up the pre-show energy.

Sunny Francois, Louisiana Horse Rescue Association, for an insider's introduction to Louisiana horse country. Thanks to Jean Lotz, AAUW, for the introduction.

Lynda Byrne, for having me out to your place and arranging my "hands-on" research experience. To riding instructor Catherine Insley, Over the Moon Farm, and her gentle retired polo pony Tesoro.

On to the criminal mind . . .

Huge thanks to behavioral neurologist—and writer—Thomas Krefft, M.D., Northlake Neurological Institute, for information on traumatic memory loss.

Bill Moran, ex-cop and hunting enthusiast, for information on shotguns, rifles, and hunting accidents.

Folsom, Louisiana, police department for the look around and answered questions. I dropped in uninvited, interrupted your lunch and you didn't shoot me—appreciate it, guys!

Captain George Bonnett, St. Tammany Parish Sheriff's Office, for the tour and the many insights.

Personal appreciation:

For Sirens Nicole Grace, Trista Hook and Amanda LaPier for allowing me to "kill" them. And to all my Sirens for the love.

Editor Jennifer Weis and the amazing SMP crew; Agent Scott Miller, Trident Media Group; Assistant (and friend) Peg Campos; and my writing gal-pals, J. T. Ellison and Alex Kava.

And finally, gratitude to my family for loving me—even when I'm on deadline—and my gracious God, for the gifts.

PROLOGUE

Friday, April 18, 2014
3:31 A.M.

Bailey Abbott's eyes cracked open. Light, so bright it stung. Pain. Her head and neck. Throbbing. She told herself to cry out, but no sound came.

Where was she?

A soft hum and ping, coming from somewhere nearby. Bailey shifted her gaze. She lay in a bed. Stainless steel rails. Clear plastic tubing that led up to a sack of liquid. The hum she'd detected from a monitor near the bed.

Hospital. The realization whispered across her thoughts as her eyes closed once more.

7:26 A.M.

The sound of voices drew Bailey back. Men's voices. She tried to open her eyes, but her lids refused to raise.

"Why hasn't she come to, Dr. Bauer?"

Urgency in the voice.

"I understand how upsetting this must be for you, but you have to be patient. Mrs. Abbott suffered a traumatic brain injury, right now she's doing exactly what she should be doing. Healing."

Brain injury? Who were they talking about? Not her. Surely.

She longed to tell them, to get their attention, but her body refused to respond to her thoughts.

"Give me something, Dr. Bauer. Please. I'll settle for an educated guess. Anything to hold on to."

"What I see looks very good. Judging by your wife's level of consciousness, the way she's responding to stimuli, her TBI is mild. It could have been so much worse."

Mrs. Abbott . . . Your wife . . .

Logan . . .

The voices dimmed. Bailey tried to grab on to something solid, but the dark rose up and dragged her back.

10:20 A.M.

Bailey became aware of voices. Jarring. Angry.

"What do you expect from me, Billy Ray? She was riding and got knocked off. That's all I know."

"Rodriquez is dead."

"That has nothing to do with her. The sheriff's detectives said—"

"She had a lot of blood on her, Abbott."

"You're telling me? I was the one who found her."

"That's right, you were."

"Which means what?"

Barely controlled fury. It frightened her.

"Like I said, it was a lot of blood."

"She busted her head open. It bled."

"Maybe it wasn't all hers?"

"What are you going to suggest next? That she shot Rodriquez? Or, wait for it, that Bailey's accident is mysteriously connected to—"

"True's disappearance."

"For God's sake! Give it a rest."

"So, let me take a look around your property."

"You're out of your mind."

"What are you trying to hide?"

"Get a warrant, you crazy son of a bitch."

"What's going on in here!"

A woman's voice. Hushed but furious.

"You'll have to leave, Officer. Family only."

Officer . . . something she . . . tell him . . .

"Fine. But know this: Abbott, as soon as she's awake, she's mine."

"That's a thing with you, isn't it, Billy Ray? Wanting what's mine?"

Important . . . now, before it was too . . .

But then the silent place swallowed her once more.

10:36 P.M.

A deep, rhythmic rumbling. It wormed its way through the fog, wrapping around her and drawing her out of her soft cocoon. Bailey's lids lifted. The dimly lit room came into focus. Sterile and unwelcoming.

She shifted her gaze in the direction of the rumble. A dark-haired man in an armchair. Asleep.

Handsome. Strong jaw, dark with several days' worth of stubble. Too tall and broad to sleep comfortably in the chair.

Logan.

She whimpered. The sound echoed in her head, like the heavy clang of a bell. His soft snoring stopped and he sat straight up.

"Bailey?" He was on his feet, beside the bed. "Baby, are you awake?"

She shrank back. Into the bedding, then deeper yet, back into her safe cocoon.

Saturday, April 19
5:24 A.M.

Light broke through. Stingingly bright. "This way!" it seemed to call. "Here to safety."

Bailey resisted. This was the safe place. Soft and close. Protected. But the light beckoned, insistent. Sound with it. And a tingling sensation, as if her entire being had come back to life.

Resistance proved futile. She ran toward the sound and light, hands outstretched.

Bailey opened her eyes and said his name.

PART ONE

CHAPTER ONE

Three Months Earlier
Grand Cayman

"Do you believe in fate, Bailey Browne?" he asked. "That two people can be destined to meet?"

They sat side by side on the beach, she and this handsome stranger she had spent the past eight hours with. The most unexpected, exciting and romantic hours of her entire life.

She turned to meet his dark, intent gaze. She should tell him she thought such notions silly. Play it cool and sophisticated. But cool and sophisticated weren't her style.

"Yes, I believe it," she said, voice husky. "What about you, Logan Abbott?"

He hesitated, a hint of vulnerability coming into his expression. "I didn't. Not until . . ."

Tonight. Until you.

The words hung unspoken in the air between them. Heady. Tantalizing.

They had been fated to meet.

He found her hand, laced their fingers. "Have you ever seen the sun rise over the Caribbean?"

"Never." She rested her head against his shoulder. "It's beautiful?"

"The most beautiful. You could stay and watch it with me?"

"Okay." Bailey tipped her head so she could see his strong profile. "You've seen a lot of sunrises, haven't you?"

"All over the world."

"Have you ever seen it rise over a Nebraska cornfield?"

He laughed. "As a matter of fact, I haven't."

Bailey liked the sound of his laugh, deep and raspy, like a growl. She snuggled closer to his side. "You might want to put it at the top of your list," she teased. "It's pretty spectacular."

He brought her hand to his mouth and kissed her palm. "Only if you promise to watch it with me?"

She could lose herself in this moment, Bailey realized. In the sound of his voice, the feel of his lips against her skin.

Simply slip away. Disappear forever.

"I promise," she whispered, and he drew her with him down to the sand.

Bailey studied him while he slept. They hadn't made love. They'd watched the sunrise, then come back to her room and slept, wrapped in each other's arms.

He took her breath away, he was so handsome. Dark hair and light green eyes, classically sculpted features, beautifully shaped mouth. Mysterious, she thought. The tortured hero of novels. Wounded deeply by someone special to him. Waiting for just the right woman, the one who could make him whole again.

Were all women as hopelessly romantic as she? Bailey wondered, fighting the urge to trail a finger over his chiseled lips. Drawn to the very thing that would eventually destroy them?

He opened his eyes. His mouth tilted into the small, lazy smile she already loved. "Good morning."

"You were sleeping so peacefully, I didn't want to wake you."

"I wasn't sleeping."

Heat stung her cheeks. "You were!"

"Nope." He laughed. "Playing possum."

She gave in and trailed a finger over his perfect mouth. "So you could tease me?"

His smile faded. "Because I didn't want this moment to end."

Inexplicably, tears stung her eyes. She blinked against them, feeling foolish.

"Don't," he said.

"What?"

"Try to hide from me. I want to know everything about you, Bailey Browne."

"I've already told you everything."

"Hardly." He cupped her face in his hands. "Why the tears?"

"Is this real?" She searched his gaze. "It's as if my dreams have conjured you, our meeting. All of it."

"I promise you, I'm real." He laid her hand over his heart. "Feel it beating."

She did and pressed closer. Thoughts of her mother swamped her. Her hopes and hurts, dreams and disappointments. Many of them for her daughter. Bailey had told him about her mother's illness, her passing. How much it hurt.

Bailey lifted her eyes to his. "I took this trip as a way to celebrate my mother's life. To honor her by . . . really living. Does that make sense?"

He combed his fingers through her hair. "It does. Completely."

A smile touched her mouth. "And here you are."

"And so are you."

"It's hard losing someone you love."

"But they're never really gone. Not if you truly loved them. They leave a little piece of themselves. Here."

He laid his hand on her breast. She wondered if he felt her heart leap at his touch.

"And what of you?" she asked thickly. "Who have you loved and lost?"

"Everyone," he said simply.

In that moment, with that one revealing word, she fell completely, irrevocably in love with him.

Before she could respond, he kissed her. She kissed him back and there, with the sun streaming through the blinds, they made love for the first time.

They sat across from each other at a small table at the thatched-roof cabana bar. A Bob Marley tune playing. Fruity drinks with tiny, paper umbrellas. Women in bikinis and see-through cover-ups. Exotic, beautiful women.

And every one of them had noticed him. Several had openly flirted, as if she weren't even there. As if recognizing, as Bailey did, that he was way out of her league.

Self-doubt swamped her and she leaned toward him. "Why are you with me?"

He looked annoyed. "Why would you ask that?"

"Why do you think? You could have any woman in this room. On this beach, for that matter. Why me?"

"You're the only woman I want."

His words, the way his gaze dropped to her mouth, thrilled. Even as the chill bumps raced up her arms, warning bells sounded in her head.

She silenced them. "You look like that character from the show *Mad Men*."

He cocked an eyebrow, obviously amused. "Don Draper?"

"That's the one. You've been told that before, haven't you?"

He shrugged. "People see what they want to see."

"And what do you see when you look at me?"

"Not Don Draper."

She laughed, liking his sudden moments of humor. "God, I hope not."

His smile faded. "I see you, Bailey."

She pouted and he frowned. "Don't do that. You don't have to and it's not you. You're not like these other women. Not a Barbie doll. Real, no artifice or games."

He leaned closer. "You still believe anything is possible. You believe in true love, in good triumphing over evil and in happily ever after."

She did, she realized. In her heart of hearts, despite a life that had time and again exhibited the opposite.

How had he learned so much about her in such a short time?

The same way she had learned so much about him.

"What about you?" she asked. "Do you believe in happily ever after?"

Shadows came into his eyes. He gathered her hands in his, leaned toward her. "Could you believe enough for the both of us?"

Her mouth went dry. A lump lodged in her throat. How many times had she told her world-weary, brokenhearted mama just that? *"I'll believe enough for us both, Mama. Everything will change for us, you just wait and see."*

It'd come too late for her mother. But not for her. "I can," she said softly. "I love you already."

He smiled, slow and satisfied. Like a cat. A big one. Sleek and dangerous.

"You're perfect, Bailey Browne. Absolutely perfect."

* * *

Bailey's suitcase lay open on the luggage rack. Tomorrow she'd be going home. Her heart was breaking.

Logan sat on the corner of the bed, silently watching her pack. He'd said little in the last few hours and she filled the silence with chatter. "All good things come to an end. That's what Mom used to say." Bailey took a stack of folded shorts and shirts and laid them in the suitcase. "Bailey," she mimicked, "if Christmas came every day, it wouldn't be a special day. Or if you ate chocolate ice cream for every meal, it wouldn't taste so good anymore. That's the nature of—"

"Don't go."

She tried not to look as devastated over this moment as she was. "My flight's tomorrow. I have to."

"No, you don't. Stay. Extend your vacation."

She met his eyes. "Just like that?"

"Yes, just like that."

Her heart began to rap against the wall of her chest. "You're serious, aren't you?"

"Dead serious. Change your flight."

"It's nonrefundable."

"I'll pay for another."

Her thoughts raced. What did she have to go back to? She'd quit her job to care for her mother and the new semester at school had just begun. She had no family and few real friends.

Bailey shook her head. "It'd cost a fortune."

"It doesn't matter. I can afford it."

"But my room—"

"I'll make arrangements with the hotel. Or you can move into my room."

Into his room and into his life, her own disappearing forever.

"Young women go missing in places like this." The

words popped out of her mouth; she hadn't even realized they'd been there.

Cold crept into his expression and he stood. "I'm sorry. I didn't know you felt that way."

"I don't. I just . . . I'm a single woman. I have to be careful."

"I get that." He started for the door, then stopped and looked over his shoulder at her. "I guess I thought this was as important to you as it is to me."

She'd hurt him. Impossible as that seemed for her, she heard it in his voice and saw it in his eyes.

"Wait!" She held out her hand. "It is, I just—"

"Don't trust me."

"No, I do. But—"

"We've only known each other five days? But you have to be smart or play it safe?" His voice deepened. "You can't have this, us, and play it safe at the same time."

He was right. Physical time didn't matter, her heart had known him forever. He was the one she had always dreamed of finding. This thing exploding between them, the love she had always longed for.

"I'll do it." She nodded her head for emphasis. "But I'm paying for it myself."

A smile tugged at his mouth. "I get you wanting to be self-reliant, but—"

"No. It seems right, spending Mom's life insurance money this way. She always wanted me to find what she never—"

Her throat closed over the last. He took her in his arms, drew her close. She curved hers around him, nestled her head on his shoulder. They stood that way a long time, his heart beating steady and strong against hers.

How could anything that felt so wonderful be anything but right?

Bailey leaned back, tipped her face up so she could meet his eyes. "My dad abandoned us when I was a baby. It broke her heart and she never found love again. But she wanted me to have what she didn't. She wanted me to find you."

"You have, Bailey. And I'm never letting you go."

The same suitcase lay open on the same bed. The same heavy silence surrounded them. The sense of loss, of her heart breaking.

No, Bailey thought, now the loss cut deeper. If he had meant to snare her in a seductive web, he had succeeded. The thought of living without him was almost more than she could bear.

"But we'll see each other," she said, voice artificially bright. "We've made a plan. It'll work."

He didn't respond and she went on. "You come to Nebraska for the sunrise, then I'll come to Louisiana for the seafood." She collected a stack of shirts from the bureau drawer. "It's not like we live on different planets. It's not—"

"Stop," he said. "Please. There's something I have to tell you."

Bailey's mouth went dry. "What?" she managed.

"I was married once," he said. "She left me."

"Oh." She didn't know what to say. The thought of him married to someone else stole her breath. It shouldn't, they were both old enough to have been married before, and he was older than she. But still, something about it cut her to the quick.

"I came home one day and she was gone. She left with nothing but the clothes on her back and the money she brought into the marriage."

Bailey cleared her throat, feeling like a deer, frozen in

the headlights of an oncoming semi. "Why didn't you . . . tell me this before?"

He looked down at his hands, then back up at her. "I don't like talking about it."

Which meant he'd been badly hurt. Because of her father, she understood betrayal by the one you loved most. The one you trusted and depended on.

"Who have you loved and lost?"

"Everyone."

She could hardly find her voice. "So . . . Why now, Logan?"

"There's more. Ugly gossip. About me and True, my family. I've put up with it most of my life, but I wanted you to know before I . . . Marry me, Bailey."

She froze, certain she couldn't have heard him right.

But she had, she realized when she looked at him.

"Marry me," he said again. "I want to spend my life with you."

The strangest sensation moved over her. Like the prickle of static electricity. But from head to toe. With the sensation came elation. And complete terror.

"You're crazy. We've only known each other—"

"Our whole lives."

She laughed nervously. "And here I was going to say twelve days."

He crossed to her, gathered her hands in his and looked deeply into her eyes. "Maybe it is crazy, but it feels as if my heart has known you forever."

God help her, it felt the same way to her. "You're serious about this, aren't you?"

"Dead serious. Listen, Bailey, we could say good-bye with all good intentions of seeing each other again. But let's be honest, we'd drift farther and farther apart. And that would be that."

He tightened his fingers on hers. "But that's not how this story goes, Bailey. It's not how *our* story goes."

He released her hands and got down on one knee. He took a small, white leather box from his pocket. "I love you, Bailey Ann Browne. Will you marry me?"

He opened the box. The most beautiful diamond ring she'd ever seen winked up at her.

She moved her gaze from the ring to his face. *He loved her.* She had told him a dozen times already, but he had waited. To make this perfect.

Happily ever after, she thought. That's how their story would go.

She believed in fairy tales. And this was hers.

"Yes, Logan," she said softly. "I love you and I will marry you."

CHAPTER TWO

Louisiana

They drove with the convertible top down and the heat
blasting. Bailey laughed out loud even as she huddled
deeper into her coat. Crazy, driving this way, bundled up
in their winter gear. But everything about this was completely and utterly nuts.

Logan glanced at her. "What's so funny?"

"We are!" She stretched her gloved hands to the sky,
the way she did when riding a roller coaster. And here she
was, in the front car of the wildest coaster of all.

"You're certifiable, you know that?"

"I married you, didn't I?"

"And I'm not about to let you forget it!" he said, then
motioned to the road ahead. "We're almost there. Don't
blink, you'll miss it."

Bailey straightened, excited. For many miles now,
every time they'd come upon another set of iron gates,
she'd asked if this one was Abbott Farm.

And each time he had smiled and told her they had to
reach Wholesome first.

Now, here it was, announced by a quaint wooden sign.

" 'Village of Wholesome,' " Bailey read aloud, " 'population seven hundred eighteen.' It looks so cute!"

He reached across the seat and caught her hand. "I hope you like it here."

"I'll love it, Logan. Because you do. Tell me again who I'll be meeting today."

"My sister, Raine."

His only family. "The artist."

"Yes. Moody and brooding."

"Obviously a strong family trait?" Bailey teased.

"Luckily, it skipped me."

They both laughed.

"She teaches art at the university," he continued. "Part-time."

"The one in Hammond. With the good elementary education program."

"Southeastern. Yes."

They rolled past the closed-up Dairy Freeze, then Earl's Quick Stop. Several patrons turned their way and stared. No doubt they recognized the car. She wondered how they would respond to the news Logan had remarried.

He didn't seem to notice their attention. "She lives in a secondary residence on the grounds."

"Don't forget, you promised she'd like me."

"I don't recall it actually being a promise." He cocked an eyebrow, expression wickedly amused. "Besides, it doesn't matter if she likes you, baby. Because I love you."

He stopped at a four-way and she sent him an arch glance. "So, you're one of those men who'll say anything to get a woman to say yes."

"It worked, didn't it?"

Bailey refused to be drawn away from the subject of his sister. "So, she's *not* going to like me?"

"Raine's a little . . . possessive, so her first reaction might be . . . cool. But once she gets to know you, and sees how happy you make me, I predict you'll be terrific friends."

Bailey rolled her eyes. "Great. I'm totally screwed."

He laughed but didn't deny it, and eased through the intersection. "Then there's August. Watch out for him, he's a womanizer and complete S.O.B."

"But you like him anyway."

"I respect him," he corrected. "He's a brilliant trainer."

Bailey imagined him. August Perez, dressage trainer. Dark and dashing. It all sounded so very romantic.

"Is this really happening?" she asked.

"It is." His eyes crinkled at the corners. "Till death do us part."

The sun went behind a cloud and a chill, like a shadow, moved over her. "How much farther?"

"A mile."

"Then quick, tell me about Paul."

"My stable manager."

"Oldest friend and right-hand man."

"Yup. And he's going to be really pissed about this."

More good news. Logan's secretiveness had bothered her. She'd called the only two people in her life who would care, her friend Marilyn and her former boss from the bookstore. Both had been shocked and had begged her to reconsider. They'd been suspicious of Logan's motives.

They didn't get it. He wasn't rushing her. *They* were following their hearts. Acting on their certainty that they were meant to be together.

But for Bailey, it was also about adventure. For once, stepping out and grabbing life by the horns. About being an active participant in her dreams coming true.

"You should have told him, Logan. To spring us on him and everyone else like this, it doesn't seem fair. I'd be pissed, too."

The light ahead turned red and he rolled to a stop. He looked at her. "I wanted this to be just ours, Bailey. For a little bit longer."

A lump formed in her throat. Not secretive. Holding on to and cherishing this special time together.

The light changed and Logan eased forward. "Besides, you'll understand when you meet everyone."

"They're a pack of hungry wolves, is that what you're saying?"

"Pretty much." He reached across the seat and caught her hand. "Look, just up on the right. Abbott Farm."

CHAPTER THREE

Logan reached the drive and turned in, rolling through the open gates, emblazoned with an ornate *AF*.

"Wait!" she said. "Stop."

He did, eyebrows drawing together. "What's wrong?"

"Nothing." She hoped he didn't hear the quiver in her voice. "I just need a moment."

To calm her thundering heart. To harness the sudden wave of uncertainty that rose up in her. This was it. Her new home. She had tied herself to this man and this place, everything familiar a thousand miles away.

She was alone here.

No, she had Logan. And as long as they were together, she'd never be alone.

Life by the horns, she reminded herself. True love and everything that went along with it.

She drew in a deep breath and let it out slowly. "Okay," she said. "Ready."

"Second thoughts?"

"No." She forced a confident smile. "Hell no, in fact."

Logan put the car in gear. The gravel drive snaked its way back to the main stable—they called them barns here, Logan had told her—and training arenas. He had shown her pictures of the estate online. It consisted of the barn and training facilities, acres of pastureland, three residences sitting on ninety wooded acres.

But the photos hadn't prepared her for how breathtaking it was.

Rolling pastures lined with white fencing. Sprawling grounds. Mature oaks, maples and birch trees. Two mares grazing in the pasture nearest the entrance, foals at their sides.

They reached the barn. Logan swung the Porsche into a spot under a tree and killed the engine. Two dogs scampered out to meet them—a corgi and a chocolate Lab—followed by a man in blue jeans, boots and a cowboy hat.

Logan glanced at her. "A word of warning. Paul has supersonic hearing. He misses nothing that's said in the barn."

"So no sex talk when I think he's out of earshot?"

"Right." He grinned. "Though it kills me to say it."

A moment later Bailey watched as the two men embraced.

"You sorry S.O.B.," Paul said, slapping him on the back. "I was beginning to wonder if you were ever coming back. One week turned into three and a half? Damn, man."

Logan smiled. "I considered living in paradise, but figured this place would go to hell without me."

Paul laughed, a deep, rumbling sound. "You wish." He looked her way and smiled. "And I see you brought a friend. Hi, I'm Paul."

She pulled off her knit cap, shook out her shoulder length, wavy blond hair and smiled. "I'm Bailey. Logan's told me so much about you."

Paul looked startled, then cleared his throat. "Hopefully nothing I have to deny too vehemently?"

"Not at all. It was all glowing."

Logan turned toward her and held out a hand. She crossed to him and took it, liking the way his fingers curled around hers. He pulled her close to his side.

"Paul," he said, "I have news. Try not to be so pissed you make an ass of yourself."

"I knew it." Paul put his fists on his hips, mouth curving into a wry smile. "You bought a horse, didn't you?"

Logan glanced at her, laughter in his eyes, then back at Paul. "In a manner of speaking."

"You son of a bitch. The two-year-old from Miami. I told you they wanted too much for him. So did August."

Bailey tried not to laugh. "The horse, it's not a him. It's a her."

"Bailey's more than a friend, Paul. She's my wife. That's the news."

Paul let out a bark of laughter. "You met on the beach, fell in love and got married. Makes perfect sense to me."

At their silence, his smile slipped. Again, he moved his gaze between the two of them, before settling it on Logan. "This isn't a joke?"

"Nope. We got married two days ago."

Paul flushed and turned to her. "I'm so sorry," he said stiffly. "I didn't mean any disrespect, I'm just . . . speechless."

"I understand," she said, and held out her hand. "In a way I am, too. It's good to meet you, Paul."

She supposed it all sounded ridiculous to him; she knew he didn't appreciate the position Logan had put him in. But instead of being a jerk about it, he ignored her hand and pulled her into a bear hug. "You're in South Louisiana now, we hug down here. Besides"—he held her at arm's length—"you're family now."

The simply stated words took her breath away. *Family. What she'd lost when her mother died.*

"That means a lot to me, Paul. Thank you."

He looked at Logan. "Does Raine know?"

Logan shook his head and Paul's eyebrows shot up. "That's one way to do it, but I would've thought that through a little more."

"I'm not scared," Logan shot back with a laugh.

"But I am," Paul said, and winked at her. "Like we always say, wind and Raine—"

"—thunder and lightning," Logan finished. "She'll get over it. She'll have to."

He led Bailey to the car, then called back to his friend, "By the way, you're coming to dinner. Bring wine. The good stuff, we're celebrating!"

A moment later, they were back in the Porsche, heading away from the barn. "What did you think of Paul?"

"I liked him. It's your sister I'm worried about."

"Raine's emotional, that's all." Logan maneuvered the vehicle up the winding gravel drive, the grounds changing from manicured to wild.

"Emotional?" She cocked an eyebrow. "Wind and rain, thunder and lightning?"

"Like I said, temperamental."

"And possessive of you?"

"Very."

"And August's a son of a bitch." Bailey mock-moaned and brought her hands to her face. "I've got a really bad feeling about this."

"Remember, Paul's nice."

"Thanks for reminding me, but I still have the feeling I'm screwed."

"I'll protect you."

"You'd better, since you got me into this." They left the sun behind. Under the canopy of trees the temperature dropped, and she huddled deeper into her coat.

They came upon another set of gates, smaller this time

with no insignia. He reached across the seat and caught her hand. "Excited?"

She nodded and he drove slowly through. The brick walls that surrounded the property looked a century old, though from what he'd told her, the house had been built less than fifty years ago.

Bailey caught her breath as the house came fully into view. She'd expected a Southern plantation or a manor house, not this sprawling . . . hacienda.

She told him so and he corrected her. "Spanish-style *cortijo.*"

"*Cortijo,*" she repeated.

"Farmhouse. My mother named it Nuestra Pequeña Cortijo. Our little farmhouse."

"Has it occurred to you, there's nothing little about it?"

"You didn't know my dad. He wanted a grand, French country manor, Mom had other ideas. As you see, she won him over."

She heard the sadness in his voice and squeezed his hand. "I love it already."

He parked. They climbed out. She stood a moment, drinking it in with all her senses. It smelled earthy and alive. But it was so quiet. Just the rustle of leaves, chirp of the birds and water trickling in a nearby fountain.

"It feels like we're in the middle of nowhere."

"Our own private world."

He grabbed her hand, lacing their fingers. "C'mon, I'll show you around."

At the front door, he scooped her into his arms and carried her across the threshold. "Welcome home, Mrs. Abbott."

As he set her down, he kissed her. She clung to him, wondering how this had happened, how her life had become the fairy tale she had fantasized of as a young girl but given up on.

"You're crying," he said as he released her. "What's wrong?"

"I'm just so happy. I just . . . I thought you'd never come."

"But here I am."

For long moments, they simply gazed into each other's eyes, then he led her from room to room. Like an eager little boy, showing off his treasures. The place was magnificent. Both rugged and elegant. Cutting-edge convenience and old-world charm. Large windows and exposed brick. Reclaimed cypress doors and heart-of-pine floors; state-of-the-art electronics and Viking appliances in the country-style kitchen.

She crossed to the French doors and peered out. A lush courtyard, she saw. Complete with a pool, outdoor fireplace and the fountain she had heard from the drive.

She looked over her shoulder at him to find him carefully watching her. "I think I know where I'm going to be spending a lot of my time."

"Other than the barn, I remember it being my mother's favorite spot as well. Come, I'll show you the rest of the house."

Moments later, he swung open a door. "My study."

Bailey stepped in, stopping at the painting that dominated the room. A portrait of a woman and a horse. The woman was beautiful, with dark hair and light skin, her mouth was curved into a small secretive smile identical to Logan's. Somehow, the artist had caught the bond between horse and his master.

"It's your mother."

"You look just like her." He circled his arms around her and drew her back against his chest. "This is the way I remember her."

"She was lovely."

"She was." He rested his chin on her head. "The horse's name is Sapphire. She raised him from a foal."

Bailey recalled what he'd told her. That horses had been his mother's passion; that she'd ridden dressage, making the U.S. team for the 1980 Summer Olympics.

"Did she medal in the games?"

"She did. Come see." He led her to the mantel. There, displayed in a shadow box were several photographs of a young Elisabeth Abbott competing and the Olympic bronze medal she had won.

"She gave up competing after. Married Dad, had us. Devoted her energy to training young riders."

"Is this the same horse from the portrait?"

"No. Sapphire was his offspring," he said softly. "He died the same year she did."

At the pain in his voice, a lump formed in her throat. His mother had died tragically young. Bailey didn't know the details, only that she drowned. Logan had been almost sixteen, Raine ten. He'd promised to share the details someday; she'd agreed, they had their whole lives to learn about each other.

Someday. It had seemed so far away a few days ago. Now, here, surrounded by his mother's things, it had arrived. Bailey longed to know everything. About his mother and everything else that had helped shape the man she loved.

She opened her mouth to ask, but as if sensing it, Logan drew her away. "Come, I'll show you the upstairs."

Three bedrooms, she discovered, including the master. Each with a balcony that looked out over the courtyard and pool.

"This is the master," he said, swinging the door open.

She stepped into the room. A king-size poster bed. Serene blues and cream, with touches of gold. Furniture that looked as if it had been made for the room. Beautiful, but . . . something about it felt wrong. Anonymous, like a well-appointed hotel room.

Bailey stopped in the center and turned slowly around.

As her gaze landed on the bed, she wondered if this was the same bed he had shared with True.

"What's wrong?"

"Nothing." She forced thoughts of the other woman away. "It's lovely."

"You can redo it, any way you like."

Bailey crossed to the balcony door, opened it and stepped out. He came up behind, looping his arms around her and easing her against his chest.

"Who's that?" she asked, indicating a man trudging through the woods beyond the brick wall. A white dog was with him, running ahead, then circling back, only to dart ahead again.

"Henry. He's worked for our family forever. When you meet him, don't be scared by the way he looks, he's a sweet, simple man."

"Why would I be frightened of his looks?"

"He was mauled by a stallion. One of ours."

"Oh, my God."

"He sacrificed himself to save Mother. By the time we got him out, his injuries were extensive. His body healed, but his brain didn't. And his face . . . well, after a half-dozen reconstructive surgeries, it seemed kinder to stop."

"Does he live here, on the property?"

"He does. He has a small cabin on the far northeastern side."

"What about the dog? What's its name?"

"Tony."

"Tony?" She tilted her head to look up at him. "It doesn't seem to fit him."

"It will, when you get to know him." He turned her in his arms. "What do you think so far?"

"That it's so beautiful, I won't ever want to leave."

"What about me, Bailey?" He tipped her face up to his, expression fierce. "Promise you'll never leave me. That we'll have babies and grow old together."

It was what she'd always wanted. A family. Meals around a big table, familial chaos with laughter and bickering siblings. What she'd never had.

Logan looked so sad it broke her heart. "Children and grandchildren," she said. "We'll raise them here, together. I'll never leave you. I promise, Logan."

He drew her to the bed. With the French doors open to the cold day, they made love.

CHAPTER FOUR

"You son of a bitch!" The woman's voice came from downstairs. "You get your sorry ass down here this minute!"

Bailey sat straight up, dragging the sheets with her. "Oh, my God, someone's in the house!"

Logan groaned. "Not someone. Hurricane Raine."

"Your sister?" Bailey squealed.

"Two minutes!" the woman shouted. "Or I'm coming up there!"

"Hold your bladder," he yelled back. "I'm coming!"

Logan sat up, a smile tugging at his mouth. "I think she heard about us."

"This is so humiliating." Bailey brought her hands to her face. "What if she *heard* . . . you know. The balcony door was open."

"It's okay, baby." He leaned across and kissed her. "Stay here, I'll be right back."

But Bailey wasn't about to hide in the bed—naked, for heaven's sake—and miss this first chance to meet her new sister-in-law. Or chance that the outspoken woman wouldn't charge up here to see her for herself.

The moment Logan exited the room, she leaped up and began throwing herself together. After finishing by pulling her hair into a ponytail and dabbing on a bit of lip gloss, she headed into the hall.

And stopped on the landing. She heard them, although they stood at the bottom of the stairs, out of her line of sight.

"How could you do this to me, Logan? I'm your sister."

"And I love you. But it's my life."

"And I like to think I'm a part of it."

"You are, Raine. C'mon."

Bailey heard the affection in his tone and smiled.

"She's so sweet," he said. "You're going to like her. I promise."

"That's what you said about True."

"And you liked her."

"At first. Then she turned on us."

"I don't want to talk about her. And I won't. Not today."

"You don't see the parallels? You thought she was sweet, too. You brought her home, just like this—"

Bailey crept closer and was just able to peek down at them.

"—surprise! 'Meet my young, beautiful wife! Love her. She's family now.'"

The bitterness and anger in Raine's voice shocked her. As did the news that Logan had done this before, gotten married in a romantic whirlwind.

Bailey had thought she was special, that their love was a once-in-a-lifetime occurrence. Apparently not, if Raine was to be believed. Bailey pushed the thought—and the way it hurt—aside and refocused on their conversation.

"They're two different people," Logan said, voice low, reassuring. "You'll see."

Raine lowered her voice; Bailey had to strain to hear. "But you're the same. I can't . . . I couldn't stand to see you heartbroken again."

Bailey stepped out into the open. "You won't have to,"

she said clearly, forcing a confident smile. "I love your brother with all my heart."

Raine looked up at her. She was beautiful—brown hair so dark it was nearly black, classic features—a feminine version of Logan save for the color of their eyes. Instead of light green, hers were a deep, rich brown.

And right now, they glittered with fury.

"Here she is," Logan said. "My beautiful bride."

His smile chased the chill away. She descended the stairs and went to his side. He drew her close, arm possessively around her.

"Bailey Abbott, meet my sister, Raine."

Bailey smiled brightly at her new sister-in-law, and held out her hand. "Hurricane Raine," she said. "I'm so happy to finally meet you."

Something in the woman's expression shifted subtly. Admiration? For her backbone? Or anticipation? As if she'd decided Bailey could prove a worthy opponent . . . or an easy target?

She took Bailey's hand. "You're right, Logan. She's not True. I think she and I are going to get along famously."

CHAPTER FIVE

The smell of grilling steak wafted on the evening air. The sound of laughter mingled with the tinkling of the courtyard fountain. Paul had arrived first, with flowers and wine. Raine had never left, instead heading straight to the bar, then out to sit alone by the pool, bundled up in her coat.

To Bailey, her sitting out there alone had felt weird. Logan had assured her that isolating herself was his sister's way and that she would join them when she was ready. Or not.

She did, finally, her smile and behavior bright, but brittle. So brittle, Bailey feared the wrong words would shatter her into a million pieces. Paul, on the other hand, was affable and generous. Smiling at her, working to include her. Even so, she could see the strain around his eyes.

She wondered if he could see the strain around hers. If they all could. These people were so different than she. Beautiful and worldly. This place, so much . . . grander. Like a movie set, she decided.

She said so, and they all looked at her. Raine smiled, clearly delighted with her naivete. "And what kind of movie will this be, my surprise sister-in-law? A comedy? Or a tragedy?"

"Why, neither, of course."

The man's voice was silky and deep, with what sounded to Bailey like a European accent. They all turned.

"August," Raine said, sounding amused. "You never miss the chance for an entrance."

He kissed Raine's cheek, then turned to Bailey. "And you must be the new Mrs. Abbott."

Physically, he wasn't a big man, yet in every other way seemed larger than life. Black hair pulled back in a pony-tail, his dark coloring a dramatic contrast to the white silk shirt he wore. Tight jeans; a brilliantly white smile.

He caught her hand, met her eyes as he brought it to his lips. "Obviously, this movie is a romance. Epic, no doubt."

Bailey smiled. "August," she said, feeling everyone's eyes on her and sensing this was a test, "you're just as charming as Logan warned me you'd be."

He laughed. "And you, Bailey, are as young and lovely as I expected."

She wasn't certain what he meant by that, but she wasn't about to let him best her. "A testament to my husband's excellent taste?"

"Something like that."

Logan announced the steaks were done and they assembled around the grand dining room table. Bailey would have preferred a more casual evening, but Logan had insisted it was a celebration, so only the finest would do. So, they had set the table, using linens and china and lighting the long white tapers inside antique hurricanes.

After only a few minutes of polite conversation, the interrogation began. Bailey had been waiting for it. How could they not be curious? Here she sat, a stranger, virtu-ally forced upon them.

And as she had also expected, it began with Raine. "Bailey, tell us about you. Where are you from?"

"Nebraska. A little town named Broken Bow."

Her eyebrows shot up. "I've never actually met anyone from Nebraska."

"Now you have. Finally, you can call your life complete."

Beside her, Logan stifled a chuckle.

"What about your family?" Paul asked.

"I don't have any."

Raine made a choked sound and grabbed her water.

August leaned forward, eyes sparkling. "How very interesting."

"I'm not certain what you mean by that."

"He doesn't mean anything by it," Raine said. "He's just trying to be clever."

He laughed and went back to his wine and Raine refocused on her. "I'm curious," Raine murmured, "how does one end up with no family at all?"

"I'm an only child, raised by a single mother. She—" Her throat closed over the words. She felt like an idiot and looked helplessly at Logan.

"Her mother passed away recently," he said. "The loss is still very fresh."

"I'm so sorry," Paul said to her. "Forgive me for bringing it up."

Raine stabbed a piece of steak. "Was it sudden?"

Bailey cleared her throat. "It depends on your definition of sudden. For me, it was. She was diagnosed with bone cancer, and six months later she was . . . gone."

Logan laid his hand over hers. "Bailey withdrew from school to care for her."

"What were you studying?" Paul asked.

"To be a teacher," Logan answered for her. "Elementary education."

"I'm going back." Bailey smiled. "Logan tells me Southeastern has a good program. And that I could easily commute."

"They do," Raine interjected. "I'm a professor there. In the art department."

"Logan told me."

"Of course, Logan and I are Tulane grads."

The subtle stress she put on the words made it clear Southeastern was fine for people like her, but not them. Bailey's hackles rose. "Why's that? It's more expensive?"

"Catfight," August murmured, bringing his glass to his lips.

"Yes, it is," Raine responded. "But it was tradition that we should go. Mother and Daddy did, their parents as well. Things like that are important down here. Family things."

Bailey bristled. "My mother studied at the school of hard knocks. And performed brilliantly."

"Touché." August looked at Raine expectantly.

But before the other woman could respond, Paul jumped in. "Do you ride, Bailey?" he asked.

"I used to. But haven't in years."

"A country girl like you?" Raine cocked an eyebrow, looking almost amused. "Why not?"

"Don't laugh, but I'm afraid of horses. Terrified, really."

No one laughed. A hush fell over the table.

"Well," August said, lifting his glass in a toast, "there's a first. Lady of the manor, ruling over all she sees, terrified of what she sees the most of. To you, Mrs. Abbott."

"Shut up, August," Raine snapped. "You're such an idiot." She turned to Bailey. "They're the most beautiful, gentle creatures on the planet, how could they scare you? What happened?"

"I was thrown. Nearly trampled." She looked at Logan. "When you told me what happened to Henry, it was all too real."

Logan curled his fingers around hers. "A boyfriend convinced her to get on a horse she had no business riding."

"Typical," August said, smirking at Logan. "Leave it to a man to convince a levelheaded girl to do something dangerous."

Logan ignored him. "She's going to give it a try again."

"When I'm ready," she added.

"Of course, when you're ready, baby." He looked at Paul. "What do you think about her riding Tea Biscuit?"

He smiled. "Perfect choice. She's a retired polo pony. Very sweet, as gentle as they come."

"We keep her around because she's good company for weaning foals," August said.

"And for children to ride," Raine added.

Paul cleared his throat at Raine's dig, obviously uncomfortable. "Logan, tell us how you two met."

He looked at her. "You tell them, sweetheart."

"It was so romantic."

"I'll need more wine for this." August held up the empty bottle. "Do you mind, Logan?"

"Of course not."

"It was the first night of my vacation"—she glanced at Logan—"both of our vacations. I was walking on the beach and was attacked."

Paul grinned. "Smooth move, Logan. Gutsy."

He laughed. "It would have been but I'm not that slick."

"He saved me," she said. "My own knight in shining armor."

Raine rolled her eyes. "God help us."

"He stayed with me the whole time, even though it took hours to wait for security, then the police. I told him he could go on, but he insisted." She sighed. "We watched the sunrise together. It was the most romantic night of my life."

"Excuse me while I retch," Raine said lightly. "Pass the bottle, August."

"We spent every moment after together," Bailey said.

"Then extended our vacations—"

"Because we couldn't bear to say good-bye."

"This could be part of a trend," August said. "Lots of trends seem to be developing here."

Paul sent him an irritated glance. "So you decided good-bye was off the table?"

"Exactly. We just . . . knew." Logan gazed into her eyes. "It was right. We were meant to be together."

"He proposed—"

"And she said yes."

Paul jumped in. "And as they say, the rest is history."

"Happily ever after," Bailey said, beaming up at Logan.

"Obviously then, he hasn't told you about True?"

The table went silent. Everyone looked at Raine.

"Why wouldn't I have?" Logan asked, voice low, vibrating with something Bailey had never heard in it before but recognized as dangerous.

"We both know why, my dear brother. In this family, there's no such thing as happily ever after."

CHAPTER SIX

The days flowed one into the other. After a week, Bailey still couldn't believe she was here, in this magical place, married to her very own Prince Charming. They had spent nearly every moment of the past days together, but today he'd had to go into New Orleans, to see to his land development and management firm.

Which left her alone in her new home for the first time. She considered finishing the arrangements to have her things shipped from Nebraska or calling and catching up with her friend Marilyn, but decided to go exploring instead.

Bailey laced up her Nikes, grabbed her jacket and headed outside. She would visit the stable, see if she could muster the courage to offer a carrot to the mare Logan had picked out for her. How could she be afraid of a horse named Tea Biscuit?

As she stepped through the gate, the white dog she had seen from the bedroom window her first day here burst out of the bushes.

"Hi there." She squatted down and held out her hand. He scurried over, his whole back end wagging with his tail. She scratched him behind his ears and he went almost epileptic with pleasure.

"Tony," she said, "you're a friendly little guy."

Not so little, she decided. But a puppy still.

A mutt, obviously. White and scruffy looking, with mismatched features, a black spot over one eye and a big, goofy smile.

"You have a bit of pit in you, don't you?"

Tony smiled and she laughed. "Where's your master? I'll bet he's missing you. Go on now. Go home."

She started in the direction of the barn; Tony followed. She stopped. "Stay. Henry will be looking for you."

The dog ignored her, loping along with her, then running ahead and circling back. Occasionally tearing off into the brush, only to return looking almost comically pleased with himself. Bailey decided she would ask about Henry at the stable and return Tony to him herself.

As she neared the barn, a couple of other dogs trotted out to meet her, the ones from her first day on the farm. In a flash, Tony had joined them in a game of tag. Bailey watched for a moment, then stepped into the barn. The interior smelled earthy but sweet, like fresh hay and clean straw. Several of the animals came to their stall doors to peer out as she passed, looking balefully at her when she passed without stopping to stroke their neck or offer a treat.

Logan had told her mornings were busy times at the barn: all the animals needed to be fed and exercised, the stalls cleaned and vet visits made. She supposed that all happened early; it was quiet now.

She had been through here with Logan, at least once every day since she arrived. Those trips had felt totally different from this one. He had been in charge. He'd pointed out each horse, which ones were boarders and which belonged to Abbott Farm. He'd explained that warmblood was a classification, not a breed, then patiently told her the differences between stallions, geldings, colts, fillies, and mares.

Each day had been another lesson; one day about naturalizing foals by handling them, another about the right age for a colt or filly to start under saddle training, and another about dressage.

For that one they had sat in the bleachers and watched August and a client. The man had been a complete son of a bitch, shouting corrections from the corner of the arena, yet his student never seemed to lose her cool, reacting with adjustments so subtle Bailey couldn't even pick them out.

Logan could. He'd been enthralled, the entire time whispering a running commentary about the skill of the rider and the athleticism of the horse. She had realized that although Logan claimed horses had been his mother's passion, they were his as well.

Which was another reason she was in the barn today. She meant to get over her fear of them. She wanted to be able to share this with Logan.

Bailey kept to the middle of the aisle between stalls, an uneasy flutter in the pit of her stomach. They were beautiful. And terrifying. She remembered being young and galloping across a field bareback, wind in her hair and against her cheeks, feeling completely alive and totally free.

And she remembered climbing onto the stallion that had thrown her, feeling his power and knowing real terror, maybe for the first time in her life. In that moment she had realized that the twelve-hundred-pound animal she perched upon was in control, not she.

And he had been in control ever since, Bailey thought ruefully. That, she promised herself, was about to change.

"Bailey?"

She whirled around, nearly colliding with August.

He reached out a hand to steady her. "I'm sorry, I didn't mean to startle you."

"That's all right." She took a step away from him. "My fault, I was lost in thought. Excuse me."

"Wait. I wanted to talk to you. To apologize for my behavior that night at dinner."

"It's forgotten."

"It's not. Not by me." He caught her hand again, his grip almost tender. "I was rude, my behavior shallow and . . . unforgivable. I know that. But I'm asking anyway. Will you forgive me?"

She studied him. He could be playing her, but so what if he was? "Forgiven and forgotten, August."

"Really?"

She slid her hand from his. "Really."

"No wonder Logan fell in love with you." He matched her steps. "Have you come to visit Tea Biscuit?"

"How did you know?"

"A hunch. And tipped off by what looks like a carrot sticking out of your pocket."

She involuntarily brought a hand to that pocket, then laughed. Sure enough, the top of the carrot poked out.

He glanced at her from the corners of his eyes. "I saw you in the stands the other day, watching. What did you think?"

"Of what?"

"Me, of course. It's always about me. Ask anyone."

She laughed again. At their first meeting she had thought him skilled at the art of laughter at others' expense. She saw now that the skill extended to himself as well.

"Do you want the truth?" she asked.

"Of course."

They reached Tea Biscuit's stall and the pretty mare came to greet them. Bailey dug one of the carrots out of her pocket. "I thought you were a total bastard. In fact, it occurred to me that I'd rather take a bullet than a riding lesson from you."

He laughed. "I knew we were going to be friends."

Friends? With this man? Bailey couldn't imagine that happening. Ever. The mare nudged her with her nose, then nickered.

"She knows you have them," he said. "She can smell them." He took the carrot from her and broke it into pieces. "Cup your hands, like this."

She imitated him, and he dropped the pieces in them. "Just like that," he said softly. "Offer them to her."

Bailey tried, but her hands shook so badly he had to support them with his. When he did, the horse took the treats, her muzzle as soft as velvet against her palms.

"See," he murmured, "she's so gentle. There's nothing to be afraid of."

Bailey laughed. She had done this as a child, fearlessly. It'd felt as natural as feeding herself. Those days were gone, but these may be better, she decided. There was something magical about reconnecting with something so elemental. She would never take it for granted again.

She fed the rest of the treats to Tea Biscuit, this time without his help. "Look, no shaking."

"I see that. Now, touch her."

"Touch her?"

"Stroke her neck."

Bailey nodded and reached out her hand. The mare moved sideways, out of reach.

"She doesn't like me."

"She takes her cues from you," he said. "She picks up on your fear and responds to it. Pet her with confidence. With affection."

Bailey tried again. This time Tea Biscuit submitted. "She's so warm. And soft."

She looked over her shoulder at him, to find his gaze on her. Something in his dark eyes had her wanting to put distance between them. Unlike the mare, she couldn't just jerk away.

She dropped her hand. "Thank you for the lesson, but I need to go."

He stopped her, a hand on her arm. "I meant it, Bailey. I want us to be friends. True and I were."

"Pardon me?"

"Friends." He lowered his voice. "I loved her."

His words shocked her. She stopped cold.

He smiled sadly. "You misunderstand. She was a beautiful person. Everyone who knew her loved her."

Insecurity shot through her. A pang of jealousy. "Oh."

"I'm sure Logan told you."

"Of course." She wondered if he could see she was lying. That she could fit what Logan had told her about True in a thimble. "We share everything."

"Except what he doesn't want you to know."

She stiffened.

"Wait! I'm sorry. I'm awful, it's why I have so few friends. It's why True's friendship meant so much to me." He searched her gaze. "You're like her, aren't you? Not just your looks. Your heart as well."

"I look like her?"

"Similar. You didn't know that?"

"No one said."

"I hope that doesn't upset you?"

"Of course not."

But it did. It bothered her very much.

"Let me help you overcome your fear of riding."

"I don't know. I was thinking Logan would want—"

"You could surprise him. For his birthday, you could ride together."

"The end of April," she said. "Do you think that's possible?"

"Absolutely."

It would be a wonderful surprise. A gift for her husband, a man who had everything.

He saw agreement in her expression and broke into a smile. "What a strange friendship we will have."

"Complete opposites. Sweet and rotten."

He laughed. "Spunk with all that sweetness, I like that. We will get along quite well, I know it."

She smiled. "Perhaps we will."

"Unfortunately, I see my client has arrived, a miserably uncoordinated girl, but I shall do my best."

Bailey watched him walk toward the woman. Tall, beautiful and lithe. And obviously, anything but uncoordinated. They embraced and August kissed her cheeks.

Bailey shifted her gaze and found Raine standing beyond them, watching the pair with naked animosity.

Or was that jealousy? she wondered. Was Raine in love with the flamboyant trainer?

"Bailey, good morning."

"Paul," she said. He'd emerged from what she assumed was his office and was walking toward her, smiling broadly. "Logan told me you might venture out and to keep an eye open for you."

She returned the smile. "And here I am."

His smile slipped. "I saw you and August, he wasn't being . . . inappropriate, was he?"

She found the question strange, and shook her head. "Not at all. Trying to make amends for the other night."

"He should. His behavior was abominable." He paused. "Just be on your guard. He can be—"

"A flirt?"

"To put it mildly."

"Logan warned me." Tony and the two other dogs came tearing through the barn; Tony saw her and charged her way. He threw himself against her legs and she laughed. "As you can see, I've made a friend."

"I see that. He's Henry's dog."

"I know. I thought I'd return him."

Paul bent to pet the pup, but he darted away, rejoining the other dogs. He straightened, met her eyes again. "That's not necessary. As you can see, there are several dogs on the farm and they all pretty much run free. Tony knows where he lives. Have you met Henry yet?" he asked.

She shook her head and he went on. "Henry has a small place on the northeast corner of the farm."

"Logan mentioned the accident."

"She had no business being in that stall with King's Challenge, not with mares in heat and another stallion nearby."

He paused, looking off in the distance. "But she thought of herself as a bit of a horse whisperer. And in truth, she was. But not this time."

Bailey swallowed past the lump in her throat. "You were there? You saw it happen?"

He nodded. "I was just a kid. Twelve, I think. Maybe eleven."

"My God."

"Henry was one of the groomers. He realized what was happening and put himself between her and the stallion. It was the most—" He shook his head. "I never looked at a stallion, any horse for that matter, the same way again. They're powerful creatures."

Bailey could only imagine how traumatic it must have been for Paul to have witnessed the attack.

Bailey rubbed her arms. "How old was Henry when it happened?"

"I'm not sure. Old enough to have been Raine's father."

"Excuse me?"

"That sounded wrong. I meant he was around the same age as Logan's parents. She never forgave herself."

He fell silent a moment. "Elisabeth took care of all his medical expenses. In fact, she promised she would take care of him forever. And she has, even though she's gone. She deeded him the land and when the time came, built him a small home, gave him a job and a salary for life. It's all legal. No one could take it away from him."

"She was something special, wasn't she?"

"Yes." A faraway expression came into his eyes. "She was more of a mother to me than my own."

He took off his cowboy hat and ran a hand through his short-cropped, sandy-colored hair, then fitted it back on. "Sorry, I didn't mean to go on that way. Is there anything I can get you, Bailey? Any questions you need answered, directions someplace?"

"I do have one question."

"Shoot."

"It's about True. August said I look like her. Do I?"

Her question had taken him by surprise, she saw. He cleared his throat. "No. Resemble, maybe. In your size and coloring."

She didn't quite believe him, but didn't know why. Most probably her own insecurity.

"One more question."

He glanced at the clock. "Shoot."

"I overheard Logan and Raine, did he and True marry as suddenly as—"

He cut her off. "You should talk to Logan about this, Bailey. It's not my business."

His brusque tone felt like a slap and her face warmed. "You're right. I'm sorry, it wasn't fair to put you in that position."

"If there's anything else I can help you with, just ask."

She stuffed her hands in her pockets. "Thanks, I will. Paul?"

He stopped and looked back.

"I'm not like True."

"I didn't say you were."

"I just wanted you to know that. I'm not going anywhere."

CHAPTER SEVEN

Bailey stepped out into the bright, cold day. She shivered slightly and drew her sweater coat tighter around her. She'd been on the farm nearly a month and had learned its rhythm. The activities here revolved around the horses and their physical needs. Food and exercise, health care. Even schooling for the young ones, discipline for the headstrong. Like a barn full of children to care for.

Her days had fallen into a predictable pattern, as well; one that revolved around Logan's schedule instead of her own. He had been busy, pulled between his land management firm and farm business.

But she hadn't been bored. Or lonely. Her things had arrived from Nebraska and a good bit of her days had been devoted to sorting and storing. She had lingered over things that had been her mother's, photographs of her, of the two of them together. She had lovingly placed the framed photos throughout the house, so no matter what room she was in, she would be able to see her.

Tony greeted her with an excited bark and ran over, his entire back end swinging with his tail.

"Hey, buddy." She bent and scratched behind his ears as best she could. In his ecstasy, he proved too much of a moving target. She had learned not to worry over where the pup was—he, too, seemed to have fallen into a pattern, splitting his time between her, Henry and hanging around the barn with the other dogs.

"You with Henry this morning? Or did you come to see me?" He stopped wiggling and sat, giving her an opportunity for a proper scratch, then jumped up, barked once and made a beeline for the garage.

She followed him and saw why. Old Henry on the far side of the garage, fiddling with a mower.

"Hi, Henry!" she called.

He didn't hear her, so she headed over. He caught sight of her then, took off his hat and smiled broadly. Between his original injuries and surgical scars, the smile stretched Joker-like across his face. "Hello there, Ms. True. Pretty day for a walk."

The first time he'd called her Logan's first wife's name, she'd been hurt. It had ceased to bother her, much anyway. Henry, she'd realized, was caught somewhere between the past and the present. "It is, but I thought I'd go for a drive today instead."

"A drive?" His bushy eyebrows lowered. "What for?"

"I thought it was time to learn my way around." He didn't look convinced it was a good idea and she patted his arm. "You and Tony have a good day."

She started to turn away. He stopped her, his grip on her arm surprisingly firm. "You'll come back, won't you?"

"Of course I will," she said, surprised. "Why would you think I wouldn't?"

"Sometimes they don't."

"Who didn't come back, Henry?"

He dropped his hand and returned to his tinkering with the mower.

"Henry?" She touched his sleeve. "Are you talking about True?"

He lifted his dark eyes, the pain in them almost palpable. "Betsy didn't. He came back without her."

"Who came back without her?"

"I don't want to talk about him." His eyes filled with tears. "Don't make me."

"It's okay." She patted his hand, realizing how upset he was. "I won't. I'll see you later, Henry."

He didn't respond, just returned to his work. She walked away, making a mental note to ask Logan who Betsy was. Whoever she was, it was obvious that Henry had cared very much for her.

Logan had left her the keys to a battered Range Rover. She climbed in and started it up, suddenly anxious to get off the farm. As she rolled past the barn, she caught sight of Paul and August in what looked like a heated discussion. They stopped when they saw her and stared. She smiled and waved, feeling suddenly as light and free as a feather on the breeze.

She drove with no particular destination in mind. Soaking in the landscape. Country. Farms, grand and modest; a smattering of businesses, not assembled in clusters, save for the village itself, but simply, suddenly *there*. A veterinary clinic. A beauty parlor called Snipz and Stylz. Several plant nurseries and a feed store. And churches. Lots of small brick or clapboard structures, some adorned with crosses, others with simple signs.

She imagined come spring it would be beautiful, lush and green. But now, at the height of winter, it all came off as gray and slightly dilapidated.

The sound of a siren broke her reverie. Bailey glanced in the rearview mirror and saw cherry lights. She'd been going the speed limit, maybe a mile or two above, surely not enough to get pulled over. An image of Hollywood's version of a small-town Southern cop filled her head—Buford T. Something-or-other.

She pulled onto a gravel drive and drew to a stop.

A moment later, the lawman was at her window. "License, registration, proof of insurance."

She handed him the items. "Was I speeding, Officer?"

Instead of answering, he said, "You visiting, Miz Browne?"

"Pardon?"

"Nebraska license."

"I just moved here." He didn't respond and she added, "It's Abbott now."

"The new Mrs. Logan Abbott."

Her hackles rose at his tone. "Is there a new one every week?"

It was his turn to look confused. "Ma'am?"

"The way you said the 'new' Mrs. Abbott suggested I might be the latest in a long and esteemed line."

He smiled slightly. "Esteemed, ma'am. Certainly."

Bad blood existed between Logan and this man, she realized. And whatever it was, it ran deep. "Are you going to write me a ticket?"

"I'll let you off with a warning. This time." He leaned down so close she saw her reflection in his mirrored sunglasses. "But I suggest you get that license changed. That is, if you plan to be around awhile."

"I do, Officer. Thank you." If he heard the acid in her tone, he didn't let on.

He held out her documents. She went to grab them, but he didn't let them go. "Did he tell you about True?"

"Excuse me?"

"I bet he only told you what he wanted you to hear."

Angry heat stung her cheeks. "If there's nothing else, Officer—"

"Or maybe only what *you* wanted to hear. Him being such a catch and all."

She caught her breath, shocked. "You're out of line, Officer."

"You look like her."

"Excuse me?"

"She and I were friends. Does that surprise you?"

"What's that supposed to mean?"

He released his grip on the documents and she snatched her hand away. "You figure it out, Mrs. Abbott. And while you're at it, grab yourself a copy of our local paper up at Faye's. I think you'll find it interesting."

Any vestige of the easygoing, Southern good ole boy was gone. He was a cop on a mission, with a gun and badge and every threat that went along with it.

But was that threat directed at her? Or Logan?

"What's your name, Officer?"

He straightened. "I suggest you be careful, ma'am. Real careful."

He was a bully, she decided. One of those cops who liked to push people around. Use his badge to intimidate. Make himself feel powerful.

She wasn't about to be intimidated by this small-minded, small-town cop. The chip on his shoulder was *his* problem, not hers.

She leaned her head out the open window. "I asked your name, Officer."

He stopped, looked back. "Billy Ray Williams. Chief of police." He smiled and tipped his hat again. "Have a good day, Bailey Abbott."

CHAPTER EIGHT

Bailey watched the lawman stroll back to his cruiser and climb in. A moment later, he was going around her, lifting his hand in a wave. As if they were old friends.

Her hands were shaking. She sucked in a deep breath, working to calm herself. He hadn't overtly threatened her or Logan. Yet the encounter had unnerved her.

She shifted into drive, and eased back onto the road. It hadn't been the badge and gun, nor the way he'd gotten in her face, that bothered her. It was the animosity he felt toward her husband. And his innuendos. That Logan was keeping secrets from her. That she didn't know the whole story about True.

He and True had been friends, he'd said. Almost defiantly. In challenge. But not a challenge to her. To Logan.

"And while you're at it, grab yourself a copy of our local paper at Faye's. I think you'll find it interesting."

Faye's. One of two restaurants in Wholesome, a diner Logan had said served the best biscuits and sausage gravy anywhere. Up ahead Bailey saw the sign announcing the Village of Wholesome. She smiled to herself. *Okay, Big-Chief Billy Ray. Challenge accepted.*

Bailey didn't have far to go; Faye's was located on the main drag, just past the town's only traffic light. The building—a low-slung, beige brick box, picture window dotted with flyers—had nothing outstanding to commend it. Except the food, which the sign in the window assured was *Real Good*. As did the nearly full parking lot, with its collection of dusty pickup trucks and SUVs.

Bailey entered the restaurant. The bell above the door jingled her arrival and conversation paused as every head swiveled in her direction.

Apparently, she had found the place to see and be seen in Wholesome.

"Seat yourself wherever there's room!" the waitress called. "I'll be with you in a shake."

Bailey picked her way to a small table in a far corner. Once seated, she took in the surroundings. Homespun. Basic. Formica tabletops matched the scarred Formica floors. On the walls were horse racing and polo memorabilia and a couple of stuffed fish. Largemouth bass, she thought.

She breathed deeply and her mouth started to water. It smelled wonderful. Like bacon, burgers and homemade biscuits.

As Bailey reached for one of the menus propped between the napkin holder and salt and pepper shakers, the waitress arrived. "Hi there," she said.

The woman looked to be in her thirties and had a handsome, weatherworn face. Not worn in a bad way, but one that spoke of fresh air and sunshine. Her long brown hair was pulled back into a ponytail.

"Hello."

"Sorry about the wait. The other girl didn't show up. Second time this week."

"Ouch."

"You're telling me. You wouldn't be looking for a job, would you?" Before Bailey could respond, she noticed her ring and answered the question herself. "No, I guess not, with a sparkler like that. It's beautiful."

Bailey glanced at it, then back up at her with a smile. "Thank you."

"I'd thank him," she said with a grin. "You know what you want?"

"Haven't even looked. Are you still serving breakfast?"

"Sorry, sugar. Just lunch after eleven."

"How about a BLT?"

"Nice compromise. Chips or fries?"

"Chips. Mayo on the side."

"Perfect. And to drink?"

"Water. With lemon."

"Anything else?"

"A newspaper?"

"I've got the *New Orleans T-P*, the *Baton Rouge Advocate* or our own little *Village Voice*."

Bailey didn't know what she was looking for—or even if there was anything—so she asked for all three. A moment later, the woman set the glass of water and three papers on the table.

As Bailey starting sifting through them, she realized how isolated from the world she had been. She and Logan hadn't watched television at night, she hadn't turned the radio on or looked at the newspaper. She hadn't even been online other than the occasional Facebook update or Tweet. She had been happily ensconced in her own little bubble of bliss.

On the front page of the *Voice* she found what she suspected Billy Ray Williams had wanted her to see.

Second Woman Disappears from Wholesome

And under the picture of a twentysomething young woman with long brown hair and a cocky smile, one word: *"Missing!"*

Bailey skimmed the article. Her name was Amanda

LaPier. She'd last been seen partying at a local bar. The next day, her car was found, keys, purse and cell phone in it. No sign of violence. As if she had been lured out by someone she knew.

Apparently, four years ago another young woman had gone missing. Trista Hook, the M.O. nearly identical.

Bailey finished the article, then skimmed the rest of the *Village Voice*. Home sales and racing stats, theft of horse tranquilizers from a vet's office, a couple of fights that led to arrests at a local honky-tonk. Nothing else that jumped out at her.

Bailey returned to the front-page article and frowned. She felt certain this was what Billy Ray Williams had wanted her to see. But what did it have to do with her or Logan?

The waitress arrived with her sandwich and set the plate in front of her. She indicated the paper. "Creepy, huh."

Bailey didn't comment and she went on. "I tell you what, I never walk to my car alone at night."

Village of Wholesome
Population 718

"Some people even believe there was a third woman. So much for the picture-perfect little village. Can I get you anything else?"

Bailey looked up. "What did you say?"

"Can I get you anything else?"

"No, not that. About a third woman."

"A sweet little gal named—"

She stopped, gaze dropping from Bailey's face to her ring finger, then back up. "I shouldn't have said that. Sometimes my mouth runs away with me and well, that's just pure gossip. My pastor preached on it just this past—"

"Steph! Order up!"

She started to go; Bailey stopped her, remembering

what Logan had said about his first wife leaving him. "Are you talking about True Abbott?"

Her stricken expression said it all.

"Stephanie!"

"I'm sorry, I have to go."

She pulled out her order pad and pen, wrote on it, then laid it on the table. "My number's on there. Call me. I'm so sorry."

CHAPTER NINE

The cold slapped Bailey in the face as she exited Faye's diner. She stuffed the ticket with the waitress's number into her jacket pocket and started toward her SUV.

Only to find Billy Ray Williams there, his cruiser blocking her vehicle, the engine running. She'd had enough of the man and his games, and strode across the parking lot and rapped on his window.

He lowered it. He'd removed his sunglasses and she saw that he had broad, even features and brown eyes, weathered at the corners from years of squinting in the sun. An everyman sort of face.

He smiled pleasantly. "Hello, Mrs. Abbott."

"Cut the crap. It's you, isn't it?"

"Me who what?"

"Believes Logan's first wife is a third missing woman."

"I'm not alone in that belief."

"What game are you playing here?"

"This is no game. Ask your husband about True."

"Don't tell me what to do in my marriage."

"Did he tell you he was investigated in her disappearance?"

He hadn't. But it didn't matter. "She left him."

"Did she?"

"Yes."

"Get in the car."

She laughed, the sound disbelieving. "You're out of your mind."

"Get in and I'll tell you everything you want to know. I'll tell you the truth."

She laughed. "The truth according to you, Chief Williams. Not interested."

"I'm the law."

"That's supposed to mean something? You can't be the law and have an agenda."

"Everyone has an agenda. Mine's uncovering the truth. Bringing it to light."

Instead of acknowledging him, she spun around and stalked to the Range Rover.

"Do you want to live, Mrs. Abbott?"

She stopped. Looked back at him in disbelief. "Are you threatening me?"

He laughed. "Hardly. Just a friendly heads-up."

She unlocked the driver-side door, yanked it open. "Leave me alone."

"Death follows him. It follows that family. You have to ask yourself why." He stuck his head out the window and called after her. "Ask him why he lied when we interviewed him. Why his story kept changing. Does an honest man do that? A concerned husband?"

"You had better move your vehicle now, or I'm going to ram it. Don't think I won't."

Bailey slid in, inserted the key and the powerful engine roared to life. Shaking with anger, she shifted into reverse. In that same moment, Billy Ray flipped on his cherry lights and tore out of the parking lot.

CHAPTER TEN

The courtyard fountain mocked Bailey with its rhythmic trickle and splash. The sun, playing peekaboo with the scattering of clouds, seemed to taunt her for her agitation.

Since returning from town, she had been unable to sit still. She had wandered, inside to outside, upstairs to downstairs. Her mind moving quicker than her feet. It spun with the things Billy Ray Williams had said, the things Stephanie had shared.

Four years. Two women missing.

Some thought True made three.

Logan had been questioned in his wife's disappearance. He'd lied to the police, changed his story. Why would he have done that? She rubbed her forehead. True hadn't disappeared. She'd left of her own free will.

True had been having an affair. Logan had told her so.

"Death follows him. It follows that family."

What did that mean?

And why hadn't Logan told her any of this?

What else hadn't he told her?

A lot, she acknowledged. But what did she expect? She had married a stranger.

No. Bailey drew a deep, steadying breath. She knew him. What she needed to know anyway—that he was strong but gentle, loving and compassionate. He understood loss, because he had lost so much. He had promised to never hurt her.

Everything else was nothing.

She would not allow Billy Ray Williams—or anyone else—to steal her happiness.

Bailey heard him arriving home, the crunch of his tires on the gravel drive. She ran out to meet him, breaking into a smile. "You're home!"

He caught her in his arms and held her tightly. "You make coming home the highlight of my day."

She lifted her face to his. "I love you."

"I love you, too."

They stood a moment, staring stupidly into each other's eyes. Love drunk, she thought. Completely ridiculous.

But wonderful. Worries over what she did and didn't know about her husband and small-town gossip melted away, and she let herself be wrapped in their love and this perfect moment.

Until even in his arms, she was cold. Bailey shivered and he drew away. "You should have grabbed a coat."

"And shoes."

He looked down at her bare feet. "Crazy wife. What were you thinking?"

Tell him, Bailey. He'll answer your questions and everything will make sense again.

Instead, she caught his hand and led him inside. "I've opened a bottle of your favorite Pinot."

"Pour me a glass. I'll get cleaned up."

"Don't go!"

He frowned slightly. "What's wrong?"

She opened her mouth to tell him, then closed it and smiled. "What could be wrong?"

He kissed her. "I'll be back in ten minutes."

"Wait!"

He stopped, frown deepening.

"How'd today go?"

Representatives from the North American Danish Warmblood Association had come to a neighboring breeding farm, Oak Hill Ranch, to inspect the two-year-olds.

"Really well. Paragon scored an eight and Paradox a nine. To give you an idea, a ten is virtually unheard of. I wish you had been there."

If only she had. "Too many horses and horse people, all talking about—"

"Horses."

"Exactly." She waved him off. "Go. I'll get the wine."

The minute he disappeared from view, her doubts returned, flooding her thoughts. Not doubts, she told herself as she poured them both a glass of wine. Concerns.

That she'd married him too fast, that the things she didn't know about him outweighed the things she did.

Stop it, Bailey.

Go to him, let him chase your doubts and fears away.

She picked up the two glasses and hurried upstairs. She entered the bedroom; from the bathroom came the sound of the shower. She crossed to the dresser and set down the glasses. Her hands, she realized, trembled.

Bailey stared at the ruby red liquid a moment, then shifted her gaze. It landed on a photograph of her and her mother. That last birthday they had celebrated together.

It was the only photo in the room. She moved her gaze over the bedroom, taking in every detail, every surface and wall. No framed photographs, awards or other mementos. Nothing personal. Like a well-appointed suite at a luxury hotel.

It's what she had felt the first time she had seen the room, but hadn't been able to put into words.

She imagined the rest of the house, searching her

memory. The portrait of his mother. The photographs of her. Her show ribbons; the Olympic medal.

But where were the pictures of them all as children? Of holidays? What of grandparents? She understood removing any traces of True, considering the circumstances, but what of everyone else? Her mother had even kept a picture of Bailey's no-good daddy, just because he was her father.

What of Logan's father? He'd mentioned him, that he'd passed . . . but not how. Not when. Why were there no photographs of him?

Bailey felt sick to her stomach. Light-headed.

She stepped into the bathroom. He stood in the shower with his back to her. Dark hair slicked to his head. The water sluiced over his wide shoulders, down to the V of his waist. He was magnificent, beautiful.

But *who* was he?

He turned, saw her and smiled. He opened the glass door, poked his head out. "Hi, babe."

"I brought the wine to you."

"Perfect." He held out a hand. "Join me?"

He smiled again. *That* smile. The one that made her melt.

"Yes," she said, her own lips curving up. "I'd like that."

Bailey slipped out of her jeans and shirt, then took his hand and stepped into the shower, still in her bra and panties.

"Nice," he said softly, trailing his finger along the cup's lacy edge, dipping his finger under the delicate fabric.

She arched against him. Greedy not just for his clever hands and mouth, but for the oblivion being with him would bring. The moments of dizzying pleasure, the certainty that came after.

That he was the man she thought he was. That their fairy tale would have a happy ending.

He pushed her up against the shower wall, hands and mouth everywhere. She shuddered and gasped, and dragged his mouth up to hers. He lifted her onto him and took her there, giving her just what she'd longed for.

Oblivion.

CHAPTER ELEVEN

Bailey and Logan lay naked under the sheet, twined together, the ceiling fan circling lazily above them. She trailed her fingers across his chest, thinking of the way she had doubted him. The way she had let her imaginings run away with her.

"Tell me about your day, sweetheart."

As if he had read her mind. She nuzzled his neck. "I spent much of it being ridiculous."

He tipped his head to see her face. "What does *that* mean?"

She sat up. "Our wine, I almost forgot."

She slipped out of bed and crossed to retrieve it.

"Nice view."

She glanced over her shoulder and struck a pose. "Glad to hear that."

"Come back here."

She collected the two glasses and returned to the bed. He sat propped up against pillows, the sheet puddled in his lap, chest, hip and thigh gloriously exposed.

"I like *that* view." She handed him a glass, then crawled in beside him.

"Did you plan anything for dinner?"

She shook her head.

"We could drive into the city?"

"Would that involve putting on clothes?"

"Unfortunately, it would."

"I could whip up a salad? Or some eggs?"

He made a face. "Faye's is open for dinner."

"No, not Faye's."

"Because you were already there today?"

She couldn't hide her shock. "Who told you that?"

"I was joking. Were you there today?"

For a moment, she didn't respond. His forehead wrinkled. "What's wrong?"

"Nothing's . . . wrong."

"So, you were there?"

"Yes."

"Why didn't you tell me?"

"I had a BLT. Hardly a crime."

"I didn't suggest you being there was a crime. You're just acting . . . guilty."

Her cheeks heated. She was. And why? She had done nothing wrong.

She opened her mouth, then shut it. This was her opportunity. Why was she hesitating? The longer she did, the stranger she felt about it. And the more uncomfortable he was becoming. She could see it in his expression.

"I was pulled over today," she said.

"You got a ticket?" He sounded amused.

"A warning. It was a local cop."

"Billy Ray Williams." He said the name flatly, but something dangerous glittered in his eyes.

"Yes. I . . . there's bad blood between the two of you."

"You could say that."

She pressed on. "What's that all about?"

"Ancient history. Did Williams harass you?"

"Why would he?" she asked, the avoidance feeling like a lie.

He didn't respond and she went on. "I heard something at Faye's—"

He snorted. "I hope you took it for what it was worth. That place's a hotbed for local gossip. And the Abbott family is always a favorite topic."

She cringed at the bitterness in his tone and wanted to drop the whole thing. Just go on as if today had never happened.

But she couldn't do that. "I saw a newspaper. I read about the missing women. Why didn't you tell me about them?"

"It didn't cross my mind." He turned to fully face her. "That has nothing to do with us, Bailey."

"Doesn't it, Logan?"

"What does *that* mean?"

"I . . . overheard some conversation. About True."

He stiffened. "You want to be more specific?"

"That she . . . that she didn't leave you. That she went missing and should have been considered a victim of foul play. Like the other two."

"I told you this would happen, I told you about the gossip."

"But not about these other two . . . I just thought we should talk about it."

"There's nothing to talk about. True left me. Those other two women, no one knows what happened to them."

"But—"

"You're going to believe gossip over what your husband tells you is true?"

"That's the problem. You haven't told me anything."

"What else do you need to know?"

"Everything! How can I defend you if I don't know—"

"Why would you have to defend me?"

"Against people who have an ax to grind." She slipped

out of bed and into her robe. "Or these small-minded gossips."

"It shouldn't matter to you."

His voice vibrated with hurt. She steeled herself against the way it made her feel.

"It doesn't." She sat on the edge of the bed. "What matters is you being completely open and honest with me. Hiding things from me—"

"Now I'm *hiding* things from you?"

"I didn't say that. I simply—"

"You, too, Bailey?" He threw back the covers and climbed out of bed. He grabbed his jeans and yanked them on. "One trip into town and suddenly I'm a monster?"

"I didn't say that, either!" She jumped to her feet. "Logan, I'd never say that."

She watched helplessly as he put on his shirt and socks, then stalked to the closet for his boots.

"Where are you going?"

"Out."

"Just tell me what happened!"

He spun to face her. "I did! I came home and she was gone. What else do you need to know?"

"Why do people say that about you? Why would they?"

"Because they found her vehicle at the side of the road!" The words exploded from him. "Unlocked, her keys in it! And I lied about the last time I saw her! Satisfied?"

She brought a hand to her mouth, took a step backward. "Oh, my God, like the others."

"I'm out of here."

"Wait! Talk to me!" He didn't and she ran after him. "Why'd you lie to the police, Logan?"

He stopped, face white with fury. "My pride," he ground out. "Ironic, isn't it? I didn't want our relationship to be on everyone's lips, and it's still all they're talking about. Even you."

Bailey flinched at the disdain in his voice. She followed him downstairs and out to the courtyard. "Stay, Logan! Please, let's talk this out."

"We shouldn't have to."

"Logan!"

Helplessly, she watched as he crossed to the truck, climbed in and left her behind.

CHAPTER TWELVE

Bailey awakened with a start. She had fallen asleep on the keeping room couch, waiting for Logan to return. Her eyes were scratchy and swollen from crying. Her head hurt.

What time was it? She reached for her phone. The display glowed 12:46.

Where was Logan?

Bailey brought the heels of her hands to her eyes. Dammit. How could she have bungled that so badly? He was her husband; they should be able to share everything. She should trust that if she asked, he would answer. Instead, she had danced around her own questions and he had gotten defensive.

"Do you think I'm a monster, too?"

"I'm your husband, you shouldn't need to defend me."

He was right. She should believe in him. Without question.

Bailey sat up. Did he really believe that? That she—or anyone else—thought he was a monster?

Billy Ray Williams did. Death follows him, he had said. It follows his family. What did that mean? His mother had died in an accident, who else? His father?

Where were all their family photographs?

"Why did you lie to the police, Logan?"

"I didn't want our relationship to be on everyone's lips, and it's still all they're talking about. Even you."

She dragged her hands through her hair. Wasn't she the one who had agreed they had their whole life to get to know each other? Bailey's Big Adventure.

He had been defensive.

And she hadn't been fair.

A sound came from the other room. A thud. Like something heavy hitting the floor.

Bailey straightened. "Logan?"

Silence answered. Frowning, she stood, called out again.

Again, nothing. She moved through the kitchen into the front hallway. Light peeked out from the partially open study door.

She reached it. Pushed it the rest of the way open. Several books, on the floor by the desk. The laptop open, a soft glow emanating from it. And Logan, his back to her as he stood in front of his mother's portrait.

She made a sound of relief. "Logan?"

He turned. He held a glass of amber-colored liquid. She caught her breath at his haunted expression.

"You're still here." His words slurred slightly and she realized he must have had quite a lot of whatever was in that glass.

"Where else would I be?"

"Thought you hated me, too."

"God, no. I love you." She crossed to him and took the glass from his hand and set it on the desk. "I was upset. I'm sorry."

"I'm sorry," he said, drawing her against him and burying his face in her hair. "I shouldn't have . . ." He straightened, looked her in the eyes. "I wanted to protect you."

"From what, Logan?"

"All the sadness."

She cupped his face in her hands. "You can't. Sadness, loss, they're a part of life."

"Not this much."

She knew he meant his life, his family. And she understood. "Come to bed."

He didn't move, just stood gazing at her, as if memorizing her image. "How do I keep you safe?"

"I'm not going anywhere."

"That's all I want." He shook his head. "I couldn't protect any of the others. None of them, not even True."

"But she left you."

"What if . . . told myself no . . . but now—"

"Sweetheart, you're not making any sense."

He rested his forehead against hers. "They were fighting."

"Who?"

"Mom 'n' Dad. That night. I should have done something."

Her pulse quickened. "What night?"

"But I didn't," he went on. "I was—"

"When, Logan? When should you have done something?"

"My responsibility . . . to stop—"

He assumed she knew what night he was referring to, or maybe he was simply too drunk for awareness of any of that.

He didn't finish, instead turned away, reached for his glass.

She stopped him. Covered his hand, brought it to her heart. "Don't. It won't help. This will." She searched his gaze. "Talk to me. Turn to me."

"Gone. Without a word. All of . . . blames me."

"Who blames you, Logan? For what?"

"I didn't stop him. I could have. I did . . . nothing. Nothing."

He started to cry. She held him, not knowing what else she could do. She wanted to ask what he could have done, but knew she wouldn't get a real answer.

He rested his forehead against hers. "Got to keep you safe."

"You will. Come to bed. You need sleep."

"No . . . afraid to . . . if I sleep who will watch over you?"

Her eyes filled with tears. "You have to sleep. How can you protect me if you're exhausted? Come to bed," she said again, coaxing.

He let her lead him upstairs. There, she helped him out of his clothes, then stripped out of hers and slipped into bed beside him, curling up against him.

"Need to tell you."

"What?"

"About True. Should have . . . told you . . ."

"What, babe? What should you have told me?"

His eyes had drifted shut.

"Babe? What about True?" She shook him gently. "Tell me about True."

His lids fluttered up, he looked at her, though she thought he was already asleep. "How . . . do I . . . keep . . ."

The words trailed off and he was asleep. Snoring softly.

Bailey gazed at him, thoughts whirling. What had he been about to tell her? About True or his parents? They'd been fighting. He felt to blame, but for what?

She frowned. What had he been doing there in the study, other than getting inebriated? She pictured the desk, the open laptop. He'd been on the computer. The books on the floor, he must have knocked them over when he stood up. That was the sound she'd heard.

How long had he been there? With that thought came

another. They'd fought, and yet when he returned to the house it hadn't been to her. He'd gone to his study and gotten on the computer. What could have been so important?

Something for work, she told herself. That had to be ready for today. She rolled carefully onto her back. Maybe he had come and checked on her, found her sleeping and decided to leave well enough alone. That's what he would tell her in the morning.

But what if he didn't? What if he didn't tell her anything? Could she live with that?

Bailey closed her eyes, breathed deeply. Yes. He was her husband. She trusted him. With her heart and her life.

Even as she repeated that promise in her head, an ugly fear gnawed at her. That something had changed between them today. And in her. Because of Billy Ray. The things he'd said about Logan. And because of those other two women. Something that would make believing for them both more difficult than she could have thought possible.

CHAPTER THIRTEEN

Bailey carefully closed the bedroom door on her way out. It was early and Logan still slept. She had awakened to the same questions that had kept her awake until the wee hours.

And sometime during those hours she had decided what she would do. Just take a look. Prove to herself her imagination was running away with her. She would feel foolish after. Guilty for not having trusted him.

Then she would let it go.

She quickly descended the stairs. At the bottom, she took one last glance back up, then headed to the study.

She stopped in the doorway, took it in. The desk, the big chair behind it turned toward the door. The books on the floor.

She crossed to the desk, slid into the chair, tapped the return key. The computer came to life.

Photos. Of the two of them. From Grand Cayman. Their wedding. She studied them, emotion choking her. Her smile. The joy shining from his eyes. The way they had lingered over their kiss. Dancing on the beach after their "I do." Their laughter.

Tears filled her eyes. She hadn't seen the pictures yet, had been waiting for the photographer to e-mail them.

When had Logan gotten them? She checked the date on the file: *Yesterday.* Yesterday, when she had been breaking his heart with her doubts. When her suspicions had kept her awake and sent him to the bottle for comfort.

"Do you think I'm a monster, too?"

"Bailey? What are you doing?"

She turned. He stood in the doorway, looking hollow-eyed and hungover. Her tears spilled, rolled down her cheeks. "I'm so sorry."

He crossed to the desk, closed the computer and drew her up. He cupped her face in his palms. "Why are you crying?"

She shook her head. "The photographs."

"You found me out." He brushed the tears from her cheeks. "I wanted to surprise you."

"I'm sorry," she said again, and pressed her face into her shoulder.

"Hey. Look at me." She did and he smiled. "What are you sorry about?"

The abbreviated truth, she thought. The whole truth would hurt him again. "Yesterday," she whispered. "Our fight."

"We need to talk."

"What about?"

"True."

She nodded and he led her to the kitchen. There, she made coffee and he drank one glass of water, then another.

"How do you feel?"

"Like hell. Splitting headache."

"Did you take something for it?"

"Upstairs."

"Want something to eat?"

"Not yet. Just coffee."

He motioned to the table. "Let's sit."

She set the mugs on the table and took the chair across from his. Her heart was rapping so hard against the wall of her chest, she wondered if he could hear it.

"I thought everything was perfect between me and True. I really had no clue that she was unhappy."

He took a sip of the coffee, then went on. "I left to go to look at a horse, up near Jackson. When I got home she was gone.

"It wasn't like her not to be here when I got back from out of town, but I thought maybe she'd gone to New Orleans to shop. But as the hours passed, I started to panic."

His voice thickened. "She hadn't returned any of my calls," he said after a moment. "Nobody on the farm knew when she'd left or where she was."

"Even Paul?"

He nodded. "Zephyr had taken ill and he was with him and the vet all day. So I went to the police."

"The Wholesome police? Billy Ray?"

"His uncle Nate was chief at the time. But Billy Ray was part of the investigation."

He went silent. Bailey gave him time, though the moments seemed an eternity.

Finally, he began again. "I was certain something bad had happened to her. An accident or something . . . then they found her car. Abandoned. Her phone and keys in it."

"Like the others," Bailey whispered. "The missing women."

"I was frantic. Out of my head with worry. Desperate to find her. But then"—his voice hardened—"things came to light."

"What kind of things?"

"Charges on her credit card, ones made to a Metairie hotel while I was out of town. And two days before she went missing, she withdrew ten thousand dollars from her own account."

Her heart went out to him. It seemed pretty obvious what had been going on.

"She left all her things. But took the cash." He paused. "To start her new life with whoever she had been seeing."

Bailey curled her hands around the warm mug. "I'm so sorry."

"You need to hear the rest before you decide what you believe. I don't want to do this again."

Speak now or forever hold your peace.

It made her feel weird. As did the way he held her gaze, almost as if in challenge. She cleared her throat. "Billy Ray, he said . . . that he and others think you—"

"Murdered my wife?"

He said the words with such bitterness, she flinched. "Why, Logan? What proof did they have?"

"Proof?" He laughed, the sound hard. "I was questioned by the police. Several times. And not just the Wholesome police. The sheriff's office as well. They searched the house and barn, and found nothing. I had an ironclad alibi. But tongues continue to wag and the legend lives on. At least in Billy Ray Williams's mind."

"Last night, you said you lied to the police."

His mouth thinned. "True and I fought before I left for that trip to Jackson. It was about something stupid, but when they asked I said everything was perfect. I denied arguing. I didn't want it to get out. The Abbott family has been the source of so much gossip, I didn't want my and True's private business to be the talk of the town."

And it had made him look guilty.

"Of course at that point, I had no idea I'd . . . never see True again."

"And they caught you in the lie."

"Yes. And no. As soon as I realized how serious it was, I came clean. But it turned out they already knew. A gardener had overheard us.

"And then there was Billy Ray, shouting from the rooftops that I was a controlling, abusive husband. He contends that when she told me she was leaving me, I killed her. And since his uncle retired in January and Billy Ray took over as chief, it's become an obsession."

"And that's it?"

"That's it."

She couldn't shake the feeling there was more, something he wasn't sharing. The suspicion lurked there, at the edges of her consciousness, taunting her. Otherwise, why Billy Ray's vendetta? Why his obsession with proving True had been murdered?

And then she realized the truth. It was so obvious, she should have seen it a mile off. Billy Ray Williams had been in love with True.

In some weird way, he still was.

"What are you thinking?" he asked.

"That Billy Ray was in love with True."

He nodded. "I've wondered that for a long time, but didn't know how that could be. They saw each other maybe a handful of times. It doesn't make sense."

The problem was, love didn't have to make sense. It just was. She should know.

"Do you have to go to the city today?" she asked.

"Unfortunately. And it will be a late one. A city council meeting."

"Oh."

"I should get cleaned up."

"How about some breakfast?"

"Sounds good. I'll shower, then eat. Will you join me?"

She said she would, then he stopped in the doorway

and looked back at her. "You never said what you were doing in the study."

She stared at him a moment, then shook her head. "Mindless Internet surfing."

"Gotcha." He smiled. "Be back down in ten minutes."

CHAPTER FOURTEEN

Logan left for the city, and Bailey decided to pay Henry a visit. She hated the thought of him out there all alone, no one to talk to but Tony. Besides, she enjoyed his company.

Bailey navigated her SUV down the narrow, twisting drive to Henry's cabin. The pine trees lining the drive were so tall and densely packed, little sun seeped through.

She had visited Henry once before, though that time she had walked, Tony leading the way. She hoped that this time, as she had then, she would find him on his porch, his ancient-looking chair creaking as he rocked.

No such luck, Bailey saw as she drew to a stop in front of the cabin. She climbed out, but before she had taken two steps toward the porch Tony began to bark. By the time she reached the door, he was pawing at it, the sound of his barks turning high-pitched and frantic.

She'd never heard him sound like that before and frowned. "Henry!" she called, rapping on the door. "It's Bailey."

When he didn't answer, she peered inside. The front room was tidy. Her gaze landed on the rug. It looked like Tony'd had an accident in the house.

That didn't make sense. He was completely house-broken. As long as she let him out when he—

He hadn't been let out.

"Henry!" she called again. "It's Bailey!" She tried the door. It opened and Tony darted past her. She watched as he reached the grass and lifted a leg.

A sick feeling in the pit of her stomach, she stepped inside. It stank of dog urine and feces. She brought her hand to her nose and made her way deeper into the cabin.

This wasn't right. The smell. The quiet. She should go for help. Call someone—

Tony barreled back inside and past her. He stopped at a doorway and looked back as if to say, "What are you waiting for?," then darted through.

She followed. The cabin's single bedroom. Henry on the bed. Unmoving.

A cry on her lips, she rushed across the room. "Henry! It's me, Bailey! Wake up!"

He didn't respond and Tony leaped onto the bed, then began licking his face.

Henry moaned.

Alive. Thank God.

Bailey shooed Tony away. Henry's scarred face was flushed. She laid a hand on his forehead, found him burning up with fever. She wondered how long he had been ill, it could have been days now.

His eyes opened. They were glassy with fever.

"True," he said.

"No, it's Bailey." He caught her hand. His skin was dry and hot. "True," he said again. "I was so afraid they had—"

He moaned again, his eyes closing and his grip going limp.

He needed water, she thought. And a fever reducer.

But when she tried to go, he clutched her hand again. "Don't go."

Tears stung her eyes. Her mother had said almost the same thing to her the day she died.

"I won't, I promise. I'll be right back." His grip didn't ease. "I promise, Henry. I'm just going to get you some water."

And then he let go. His eyes closed and she saw the tension slip out of him. For one terrifying moment, she thought he had died. Just slipped away, the way her mother had.

No, she realized as she saw his chest rise and fall.

She hurried for the water. Then rifled through the bathroom for some Advil. She found some, said a silent prayer and returned to the old man's side.

She got the fever reducer and some water down him, then went for a cool, damp cloth.

Minutes passed as she alternated between offering him sips of water and replacing the cloths. He moaned and stirred. Occasionally he flailed, batting at imaginary demons. Each time, she would speak quietly and softly and he would again fall into a fitful sleep.

Finally, his skin cooled and he slipped into what appeared to be a peaceful sleep, Tony curled up beside him.

When she was certain she could leave his side, Bailey cleaned up Tony's messes, scrubbing the floor and rug and depositing the refuse in the outside bin, then went back to sit by the bed.

A photo there on the nightstand caught her eye. Logan's mother, she realized. Young and lovely, standing beside a horse, smiling at the camera. Bailey picked it up, squinting at the grainy image. Not at the camera. At Henry. Totally relaxed and happy.

She replaced the photo, then crossed to the dresser, to a couple more. Another of Elisabeth Abbott, with babies in her arms. Two babies. Another, of Logan and another boy. Logan looked to be ten or so, the other boy half that. They stood side by side, shirtless, broad smiles on their faces.

She studied the photograph. The other boy looked eerily similar to Logan. In fact, their faces were near replicas of each other's. They could be twins save for the fact Logan was clearly older.

Her legs went weak. A brother? Logan had a brother he hadn't told her about? They looked so similar, it had to be.

How could he not have told her about a brother? It took her breath away.

What else hadn't he told her?

She shifted her attention to the next photo. Logan, Raine and the other boy. Raine, also smiling. Looking carefree and truly happy, Bailey thought. They all did.

That hurt, too. She wondered what had happened to steal their happiness.

Bailey ventured out of the bedroom. As she had suspected she would, she found more photographs. The kind missing from the big house. Of children growing up. Events in their lives.

Of a family, proudly displayed.

Henry thought of Logan's family as his own, she realized. Tears pricked her eyes and she moved on. Among the shots of the Abbott kids were several of another girl. In first communion white; atop a horse with a big, blue ribbon affixed to its bridle; in a high school graduation cap and gown. She looked familiar, Bailey thought, though she didn't know from where.

The last photograph caused her to stop. True. At least that's who she suspected the lovely blonde in the photograph was, her arms around Logan.

She and True did look alike. Bailey cocked her head,

studying the image. The woman's bright, beautiful smile. Her hair and eyes, the shape of her mouth and tilt of her chin. Perhaps, from a distance, each could be mistaken for the other, or by a mere acquaintance. But those familiar with the women would immediately realize the truth: Bailey was a pale imitation of the other woman.

The realization brought more than a pinch of jealousy and the horrible question: When Logan said he had eyes only for her, was it because she looked like True?

A sound came from the bedroom. Henry stirring. Muttering something. She hurried back. "It's all right," she murmured. "You're going to be just fine."

But was he? she wondered, laying her hand gently on his forehead. She had no idea how long he had been sick, whether what he had was viral or bacterial. She couldn't leave him out here alone; he could very well need professional care. At his age, maybe a hospital.

A hospital. But how would she get him into the Range Rover? Logan wouldn't be home from New Orleans for hours and by then— Paul, she thought. Paul could help her.

CHAPTER FIFTEEN

Paul took one look at Henry and decided they needed to get him to the emergency room. He had to carry the man to the truck; the emergency room doctor immediately admitted him.

Bailey sat in the waiting room, Paul at the nurses' station, trying to get ahold of Henry's niece. In the meantime, she had left Logan a message about what was going on.

"Steph's on her way," Paul said, stepping back into the room. "She was pretty upset."

"Where's she coming from?"

"Wholesome." He settled into the seat beside her. "You haven't met?"

She shook her head. They fell silent.

After several moments, Paul broke it. "You let Logan know where you were?"

"I did."

"Good."

Bailey glanced his way. "How'd you two become friends?"

"Logan and I?" She nodded. "We've known each other since elementary school."

"Which doesn't answer my question."

The corner of his mouth lifted in a rueful grin. "He championed me."

She eyed him. Tall and strong. An air of solid confidence. "You hardly look like you would need a champion."

"I did then. I was this funny-looking kid. All freckles and bones."

She laughed. "You were not!"

"Oh, I was. And weird, too. A total weirdo."

Her laughter faded. "You got picked on."

"They more appropriately call it bullying now, but yeah, I did." He shrugged off her sympathy before she could even express it aloud. "One day Logan stepped in. Nobody bothered me again."

"Just like that?"

"Pretty much. He was the school yard stud, even back then."

She couldn't help but smile, imagining Logan in that role. "But it still doesn't explain your friendship."

"You're a little pushy, you know that?"

She smiled. "But in a good way."

He snorted. "Logan decided he liked me, though at the time I was straight-up starstruck. But it turned out we had things in common. Horses, for one. We'd both have lived in the barn, if we could have."

She loved hearing about Logan as a child. Loved picturing him that way. "How old were you?"

"Eight, I think. Things really changed when he brought me to Abbott Farm. Elisabeth took one look at—"

"His mom?"

"Yeah, sorry. That's what she wanted me to call her. She took one look at scrawny little me and that was that."

"What was that?"

"I had a new family. Metaphorically speaking."

"What does that mean?"

"I went home at night, most nights anyway. But my heart wasn't there, it wasn't where I belonged." His tone changed subtly, became harder. "They didn't deserve me. That's what Elisabeth told me."

"Paul!"

Bailey turned. Paul got to his feet and crossed to meet the woman rushing toward them. She had met her before, Bailey realized as the two hugged. Stephanie was the waitress from Faye's Diner—and the girl from the photographs at Henry's, all grown-up now.

"How is he?" she asked.

"Dehydrated. Weak. Blood work's not back yet, but the doctor suspects it's the flu that's been going around. But he's stable."

Her eyes flooded with tears. "Can I see him?"

"Absolutely." Paul looked her in the eyes. "He's going to be okay, Steph."

"But if you hadn't— It's my job to make certain—"

"Don't thank me, thank Bailey. She's the one who noticed she hadn't seen him and went to check on him."

She turned to Bailey, though she didn't quite meet her eyes. "I can't tell you how appreciative I am. Uncle Henry's all I— Thank you," she whispered. "Excuse me."

Bailey watched her duck into Henry's room, then turned to Paul. "What now?"

"I've got to get back to the farm."

"I think I'll stay."

"Stephanie's here now, Henry's in good hands. He'll be fine, Bailey."

"I know, but she seemed pretty upset. I hate to leave her alone."

He checked his watch, then nodded. "Do you know your way back?"

She assured him that even if she didn't, her GPS did,

and promised to call if she ran into trouble. And then she sat and waited for Stephanie to return.

Which she did after thirty or forty minutes. "Hey," she said.

"How's Henry?" Bailey asked.

"He's asleep. Resting comfortably, as they say in places like this."

"That's good."

"The doctor said"—she cleared her throat, her eyes welling with tears—"if you hadn't shown up when you did, he might have died."

Bailey crossed to her, and gave her a hug. "But I did. He's going to be fine. Right?"

"Right." She smiled weakly and indicated the bank of chairs. "Do you mind? I feel a bit weak in the knees."

Bailey got her a cold drink, then sat beside her while she sipped.

"Henry's my dad's brother. He never married." She paused, then said almost to herself, "Of course he didn't."

"Because of what happened to him?"

Stephanie looked at her strangely. "I'm so sorry about yesterday."

"You shouldn't be."

"Yeah, I should. As a kid I spent a lot of time at Abbott Farm. Logan's my friend."

"So you don't believe the rumors?"

"No," she said, "I don't." She looked down at her hands, then back up at Bailey. "There's something I need to tell you."

"Tell me? What?"

"I watched you leave Faye's yesterday. I saw you talking to Billy Ray. Saw what he was doing."

She paused. Bailey waited.

"At one time, Billy Ray and I were in a relationship."

She looked away, then back. "In fact, I was in love with him."

Bailey didn't know how to respond, so she said nothing.

"He didn't love me back," she finished, words thick with emotion.

"He loved True, didn't he?"

"Yes. He still does." Again she stopped, but this time as if to collect her thoughts. "I finally admitted the truth and broke it off.

"There's something else. I've never told anyone. It's something that happened when he and I were together."

A heaviness settled in Bailey's chest. A feeling that she wouldn't like what the other woman had to say, that once she said it there would be no going back. She didn't know why—the seriousness of Stephanie's tone or a premonition—but it took all her control not to just walk away.

"We were lovers. At his house, there's a room he keeps locked. He said he used it for storage, but I knew he was lying. I caught him in there once, he closed the door before I could see much. But—"

"What?" Bailey prodded. "Tell me, please."

"I got a peek inside. A board with diagrams and photos. There were pictures of True." She paused. "And one of Logan. At the center of the board."

Pictures of True. A picture of Logan. At the center. For a moment, Bailey felt as if she couldn't breathe. "Did you ask him about it? What did he say?"

"I pretended I didn't see anything. But it really freaked me out."

"What do you think it means?"

"I don't know for sure, but . . . I think he's trying to build a case against Logan."

"I don't understand."

"A case proving that Logan not only killed True, but is also responsible for the women who've gone missing."

Bailey felt sick. "That's crazy."

"That's Billy Ray. Crazy."

"He can't have proof Logan did that. Because he didn't. I know he didn't."

Bailey heard the frantic edge in her voice and struggled to control it. "If he really did have evidence, he'd have used it a long time ago."

"He won't quit trying. He's obsessed. I just . . . thought you should know."

Bailey knew she should respond, thank her. Instead, she stood. "I need to be getting back to the farm."

Stephanie reached up and grabbed her hand. "It hasn't been easy for Logan. He takes so much on himself. Responsibility for everything from his mother's murder to his brother's suicide." She shook her head. "Just love him, Bailey. That's what he needs from you."

CHAPTER SIXTEEN

For a long time after she exited the hospital, Bailey sat in her vehicle, engine running, thoughts whirling. Logan's mother murdered? A brother who committed suicide? She pictured the boy from the photographs at Henry's and shuddered. No wonder he didn't speak much of the past. No wonder he was guarded to the point of secretive.

True's desertion. Another betrayal. The horrible rumors. Being investigated by the police.

"Death follows him. It follows that family."

Not death. Tragedy. How unfair to point at Logan that way. He was the victim, not a perpetrator. One of the victims. Raine was another. Anyone all this sadness had touched.

Her, too, now that she loved him.

Tears stung her eyes. *"Just love him. That's what he needs from you."*

Bailey rested her head against the seat back. But how did she love someone she didn't know? Who kept so much of himself locked away?

She could be *in* love with him, but it wasn't the same as love in the transformative sense, where two people became as one. Sharing everything. Leaning on each other for everything.

In sickness and in health.

Until death do us part.

The chirp-chirp of a car's auto lock came from the car beside her. A man and a woman arriving. Bailey realized she was crying and sat up, pretending to be searching for something in her purse on the passenger-side seat.

She felt the couple's curious gazes, and knew they probably thought someone she loved was ill. That she had been visiting. Or saying good-bye.

Maybe she should. Say good-bye. Leave Logan and Abbott Farm behind. He'd kept so much from her. Deliberately. His choice. If she stripped it down, took away all the romance, the sex and sunrises, he had deceived her. Manipulated her, stolen *her* right to make an informed decision about marriage to him.

Bailey wiped the tears from her cheeks. She wanted to be angry. Indignant. That would be so much more palatable than this hurt. This feeling of betrayal.

She could confront him. Demand he tell her everything, spill his guts. Or else.

She let out a long breath. She'd find no satisfaction in that. She wanted him to fully trust her. To let her in, without tears or ultimatums.

The way she had him. She had told him about her father leaving, her mother's illness and the toll caring for her had taken. She'd shared her hopes and dreams, her fears. Before they'd left the island. Before I do. Before, before, before.

What he had shared with her would fill a teacup.

But she loved him anyway. She had tied her life to his, had chosen to believe their fairy tale. For better or worse, crazy or not.

Happily ever after.

She could believe enough for the both of them.

Bailey straightened. She wouldn't let their love slip

away. She would love him hard enough, completely enough, to burrow through his defenses.

But she needed help. Someone who knew everything about him and his past. Who understood and loved him. Two people came to mind. One whose loyalty made him tight-lipped, the other whose emotional instability made her dangerous.

But Raine loved him the way only a sister who had suffered the same blows could.

Of course, Raine. Although it might take a miracle.

Bailey punched "Home" into her GPS; the system directed her to *"proceed to the highlighted route."*

Good advice, she thought. And exactly her plan. She shifted the Range Rover into gear.

The sun had begun its final descent as Bailey made her way up the drive to Raine's cottage and studio. The landscape was wild and lovely, very much like the woman. Several pieces of abstract sculpture adorned the green spaces near the buildings—one of which was lyrical, with colorful pieces that caught the light and spun in the wind like pinwheels. Bailey detested the other two on sight—muscular and somehow threatening, like New Age gargoyles.

She parked in front of the two buildings. It wasn't difficult to pick the house from the studio—the house looked like many of the cottages Bailey had seen around town, with a wide front porch and Victorian trim; the other was modern and minimalist, incongruent with the natural setting.

Lights burned inside the latter, and pasting a friendly smile on her face, she approached. Raine opened the door before Bailey knocked. She wore a painter's apron, decorated with what looked to be a lifetime of paint; shorts and a T-shirt under the apron. Latex gloves, also smeared with paint, covered her hands.

Her eyebrows drew down into a frown. "This is a surprise."

"Hello, Raine." Bailey handed her the bottle of wine she had purloined from Logan's wine closet. "I hoped we could visit."

Raine looked at the bottle's label, then back up at her. One corner of her mouth lifted in amusement. "You chose well. Just hope Logan doesn't miss it."

She moved aside and Bailey stepped into the studio, little more than a large box with windows and a vaulted ceiling, a half-dozen fans suspended from its rafters. The smell of the oil paint and turpentine stung her nose, though it wasn't overpowering. Obviously Raine had taken care to install good ventilation.

Bailey moved her gaze over the space. Color and texture, light and dark, line and shape. Surrounding her, on every wall and easel, stacked in vertical racks were the most grotesque paintings she had ever seen.

"They're awful, aren't they?"

"No, of course not." Bailey meant it. They were powerful. And powerfully disturbing. Dark, violent and raw.

"I'm not a favorite of interior designers."

"Which pleases you."

It wasn't a question, but Raine answered anyway. "Art is supposed to arouse emotion. Stimulate thought. Not lull one into a well-coordinated stupor."

"I get that."

"Do you?"

"Despite what you might think of your brother's choice, Raine, I'm neither stupid nor completely uncultured. And this may shock you, but there are even art museums in Nebraska."

Raine laughed. "You do have fire. I'm not sure it's

enough for the long haul, but it'll make for interesting viewing."

"Such cynicism. Don't you believe in love?"

"Careful, darling sister-in-law, you'll make me puke."

Bailey watched as she crossed to a workbench, removed her gloves and retrieved a corkscrew. "This is way too good of a wine for a Tuesday afternoon, but let's live dangerously."

She expertly extracted the cork, then poured some into two colorful plastic cups. "Mardi Gras cups," she said as she handed her one. "They throw them from the floats. Cheers."

Bailey studied the cartoon-like image on hers, of a bearded man wearing a crown of grapevines.

"Krewe of Bacchus," Raine offered. "God of wine and revelry. Appropriate, don't you think?"

Bailey took a sip, although the last thing she felt like drinking on a warm afternoon was red wine.

"Do you like it?" Raine asked.

"It's delicious."

"It should be. Street value is about two-fifty."

Bailey almost choked. Raine laughed. "The perfect butter-me-up gift. I did say you'd chosen well."

Bailey set down her cup and returned to her question from a moment ago. "You never answered, do you believe in love?"

"The romantic version? Death do us part and all that?"

"Yes."

"Do you?"

"Obviously."

"How lucky you are to be such an innocent." Raine crossed to the sink and donned another pair of gloves, these brand-new. The kind TV detectives wore.

"Which answers my question," Bailey said.

"I'm afraid so."

Bailey reached for her cup. "Why do you dislike me?"

"I don't like having people forced down my throat. And that's exactly what Logan is doing—again—and it pisses me off."

Bailey tried another tack. "But you do want him to be happy?"

"Happiness is illusory." Raine began to clean the paint off her brushes. "But, yes, more than anything. More than my own happiness."

"Then help me. That's all I want."

"Be the adoring little wife and he will be."

"Why are you so mean?"

She laughed but didn't look up. "I think that's why you're here, isn't it? You're wondering about all the things he won't talk about? Why he won't and how you can get him to let you in?"

How had Raine known? Was she that transparent, or Logan that predictable?

"Only partly," she said. "I really would like us to be friends."

Raine snorted at that and Bailey went on. "Tell me about your other brother."

"Roane?"

Bailey worked to keep her excitement from showing. His name had been Roane. "Yes."

"Why?" She stopped and looked at her. "What does it matter if you know about my poor dead twin? How will that make Logan happy?"

The two babies in the photograph at Henry's. Twins. Raine and Roane.

"You said it yourself, I need to understand him. So I can help him."

"Help him?" she repeated. "Change him, you mean." She laughed. "Just let him be. Enjoy your good fortune while you can."

She was so very brittle, Bailey thought. And angry. It glittered in her eyes and vibrated in her acid tone.

Bailey's heart went out to her, for all the loss she had suffered. But it was her husband she meant to save. "What does that mean?"

"Nothing."

But Bailey had a good idea what it meant, and she wasn't about to let it pass. "I love him," she said again. "And I'm not going to stop loving him."

"And to do that, you have to peel back the layers." She finished with the brushes and laid them out on a rack. "Peek under the rock and see what's lurking there?"

She had begun moving around the studio as she spoke, touching this and that. She stopped now and looked directly at Bailey. "You won't like what you find."

"You can't scare me."

"Oh, but I think I can."

Raine took up her cup, sipping as she went from one painting in progress to the next. Pausing a moment to study, then flitting on to the next. Genuine nervous energy? Bailey wondered. Or artifice? Meant to prove how bizarre she was?

"You sound like someone else. 'I *love* him,'" Raine mocked, refilling her cup. "'I want him to be *happy*.' We see how well that worked out."

"True."

"Of course True." She stopped and looked at her again. "You even look like her. Not as pretty, but similar."

"I've seen pictures of her."

"Really?" She looked surprised. "Where?"

"Henry's."

She nodded, her expression becoming faraway. "True was beautiful. And sweet." Longing in her tone. An ache. "Like a butterfly. Too vulnerable for this shark tank."

Raine laughed again, then shook her head. "She was

ten years younger than Logan. You're ten years younger, as well. Why do you think he keeps marrying younger women?"

Bailey tried not to get her back up, tried to hide how offended she was. Raine had gotten enough points this go-around. "It's not that unusual," Bailey said. "People do it all the time."

"Men," Raine said. "More than women. For obvious reasons."

"Logan isn't just any man."

"No, he's not. And he could have anyone." She stopped again. Pinned her with that somehow feral gaze. "Why you?"

Bailey tried not to flinch. Unsuccessfully, she knew by the gleam that came into Raine's eyes.

"Bull's-eye." Smiling, Raine brought her glass to her lips. "You're not a dumb woman, at least."

"And you're not a nice one."

"You didn't answer my question. Why you?"

"I have no idea. But you do. Or you think you do."

"You won't like it."

"I can handle it."

"Because young women are starry-eyed. And gullible. And fall so very easily into love."

"We're dumb, is that what you're saying?"

"Some are. Not you. Impetuous maybe. A bit desperate."

That last hurt, Bailey hoped she kept it from showing.

"Did he tell you that he kept True a secret from us, as well? Oh, I see by your expression that he didn't." She smiled. "No worries, sweet Bailey, their courtship was quite different. He didn't fly off to a Caribbean island and come home with a wife."

"That's a relief."

Raine smiled at Bailey's sarcasm. "She was a nail tech.

Another under-achiever. Like you, no family. Or almost none. A crazy, drug-addled mother. True was a Mississippi girl. The Jackson area. They met when Logan was there on business. Dated several months, married in Vegas, then voilà! Raine had a sister."

"You didn't like her."

Her eyes filled with tears. She blinked against them and whirled away. "Everyone loved True. Me included."

"Why'd she leave him? What went wrong?"

She stopped, her back to Bailey. "Do you really want to do this?"

"This?"

She looked over her shoulder. "Peek under that rock? See what's hiding there in the dark?"

"Yes."

Raine's shoulders drooped, as if all the fight had left her. She sank onto the stool in front of a large, dark painting. The one she had been working on, Bailey thought.

For long moments, she simply gazed at it. Then she spoke. "I don't know. Though it nearly beat him."

"I won't hurt him, Raine. I promise you."

"But what about you?" She looked over her shoulder at Bailey. "Death follows him. That's what they say, you know. That death follows us, this family."

Chill bumps raced up her arms. Bailey steeled herself against them. "I know. I think people are being cruel, saying that."

"You heard it in town."

"Yes."

"I'm not surprised." Raine turned back to the painting. "All dead. Mama and Roane. Daddy. True," she added, voice barely a whisper.

The blood began to thunder in Bailey's head. "What did you say?"

When Raine didn't respond, Bailey took a step toward her. "You said True's name. But True's not dead."

For a moment, Raine simply gazed at her painting as she sipped her wine. Then, without looking at her, she said, "Or so you've been told."

"Stop it."

"Who will be next? You?"

"Enough!"

"I'm just being honest. Isn't that why you came here today?"

"That's not what you're doing and we both know it."

A smile touched her lips. "Shaken, I see. Poor little Bailey. You should run now. While you still have the chance."

This had been a mistake, Bailey acknowledged. Coming here. Thinking anyone both as brilliant and unstable as Raine would do anything but toy with her.

"I thought you might care enough for your brother to help me. But I did learn something and I thank you for that."

Bailey set her cup on a workbench and crossed to the door. When she reached it, she stopped. "Just so you know, you can't chase me away. I'm here to stay."

"Bailey?" She met the other woman's eyes. "Roane hung himself. On our sixteenth birthday."

CHAPTER SEVENTEEN

The night had gobbled up the last of the sun. The cold, damp air chilled Bailey clear to her bones. She climbed out of her SUV and hurried to her front door.

"Roane hung himself. On our sixteenth birthday."

She stepped inside. Darkness greeted her. And cold. She shivered and flipped on the foyer light. Light washed over her, but not warmth.

What must that feel like? Every new birthday, being reminded of the twin you'd had. And lost. Even the thought of it grabbed tightly ahold of her diaphragm.

Bailey struggled to breathe past it and crossed to the thermostat, nudged the temperature up.

And what of Logan? How had the loss affected him?

Tears stung her eyes and she glanced at her watch. Just after six. Logan had said the council meeting was at seven, maybe she could catch him before he went in?

She dug her phone out of her purse and dialed. He answered immediately.

"Logan, it's me."

She sounded shaky, even to her own ears.

"Are you okay?" Immediate concern, an edge of panic in his voice.

She shouldn't have called until she'd pulled herself together.

"Bailey?"

"Yes." She cleared her throat. "I'm fine. I just . . . needed to hear your voice."

"I miss you, too. How's Henry?"

"Stable. They're keeping him overnight. Stephanie's with him."

"Good. You're home?"

"Yes." She paused. "But it's cold."

"Light a fire in the keeping room. It's gas. The key's on the mantel."

"I wish you were home."

"Are you sure you're okay? You sound very strange."

"I went to see . . . Raine. She told me about your brother. About Roane."

He was silent. She heard the murmur of voices coming from around him. Finally, he cleared his throat. Even so, when he spoke, his voice was thick with emotion. "I'm sorry, I . . . hate that you found out that way. I should have—"

"It's okay. I get it." She realized her lips were trembling and she pressed them together a moment. "It's me who's . . . I'm so sorry, Logan. I can only imagine how much that hurt. How much it still must hurt."

Someone said his name, called him into the meeting. "You have to go."

"I do, baby. I'm sorry. About this and now. It's going to be a few more hours."

"I'll wait up."

Then he was gone. And she was bereft. Left with nothing to hold on to but Raine's ugly words. The image they cast in her head. The terrible things she had learned earlier. The feeling of betrayal.

She needed Logan. His reassuring arms. The warmth of his body, driving away the cold.

Their wedding pictures.

Bailey dropped her purse on the entryway table and headed into the office. She switched on the desk lamp, then sank into the chair. The computer was still on, and when she lifted the cover the photos of her and Logan filled the screen. Visual confirmation of their love. That she hadn't made a mistake. She scrolled through them, marking her favorites, losing time. Raine's words becoming further away.

Her stomach growled and she realized the time. That she hadn't eaten since early in the day. That Logan would be home soon. She moused up to close the computer window and accidentally clicked on the edge of one behind it.

The face of Amanda LaPier stared back at her. The young woman who had recently gone missing.

She scrolled down, hand trembling. The photo was connected to the same news story she had read in the *Wholesome Village Voice*.

Deep breath, Bailey. It doesn't mean anything. Considering their argument, it even made sense.

Another open window, she saw. Behind this one.

Even as she told herself to close the laptop and walk away, she tapped it open.

A Web site. NecroSearch International—an outfit dedicated to helping law enforcement locate clandestine graves.

Clandestine graves.

She stared at the image, confused, light-headed. The moment felt surreal. Like something out of a novel. In the blink of an eye, everything changed. The world stopped. And shrank. Zeroed in until it consisted of her, the laptop, a digital image of a woman she didn't know.

And a Web site she could think of only one reason her husband would be interested in.

She moved the cursor up to recent history. More stories. About LaPier. And Trista Hook, the woman who had previously gone missing. And not just one, many. As if he had been scouring the media for any news of the investigation.

Bailey swallowed against the bile that rose in her throat. Last night, this entire search. This was what he had been doing down here. Searching. Studying. Why?

She heard the slam of a car door. Her gaze flew to the clock. *Logan. Home.*

She couldn't talk to him. Not now. Couldn't look at him. He would know. What should she—

Think, Bailey. Think.

Go to bed. Quickly, heart racing, she closed the windows and shut the laptop. She snapped off the desk lamp, leaped to her feet, darted into the foyer.

And paused. She heard him in the kitchen. The sound of ice dropping into a glass, the water running.

Bailey flew up the stairs to the bedroom. There, she stripped out of her clothes and slid into bed. She curled up on her side, pretending to be asleep.

He entered the room. She heard the soft whoosh of his breath being expelled.

"Bailey?"

She lay quietly, breathing as deeply and evenly as she could with blood pounding and thoughts racing. She heard him cross to the bed, felt him standing over her. He bent; his breath stirred against her cheek.

In the next moment, the bedroom door clicked softly shut and she was alone again.

CHAPTER EIGHTEEN

The next morning, Bailey threw up. She bent over the commode and heaved, though nothing came up but bile. She rinsed her face and brushed her teeth, then turned to find Logan in the doorway. Fully dressed, ready for the day.

"Are you all right?" he asked.

"Yes, I—" She laid a hand on her stomach. "I must have eaten something that didn't agree."

But she hadn't eaten. Food, anyway. What she'd ingested was suspicion. And doubt. She was sick with it.

"Maybe you picked up a bug?" He crossed to her and laid a hand on her forehead. "You feel a little clammy. But cool."

She took a step back. "I'm fine, really."

He frowned slightly. "You didn't wait up last night."

"I just . . . couldn't." *Not a lie. None of it. Her heart was shattered.* "I'm sorry."

He gazed at her a moment. "I bought you something." He said it stiffly. Retreating from her. As if she had become a stranger to him.

She had, Bailey thought. This woman sick with doubt, a stranger even to herself.

"Thank you."

"You don't even know what it is. Come see."

An iPad, she saw a moment later.

"It's all set up. E-mail, Internet, everything. I even loaded our wedding pictures."

She held it in her hands. Stared at it as if it were a snake. *So she wouldn't use his computer. So she wouldn't have access to his secrets.*

"What's wrong?"

"Nothing," she lied. "I love it."

"I thought you'd like to be able to connect anywhere. Especially with me gone so much." He paused. "Would you rather have a laptop?"

She shook her head. "This is perfect. Thank you."

They stood there in the bedroom, awkwardly silent. He cleared his throat. "I'm afraid it might be another late night."

Bailey wasn't sure what to say. What to feel: despair or relief. "Okay. Just . . . let me know."

He hesitated, then bent and brushed his mouth against hers. "I'll miss you."

"I miss you, too."

"I haven't left yet."

"You know what I meant."

"I think I do." He held her gaze until she looked away. "I'll call you later then."

He left the bedroom. It felt as if the best part of her were going with him. A cry flew to her lips and she started after him.

"Logan! Wait!"

She ran down the stairs and into his arms. Bailey clung to him, face pressed against his chest. "I love you so much."

He shuddered; his arms curved around her. He held her silently.

"I'm not myself today," she said. "That's all."

"Rest. You'll feel better."

She walked him to the door, watched him drive off. When she turned back, her gaze landed on his office, door open to the hallway. His desktop.

The laptop was gone.

CHAPTER NINETEEN

As the days passed, the awkwardness between Bailey and Logan grew. They approached each other cautiously, married strangers, she with her unspoken fears and he with his secrets.

He had to know she'd viewed his Internet search history. It's why he'd bought her the tablet, why he now took his laptop to and from the city with him each day.

But he hadn't mentioned it.

And she hadn't brought it up.

The proverbial elephant in the room, which they danced around, the distance between them growing.

"Pay attention!" August ordered, sounding frustrated. "Elbows back. She's leading you. When a horse figures out they're in charge, you're in trouble."

Bailey had taken August up on his promise to get her back in the saddle and comfortably riding by Logan's birthday. After her initial terror, she had begun to relax and trust, then actually enjoy being on a horse again.

Now, she made the adjustment, working to concentrate. Elbows slightly bent. Hold the reins lightly but with control. Sit bones firmly planted. Eyes fixed straight ahead. The horse followed her, not the other way around.

August made a sound of disgust. "This isn't like riding a bike, Bailey. If you forget to pedal, the bike doesn't take over. It's how people get hurt."

How people get hurt.

A broken heart. A clandestine grave.

"Death follows him."

She shook her head, trying to focus. Failing miserably.

"Bailey, for God's sake! Pay attention!"

She drew back on the reins and Tea Biscuit stopped.

August strode over. "You look like a rag doll up there."

"I'm sorry," she said automatically, forcing a wan smile. "At least I'm not afraid anymore."

"Maybe you should be."

He held her gaze. She suddenly felt as if she couldn't breathe.

"Do you really want to peek under that rock? See what's lurking there?"

"I need to get off."

"Don't overreact. Just put your mind—"

"Now. I need to get off now!"

Without waiting for his reply, she swung out of the saddle. As her feet landed on the ground, she realized her legs were shaking. She tried to hide it from August.

But August Perez missed nothing. "What's wrong with you?"

"Nothing." She led Tea Biscuit back to the barn. He fell in step beside her.

"Are you and Logan fighting?"

"No."

"I could always tell when he and True had fought. She radiated it, poor darling."

"I don't want to talk about True. And I'm not in the mood for your nonsense."

"Now *my* heart is broken."

Bailey ignored the subtle stress he put on the sentence. The only way to win a verbal sparring with August was to not play.

They reached the barn. She tied up Tea Biscuit, then removed the bit. The horse responded by stretching her jaw. "Poor baby," she said, and stroked her. "I wouldn't like that thing in my mouth, either."

She offered her a treat—her favorite, a Starlight mint. Watching the horse suck on it always made her smile. She removed the saddle, but left the blanket on for now, not wanting the horse to get chilled.

Once she cooled down, she would brush her out. Until then, Bailey busied herself with the hoof pick, cleaning out dirt and debris. August stood by, watching her.

She usually loved grooming the animal, usually responded in an elemental way to it. Tea Biscuit did as well, evident in the way she nickered or neighed when she saw her, the way she picked up on Bailey's mood.

"I know you went to see Raine."

Bailey paused, looked up at August. "She called you."

It wasn't a question; he answered anyway. "Yes. Practically gleeful. Don't let her get to you, darling. She's evil, you know that."

"She's not evil," Bailey said softly. "She's sad. Terribly sad."

"Is that what's wrong with you today?" August asked. "Raine's malicious agenda?"

"No. And yes." She paused. "I know about Roane. That he hung himself."

"I'm impressed. I was here a year before I learned there'd been another Abbott sibling. Of course, now I know where all the bodies are buried."

"What did you say?"

"A figure of speech, darling."

He was playing with her. A cat with a vulnerable mouse. The way they all did here.

No, she thought. Not Logan. Instead, he said nothing at all.

Bailey ran her hands over the horse, checking for bumps or wounds. Finding none, she looked back up at August. "Will you help me?"

He cocked an eyebrow. "I thought that's what I was doing?"

She shook her head. "What was True like? Really?"

"Beautiful and kindhearted. Completely devoted to Logan. Madly in love."

Bailey snorted. "Right."

"She was."

"Madly in love but having an affair? Completely devoted, yet she runs off when his back is turned?"

He met her gaze. "Maybe she didn't run off?"

She stiffened. "Not you, too?"

"Keeping it real, beautiful. That's all."

"What about the money she withdrew? What about those nights at a hotel, while Logan was out of town?"

"Maybe there's an explanation for those other than infidelity."

Bailey narrowed her eyes on him. "If you know something, you should tell me. Or better yet, Logan."

He laughed, the sound hard. "I don't know anything." He leaned toward her. "I only know what I believe."

Her mouth went dry. "And what is that?"

"I think True's dead. I think they're all dead."

The words, what they meant, affected her like a gut punch. For a moment she couldn't breathe. When she could, she managed to ask, "Why?"

"It's just my opinion, darling."

She realized she was shaking with anger. She must

have transmitted the emotion to Tea Biscuit, because the animal whinnied and pranced sideways.

"It's okay," Bailey murmured, drawing her back, stroking her neck. "Shh, everything's all right."

Even as she crooned to the horse, Bailey wondered if it wasn't herself she was hoping to reassure. She saw by the gleam in August's eyes that he was wondering the same thing. She disliked him for it.

"I'm not trying to hurt you, Bailey."

"Just scare me?"

"I care about you. I don't want to see you hurt."

"What a crock, August. You only care about yourself."

"What if Logan thought he was going to lose her?"

"Stop it."

"That she was going to leave him for another man? If it was you who was leaving, how do you think he'd react?"

She didn't know. But he wouldn't hurt her. She told August so, then removed the saddle blanket and began brushing the horse. "You've spent too much time listening to gossip. Or Billy Ray Williams."

"Billy Ray?" He snorted. "I don't need that little man thinking for me. I've trained some of the best riders in the world. I've worked with horses that belong to kings and are worshipped like Gods. The way I was worshipped. Billy Ray Williams isn't good enough to be a fly on one of their asses. He's not good enough to be a fly on mine."

She'd never seen him angry. His dislike of the other man ran deep and personal. What happened between them? And what had brought August here, so far from kings and the horses they owned?

She stopped brushing the mare and looked up at him. "Why are you here, August?"

The fire of indignation died in his eyes. Replaced by something sad and slightly bitter. "Because I'm just a man. Not a God."

He squatted so he could look her in the eyes. "Why would True have left her car that way? Like the others? She would have known what everyone would think. Would she want that? For her husband . . . her friends to think . . . that?"

She wouldn't. Not the woman whom everyone had described to her.

But that woman wouldn't have had an affair, then run out on her husband and family without a word.

A clandestine grave.

"You knew her, you said you were friends. Was she going to leave him?"

"She never said anything that made me suspect that." He paused. "Anyone could have killed her. Not just Logan."

Was that supposed to make her feel better?

"Even you?" she asked, then resumed grooming the horse, though her heart wasn't in it.

"Of course." He straightened. "But I didn't."

"Which is what every killer says."

"If it helps, I don't think Logan killed her, either."

She stopped again, surprised. "You don't?"

"Logan's my friend, Bailey. He took me on when I'd burned every bridge within a thousand miles. I'd never betray him."

Which wasn't the same as believing in a man's innocence. She pushed the thought away. "Who killed True?"

"I don't know. Maybe you can figure that out."

CHAPTER TWENTY

Bailey sat curled up on the keeping room sofa. She couldn't stop thinking about her conversation with August. He'd been toying with her. But no. He was nothing if not a troublemaker, but he also had heart. And a sense of loyalty toward Logan.

"I'd never betray him."

She rubbed the bridge of her nose, at the beginning of a headache lurking there. True had been his friend. He believed she was dead. Murdered. Along with Amanda LaPier and Trista Hook.

Bailey replayed the things he had said about True. The things others had said. About the kind of person she had been. That she had been completely devoted to Logan. Madly in love.

She hadn't had an affair. There was another explanation for the hotel rooms and missing cash. There had to be.

August didn't believe Logan a killer.

And neither did she.

In the hours that had passed since that conversation Bailey had tried to put herself in Logan's head that night in the office. His mind-set after their argument. She'd come to the conclusion, he'd seen the cloud hanging over their heads. Of suspicion and accusation. The unanswered questions. He saw how it could kill their love.

Maybe he wondered, too? Maybe he had begun to doubt?

What really happened to True?

The truth took her breath. He had been searching for answers. Trying to figure things out himself.

It had made him look guilty. But just as easily, by her thinking, made him look innocent.

They'd fought about True, her disappearance, the other women who had gone missing. The things Billy Ray had said and believed.

Billy Ray Williams.

Logan's number-one detractor. Who believed Logan a killer and had done everything but shout it from the rooftops.

"Who killed True?"

"I don't know. Maybe you can figure that out."

Billy Ray had given her his card, that day at Faye's. She had been furious. Disgusted. She had wanted it out of her sight and had tossed it into the console. Snapped the console lid shut.

And hadn't thought about it again until now.

She jumped to her feet and ran outside. To the garage. Her SUV.

Sure enough, the card was there. She snatched it up, found her phone and dialed.

Her voice shook when he answered. "It's Bailey Abbott. You said you'd tell me everything I wanted to know about my husband. I'm ready to listen."

CHAPTER TWENTY-ONE

Billy Ray lived in a small, brick home only a couple of blocks from the police station. Bailey had felt a small measure of relief as she passed the station, though since Billy Ray was the law, the proximity wouldn't do her much good. If he meant her harm, there would be no help coming.

Billy Ray would know how to make her disappear.

Bailey's mouth went dry. A half-dozen times during the drive here, Bailey had nearly changed her mind. But here she was, heading willingly into the enemy's camp.

She parked on the street and climbed out of her vehicle. There, she stopped, drew a deep breath. She had to do this. She had to know what "evidence" Billy Ray had against Logan.

As she climbed his porch steps, Billy Ray opened the door. "Hello, Bailey."

The familiarity felt wrong. It grated. This man was not her friend. "I prefer you call me Mrs. Abbott."

He cocked an eyebrow. "If that makes you more comfortable."

She folded her arms across her chest. "It does."

"Why'd you change your mind?"

"That's not really any of your business."

"Fine."

"So, talk to me."

"It's not what I want to say. It's what I'm going to show you."

His secret room. The one Stephanie had told her about. *Diagrams. Pictures of True. A picture of Logan, at the center.*

"But I need something from you first," he said. "Your promise. To look at what I have with an open mind."

"The way I see it, you're not in a position to make demands."

He smiled slightly. "If you have any doubt, any doubt, about your husband's guilt, you'll work with me."

"Work with you?" She shook her head. "You mean help you prove my husband's guilty of murdering his first wife?"

"No." He leaned closer. "You'll be working to prove to yourself that he didn't."

He knew why she was here. Of course he did.

The screen door squeaked as he swung it open; the heavy wooden door followed, swinging in like the invitation to a tomb.

She followed him inside. When Billy Ray moved to close the wooden door, she stopped him. "Leave it."

He looked surprised. "Seriously?"

"Yes."

He shook his head. "It's your husband you have to fear, not me. But if that's what you want."

He led her through the living room to a bedroom hallway. He stopped at the only closed door, and from his ring he selected a key, then unlocked it. He stepped inside, flipped on the light.

Bailey hung back. Peered into the room. Like something out of a cop show. Dry erase board that ran the entire length of one wall. A diagram—part timeline, part spiderweb. Places and dates. Photographs. Notes, clippings.

"Come in."

Her being here was a betrayal of her husband. It put their relationship, their future together, at risk.

But not one as great as the doubt that hung over them now.

She stepped into the room, looked him in the eyes. "You can go now."

"Excuse me?"

"I'm doing this alone. I want thirty minutes. From the moment you're in your car."

"My car?"

She nodded. "You take a ride. I'll watch you go. Time starts then."

She could tell he wanted to balk, but didn't. Bailey waited until he had pulled out of his driveway, then hurried back to his study. Thirty minutes. She planned to be gone in twenty, before he got back. She set the timer on her cell phone and, sucking a deep, resolute breath, entered the room.

And took it all in, though it felt like it took *her* in. Swallowed her up. A tsunami of dates and times, notes and photos.

And her husband's photo occupied the very center.

Bailey couldn't take her eyes off it. Like a spider in his web, all threads radiated to and from him. Damning him.

Bailey fought to steady herself. Billy Ray had known she would react this way; he had counted on it. The more emotional she was, the less objective she would be. He had planned to be here with her, whispering in her ear, feeding her fear.

She was in control of herself and her life, she reminded herself, what she felt. What she believed in. Who she believed in.

Start at the beginning, Bailey. The first girl, one she hadn't heard of before.

2005. Her name had been Nicole Grace. Fifteen years old. Found dead. Strangled. Billy Ray had noted that her mother had worked for the Abbotts. She had spent a good bit of time at the farm when she was young.

Billy Ray had added in a different color: *"Nicole would have felt safe with Logan Abbott."*

The thought of it made Bailey's stomach roll. She pressed on anyway, doing the math. 2005. Three years before he had married True. Logan would have been twenty-seven.

Bailey shifted her gaze to the next young woman. Trista Hook. 2010. Twenty-eight years old. According to Billy Ray's notes, Logan and Trista had dated briefly, he in college, she still in high school. A summer romance, that ended abruptly. He had "broken" her heart.

She skipped over True, fixing her attention on twenty-one-year-old Amanda LaPier. Four years had passed between her and Trista.

Billy Ray's note read: *"Two years previous, Logan Abbott picked LaPier up; gave her a ride. LaPier had bragged to friends about riding in his Porsche."*

Both Trista and Amanda had gone missing after having been out partying. Neither arrived home after. The following day, their unlocked vehicles had been found, keys in the ignition, purses, wallets and I.D.'s in them. No sign of a struggle.

Billy Ray's note: *"Obviously the women knew and trusted their abductor. They went willingly—up to a point."*

Bailey saw where he was going with this. Logan had a connection to all the women. They would have trusted him. Enough to climb into his car. Or get close enough to be pulled in.

Bailey then focused on True. Here, Billy Ray had more information than anywhere else: photographs, notations, some looked lovingly, painstakingly written, others scribbled in a frenzy.

He'd followed True, Bailey realized. There were photos he wouldn't have had access to otherwise. Inappropriate. Obsessive.

Hands shaking, Bailey checked her phone. Nearly twenty minutes had passed. *How was that possible?* She reset the timer, adding eight more minutes.

On either end of his diagram, Billy had included other information. On the one, the tragedies that had befallen the Abbott family, starting with his mother's drowning. She read each, the scribbled notations: "*Logan was on the boat that night*"; "*Logan was the one who came forward about his father*"; "*he was the one who found Roane.*"

Clearly, Billy Ray was somehow convinced that Logan had orchestrated each tragedy, a dark force destroying all their lives.

Flimsy. Overreaching. Even she, untrained in investigative techniques, could see that. The musings of a man with an agenda. A man desperate to believe his own agenda.

Relief swept over her. Tears stung her eyes. Nothing, it was all . . . nothing. Logan had lost so much. Mother and father. Brother. His wife. Then he'd had to suffer suspicions and accusation.

Even from her. Unspoken but loud and clear anyway.

Bailey glanced at the timer, saw she had only a couple of minutes if she wanted to get out without confronting Billy Ray, and hurried to the opposite end of the diagram.

Three women's names. A photograph beside each. All three had gone missing in the years between Trista Hook and Amanda LaPier. One in Jacksonville, Florida, one in Houston, Texas, and the last, Atlanta, Georgia. All three with a brief connection to Louisiana: one a stint as a bartender in the French Quarter, two had attended LSU.

That was it. No other information about them or their abductions. If in reality they even had been. She only had this, Billy Ray's written ravings, to go by.

Grasping at straws, she told herself. Trying anything to pin these abominations on her husband—going so far as to access law enforcement databases for like crimes. For all she knew, these women had been recovered, or a suspect apprehended.

She should follow up. Bailey dug a pen and a scrap of paper out of her purse, jotted the three names on the paper and slipped it into her pocket.

From outside she heard the slam of a car door. *Billy Ray, returning. Three minutes early.*

Bailey didn't want to be here, in this room, with him. She slung her purse strap on her shoulder and hurried to the front porch. He looked anxious. And hopeful. For a moment, Bailey felt sorry for him, then reminded herself of his vendetta against her husband.

"Well?" he said. She didn't respond; he searched her expression. "You see now, don't you?"

"No, Billy Ray, I don't. At least not what you want me to see."

"You're lying, I can tell. I see how upset you are."

"For a moment, I was. For a moment, I doubted him. But only a moment."

"You're blind to what he really is. Because of his looks. And money. Because of his—"

"No," she said softly, "you're the one who's blinded. I'm going home now, Billy Ray."

"No." He caught her arm. "Not until you tell me the truth."

His voice rose slightly. His grip on her arm hurt. She kept her own voice low, soothing. "I think you've been told the truth before. You don't have anything substantial here. It's circumstantial, wishful thinking. I'm sorry."

His fingers tightened on her arm. "I'm not going to stop."

"Let me go, Billy Ray. You're hurting me."

"I know I'm right. It's so obvious."

"Only to you." She covered his hand with hers, gave it a gentle squeeze, then removed it from her arm. "Logan loved True. He didn't hurt her."

"She was afraid of him."

"You're grasping at straws. No one else saw that."

"I saw it in her eyes. Her posture. She radiated it. I saw because I was witness to the same thing all my life."

"Your mother and father."

"And the whole world thought they were a happy couple, too. My dad the greatest guy in the world. But I knew better. I saw what no one else did. I don't know why she stayed with him."

He said the last almost to himself, and Bailey wondered whether he was talking about his mother or True. Even as compassion washed over her, she acknowledged that it didn't matter. Logan was just who she thought he was, the man she had fallen in love with.

"I'm so sorry, Billy Ray."

"I don't need your pity." An angry red stained his cheeks. "Yours, my uncle's or anyone else's! I'm right about this. These women were murdered."

"Maybe so, but not by my husband."

Bailey turned and walked away. He called after her. "The bodies are there. Buried on Abbott Farm. Why won't he—"

She reached the SUV, unlocked the door.

"—allow a search of the property? What's—"

She slid inside, started the engine.

"—he hiding?"

Nothing, she thought. He was hiding nothing. Lips curving into a smile, she headed home.

CHAPTER TWENTY-TWO

"Okay, Tony," Bailey said, tugging on her rain boots—shrimp boots they called them down here, which always made her laugh. "Almost ready. Are you?" He barked once, ran in a circle, stopped, then barked once again. She laughed. "I'll take that as a yes. Let's do this."

She slipped into her hooded windbreaker and headed outside. The sky had finally cleared, and the wet world glistened in the sunlight. Bailey had discovered it rained a lot in South Louisiana. Dramatic thunderstorms, sudden showers and all-day soakers. Or three-day soakers, like this one had been. She couldn't wait to get some fresh air and exercise.

Obviously, Tony felt the same way. He'd been racing around the house, getting into one thing after another; a war with a down pillow—the pillow had lost—a game of hide-and-seek with every shoe in her closet and an imaginary grand prix, in which the course was a perfect loop through the dining and living room, kitchen and front hall.

It had ceased to be amusing after the first two hours.

Now, time for some fresh air and exercise. She wasn't sure who needed it more—her or the dog.

A hike to Henry's, she had decided. She patted the

jacket's inside pocket to make certain the candy bars were there—Henry's favorite, Baby Ruth.

He'd been home from the hospital nearly two weeks, growing stronger every day. Stephanie had stayed with him at first, then she and Bailey had shared daily check-ins. In the process they had become fast friends.

Bailey stuck to the path. She'd expected it to be wet, but not this soupy. Now she understood the boots. When Logan had proudly handed them to her, she hadn't gotten it. She sure did now.

Logan. She smiled, thinking of him. She hadn't told him about going to Billy Ray's, not about his dry erase board, none of it. He would be hurt by what he'd perceive as her doubt and furious at Billy Ray. They didn't need all that; things were good. They were good.

Tony, obviously, found the conditions to be very much to his liking. The wetter, the muddier, the better. He ran ahead, then barreled off the path and through the underbrush after his imaginary prey, then circled back looking like a four-legged swamp creature. Bailey laughed and wondered what Henry would think, showing up with his dog in this condition—although she suspected he had seen the dog this way many times before.

Bailey stopped suddenly, realizing she hadn't seen Tony in several minutes. "Tony!" she called. "C'mon, boy!"

Instead of the telltale crunching of the underbrush, he barked. Once, then twice. She called him to come again. This time he responded with frenzied, continual barking.

She glanced ahead. The moisture had begun to seep through her jacket and jeans, chilling her. Henry's cabin wasn't that much farther, located in a clearing. Here the sun barely peeked through the forest canopy, but there it would be bright and warm.

Tony knew where he lived. Of course he did. He was

a dog, not a child, and traveled these woods almost every day. She was the one who would get lost if she wandered, not him. Even as she told herself to stick to the path, she went in search of the dog.

Something didn't feel right to her. She'd made this trip a dozen times before, and never once had Tony run off and refused to come when called. Maybe Tony was hurt?

Bailey caught her bottom lip between her teeth. Or maybe it was Henry? Maybe Henry had been out walking, fallen and been incapacitated?

Or Tony was just being a crazy puppy and had discovered a new trick?

Muttering an oath, she struck off in search of the dog, following the sound of his barking.

The forest played games with her, leading her one way, then another. Just when she realized she was hopelessly lost, the woods opened into a small clearing with a pond.

She stopped, surprised. Logan hadn't mentioned a pond on the property and she could see that in better weather it would be a pretty spot. Secluded and shady, with grassy areas perfect for picnics or sunning. She wondered if as kids, he and his sibs had used it as a swimming hole.

Tony was on the far side of it, apparently digging a route to China from a Louisiana swimming hole.

"Tony!" she called sharply. "Come!"

This time he didn't even acknowledge her existence. As annoyed with herself as with him for being in this predicament, Bailey looked over her shoulder. Obviously, the dog could find his way to Henry's, but could she?

Doubtful she could, she scanned the ground around the swollen pond. She really had no desire to trek around it, but she wasn't leaving without Tony. The little shit had to help her find her way out of here.

She picked her way to him, choosing her steps carefully. She envisioned slipping and falling in or twisting an ankle. How long before Logan would come searching for her? And how would he find her way out here?

She reached the far side of the pond, managing to avoid both scenarios. Tony paid no attention to her, intent on digging up whatever treasure he'd uncovered.

Something red, she saw as she neared him. Candy apple red. Hardly a color indigenous to the area ever, let alone at this time of year. Bailey frowned. What was it?

She squatted by Tony. "Let me see what that is, buddy. That's right," she said, grabbing his collar and pulling him back.

The toe of a shoe, she saw. Peeking out from the embankment. A lady's shoe, with a peekaboo toe.

The hair at the back of her neck prickled. With the sensation, a metallic taste filled her mouth. How had it gotten out here, buried in the muck?

Bailey swallowed hard. She was being an idiot. It was probably a sandal. Undoubtedly this pretty little pond was known to all the locals, and she'd bet it was popular with young people. Someone had left it behind.

Simple.

So, why didn't it feel simple?

Bailey released Tony, stood and went searching for a sturdy stick. She found one and returned to the dog who had apparently decided it would be much more entertaining to watch her. He sat on his haunches, as if patiently waiting for her to retrieve *his* prize.

She knelt and the wet seeped through her jeans. Using the stick, she started digging out the shoe.

Not a sandal, she realized. A high-heeled pump.

Bailey sat back and stared at it, heart beating fast, mind whirling.

Two women missing from Wholesome. Some people thought True had brought that number to three.

And now, here on Logan's property, she had found this candy apple red, high-heeled shoe. In a place she could think of no logical reason for it to be.

What else could be buried by the pretty, little swimming hole?

Fear coiled inside her, stealing her breath. Any notion of staying calm and collected evaporated.

Get out of here, Bailey. Now.

She jumped to her feet, slipped on the wet grass, then scrambled back up. She swung around and stopped, a sound of terror on her lips. A figure in the wooded area beyond the clearing. Watching her.

Had he seen her unearth the shoe? she wondered. What if it was his handiwork, something he didn't want revealed to anyone?

Two women, missing from Wholesome.

And True had made three.

PART TWO

CHAPTER TWENTY-THREE

Saturday, April 19
5:25 A.M.

Bailey opened her eyes. The light stung. Her head throbbed. It all came crashing back. The hospital. Bits and pieces of conversations. Her husband.

She turned her head, wincing at how much that hurt. Her gaze settled on him. She said his name.

"Logan."

He stirred, opened his eyes and looked at her. She said his name again and he made a sound. Broken, and raw. In the next moment, he was clutching her hand, kissing it. "I was so afraid . . . I thought . . . I thought I'd lost you."

She tried to smile, but couldn't. "What's . . . wrong . . . with me?"

"Now that you're awake, nothing. You took a fall and bumped your head. That's all."

That wasn't all. There was something else, but she couldn't remember what.

Queasiness rolled over her, and he suddenly felt too close. His mouth on her hand too familiar. She shrank back against the pillow. "Don't."

He looked devastated but loosened his grip on her hand. "Baby, what's—"

"Good morning, Mr. Abbott!" a nurse called cheerfully

as she entered the room. "There's a fresh pot of coffee at the nurses' station, if you're interested."

He glanced over his shoulder at her. "She's awake."

The broad-faced woman crossed to the bed and smiled down at her. "My goodness, she is! Welcome back, Mrs. Abbott. It's good to see those pretty, blue eyes open."

The nurse looked back at Logan. "When did she wake up?"

"Just before you arrived."

She nodded and returned her gaze to Bailey's. "Dr. Bauer's here for rounds, I'll get your vitals, then let him know you're up."

She busied herself, chatting the whole while. "How are you feeling? Any pain?"

"Thirsty," Bailey answered, the word coming out a croak. "Headache. Bad."

"I'll bet you do have a headache. That was some tumble you took." She raised the bed slightly. "I'll get you a cup of water."

"Wait." Bailey touched her sleeve. "How long . . . was I—"

"Out? About three days." The woman patted her hand. "And this sweet man of yours never left your side."

A shudder rippled over her. Something . . . there was something she should remember. About her husband? To tell him? Or—

No, that wasn't right. Bailey squeezed her eyes shut. About True? Was that—

"Mrs. Abbott? Are you all right?"

She looked into the nurse's kind eyes. "I don't remember . . . I need to—" She choked back a sob. "What's happening to me?"

The woman's expression altered subtly. She exchanged a glance with Logan. "I'll call Dr. Bauer." She smiled reassuringly. "He'll be able to tell you everything you need to know."

A moment later, Logan held the cup and straw to her lips. His hand shook slightly. "Tiny sips," he said. "That's right. Take it slow."

After several, she turned her head away and closed her eyes. Like a dripping faucet somewhere in the back of her brain it plucked at her. *Remember . . . Remember . . . Remember.*

Why couldn't she?

"It's going to be all right, baby. I promise it is."

She opened her eyes, looked at him. "Are we going to be all right?"

"Yes." He squeezed her hand. "Of course we are."

"Were we fighting?"

"Fighting? When?"

"Before my accident."

"Why do you ask that, Bailey?"

She shook her head slightly. Even the small movement hurt.

"No, baby. Everything was perfect between us. The way it always is."

Then why did she feel this way?

"We were happy?"

He seemed to flinch at the question. "We *are* happy. You'll see. You need to rest—"

"No." Her voice rose; her head throbbed. "What happened to me? Why can't I . . . I *need* to know, Logan!"

A song popped into her head. Her own off-key voice singing with it.

Shatter every window 'til it's all blown away . . .

Carrie Underwood on the car radio, she realized. A brilliantly sunny day. She'd been happy. Deliriously happy.

Even as the memory spilled over her, realization struck.

A car accident. She must have been in a wreck.

Bailey imagined it. Imagined the crunch of metal and glass shattering. Imagined hurting someone, their blood on her hands. Spilled across the pavement.

Her pulse began to race; it felt as if her heart were flinging itself against the wall of her chest. The monitor by the bed screamed.

"The accident . . . Did I hurt—"

"Calm down, sweetheart. You have to calm—"

She clutched his hand, the screaming monitor like a knife in her skull. "Please . . . you have to tell—"

"Nurse!" he shouted.

The nurse from earlier flew into the room, an aide with her. "We were just talking," Logan said, jumping to his feet. "She got upset. I didn't know what to do!"

The nurse instructed him to move aside. "Mrs. Abbott," she said firmly, "look at me." Bailey did. "You're going to be all right. Calm down."

The aide took the other side of the bed. "Nurse Flynn's administering a mild dose of Ativan, it'll help. Everything's going to be just fine."

"But I . . . please . . . I need to— So . . . much . . . blood . . ." The medicine's effect was almost instantaneous. Her heart slowed and her anxiousness melted away. She rested her head against the pillow and closed her eyes.

When Bailey reopened them, only she and Logan remained in the room. He stood by the bed, looking hollow-eyed and anxious. "Hey," he said softly.

"Hey."

"How do you feel?"

"Groggy. Head still hurts."

"Want a drink of water?"

"Yes, please."

He held the cup and straw to her lips; she sipped, then rested her head back against the pillows. "What did they say they gave me?"

"Ativan. Nothing that would hurt the— They were afraid you would hurt yourself."

"Logan, tell me what happened. Please."

"Let's not do this now. You've been through a terrible trauma. We both have."

"I won't get upset this time. I just . . . I need to know."

He hesitated, then pulled over the chair and sat. He gathered her hand in his. "No one was hurt but you."

Her breath came out in a soft whoosh. She closed her eyes. "Thank God."

"But you weren't in a car accident, Bailey."

She looked at him. "But I just . . . I remember being in the car. I was singing to the radio."

"No. Bailey, sweetheart, you were on Tea Biscuit."

Bailey stared at him, struggling to come to terms with his words. She was scared of horses. To the bone terrified.

"You were in the woods, off trail. Knocked off by a low-hanging branch."

A low-hanging branch? Knocked off? She frantically searched her memory. The incident wasn't there.

She looked at him helplessly. "But I don't ride."

"August was helping you overcome your fear. So you could surprise me."

She remembered. "That's right. But how—"

"Paul told me. He overheard you and August talking about it." A smile touched his mouth. "No more surprises, okay?"

"Okay." Tears filled her eyes. "I remember now, working with August, but not the accident."

A frown creased his brow. "Not how you came to be on Tea Biscuit? Or why you were in the woods?"

She brought a trembling hand to her head. To the bandages. She felt faint, and breathed deeply and slowly, in and out. How could she not remember?

"Bailey, there's something else about your accident. Something I haven't told you."

Something bad. It was there, in the deep recesses of her brain, taunting her.

"The police, they're going to need to question you. It's about Henry." Logan paused, his expression stricken. "He's dead, Bailey."

Bailey stared at him, the strangest sensation moving over her. Of being lost in the middle of an ocean, pushed and pulled with the movement of the water. Helpless to change her own course.

Tears filled her eyes, blurred her vision. She pressed her trembling lips together, overwhelmed. "I don't understand. I just saw him."

His grip on her hand tightened. "When?"

She thought back. Or tried to. It made her head hurt. "I don't know. I can't recall what day."

"It's okay. It'll come."

"What . . . happened to him?"

"Somebody shot him. A hunting accident is what the sheriff's deputy thought." He looked away, then back. There were tears in his eyes. "Damn poachers."

"Then . . . I don't understand. Why do the police want to question me?"

"You were in the woods around that time. It happened the same day as your accident. Maybe you saw something?" He paused. "Or someone?"

Was it her imagination or had his expression sharpened? She looked away, uncomfortable with the intensity.

"Bailey, it's important for us that you—"

A tap on the door interrupted him. A small, square

man in a white coat. "Good morning, Mrs. Abbott," he said. "I'm Dr. Bauer."

He crossed to the bed and smiled down at her, the twinkle in his eyes comforting. "You gave us all a terrible scare. But you're awake now." He patted her hand. "How do you feel this morning?"

"Sore. Confused."

"I'm not surprised by either." He flipped through her file. "You took a serious blow to the head."

Logan moved to the head of the bed and laid a hand on her shoulder. "She can't remember what happened, Dr. Bauer. None of it."

The physician made a notation on her chart. "When you came to, did you know where you were?"

"In a hospital, yes."

"But not how you came to be here?"

"That's right."

"Did you recognize your husband?"

"Logan. Yes."

"Do you know where you live?"

"Wholesome, Louisiana. Abbott Farm."

"How long have you lived there?"

"Since January." She looked at Logan. "We got married on New Year's Day."

"Congratulations." He flashed a quick smile. "Before that, your childhood? What do you remember?"

"Everything, I think."

"Your full name?"

"Bailey Ann Abbott."

"Maiden name?"

"Browne."

"Mother's name?"

"Julie. She died recently." Tears stung her eyes. "Cancer."

"I'm sorry to hear that. Father's name?"

"Gregory. He left us when I was little."

He asked her a series of other questions: her birth-date—February fourteenth, she was a Valentine's baby—elementary school—Kennedy—childhood best friend—Meredith—and the name of a childhood pet—she never had one.

"Good," he said. "What's the last thing you remember before coming to this morning?"

Logan answered for her. "She was driving."

"No." She shook her head, then winced as pain knifed through it. "That's not right."

"But before, you said—"

"I know." She brought her hand to the bandaged head, trailed her fingers over the bandages, as if it would help her remember. "I was wrong. I wasn't in the car. That song's stuck in my head but . . . It'd been raining. For days. But had finally stopped. I was with Tony."

"Who's Tony?" the doctor asked.

"The dog. He— We were going for a walk. He was ex-cited. Dancing around. We'd both been cooped up too long."

"Because of the rain." The doctor nodded, looked at Logan. "We had all that rain last weekend."

"Yes. It started Sunday and didn't stop until early Wednesday."

"Mrs. Abbott, the day before the rain started, do you recall it?"

She thought a moment. "Yes. Saturday." She glanced at Logan. "I did some planting, in the front garden. Im-patiens. Blue and white."

"Sounds nice." He jotted her comments on her chart. "That night, what did you have for dinner?"

"Mahi. We grilled out. We figured it'd be our last chance before the rain came."

He looked at Logan in question. "Is she describing the events of Saturday, April twelfth?"

Logan nodded. "Perfectly."

"Do you remember anything else?"

Bailey thought back and came up blank. "That's it. Next thing I remember is waking up here."

The doctor nodded, made a notation on her chart, then looked at her once more. "And since waking up? What do you remember?"

"Everything, I think. Logan, the nurse, getting upset, how I felt, what I was thinking." Her hands trembled and she clasped them together in her lap. "What's wrong with me, Dr. Bauer?"

"Nothing dangerous. Or permanent. You suffered a traumatic brain injury, Mrs. Abbott. In your case a mild one. Amnesia with this type of injury isn't uncommon. In fact, it's called traumatic memory loss. In your case it's retrograde amnesia, meaning you can't recall events immediately preceding the accident."

"But three days preceding?" Logan asked.

"Not unusual. I'm sure you've heard stories of people who come to in a hospital with no idea who or where they are. It happens. The good news for you, Mrs. Abbott, is that retrograde amnesia is typically short-lived."

Tears stung her eyes and she blinked against them. "What does that mean, Dr. Bauer?"

"I'm a neurologist, not God, but there are a couple of ways we determine when memory will return, and both have to do with the injury itself, its severity and the amount of time you were out. Yours, Mrs. Abbott, was mild, and you were out approximately three days. I'd say memory recovery should be within a couple of days to a week. It might even be today."

"That soon?" Bailey looked up at Logan, excited. "Did you hear, Logan?"

But he looked at her strangely, as if he hadn't heard. As if his thoughts had drifted far from this room.

Bailey frowned slightly. "Logan?"

He looked at her; his gaze cleared. "Yes. Great news."

"One caveat," the doctor went on. "If you failed to make the memory, there's nothing to retrieve."

"I don't understand," she said.

"With traumatic memory loss, you haven't actually lost memories. All the events of those three days are stored in your brain. Right now, you're just unable to retrieve them."

"But?"

"Sometimes, with an injury like this, the brain fails to make a memory."

"What does that mean?" she asked.

"That you can't retrieve what's not there," Logan offered, eyebrows drawn together in thought.

"Exactly. You may never remember the accident, the moments before or after."

"Never," she repeated, a sinking sensation in the pit of her stomach.

"It's a possibility. If your brain didn't lay those memories down."

Henry was dead. Somebody shot him.

She had to remember.

Bailey frowned slightly, the queasy feeling from earlier returning.

"What, baby?"

She glanced up at Logan. "Nothing."

He held her gaze a moment; she saw doubt in his. Concern.

He turned his attention to the doctor. "What now?"

"I want her to stay one more night. For observation. And rest. No stress." The doctor smiled reassuringly at her. "You're going to be fine, Mrs. Abbott. Don't try to force the memories. Let your brain heal, there's no rush."

But there was, Bailey thought as she watched him leave the room. She felt the urgency to the very core of her being.

CHAPTER TWENTY-FOUR

Saturday, April 19
4:25 P.M.

Bailey spent the day drifting in and out of sleep. She had insisted Logan check in at the farm and his office; other than the nurses and activity outside her room, it had been quiet. Each time she'd awakened, she had gone over and over the days leading up to her accident, hoping something would jog her memory. All she had to show for it was a splitting headache.

"Bailey, baby, are you awake?"

Logan. In the doorway. Looking freshly showered and changed. An arrangement of delicate yellow roses in his hands. Tears stung her eyes. A part of her wished she could pull the covers up over her head and shut him and everything else out. Hide until her memory returned.

But then what?

"I'm awake." She forced a wan smile. "The flowers are beautiful."

"You're beautiful."

He crossed to the bed, set the vase on the table beside it, bent over and kissed her. "Did you get some rest?"

"A little."

He seemed so tall, standing there beside the bed looking down at her. And she felt so small. So vulnerable. He tilted his head, eyebrows coming together with concern. "What's wrong?"

"I have a headache."

"I'll call the nurse."

"Don't. She'll just give me something that'll make me feel cotton-headed. I don't want to feel that way anymore."

He pulled the chair over and sat. "There's something I have to tell you."

"About True."

He frowned. "No, Bailey, why would you— About us. You and me." He took her hand. "Our dreams."

Their dreams. She couldn't remember them, she realized. If she and Logan had them, they were now residing beside her nightmares.

He leaned closer; there were tears in his eyes. "It's something wonderful."

"Wonderful?" she repeated, heart in her throat.

"We're having a baby."

She stared at him. "What did you—"

"A baby." He covered her hand with one of his, lacing their fingers. "We're pregnant. It's a miracle you didn't lose it. That fall—" His throat seemed to close over the words; he cleared it. "We could have lost it." He bent and gently rested his cheek against her belly.

She gazed down at his head, thoughts spinning. *A baby? She was having a baby?*

"But how . . . I mean, I didn't know before the accident. Did I?"

He lifted his head, met her eyes. "Neither of us did."

"Then how—"

"The hospital did a pregnancy test, protocol when women of childbearing age are admitted."

She struggled with that. "And it was . . . positive?"

"You're five weeks along, Bailey."

Worries over what she remembered and what she didn't lost their power. Her confusion melted away, replaced by a wonder, a sense of purpose like she had never known.

She met his eyes. "This is really happening?"

"It is."

"We're having a baby," she said. She brought her hands to her abdomen. She imagined the life there, a part of her and this man. Logan. Her husband.

A family. What she'd always wanted.

What she'd never had.

Until now.

A wave of protectiveness rose up in her, fierce, primal. This was *everything.* Bailey reached up, cupped his cheek, liking the just-shaved feel against her palm.

She smiled. As it broke across her face, she realized it was the first time she'd smiled since awaking. "I'm going to be a mother. We're going to be parents."

"We are." He bent and kissed her. "I love you."

"I love you, too."

The words passed her lips, bringing emotional clarity. With it, a full, all-senses, to-her-core memory of loving him. As if she had only now emerged from her coma.

Everything else she had been feeling was inconsequential. Logan was her husband. They were going to be parents, raise a child together. If she should trust anyone, it was him.

A nurse came in with her cart. "Time to check your vitals, Mrs. Abbott." She busied herself, making small talk as she checked Bailey's temperature, blood pressure and pulse, not seeming to notice she and Logan only had eyes for each other.

When she'd finished and reached the door, she stopped. "By the way, there's a policeman here to speak with you, Mrs. Abbott. A Chief Williams, from the Wholesome Police Department."

CHAPTER TWENTY-FIVE

Billy Ray waited outside room 410. Inside, Bailey Abbott was awake and communicating. Finally. The moment he'd gotten word, he'd hightailed it over here.

He flat out didn't like hospitals. He was a lawman, admittedly small town, but he still dealt with some seriously unpleasant shit. Accident victims. Fights. Drunks lying in a pool of their own vomit.

But hospitals made his skin crawl. Go figure.

He'd arrived just as the nurse had been going in. She'd snapped the door closed in his face, unimpressed with both his credentials and sense of urgency. What he'd done to piss her off, he hadn't a clue.

Abbott, he thought. Probably directed the woman to stall him.

A smile touched Billy Ray's mouth. He could stall all he wanted, but this was it. His chance to nail Abbott, after three long years.

It's going to happen, my love. I'm going to make him pay.

True.

He didn't allow himself to think of her often, or to linger on what might have been. But when she popped into his mind, she came with a wisp of something both tender and bitter.

Tender. And bitter. He mostly focused on the bitter. Or tried to. That he could hold on to. It didn't tease or torment.

Billy Ray thought again of this moment. Henry Rodriquez shot to death. Logan's pretty new wife, red with blood. Too much to be from her head wound.

His gaze drifted back to the clock. And to True. In his mind's eye, the clock turned back. Back to that first meeting. And to that moment when he'd realized how desperately she needed him.

He'd been on patrol that morning. Cruising with the windows down, enjoying the breeze through the windows. It reminded him of being a kid, riding along with his uncle Nate, feeling free and happy. He hadn't had a whole lot of happiness in his childhood, but those ride-alongs with Uncle Nate stood out in bright contrast to his otherwise grim memories.

They'd cruise the winding country roads talking about the world, life or sometimes nothing at all. He'd felt safe with Uncle Nate. No wonder he'd followed in his footsteps and become a cop.

Up ahead he saw a woman sitting slumped by the side of the road, her head in her hands. He tapped the siren, slowed and pulled up alongside her. Her long blond hair was pulled back into a high ponytail; she wore hot pink and black exercise gear.

"Ma'am, you okay?"

She lifted her head and he realized who she was. Logan Abbott's young bride.

Lordy, she was beautiful. Take-your-breath-away gorgeous. At the moment, however, she was as pale as a ghost.

"Miz Abbott? It's Officer Williams, remember me? Billy Ray. We met down at the Stop and Shop."

She nodded. "I remember."

Her voice was like a breath of spring. Light and sweet. The sound of it just made him feel good. "Can I help you?"

"Yes, please. I don't feel so good."

Billy Ray grabbed a bottle of water from the cooler on the floor of the cruiser and brought it to her. "Here you go, ma'am." He twisted off the top and handed her the bottle. He noticed her hand shook as she took it.

She tipped her head back and drank. Billy Ray found himself staring at the smooth arch of her neck and jerked his gaze away, embarrassed.

"Thank you, Billy Ray," she said softly, cradling the now-empty bottle in her hands.

"You're very welcome, Miz Abbott. I'll take that, if you're finished?"

"I am." She handed it over. "And please, call me True."

Blue eyes. Clear and guileless as a summer sky. "I'd be happy to, True." Her name felt like poetry on his lips and he longed to say it again. He resisted and carefully deposited the empty bottle in the cooler, then held out a hand. "You feel strong enough to stand?"

She nodded and laid her small hand in his. He curled his protectively around it and helped her up.

"Good as new," she said lightly, "thanks to you, my knight in shining armor."

He smiled. "You look a little wobbly to me. Climb in, I'll give you a ride home."

She hesitated, something apprehensive moving across her expression. "I'm fine now. Really."

"Abbott Farm is more than a mile up the road."

"Logan won't like it."

"Pardon?"

"You bringing me home. He's a little jealous."

"Well, look here, True. I'm the law and I'm just gonna insist."

He helped her into the cruiser, then went around and climbed in. "Buckle up."

She did as he asked and he pulled onto the road. "What happened, True?"

"I went for a run. I didn't intend to go so far and suddenly I was just overcome. I thought I was going to faint."

"You didn't bring water?"

"No."

"Or a cell phone?"

She shook her head. "I just wanted some time to myself. To clear my head. You know what I mean?" She looked at him, the expression in those wide blue eyes hopeful.

A lump formed in his throat. "I do."

"Pretty dumb, huh."

"Not at all. Overconfident."

She laughed. "That sounds a whole lot better, but it's not true. I just wanted to . . . go. Dumb," she said again.

He reached the Abbott Farm gates, with its ornate logo. They stood open and Billy Ray turned in. He followed the drive to where it split: to the right lay the stable and training facilities, to the left the main house.

"House or barn?" he asked.

"Barn."

Moments later, he rolled to a stop; Logan stepped out of the stable, a commanding figure in riding breeches and boots.

True flew out of the car and ran to him; Billy Ray followed more slowly. Something about the way Abbott pulled her against his side had Billy Ray seeing red.

"True, baby, are you all right?"

"I'm fine." Her voice shook slightly. "Officer Williams here rescued me from the side of the road."

"Is that so?" He turned his gaze to him. "Then I'm indebted to you, Billy Ray."

He held out a hand; Billy Ray took it. It seemed to him Logan held it a bit too tightly and for a moment too long before letting go. "Just doing my job, Logan."

"What happened, baby?"

"I went for a run and felt sick. I thought I might faint and sat down. That's when Officer Williams came along."

"Why didn't you call me?"

"I forgot to bring my phone."

Billy Ray noted the untruth. She had told him she'd deliberately left it. Why lie?

Logan frowned. "That's not safe, True. We talked about that." He shifted his gaze to Billy Ray. "She leaves her phone behind all the time."

"I do." Her smile looked stiff. "I'm sorry, Logan."

Billy Ray stepped in. "What's not safe, Miz Abbott, is exercising in this heat without water. Remember the H_2O and you'll be fine."

"Maybe I just won't let her go without me." Logan drew her closer to his side. "That way I'll know she's safe."

Billy thought he saw her shudder and he frowned. *What was going on here?*

"If you folks don't need anything else from me, I'll get back to it."

"Wait!" True called.

Billy Ray stopped and looked back at her. Logan frowned.

"Let me get you a bottle of water. To replace the one you gave me."

He smiled, thinking her one of the sweetest things he'd ever met. "That's not necessary, Miz Abbott. I keep a cooler in the cruiser, just in case."

"Thanks for your help, Billy Ray," Logan said, smiling. "Tell your uncle Nate I said hello."

As he drove off, Billy Ray glanced in the rearview. The pair stood as they had been, Logan holding his wife tightly to his side, her smile stiff.

Something fierce stirred up in him. With it the urge to turn back, swoop True Abbott up and take her away. Save her.

But he hadn't been able to. Money, power and influence had won the day. The way it always did.

"You can go in now, Officer."

He blinked. The nurse stood at the door, scowling at him.

He forced himself to smile pleasantly at her. She didn't know, didn't understand about Abbott. Like the rest of the world, she only saw what he wanted her to.

For True, he silently promised and turned toward the door. No matter what he had to do, if it took his very last breath, he would make Logan Abbott pay.

CHAPTER TWENTY-SIX

Saturday, April 19
5:10 P.M.

Bailey looked up as Billy Ray entered the room. Her stomach clenched and she shrank back against the pillows. She wasn't ready for this. It was too soon.

Logan curled his hand around hers. He leaned down. Murmured so just she would hear, "It's okay, baby. You'll be fine."

Billy Ray stopped at the end of the bed. The intensity in his eyes made her uncomfortable. He shifted that gaze from her to Logan and back.

"It's good to see you awake, Mrs. Abbott."

She couldn't find her voice and Logan stepped in. "What do you want, Billy Ray?"

The lawman glanced at him, expression dismissive. "Give us a couple minutes."

"Alone?" One corner of Logan's mouth lifted. "Not happening, Williams."

"As a sworn officer of the Wholesome Police Department, I have every right to interview your wife regarding the events of Wednesday, April sixteen."

"And I have every right to refuse to leave her side."

"I don't want this to get ugly."

"And neither do I."

"Stop it, please. It doesn't matter because I don't re-member anything!"

Billy Ray seemed to freeze. "What did you say?"

"She has traumatic amnesia," Logan said. "She doesn't remember any of it."

Billy Ray looked as if he had been punched in the gut. He turned to her. "Is that true, Mrs. Abbott?"

She nodded. Her chin trembled.

"Bailey, Mrs. Abbott, you came into the hospital with a lot of blood on you."

"I had an injury. My head—"

"A lot of blood."

"I told her," Logan said.

"Do you have any memory of how that came to be?"

"My head injury?"

"Yes, but not what your husband might have told you. Not a guess. Your own memory of the event."

"No. The last thing I remember is three days before the accident."

"Three days?" He all but snorted in disbelief.

"It's true!" She glanced at Logan, then back at him. "I'm sorry."

"Henry Rodriquez is dead, did your *husband* tell you that?"

"Yes," she whispered.

"Did he tell you he was murdered?"

"Williams! That's enough—"

"I bet he told you it was a hunting accident."

"Yeah, I did. Because it's what the Saint Tammany sheriff's detective told me."

"Even though it's not hunting season. You don't find that strange?"

Bailey's head hurt. She wanted them to stop.

Please . . . please . . . stop . . .

"No, I don't. My property is posted no hunting and no

trespassing, and that doesn't stop folks from doing both. A month ago, I found deer parts dumped in the creek. Just last week, Henry found a wounded hog not far from his cabin."

"And you reported both to the sheriff's office."

"Of course! For this very reason."

Please . . . it hurts . . .

"Touché, Abbott. Very well thought out. Down to the little woman's amnesia."

"What the hell are you trying to say? That she's faking it? Talk to her doctor, you son of a bitch!"

"I will, believe me. But right now—"

"Stop it!" she cried. "My head hurts! That's all I know."

Both men stopped and looked at her. She blinked, seeing them both clearly, her thoughts flooding with something dark. Disturbing. She shuddered and turned her face away. "I'm tired," she managed, voice quivering. "Please go."

"Mrs. Abbott, if you remembered something—"

"You're done here, Williams." Logan left her side, crossed to the door and opened it. "Get out."

Billy Ray looked like he wanted to argue. Instead, he said, "You and me, Abbott. In the hall. Now."

CHAPTER TWENTY-SEVEN

Saturday, April 19
5:25 P.M.

The door snapped shut behind them. Billy Ray faced Logan. "What kind of bullshit is this, Abbott?" he said, keeping his voice low. "Amnesia?"

"Not bullshit. Sorry for your great disappointment."

"Forgive me if I don't believe you."

"I don't care what you believe. Talk to Dr. Bauer. He'll give you the details."

"I will. Count on it."

"Grow up, Billy Ray. This isn't a school yard competition."

Billy Ray smiled. "That would imply this is a game. I assure you, it's not."

"Oh, yes, it is." Logan leaned closer, so close Billy Ray felt his breath on his face, saw the glitter of fury in his determined gaze. "You're playing a very dangerous game with my wife and my life. If you think I'm going to stand back and let you destroy what I have, you're in for a very nasty surprise."

"That's the thing, Abbott. Nothing you could do would surprise me. Not anymore." Billy Ray smiled. "Excuse me, I've got a neurologist to talk to."

Luckily, the neurologist had just finished evening rounds when Billy Ray caught him. "Dr. Bauer? Chief

Williams, Wholesome P.D. Could I have a moment of your time?"

The doctor checked his watch, then nodded. "This must be about Bailey Abbott."

"How did you know that?"

"You were standing outside her door earlier."

"Of course." Billy Ray cleared his throat, feeling foolish. "I understand you diagnosed Mrs. Abbott with amnesia."

"Yes." He motioned to the nearly empty seating area behind them. "Why don't we sit down?"

They did and Bauer picked up where they'd left off. "Mrs. Abbott is suffering from an amnesia associated with a traumatic brain injury."

"Basically a bump on the head."

"Basically." The neurologist's eyebrows rose slightly. "Times a hundred. People die from these kinds of 'bumps' on the head."

"I get it, they're serious."

Bauer hesitated a moment, as if irritated, then continued. "It's called TML—"

"Which is?"

"Traumatic memory loss. There are two types. Retrograde and anterograde. With retrograde amnesia, the patient loses a portion of memory of events before the injury, with anterograde, events after the injury."

"And Mrs. Abbott is suffering from retrograde amnesia?"

"That's my diagnosis."

"And how did you come to that diagnosis?"

The neurologist smiled slightly. "She took a serious blow to the head. She was unconscious for seventy-two or so hours and she doesn't remember the events leading up to the accident. It's pretty simple, Chief Williams."

Condescending. Typical doctor. But what Dr. High-and-Mighty didn't understand was that it was never simple. Not when Logan Abbott was involved.

"Will her memory come back?"

"In her case, almost certainly. Her TBI was mild, which doesn't negate the seriousness of it, but speaks to long-term prognosis. And how quickly her memory will be retrieved."

Billy Ray made a note. "The milder the trauma, the more quickly she will retrieve those lost memories?"

"Yes. In Mrs. Abbott's case it will be relatively quickly. A day. Maybe a week."

"So, how does it happen? Does she just wake up one morning and remember?"

"Maybe in the movies. In real life, the memory loss becomes shorter and shorter and typically returns in bits and pieces, jogged by some sort of memory key."

"Such as?"

"A word or phrase. A sight or sound. And actually, Chief Williams, the memories don't 'come back.' They're there the whole time. The patient is simply unable to access them."

Billy Ray digested that. "Could Bailey Abbott be faking it?"

"Pardon me?"

"Mrs. Abbott, could she simply be pretending not to remember?"

His eyebrows shot up. "And why would she want to do that?"

"It's just a simple question, Doctor. Could you be fooled?"

The doctor's expression went from patient to irritated. "Chief Williams, I have over twenty years of experience in the field of memory loss. And in that time, no one has faked a case of amnesia."

"As far as you know."

His face reddened. "Why would she pretend not to remember?"

"This is a police investigation, Dr. Bauer. A man is dead. You tell me."

"I suppose someone could. But it would be difficult to pull off."

"Why?"

"Let me ask you a question, Chief Williams. You're a professional lawman, correct?" Billy Ray nodded and Bauer went on. "As such, how easy is it for a criminal to fool you?"

"Difficult."

"You see my point then." He glanced at his watch. "If there's nothing else, it's my wife's birthday and we have reservations."

"Just a couple more questions. A few moments ago, you said Bailey Abbott's amnesia was brought on by her fall. Can this kind of memory loss be caused by anything else?"

"Absolutely. It can be brought on by highly emotional, stressful or traumatic events. We see it a lot in soldiers with PTSD. Victims of crimes, horrific accidents, things like that."

Billy Ray gazed at the man, the information reverberating through him. As if plucking a chord. "And it's called the same thing?"

"It is. Although that type of TML falls to treatment by a psychiatric clinician."

"Because it's emotional, not physical."

"Exactly. The loss of memory is a form of self-protection. The event, whatever it was, is simply too painful for the conscious self to deal with. So the psyche hides it."

"But it's still there."

"Yes."

Choosing not to remember, Billy Ray thought. Conscious or not, he could see Bailey Abbott doing that.

After all, how did you admit you married a monster?

"Is there a chance Mrs. Abbott's amnesia is stress induced rather than injury induced?"

Bauer looked surprised. "Certainly. However, my professional opinion is that it's not."

"Why?"

"Because the pieces all fit. The accident. The force and location of her injury. The amount of time she was unconscious, her responses on the Glasgow coma scale, the fact that although she has bruising of the brain tissue, there's neither bleeding nor swelling." The neurologist stood and held out his hand. "Good luck with your investigation."

Billy Ray took it. "Thank you for your time."

The doctor started toward the elevator, Billy Ray stopped him. "One last thing, have you ever had an amnesia patient who's also the suspect in a criminal case?"

"I can't see how that's pertinent."

"You don't have to, Dr. Bauer."

The man's expression hardened with dislike. Billy Ray didn't care if the man hated his guts, he had a job to do.

"No," Bauer said. "Not to my knowledge."

"What about a witness to a crime?"

"Again, not to my knowledge."

"Thank you, Dr. Bauer."

"Chief Williams?"

Now it was Billy Ray's turn to stop and look back.

"Time's on your side. Just be patient, she'll remember."

But Billy Ray had been patient for three frustrating years. That time had come to an end.

Billy Ray exited the hospital and made his way to his cruiser. He climbed in, started it up and just sat, engine running, thoughts racing. Choosing to forget things that were too painful to remember. He'd made a lifetime of it. Like the sound of his father's rage. Or the smell of whiskey and sweat, and what often came with the mingling of those two.

Billy Ray shifted into reverse and eased out of the parking spot. And what of letting go of the unbearably sweet? Memories so pure they brought an ache a thousand times more brutal than his old man's drunken rage.

Memories of True.

No, he amended. She had been sweet. But his memories of her were bittersweet, indeed. Of not being able to put her out of his thoughts. Of thinking of her day and night, dreaming of her. That she needed him. That she was in danger.

And in the end, it seemed, she had been. If only he'd done more. Been more insistent. Whisked her away. She would be here today. Safe.

But he hadn't been insistent enough, hadn't whisked her away. So now, all he had left was the ability to make it right.

Something terrible had happened in those woods, something just too painful for Bailey Abbott to remember. And he meant to find out what.

CHAPTER TWENTY-EIGHT

Sunday, April 20
11:15 A.M.

Sunday mornings Billy Ray slept in. He worshipped at First Baptist's nine-thirty service, then stopped and ate a big breakfast at Faye's. She always had a place at the counter waiting for him; he always left the waitress a big tip and on his way out always stopped at a half-dozen tables for a hello and handshake. Today had been no different.

Now he stepped out into the bright spring day, slipping on his shades. It was going to be a muggy one, he thought, ambling to the cruiser. The radio crackled as he settled behind the wheel.

"Chief, you there?"

He snatched it up. "Ten-four, Robin. What's up?"

"Travis Jenkins just called. He's worried 'bout his youngest, Dixie."

"What about her?"

"She didn't come home the last two nights and Jo-Jo from the Dairy Freeze told him she'd seen Dixie's Mustang parked up at The Landing. Saw it on his way to work yesterday and on his way home, too. Travis doesn't think that's right. He called the friends she went out with Friday night, Katie Walton and Lea Johnson, but they hadn't seen her since then."

"I'm heading that way now. Have Earl meet me there."

The Landing was a honky-tonk just inside the Wholesome city limits. A popular spot for farmhands and horse folk, the down-on-their-luck and the high-and-mighty. They served up cold beer and country music, a powerful combination after a long, hot day in the sun.

He should know, a Saturday night didn't go by without at least one call to break up a fight.

He had a pretty good idea how this was going to turn out. Dixie had a wild streak about a mile wide and liked men, probably more than she should. No doubt she hooked up with someone and the last thing on her mind had been Daddy worrying over her whereabouts.

Billy Ray reached the bar and saw that Earl had beat him there. The youngest officer on the force, Earl Stroup had graduated from Covington High a scant two and a half years ago. Tall and gangly, the twenty-one-year-old hadn't even grown into his frame yet.

Billy Ray stopped his cruiser beside Earl's. Sure enough, Dixie Jenkins's battered red Mustang sat all by itself in a back corner of The Landing's parking lot.

Earl met him and together they crossed to the 'stang. They reached the passenger side first, and Billy Ray peered inside. Keys in the ignition, driver's-side door cracked open.

His heart sank. It was too soon for another one. It'd only been since January. Less than three full months.

Earl looked at him. "She left the keys in the ignition."

"Yup."

"And her cell phone, there on the seat."

Earl had a habit of stating the obvious. Usually, it didn't much bother him, but at the moment it was bugging the crap out of him.

"What'd she do that for?"

Billy Ray didn't answer, just went around to the driver's side. "Look here, Earl, door's not shut tight."

Earl stared stupidly a moment, then the color left his already pale face. His mass of freckles stood out starkly against the white.

"Oh, shit," he said. "This is like Amanda LaPier. And the other one."

Two others, unless you counted True. Most folks didn't, 'cause they were scared, but Billy Ray had heard their whispers.

He turned to Earl. "Listen to me, Stroup, you are a sworn officer of the Wholesome Police Department. If you're going to work this case you damn well remember that."

"Yessir."

"You don't talk about this with anybody."

"Yessir."

He looked terrified. Billy Ray remembered looking that way himself, once upon a time. And his uncle giving him the exact same speech.

"This is a small town, and people talk. They ask questions. You just keep your head down and do your job. None of that concerns you."

"Yessir."

"Now, go grab us some gloves. If you don't have any, I've got extra in my console. And bring me my camera, it's there, too."

Moments later, gloves on and camera hanging from a strap around his neck, he examined the driver's-side door panel.

"This could be nothing, Earl. But since this scene is so similar to the others, we have to take every precaution." He indicated the door. "When you got here, the door was open?"

"I don't know if it was open, but I didn't touch it. Or anything else. Just waited for you."

"This doesn't mean she didn't go home with somebody.

Dixie likes her beer and she's not shy, if you know what I mean."

Earl nodded and Billy Ray opened the door the rest of the way. It didn't hold and tried to swing back shut. Billy Ray stopped it and pushed it until it set. He leaned into the vehicle. It smelled of cigarettes and cheap perfume. Sure enough, the ashtray was filled with butts, each of them with a red lipstick stain on the filter.

He shifted his attention to the floorboards. An empty Rockstar energy drink can, a bag from the Sonic Drive-In, a couple of water bottles. Another Rockstar in the cup holder. In the back, a change of clothes and a pair of sneakers.

He went around to the passenger side, to get a better look at her cell. Looked like she had just tossed it there. He wondered who her last call had been to; if she had been on it when the perp pulled up, made his offer?

He looked over his shoulder at Stroup. "I'm going to document the condition of the vehicle and its contents. I'd like you to watch my every move, so if need be you can verify my actions in court."

Stroup opened his mouth, then shut it, obviously thinking better of whatever he'd been about to say. Good thing, Billy Ray thought. Because he wasn't in the mood to justify his actions or play teacher.

He started snapping pictures. When he'd finished with the inside, he went around the outside again, this time with the proverbial fine-tooth comb.

"It pays to be careful, Earl. I fully expect her to show up here with a hangover and wearing last night's panties, but just in case she doesn't, we'll have this."

Earl nodded. "What're you thinkin' happened, Billy Ray?"

"What does it look like to you?"

"Like she was fixin' to head home."

"Good. What else?"

"Drunk as a skunk, no doubt."

Again, Billy Ray agreed.

"She climbs in, gets the key in the ignition but doesn't start the engine."

"Why?"

"I don't know." Earl drew his eyebrows together. "It's got me guessing. Could be a number of things."

"That it could. But here's what I think. Somebody calls to her or taps on the window, something like that. Maybe one of her girlfriends, but most probably a guy."

"That makes sense."

"He asks her if she wants to party some more—"

"And of course, she does."

"Right. So she climbs out of the Mustang and in with the guy."

"Our Unsub."

"You've been doing your homework, Earl."

"Watchin' TV, Chief. *CSI.*"

Billy Ray let that one pass. "She's so wasted, she doesn't even remember her keys are in the car."

"She's holed up someplace, still sleepin' it off. Or still partying."

"That's scenario number one."

"And number two?"

"It begins the same way," Billy Ray said. "Someone she knows calls her over to their vehicle. Only this time, they force her inside."

"I don't see any signs of a scuffle." Earl frowned. "There would've been plenty of folks around to see her."

Billy Ray nodded. "Unless she was last to leave."

"Bartenders and waitresses are always the last to go."

"Exactly, Earl. I want you to find out who was working the bar Friday night, and who was serving. Your best bet would be giving Joe a call."

"Yessir."

"Joe runs a tight ship; my guess is he stopped in Friday, checked on things. Particularly the till. If he did, ask him about it. Whether he saw Dixie."

"What should I tell him?"

"The truth, but nothing more. That Travis is lookin' for Dixie and her car's in his lot. Think you can do that?" Earl said he could and Billy Ray went on. "Tell him I'm gonna need to have a look at the security tapes. If he knows anything, write it down. You got your notebook?"

"And a pen." He patted his shirt pocket and smiled, obviously pleased with himself.

"Good man. Call me the moment you're finished."

"What're you going to do, Chief?"

"Have a talk with Travis. Try to get him settled down. By then, I'll have heard back from you."

Earl nodded and started for his vehicle, then stopped and looked back at Billy Ray. "You don't think this is the same as those other times, do you? I mean, I went to school with Dix. She was in my sister's class, they used to hang out sometimes."

"Course not, Earl. Dixie is sleeping it off someplace, thinking she's found Mr. Wonderful. But we've got to be sure it's nothing else."

Billy Ray watched as the young man climbed into his cruiser and started it up, before heading back to his own vehicle. He slipped into the Ford, hesitated a moment, then started it. He hated having lied to Earl, but the young man didn't need to know his thoughts, not quite yet. No one did. One step at a time. One piece of evidence after another.

Build a case. Nail the bastard.

CHAPTER TWENTY-NINE

Sunday, April 20
12:45 P.M.

Travis Jenkins was a hard man. A man who didn't have the luxury of soft edges or sentimentalism. He'd raised his three children without a wife while scraping out a meager living doing whatever somebody needed done. He'd mucked out stalls and repaired fencing, painted barns and delivered feed.

But he was scared. His eyes filled with tears. Those tears cut Billy Ray like a knife. Accusing him. *Couldn't he have done more? Couldn't he have ended this before Dixie?*

"Settle down, Travis," he said. "We don't know anything but that she left her car in the Landing parking lot."

"She loves that car. It's her baby. Why would she leave it like that, the keys in it?"

"You know Dixie, she likes her tequila and most probably had plenty of it. She wasn't thinking clearly. But I need *you* to think clearly, Travis. What else can you tell me about Friday night?"

"Not much. It was the same as every night. She was going out. Meeting her friends."

"Did you argue?"

"We always argued. Hell, Billy Ray, you know that. Raised two others, but my Dixie, she has her own mind."

"Did she mention anyone in particular she was meeting?"

"A couple of her girlfriends. You know Katie, John Walton's girl. And Lea Johnson."

"Steve's oldest?"

"Yeah."

"What about guys? Was she seeing anyone? Romantically?"

He shook his head.

"Did she mention being at odds with anyone?"

"Just her sister."

"Patsy."

"Yes." His eyes grew glassy with tears again. "For trying to mother her. Get her settled on the right path. Now—" His throat closed over the words.

Billy Ray patted him on the shoulder. "You've got to keep it together, Travis. We'll figure this out. Okay?"

He cleared his throat and nodded.

"I'll talk to Patsy next, she might know something."

"I called her. She hasn't heard anything from her."

"But she may know something and not realize it. Then I'll talk to folks who were at The Landing and saw her. Like I said, we'll figure this out."

Travis seemed to pull himself together. "And if she comes home? What do I do?"

"Hug her. Then call me."

Travis tugged at the brim of his cowboy hat. "I'll kick her ass, that's what I'll do."

And maybe he would, Billy Ray thought as he headed back to his cruiser, but only after he hugged her.

Through the vehicle's open window, he heard the crackle of the radio. He reached through and grabbed it. "Chief Williams."

"Billy Ray, it's me, Earl."

"Ten-four, Officer Stroup."

For a split second, the other man went quiet. As if with surprise. Billy Ray climbed into the cruiser. "You have that list for me?"

"I do. Talked to Joe. He said the surveillance video is ours anytime we want it. Ricky, Elaine and Annie were on the bar, Bubba T at the door. Ricky opened at eleven. Want me to go by, question him?"

"I'll do it."

"What do you want me to do now, Billy Ray?"

"You know, Earl, I got my promotion more than a year ago. I'm thinking you need to call me Chief."

His deputy was obviously taken aback. "Sure, Billy— Chief. Didn't mean any disrespect."

"I know, Earl. Didn't take it that way. Just figure we might need a little more formality around here. Things being what they are."

"Yessir, Chief."

"While I follow up at The Landing, give the boys over at the sheriff's office a call. See if there's anything new on Henry Rodriquez."

"Should I tell them about Dixie?"

"Lordy, no. And have those know-it-alls climbing our frames? That's the last thing we need. Besides, there's nothing to tell, not yet." Billy Ray paused a moment, sorting his to-do list. "When you hang up with them, give the lab a call, see if they've got anything yet on the blood samples I sent over. And keep me posted."

CHAPTER THIRTY

Billy Ray sat at The Landing's bar. Joe Cooper didn't hire kids to run his business. He didn't need to. Lots of folks around Wholesome needed steady, good-paying work. Seasoned professionals, Joe had told him once. Instead of putting the eye candy behind the bar—the very heart of the money-making operation—have them wait tables.

Ricky St. James had turned thirty-five around the same time Billy Ray had. He had a family to support. There'd be no messing with the till or offering free rounds from him or his crew.

"Tell me about Friday night, Ricky. What time did Dixie show up?"

Ricky leaned on the counter. He looked tired. He'd brewed them both a cup of coffee, and it sat on the bar in front of him, steam curling toward the ceiling.

"About nine. That's the first time I recall seeing her anyway."

"Is that her usual time?"

Ricky nodded. Sipped his coffee. "Things don't get really cranked up until then. And Dixie's one of those stay-to-the-bitter-end girls."

"And Friday?"

"Nope. Band was still playing and she was gone."

"She leave with anybody?"

"Not that I noticed. Surveillance might show different." He took another sip of the coffee; Billy Ray noticed his hand was steady as a rock.

"What about while she was here? She spend a lot of time with one particular guy?"

"Again, not that I noticed. Friday nights are crazy." He paused as if to search his memory. "Saw her dancing with her friends at one point."

"Names?

"Katie Walton and Lea Johnson."

"Those her two BFFs?"

"It seems that way. They're here together almost every night."

"Anyone new in that night? Anyone you didn't recognize?"

"Nope." He drained his cup, then refilled it. "You probably want to talk to Bubba T. Anyone comes through the door, he eyeballs 'em."

"Anyone unexpected come in?"

"What d'you mean?"

"Folks you recognize from the community, but don't come in much? Maybe ever. And suddenly there they are?"

He frowned slightly. "Come to think about it, I was surprised to see one of the Abbotts—"

"Logan Abbott?" Billy Ray heard the excitement in his voice and knew, by the strange way Ricky looked at him, that the bartender had as well.

"No, his sister. Raine."

"Raine was in Friday night? You're certain?"

He nodded. "With that fancy, foreign trainer. August something."

Billy Ray could tell he wasn't Ricky's favorite. "Perez?"

"Yeah. They were together."

"No kidding." He brought the cup to his lips. "How was that?"

"Bizarre. They ended up getting in a fight."

"Some folks can't hold their liquor."

"Exactly."

"They leave together?"

"Yup." He lifted the cup, then set it back down. "I kicked them out and suddenly they were best friends again."

"And you were the bad guy?"

"Uh-huh."

"No Logan Abbott, though?" When the bartender's eyebrows rose slightly at the question, Billy Ray added, "Come looking for his crazy sister or something?"

He shook his head. "Logan Abbott hasn't been in here since . . . hell, not since his first wife ran off. They used to come in sometimes and dance." He brought his coffee cup to his lips but didn't sip. "Besides, I hear he was in the hospital all night. His new wife was in some sort of riding accident."

The perfect alibi.

Or the perfect way to catch him in a lie. With cell phone records or the hospital's security video. Problem was, at this point a judge would deny any request for a search warrant. Which meant the cell carrier was out. He may, however, be able to sweet-talk the hospital into a little peek.

He returned his focus to the interview at hand. "Can you remember anything else about Dixie from that night? Anything that jumps out at you?"

He thought a moment. "Just that her Mustang was in the lot when we left."

"You didn't find that strange?"

"Nope. It wasn't the first time, if you know what I mean."

"Even when it was still there yesterday?"

"Nope."

"Did you check the car out, take a look inside, anything like that?"

Ricky shook his head. "Like I said, wasn't the first time. Although I don't believe it's ever still been here this long."

Billy Ray nodded and stood. "Joe said I could look at Friday night's surveillance video. Mind if I do that now?"

"Not at all. I'll get you set up in his office."

CHAPTER THIRTY-ONE

Sunday, April 20
3:30 P.M.

Dr. Bauer had released Bailey. Now, as they neared the farm, she asked Logan to lower the windows. "I want to smell the air," she said. "Then I'll know I'm almost home."

The fresh, warm breeze rushed into the car, whipping at her hair. She breathed it in, letting it fill her senses and chase away the institutional smell of the hospital.

The neurologist had warned her not to expect too much of herself at first. She had suffered a brain trauma, she needed time to heal. He had assured her the memory of what happened would return, and had cautioned her not to try and force it.

"Just let it happen, Mrs. Abbott."

Easy for him to say, she thought. It wasn't a piece of his life that had gone missing. It wasn't him existing in this constant state of uneasiness. As if some terrible surprise lurked up ahead, one she couldn't predict—or avoid.

They reached the iron gates and rolled through. "Welcome home, Bailey."

Weirdly, even her memory hadn't prepared her for how beautiful it was. The rolling green hills and blue sky, the white fencing and azalea bushes, exploding with pink, white and fuchsia blossoms. The horses, with their rich brown coats shimmering in the sun.

Bailey let its magic wash over her, the memory of her antiseptic hospital room fading away.

The barn and arena came into view. Jo-Jo and Max, the chocolate Lab and corgi, trotted out to greet them. She didn't see Tony and asked Logan about him.

"He's fine." Logan squeezed her hand. "Stephanie has him."

A moment later, Paul appeared, followed by August.

"Do you want to stop?" he asked.

She shook her head. "I'm not ready."

The men watched them roll past, hands lifted in greeting.

"They were worried about you. Everyone was."

"Even Raine?"

He smiled. "You are feeling better."

"Wind and Raine—" she said.

"Thunder and lightning," he finished, and they both laughed.

"Do they know?" she asked.

"The details of the accident?"

She shook her head. "About the baby."

"No. No one knows but you, me and the medical staff."

"Thank you."

They came upon the second set of gates, and Logan drove slowly through. Moments later, she stepped out of the car and stood a moment, drinking it in with all her senses. As if they had been newly awakened. The smell of earth and plants, the sun warming them. The rustle of the leaves and chirp of the birds. The trickling of the fountain.

She held out her hand. "Home."

He took it. "Our home."

"I want to see it all again. Just to know I remember it. Do you think that's weird?"

He smiled. "I think it's nice."

So, they went from room to room, the country-style kitchen and keeping room, the formal living room and Logan's study. Bailey stopped in front of the portrait of his mother. "You look exactly like her."

"That's what you said the first time you saw it."

"I know." She glanced over her shoulder at him and smiled. "And I really meant it."

He laughed and together they headed upstairs, holding hands. In their bedroom Bailey stopped, her gaze on the bed.

The bed they shared. Husband and wife. She recalled how it felt to lie there, enclosed in his arms. Warm and protected. She brought a hand to her abdomen, to the life growing inside her.

"What are you thinking?"

"About us. Making love, creating this baby. Here. In this bed."

Tears stung her eyes and feeling silly, Bailey turned quickly and crossed to the balcony doors. She stepped through them and gazed out beyond the wall, to the woods beyond.

Her accident. Henry, shot dead. Emotion choked her.

He followed her and drew her snugly back against his chest. "To keep you warm," he murmured, resting his chin on her head.

This was where she'd seen Henry for the first time. With her mind's eye she saw him walking along the path, Tony, with him, running ahead, circling back.

Henry, with his scarred face and kind eyes. His ready smile and childlike wisdom. With a heart as wide as the sky.

Her friend. Shot dead.

Dead, she realized, the truth of it swamping her, bitterly real. She brought a hand to her mouth. "No. It can't be. Not Henry, he . . . I can't—" She started to cry, great, wracking sobs of despair.

Logan turned her in his arms and held her against his chest. "I'm sorry, baby," he murmured over and over, rubbing her back. "So sorry."

She cried until her eyes burned and her throat ached, until she hadn't the energy for more. "I'm going to miss him so . . . Just a moment ago, I was thinking how wonderful it was to remember. How beautiful to reexperience it all. But now . . . this . . . I wish I didn't remember." She tipped her head back to meet his eyes. "It hurts, Logan."

He cupped her face in his hands, brushing her tears away with his thumbs. "I wish I could take it away."

"But you can't. No one can."

"Why don't you lie down? You're tired. I could bring you some tea? And a magazine?"

"The courtyard," she said. "I need the sun."

He set her up on one of the chaises. He worried it was chilly, so he brought a blanket along with her sunglasses and iPhone and a magazine.

"There are a couple of things I have to take care of," he said. "The office, I've been away—"

"Go. I'm not sick. And I'm not made of glass. Obviously, considering the knock I took to my head."

He didn't smile and she went on. "I'm fine. Really."

He bent and kissed her. "I'll be in the study, answering e-mails. Call if you need anything. Anything. Promise?"

She did, but still he lingered. "Enough, you. Just go—" She waved him off. "I won't be able to nap with you hovering like this."

So he left her. Bailey laid her head back and closed her eyes, letting her mind drift, like the puffy clouds above.

A sharp sound broke the gentle day. *A gunshot*. Her eyes snapped open, fear gripping her. She looked down at her lap, her hands.

A cry of terror escaped her. Blood. Where had all this blood come from?

"There you are."

Bailey jerked her head up, and pain shot through it. Raine, standing just inside the courtyard gate, a huge arrangement of flowers in her arms.

"My God, Bailey, what's wrong?"

"I was dreaming. I thought . . . Did you hear a gun go off a moment ago?"

Raine went white. The arrangement slipped from her hands, the vase shattered as it hit the brick patio floor. "Where's Logan?"

"His study. Raine, what—"

But the other woman was gone before Bailey could get the words out, running into the house, calling Logan's name.

And then it hit her why. No. He couldn't . . . he wouldn't. Panicked, Bailey leaped to her feet and ran after the other woman. She flew through the kitchen and into the foyer, then stopped short. She grabbed the banister for support, dizzy, head throbbing.

Logan, alive and well, his sister, clinging to him and shaking. He looked befuddled.

"Raine, it's okay." He patted her back, then drew away from her, looking her in the eyes. "What brought this on? I'm fine."

"Bailey said she heard a gunshot."

"I did." Bailey stepped into his line of sight. "I'd dozed off and it woke me up."

"When?"

"Just now. Right before Raine arrived."

"I didn't hear anything." He looked at his sister. "Did you?"

She shook her head. "But I had the radio on."

"I'd better call down to the barn, see if they heard it." He quickly dialed. "Hey Paul— Yeah, she's fine. Look, she was outside and thought she heard a gunshot. You hear anything down there?" He paused, obviously listening, then nodded. "That's what I'm afraid of. If so, it was damn close to the house." He stopped to listen again. "I agree. But let me get a little more information from her first. Thanks, man."

"Did he?" Bailey asked.

"No, but it wouldn't surprise him if you did. Considering recent events."

Henry.

"Paul's going to call the sheriff's office, but I wanted to get as many details from you as possible first."

"The sound awakened me. I opened my eyes and I—"

Saw blood. A lot of blood.

"What?"

She brought a hand to her head. "I don't feel so good. My head hurts really bad."

He was by her side in an instant, helping lower her to sit on the stairs. "Deep breath, baby. Everything's all right. Just calm down."

He looked at his sister. "Could you get a cool cloth for the back of her neck?"

Moments later, Raine returned with it and Logan laid it on the back of her neck. "That's it," he said. "Breathe. In your nose, out your mouth."

She did and after several seconds the pain eased and the dizziness passed. She took the cloth from her neck. "I feel better now. Thanks."

"So stop scaring us, please," Raine said. "I don't think I can take any more."

The image of red filled her head. "Logan, I—" Her throat closed over the words; she cleared it. "I may have remembered something. Or—" She bit the last back, moved her gaze between Logan and Raine. "Or maybe I was dreaming."

He curled his fingers around hers. "Tell us."

"I opened my eyes and saw . . . blood. On my hands and my jeans."

"Anything else?"

"No. There was Raine—"

"Having the life scared out of her, thank you very much."

Logan ignored his sister and squatted in front of Bailey. "You were dreaming," he said.

"Why do you think so?"

"I told you about Henry in the hospital and you were really upset about it right before your nap."

"But the blood—"

"Remember what Billy Ray said? That you had a lot of blood on you. Of course it was on your mind."

That's right. Of course.

From out front came the slam of a car door. Bailey jumped. She noticed Raine did, too. The other woman's nerves seemed to be just as fried as hers.

Raine started toward the door. "Maybe what you heard was me slamming the car door? It certainly made us both jump just now." Raine peered out the sidelight, then looked over her shoulder at Logan. "We have company, and it's your very favorite person."

CHAPTER THIRTY-TWO

Sunday, April 20
4:05 P.M.

"Hello, Billy Ray," Raine said, cracking open the door. "Isn't this a lovely surprise."

"Give it a rest, Raine. I'm here to speak to Logan and Bailey."

"I don't think they want to speak to you." She looked over her shoulder at her brother and grinned. "Do you?"

Without waiting for an answer, she turned back to Billy Ray. "He said to go screw yourself."

Logan strode forward. "That's enough, Raine."

"After all the trouble he's caused our family? Not near enough."

Logan yanked the door the rest of the way open. "Now's not a good time, Williams."

"I'm sure it's not, but I'm here anyway. Just came to check on your wife. See how she was feeling."

He looked past Logan to her and smiled. "The doctor let you go home. That's good news."

"Yes, it is," Logan said. "Now, if you'll excuse us—"

But the man ducked past Logan and into the foyer. "How about your memory, Mrs. Abbott? Has it started coming back?"

Blood. On her hands and lap.

A dream? Or a memory?

Logan answered for her. "Not yet, Billy Ray. You'll be the first person we call."

Bailey frowned slightly. Obviously, he hadn't wanted Billy Ray to know about the gunshot or blood. Because it might have been her imagination? Or because of something else?

"Bailey was just going up for a rest. I'm afraid you'll have to come back another—"

"I have news."

She looked at Logan, then back at the lawman. "What news?"

"About Henry's blood."

Red. Everywhere. Her hands and jeans.

"I got a report back from the lab. I was right. Not all that blood was yours."

The strangest sensation came over her. A chill that started at the top of her head and eased downward.

"Blood belonged to a male. Type matched old Henry's."

"Oh, my God."

That had come from Raine. She stood as if frozen, face as bloodless as a ghost's.

"He's guessing it's Henry's," Logan said. "DNA profiling takes weeks. Even months."

Billy Ray smirked. "But basic serology is quick."

Bailey looked up at Logan. "I can't . . . Do you think . . . Could I have seen Henry . . . shot?"

"Must have been more than saw him," Billy Ray said. "Otherwise how'd you get all that blood on your—"

"Shut up, Billy Ray! You don't know for sure it's even Henry's blood."

"Who else's could it be!" Bailey got to her feet, legs shaking so badly, she feared she might fall. She grasped the banister for support. "It must be his. . . . How did I end up with Henry's blood all over me!"

"My question exactly, Mrs. Abbott."

"I told you, I don't remember!"

"How about the last time you saw him alive?"

Henry. Alive. She brought a hand to her head, to the bandages that covered her wound. "I don't . . . recently . . . it must have been. We talked about True."

The words landed with a silent roar. All three looked at her.

Logan held a hand out. "What did you say?"

She stared at him, heart thundering. Head pounding. "Nothing. I didn't say . . ." Her vision blurred. "No. That was a mistake. I don't know why I said that."

"Yes, you do," Billy Ray said. "Tell me, when did you last see him?"

"He was my friend." Her tears spilled over and she brought a hand to her mouth. She'd always wondered why people did that, and now she knew. To hold back the sounds of their pain, as if holding them back somehow kept the hurt at bay. "I don't remember."

Logan moved to take her into his arms. "Sweetheart, I'm so—"

She pushed him away. "Don't touch me. You must have known this. All that blood . . . how else . . . you must have—"

"I didn't want to upset you."

"You see why it's so important you talk to me," Billy Ray said, taking a step toward her. "Who knows what he will or won't tell you?"

"You son of a bitch!" Logan lunged at Billy Ray, knocking him into the entryway table. A lamp crashed to the floor.

Raine jumped in, dragging Logan back. "Don't! He wants you to hit him!"

Bailey stared at them.

"Who knows what he will or won't tell you?"

"Ask him about True."

Ask him.

About True.

True. What happened to True?

"Stop it!" she shouted, and pain knifed through her skull. She did it again anyway. "Both of you! Leave me alone!"

She turned and ran up the stairs to the bedroom and locked the door behind her. There, pain crashed down on her.

CHAPTER THIRTY-THREE

Billy Ray stared after Bailey, her words reverberating in his head. To leave her alone, go away. He couldn't breathe. As if something from the depths of his being was spilling forth, like helium filling a balloon to bursting. Until there was room for nothing else in its skin.

"You son of a bitch."

Billy Ray jerked his gaze to Logan.

"You leave her alone. Do you hear me? You leave us alone!"

Billy Ray didn't respond. He turned to go; Logan grabbed his arm, stopping him. "That's my wife, and she's carrying my child. And I swear to God, I'll do whatever it takes to protect what's mine."

He released him. "Now get the hell out of my house!"

Billy Ray half stumbled, half ran to his cruiser. He felt sick. If he puked in front of Abbott, he'd know just how personal this was.

"You've got to stop this, Billy Ray."

"You've got to leave me alone now."

He started the vehicle and tore out, spitting gravel up as he did. He made it past the barn and through the main gates and onto the road before he had to pull the cruiser over. He climbed out and stumbled to the side and vomited.

Billy Ray retched until he thought there could be nothing left inside him. Empty. He was completely empty.

He made it back into the vehicle and slumped behind the wheel. The image of Bailey Abbott's stricken face taunted him. The way True's did. Expression afraid. And lost. So very vulnerable it tore him apart.

True. She was right there, where she lived in his head, so real he was sure that if he could find a way to crawl inside himself, he could hold her in his arms.

She was beckoning him. To try. To open the door, step through. Join her.

Billy Ray looked at his hands. They were shaking. He was so tired of fighting the memories and feelings, stuffing them deep down, so deep they occupied the very marrow of his being. Holding them there. He was tired, so tired.

So he let go, and she was opening her front door. His knees went weak at the sight of her.

"What are you doing here, Billy Ray?"

She looked over his shoulder as if expecting to see someone else with him.

"Just checking on you, True. Making sure you're okay."

Her smile looked stiff. "Of course I'm okay. Why wouldn't I be?"

Was she teasing him? Or did she really want him to spell it out for her? "Can I come in?"

"I don't think that's a good idea. Logan wouldn't like it."

"But he's out of town."

A wrinkle formed between her eyebrows. "How'd you know that, Billy Ray?"

He hadn't meant to make her feel uncomfortable. "This is a small town, everybody knows everything."

"You still can't come in. Logan's my husband, and if he wouldn't like something, I don't do it. Out of respect."

No wonder he loved her. "Can we talk out here?"

She hesitated, then nodded. "I suppose so." She stepped the rest of the way out onto the porch and closed the door behind her. "What's on your mind?"

"You, True."

"You've got to stop this, Billy Ray—"

"No, wait! I know some things about this family and I think you need—"

"No." She held up a hand, obviously upset. "I know about this family. I know how sad—"

"And about Logan. He's a bad guy, True. You've got to believe me. The woman who went missing, she wasn't the only one. Five years ago—"

"No." She shook her head. "I love Logan. He wouldn't hurt me or anybody else."

"Please, True. Just listen to me."

"I'm sorry, but I can't. You'll find somebody. The right girl."

He didn't respond and she squeezed his hand. "You've got to leave me alone now. And if you don't, I'm going to have to do something about it."

"I have to save you, True."

"I know, Billy Ray," she said, her expression as sad as any he'd ever seen. "And you are a sweet, sweet man. But you have to believe me now, I don't need saving."

A truck rumbled past, the driver honking in greeting. Billy Ray snapped back to the present. He realized he had been crying and wiped his eyes and sat up straight. He couldn't save True. Not then and certainly not now.

But Bailey, he could. And her unborn child. It wasn't too late for them. He fastened his safety belt and pulled onto the highway. If it cost him his last breath, he would see to it that Logan Abbott never hurt another woman.

CHAPTER THIRTY-FOUR

Sunday, April 20
6:05 P.M.

Stephanie Rodriquez sat on her small front porch, a drink cradled in her hands, staring out at the pasture and the waning day. An idyllic scene: the three mares grazing, her chestnut, Molly, stopping every so often to whinny softly at her.

The animal had picked up on her distress. They were amazing creatures. Sensitive. Capable of a range of emotion. Of devotion.

If Stephanie would allow herself to be soothed, Molly could do it. But Stephanie wasn't ready to feel better. Tears stung her eyes and she brought the glass to her lips and sipped. The alcohol burned, but she welcomed its sting.

Uncle Henry was dead. Shot in the back by some idiot with a rifle and more than likely a belly full of beer.

She took another sip, acknowledging anger. At the gun-happy, trespassing son of a bitch who did it. But also at herself. Why had she allowed him to continue to live out there alone? She should have convinced him to come live with her here, at her farm.

Truth was, she'd hardly even tried. Asked when she should have insisted. Bought into her own self-assurances. If she was vigilant, all would be well.

But it wasn't well. Now he was gone.

And she was alone.

From inside came the sound of the phone. She left the call for voice mail to answer; she didn't have the heart for another condolence or the inevitable questions that followed. The calls had been coming nonstop. As much with concern as curiosity.

From one of the callers she'd learned about Bailey's accident. Her amnesia. The fact it had happened the same day as Uncle Henry had been shot. One neighbor had actually posed aloud what the rest of them had been salivating to know: What really happened out in those woods?

The sound of tires on her gravel drive drew her attention. A Wholesome police cruiser.

Billy Ray.

Once upon a time she would have waved and waited for him, or run to meet him. Flung herself into his arms. Stephanie closed her eyes, and pushed aside the memories of those times. She couldn't change the past. She understood that just as clearly as she believed she *could* control the present—and the person she would become.

Billy Ray no longer had the ability to hurt her. Because she wouldn't allow him that power, and it was her choice how the next few minutes would go.

She stood as he drew to a stop, watched as he climbed out of the cruiser and crossed to her.

"Billy Ray," she said when he stopped at the bottom of the porch steps and looked up.

"Hello, Steph."

"What're you doing out here?"

"Came to make certain you were doing all right."

"Seeing is believing. I'm dandy. You can go now."

He nudged his hat back so he could see her better. "I'm really sorry about Henry."

Tears pricked her eyes and she cursed them. She would

not cry in front of this man. Never again. "Why are you really here, Billy Ray?"

"I tried to call. You didn't answer."

"Because it was you calling." She folded her arms across her chest. "What do you want? If this is just more of your nonsense, I really don't have time for it."

"It's an official visit from the chief of police. If you call that 'nonsense.'"

She cocked an eyebrow. "Village of Wholesome, population seven hundred."

"That used to be good enough for you, Steph."

"And so was baby food."

His mouth tightened. She'd hit her mark. "I came to talk to you about Bailey Abbott."

"Surprise, surprise."

"I don't want to fight with you."

Of course he didn't. To him, she'd never been worth fighting for.

"When'd you see her last?"

"A little over a week ago. Right before all that rain."

"Friday."

She thought a moment. "That's right."

"Here?"

"Yes."

"What was the purpose of her visit?"

"The purpose of . . . Really? You have to ask that?" Stephanie made a sound of disbelief. "We're friends. You know that. Obviously."

"And friends talk."

"Of course."

"What did you talk about that day?"

"None of your damn business!"

He flushed slightly. "You heard about her accident?"

"Yes. No way to keep a juicy tidbit like that quiet."

"She was riding. Caught a low-hanging branch in the

temple." When she frowned slightly, he added, "Doesn't sound right, does it?"

"It doesn't sound like Bailey. She's cautious."

"As I understand it, she doesn't ride. She's terrified of horses."

He sounded smug. Of course he would, he prided himself on knowing everything about the man he hated most in all the world. "Yes, she does. Sorry to disappoint you, but she's actually a competent rider. Just rusty." She smiled slightly at his surprise. "And no, she's not terrified of them. Not anymore."

"You're lying."

She flushed. "That's not something *I* do."

"Did Logan know?"

He always brought it back around to Logan. "No. She wanted to surprise him for his birthday. It's one of the things we talked about that Friday."

She saw his consternation. Obviously this news had forced him to rewrite whatever nefarious plot he'd composed in his head.

"Bailey has no memory of what happened. You don't find that odd?"

"Give it a rest."

"There's more about her accident, you want to hear it?"

She did, but not from him. "I'll call Logan. I'm a family friend, I don't have to rely on gossip."

"It's not gossip. It's right from the police report."

"One you wrote up yourself, no doubt. I'll take my chances."

"It has to do with your uncle."

She stopped on that. "Uncle Henry?"

"When they found Bailey, she had a lot of blood on her. It wasn't all hers."

Stephanie felt as if the wind had been knocked out of her. "Oh, my God."

"A week ago, besides her riding, what did you talk about?"

"We're friends, Billy Ray. We just talked."

"That's what girlfriends do, isn't it? Talk about everything. Their husbands, trouble they may be having in their marriage, their concerns—"

"You're so full of shit."

She turned to go inside; before she could, he was up the porch steps, hand on her arm. "Did she? Talk about Logan? Was she worried about anything?"

"No, she was happy. Ecstatic even. Now, take your hand off me."

He tightened his grip instead. "You're lying."

"And you're obsessed!" She jerked her arm free. "She's not True. She doesn't need you to 'save' her."

"How good a rider had she become?"

"I told you, she's competent."

"Confident enough to be galloping through the woods?"

She couldn't imagine it. "I'm not in her head."

"But I need you to be."

"For God's sake, Billy Ray—"

"I need you to talk to her, Steph. Get the truth. She claims to have amnesia. But what if it's a ruse? Because she's scared. You can talk to her. She trusts you—"

"That's right, she does trust me. That's why I won't do it, Billy Ray."

"Henry's blood was all over her, Steph. What do you think that means?"

He was manipulating her. The way he always had. Pulling her strings. Pressing her buttons.

If he had something real, he wouldn't be here.

"It's time for you to go."

"If you'd just listen."

She opened her screen door, stepped through it, then

looked back at him. "I've done all the listening to you that I'm ever going to do."

She shut the door, twisted the lock. Billy Ray hesitated on the porch a moment, then walked off. When she heard the crunching of his wheels on the gravel drive, she sank to the floor.

And fell apart.

CHAPTER THIRTY-FIVE

Monday, April 21
8:30 A.M.

Billy Ray had officially started his day five minutes before the hour of eight. Unofficially, he had been at it most of the night. In his war room, reviewing every report, every piece of evidence from Wholesome's three most notorious mysteries. The way he did anytime he couldn't sleep.

Last night he had added two new photos to his time-line: Dixie Jenkins's and Henry Rodriquez's.

As tragic as both cases were, he was grateful for them. Fresh blood meant new evidence and witnesses. It offered a real opportunity to move his agenda forward.

But as much as it pained him to admit it, he needed help. The sheriff's office had both the resources and clout to make things happen. Abbott wouldn't dare pull his high-and-mighty act with them. All he had to do was get them onboard.

Located in Slidell, forty miles south and east of Wholesome, the sheriff's complex was state-of-the-art, down to the new on-site crime lab due to open later this year.

Billy Ray had to fight the envy that surged up in him every time he entered the building. The feeling that maybe he'd sold himself short by sticking with the Wholesome

P.D. But he'd had his reasons and made his choices; the way he figured, it was way too late to go back now.

He caught Rumsfeld and Carlson, the two detectives working Rodriquez, in the lobby. He called their names, stopping them from stepping into the elevator.

"Glad I caught you," Billy Ray said when he reached them.

They looked tired. And anything but happy to see him. "What can we do for you, Williams?"

"I was hoping we could chat a minute."

Rumsfeld looked at his watch. "A minute."

The attitude pissed Billy Ray off, but he held it back. "Rodriquez autopsy was yesterday. It turn up anything?"

"No surprises. Confirmed what we suspected."

"That a hunter mistook Rodriquez for a deer or hog and killed him?"

"It all fits. The location of the body. The bullet's trajectory. One shot. Shooter used a rifle, the Remington 700. Bullet made a small entrance and a huge exit, consistent with the .308."

Billy Ray pursed his lips in thought. A .308 entered the target, then mushroomed, causing massive destruction upon exit. "The 700's also known as a sniper rifle, correct?"

Rumsfeld's eyebrows shot up. "Are you suggesting someone took a hit out on simple, old Henry Rodriquez?"

"Just thinking out loud."

"We're releasing the body to the family this morning. And now, Williams, if you'll excuse us, we've got a half-dozen other cases with our names on them."

"Rodriquez is still a homicide."

"Pardon?"

"Whether the homicide was accidental or not, it's still murder."

"We get that, Williams. And we have no intention of

closing this case. But right now, we've taken it as far as it can go."

The elevator door swished open; the two stepped on. Billy Ray stopped the doors from closing. "Are you aware that three days ago Abbott's wife was found unconscious and covered in blood?"

He had their attention and went on. "That's right, Bailey Abbott, Logan Abbott's wife, was found the same day, in the very woods where Rodriquez was shot, unconscious and covered in blood."

"Why didn't we hear anything about this?"

"My jurisdiction, no reason to. Until now."

"Why now?"

"The story is, she was out riding, took a low-hanging branch to the head and went down. Horse returns to the stable without a rider; a search ensues. Abbott finds her unconscious, gets her to the hospital. Meanwhile other members of the search party came across Rodriquez and called you."

Rumsfeld let out a long breath. He glanced at his partner, then back at Billy Ray. "Who called you?"

"That doesn't matter. The point is, we both have pieces of the puzzle."

"You've interviewed her?"

"Tried. Supposedly she has TML."

"In English."

"Traumatic memory loss. Amnesia."

"You said 'supposedly'? Why?"

"Awfully convenient, don't you think?"

"She was hospitalized?"

"Yes."

"And a doctor confirmed the amnesia?"

He was losing them. "Yes."

"Then keep us posted. The amnesia will pass and if she knows something—"

"Oh, she does."

Carlson snorted. "Something pertinent, Williams."

"I think she may have a reason not to remember."

Rumsfeld narrowed his eyes. "And what would that be?"

"Protect someone she loves."

"Go on."

"Mrs. Abbott had a lot of blood on her. I sent samples from her clothes to the lab. Got the preliminary results back. Two different blood types. Hers. And Henry Rodriquez's. Now, I know that doesn't prove it was his blood, but as coincidences go, it's a doozy.

"At least," he went on, "pay her a visit. Maybe she saw the shooter. Maybe her amnesia was caused by the trauma of witnessing the event, not the blow to her head."

It sounded like he was begging, and he despised himself for it.

But he'd do it for True. Anything for True.

"When's the last time you spoke with her?" Carlson asked.

"Tried to talk to her yesterday afternoon. Abbott threw me out."

"Interesting." Rumsfeld rubbed his jaw. "They ever find his first wife?"

"Nope. Disappeared without a trace."

"I sat in one of his interviews back then. His story never quite added up for me."

Billy Ray hid his glee. "Hit a lot of folks around Wholesome that way. They're still talkin' about it."

The two sheriff's detectives exchanged glances. Rumsfeld nodded. "Thanks for the lead, Williams. We'll pay her a visit."

"One more heads-up. Abbott hovers over her like a hawk. I get the sense she only says what he wants to hear."

The detective cocked an eyebrow and Billy Ray hoped

he hadn't pushed too hard. "Just want you to have everything."

"We appreciate that, Williams. We'll be sure to return the favor."

He'd done good, Billy Ray thought, relief flooding him. He smiled at the two detectives. "I'll count on it."

He started off; they called after him. He stopped and looked back. "Yeah?"

"Heard you had another woman go missing."

Bad news traveled fast. "It's not official. We're still hoping she's holed up somewhere with someone. I'm moving forward with the investigation anyway. Video surveillance turned up squat, so we're questioning everyone who set foot in the bar that night."

"We're here, Williams. Call us if you need us."

CHAPTER THIRTY-SIX

Monday, April 21
9:45 A.M.

Bailey stood under the hot spray, letting the water course over her. Logan had gotten up hours ago. She had stirred, tried to will herself to arise with him, but had fallen back to sleep.

She wanted to apologize to him this morning. For her outburst, for charging up the stairs and locking herself in their bedroom. She didn't understand what had come over her. Her head had hurt so much; Logan and Billy Ray's back-and-forth, the thought of Henry, his blood on her hands . . . She just hadn't been able to take it. But to storm from the room that way, slam the door behind her? It was all so . . . junior high.

Maybe her hormones were messing with her? She'd heard other women talk about seesawing emotions during pregnancy, and last night's behavior had surely been that.

Bailey cut off the shower, grabbed a towel and stepped out. As she dried off, she caught sight of herself in the mirror and stopped. Did she look different? she wondered, turning sideways. It was too early to be showing, but it felt as if she were. She suddenly felt . . . pregnant.

She laid a hand on her still-flat stomach. A baby. She was going to be a mother. A fierce protectiveness rose up in her. It wasn't just about her and Logan anymore. Not just their lives, their love story to protect.

"I couldn't protect any of the others. Not even True."

Logan had said that to her, that night they'd fought and he'd gotten drunk. What had he meant about not being able to protect True? She'd left him. He'd said so. But that statement suggested, maybe, he thought she was dead.

Red. Everywhere. On her hands and jeans.

A chill rolled over her, and Bailey wrapped herself in the towel. No. He didn't think that. If he did, he would have moved heaven and earth to find her killer.

She finished dressing, then carefully arranged her hair over her bandages. That done, she headed downstairs to find Logan.

She found him in the kitchen, dressed and ready to go. "You're leaving?" she said, crestfallen.

"I'll stay with you while you eat, then I have to run out."

Bailey couldn't hide her disappointment. "Where?"

He hesitated. "The sheriff's office."

She felt as if he'd doused her with cold water. "Why?"

"About Henry, they said."

"I'll come with you."

"Absolutely not. In fact, they asked about you and I told them you were still recovering from your accident."

"They wanted to talk to me?"

"It's nothing. I explained about your amnesia and directed them to speak with Dr. Bauer about it."

Obviously, he didn't want her talking to them. Was he protecting her? Or someone else?

Maybe he was protecting himself?

She shook her head slightly, wondering where that had come from, chasing it away. "Thank you. Have you eaten?"

"I have. Can I get you something?"

"I can do it. I'm thinking a big bowl of oatmeal."

She was aware of him watching as she busied herself making it. Like he was counting every step, measuring every move. It made her feel oddly uncomfortable. She thought of asking him why or to stop, but didn't want to hurt his feelings.

She turned toward him. They said each other's names simultaneously.

"Logan—"

"Bailey—"

They stopped, laughed, then said in unison. "I'm so sorry about—"

They stopped again. "You first," he said.

"No, you."

He crossed to her and took her hands. "I'm sorry I acted like an ass with Billy Ray last night."

"I'm sorry I acted like a petulant teenager. Stomping upstairs that way."

"It's my fault. Besides, you have a legitimate excuse." He tenderly touched her bandages. "How's your head this morning?"

"Better. A rubber mallet's replaced yesterday's hammer."

He bent and kissed her. "Did you take something for it?"

Before she could answer, his cell pinged the arrival of a text. "Hold on, I need to check this." He did, then stepped away. "I've got to go. My attorney's on his way."

"Your attorney? On his way where?"

"To meet me at the sheriff's office."

She blinked, confused. "I don't understand. . . . You're just going in to answer a few questions about Henry. Why do you need a lawyer?"

"Because there are people who think I have something to hide."

Like Billy Ray.

And his own wife.

Why had she thought that? She had seen and heard Billy Ray's arguments, they added up to nothing more than wishful thinking.

He lightly touched her brow. "Why the frown?"

She hadn't realized she was frowning and tried to relax it. "I wish you didn't have to go."

"I know. Me, too." He kissed her again, lingering, then groaned and stepped away. "I better go."

"Yes."

He started for the door, then stopped and looked back. "It doesn't mean anything."

"What?"

"That I want my lawyer with me."

But it did. To her. It felt wrong.

She clasped her hands together. "Call me when you're finished."

He said he would and she watched him leave, then reheated her oatmeal. Although she had lost a taste for it, she forced herself to eat every bite.

Something nagged at her, like a sliver or a bug bite. Irritating, festering.

What happened the day of her accident? The two days before? Why couldn't she remember?

The bump on her head, Dr. Bauer said. She had no reason not to believe him, yet she had this terrible feeling . . . this sensation of something terrible and dark hanging over her.

Bailey stood, carried her empty bowl to the sink. She told herself to shake it off. It was the memory loss making her feel this way. The big blank spot where those three days were supposed to be. She rinsed her bowl and set it in the dishwasher. Maybe she'd give Dr. Bauer a call? Ask him about it, ask if most of his patients felt this way.

The doorbell pealed. She dried her hands, then went to answer it. Two men, both in sport coats and ties, one young and the other middle-aged, stood on her front step.

She didn't open the door and the older of the two held up a shield. "Mrs. Abbott? Detectives Rumsfeld and Carlson, Saint Tammany Sheriff's Office."

She cracked it open. "There must be some mistake. My husband is on his way to your office."

"No mistake, ma'am. May we come in? We'd like to ask you a few questions."

"I thought my husband already told you that I—" She stopped, realizing they knew very well what they were doing. "I see," she said, stepping away from the door to allow them in. "He's being questioned there, and I'm being questioned here."

"Yes, ma'am," the older one replied. "May we sit down?"

"Of course. This way." She led them to the keeping room, with its windows facing the gardens. The sun tumbled through, warming her.

The detectives sat directly across from her. She found their gazes uncomfortably intense. "We understand you had an accident on Wednesday?"

"Yes." Her hand went instinctively to the bandages. "I was riding. I fell and hit my head."

"How? What caused the fall?"

"I don't remember. In fact, I don't remember any of it." She moved her gaze between the two. "But I think you already know that. Am I right?"

Neither responded. The older of the two glanced down at his notebook, then back up at her. "You're suffering from Traumatic Memory Loss, TML."

"Yes," she said. "Retrograde. That's what the neurologist called it."

"His name?"

"Dr. Bauer."

"First name?"

She got the feeling the detectives already knew it. They were one up on her—she didn't have a clue. She told them so. "I'm sure that information would be easy enough to come by."

"Of course." He looked at his notes. "What, exactly, does 'retrograde amnesia' mean?"

"Actually, Detective Rumsfeld, I'm sure Dr. Bauer could explain it much better than I."

She saw something sly in the detective's expression; it caused a shudder to ripple over her. This man was not her friend. "And I will ask Dr. Bauer, but right now I'd like to hear it from you."

"It means the blow to my head affected my memory."

"Does it?"

She met the detective's gaze evenly. "Yes. That's what Dr. Bauer said."

"But just that small space of time?"

"Apparently. Like I said, when I woke up, I had no recollection of what had happened. The last clear memory I have was of getting ready to go for a walk. That was last Wednesday, after all the rain."

"Anywhere in particular?"

"What?"

"The walk, heading anywhere specifically."

Henry's, she realized. No one had asked her that until now. A shudder passed over her.

"What's wrong?"

"Nothing, I—" She stopped, clasped her hands in her lap. "I just realized I'd been going to check on Henry. And now he's . . ."

"Dead."

She nodded, blinking against tears.

"I wondered if you saw him that day?"

"I don't remember."

"There's no reason you wouldn't have, is there?"

Would there be? The gaping hole in her memory shouted, "Yes!" but she shook her head. "I don't imagine."

"I wonder if that was the last time you saw him alive? I wonder what you talked about?"

She didn't have an answer and after a moment he went on. "Actually, Mrs. Abbott, I'm not a complete stranger to TML," he said. "As you can imagine, many a criminal has suffered from 'amnesia.'"

"I'm not a criminal."

"I'm not saying you are."

Subtle stress on the "*you*." Implying someone else involved was. Someone close to her.

Logan.

Rumsfeld went on. "The way I understand it, traumatic memory loss can be caused by a physical trauma, but also a psychological one. For example, an experience so disturbing or upsetting, the subconscious suppresses it."

A psychological trauma. Could that be the cause of her amnesia?

"What do you think, Mrs. Abbott?" The detective looked her in the eyes. "What could have been so very traumatic, you had to block it out?"

Bailey stared at him. Her heart pounded heavily; her mouth had gone bone dry. "Henry," she said. "Finding him. His blood was on my clothing."

"What else?"

"I don't know." She twisted her fingers. "That wouldn't be enough?"

"You tell me. Would it take something you would want to deny with every fiber of your being, Mrs. Abbott? What could that be?"

"I don't understand what you're saying, Detective. I don't remember anything else. Just Henry's blood!"

He leaped on the comment. "So, you do remember something?"

"Yes . . . no . . ."

The other detective spoke up. "You look pale, Mrs. Abbott. Could I get you a glass of water?"

She looked at him, grateful. "Yes, thank you."

Rumsfeld went on. "Just a moment ago, you said you didn't remember anything."

"I don't . . . didn't, I mean. Yesterday I awakened from a nap. . . . I thought I'd heard a gunshot and I looked down and saw . . . blood."

He frowned. "There was blood on you?"

"Not right then." She brought a hand to her throbbing head, the bandages, then dropped it. "I might have been dreaming it or remembering it, I don't know. You can ask Logan about it. Or my sister-in-law. She was here."

Carlson handed her the water. She brought it to her lips, hand shaking. She took a few sips, then looked up at the young detective. "Thank you."

He squatted in front of her. "I'm sorry if we upset you," he said gently. "I know you cared about Henry Rodriquez, Mrs. Abbott. I'm sure you would want to help us find his killer."

"Of course," she said. "I loved Henry."

"You may have seen the shooter. You may have heard something important. A clue that will help us find who did this." He handed her his card. "Will you call me as you remember? Anything, even something you think is unrelated?"

"I will."

Carlson stood back up; Rumsfeld followed him to his feet.

"Thank you, Mrs. Abbott. That's all for now."

Bailey nodded mutely and showed them to the door,

still holding the glass of water. They drove off, the truth of the young detective's words ringing in her head.

She might have seen or heard something important. Something that would lead them to Henry's killer.

To hell with Dr. Bauer's warning, she decided. She couldn't just wait around to remember what happened. She needed those memories now.

CHAPTER THIRTY-SEVEN

Bailey hurried up to her bedroom. She had a plan. Dr. Bauer had said her memory could be triggered by a sight, smell or sound. The last thing she remembered was being on her way to Henry's. It seemed to her that his cabin might be the best place for her to start. If the cabin didn't do the trick, she'd try the woods around it.

Where Henry had been shot. Where she must have found him.

She changed into jeans and a long-sleeved, chambray shirt, donned socks and boots. Hiking out there might be a better choice for jogging her memory, but she didn't feel strong enough.

Bailey headed back downstairs and outside. The way she figured it, she had about an hour until Logan returned. She was certain he wouldn't approve of her plan, and didn't want to give him the opportunity to talk her out of it.

She fired up the Range Rover and headed out. The closer Bailey came to Henry's cabin, the more her feeling of dread grew. Her every instinct urged her to turn back.

But that didn't make sense. How could she hide from what she already knew?

Apparently, quite efficiently.

No more. She had lived through whatever it was once, she could do it again.

The small house came into view. The Cajun cabin was exactly how she remembered it, save for the bright yellow crime scene tape stretched across the front.

At the sight of that tape her stomach clenched.

Henry. Gone. Shot in the back.

Her friend. Dead.

A sob rose in her throat; she fought it back. Sweet, sweet Henry. Of all people, he least deserved that.

Bailey resolutely closed the distance to the cabin. She braked directly in front, cut the engine. Climbed out. And collected herself, her thoughts.

Three little steps. The garishly bright crime tape. The short walk across the porch to the front door.

Remember, Bailey. All of it. Rip the Band-Aid off.

She closed her eyes, waited a moment for a memory to come tumbling back. To save her from having to step into the house. Or worse, visit the place Henry's blood had spilled out.

None did.

Releasing a pent-up breath, Bailey made her way to the front door. She let herself inside. For the first time, she wondered if being here was breaking the law. In the same instant, she acknowledged that even if she was, it would change nothing. She had to do this.

The three-room house was unnaturally quiet. The emptiness seemed to shout at her, like an obscenity. She longed to break that silence. To call out a greeting. It sprang to her lips and she bit it back. Never again.

Bailey closed the door behind her and moved deeper into the living room. Here were the framed photographs she had studied before.

She went from one grouping of them to the other. This is how she'd learned Logan had a brother. Here, looking at these photographs. She remembered her shock. Her feeling of betrayal.

Bailey pushed those thoughts away, focusing instead on the reason for her being here.

Henry had been part of this family since the beginning. He had known everything about them. All their secrets.

He had known where all the bodies were buried.

She stopped on that, momentarily off-balanced. No, it was August who had said that to her. In an attempt to upset her. Henry had been kind. Wise in an uncomplicated way, an open book. No secrets or subterfuge.

Nothing in the front room triggered a memory, nor in the kitchen. Bailey made her way to the bedroom. The door stood partway open. She started through, then stopped, shocked.

Stephanie lay in Henry's bed, curled into a fetal position under the blanket. Nothing but the top of her head poked out from the covers and she shook, as if with silent tears or shuddering.

On the floor beside the bed lay a cluster of loose photographs and what looked like letters.

Bailey stood frozen, uncertain what to do. They were friends, the decent thing would be to offer comfort. Or would it? Stephanie wouldn't have come out here if she had wanted the company of others.

She couldn't leave her this way.

Bailey took a step closer, her friend's name on her lips when she stopped again, a smell filling her head. She wrinkled her nose. What was it? She'd smelled it recently, someplace else—

Turpentine. Raine's studio.

The person in Henry's bed wasn't Stephanie, it was Raine.

She must have made a sound, because Raine sat up, face blotchy from crying. "What are you doing here?"

Bailey took a step backward. "Excuse me. I didn't—"

"Why are you doing this to me?"

Bailey shook her head. "I came here hoping to jog my memory. I had no idea you'd be here. I'm so sorry for your loss."

Her sister-in-law stared at her, eyes glassy and bloodshot. "You did this."

She shook her head. "You're upset."

"Everything was fine before you got here."

Clearly it hadn't been. Nothing had been "fine" in this family for a very long time. But Bailey didn't correct her. "I'm leaving now, Raine. I didn't mean to intrude."

"She loved him," Raine said. "That's why he killed her."

Bailey's blood went cold. She stopped, turned back. "What did you say?"

"I don't want you here."

Bailey shook her head. "You said he killed her. Because she loved him. Who are you talking about?"

"No one. Nothing." She curled back into a ball of misery. "I lose everyone I love."

It occurred to Bailey that Raine might be manipulating her, at least partly. Tossing out provocative statements, then refusing to expand on them. But she had no doubt her emotional distress was real.

"You still have Logan. Your friends. Paul and—"

"We're poison, that's what we are. This family . . . murder . . . adultery . . . no wonder Roane—" She looked up at Bailey, dark eyes anguished. "He knew. He must have!"

Bailey squatted beside the bed. She didn't know how to calm the other woman, if she should even try or just call for Paul or Logan. "What are you talking about? Raine, please, let me help you."

Raine's tears turned to sobs. "There's no help for me. Don't you see?"

"I don't." Bailey's voice shook. "It's never as bad as it seems. I promise you—"

Raine sat up again, face twisting into a mask of hatred and rage. Startled, Bailey fell backward, landing on her bum.

"We're poison," Raine all but spit. "Run. Get out! I don't want you here!"

Bailey struggled to her feet, slipping on the spray of photographs, sending them skidding. "I'm sorry," she said. "Let me—"

"Don't touch those!"

Bailey jerked her hand back. "Raine, please . . . let me help you."

She stared at her, fury fading. Once more replaced by despair. "Leave . . . me . . . alone." She lay back down, drawing the covers to her chin, curling into a tight ball. "Please . . . go."

Bailey hesitated, uncertain what to do. What if she left her and she did something desperate? The way her brother had.

But Raine didn't want her here. She needed Logan. Or Paul. Raine would respond to them.

Bailey turned and ran for the car.

CHAPTER THIRTY-EIGHT

Monday, April 21
12:50 P.M.

She started the SUV and tore down the gravel drive. She gripped the steering wheel so tightly her fingers went numb. Her stitched-up head throbbed. The image of Raine's anguish—and fury—played over and over in her mind.

Along with her words. *"We're poison . . . This family . . . murder, adultery . . . She loved him. That's why he killed her."*

Bailey almost lost it on the drive's last turn. She righted the vehicle, and eased her foot off the accelerator. *Slow down, Bailey.* Ending up in a ditch wouldn't help Raine. Or Logan.

Logan couldn't lose his sister. He had lost too many loved ones already.

She reached Abbott Farm and drove through the gate. Paul stood at the barn's entrance, talking to August and one of the grooms. She stopped, lowered her window. "Paul!"

At the alarm in her voice, he came running.

"It's Raine!" she cried. "She's at Henry's. She's hysterical, talking crazy—"

"Logan's at the house. Tell him I'm on my way."

Bailey didn't waste time with a reply. Two minutes

later the house came into view and she roared through the open gate. And stopped short, so short the seat belt snapped hard against her chest.

Logan and Stephanie. They stood between their two vehicles, embracing.

They sprang apart and looked guiltily her way. Logan's expression became concerned. He was beside her in a flash. Opening the door, helping her out.

"Bailey, my God, what's wrong?"

For a moment, she couldn't find her voice. "I went to Henry's . . . I saw—"

"Uncle Henry's?" Stephanie said, voice unnaturally high. "Have you remembered something?"

She shook her head. "Raine's"—she sucked in a deep breath—"she's there. She's hysterical. I'm afraid she might try to—"

She didn't finish. She didn't need to; Logan understood. He started for the Porsche.

"I told Paul!" she called after him. "He's on his way, too."

Logan looked over his shoulder at Stephanie. "Keep an eye on her, would you? I'm starting to think I can't let her out of my sight."

They watched him go, then Stephanie turned to her. "Believe it or not, Raine has a highly developed sense of self-preservation. She'll be fine."

She must, Bailey thought. Otherwise, how could one survive in this family?

Bailey curved a hand protectively over her belly. Stephanie saw the movement and frowned. "Are you okay?"

"Yes. Just winded."

Stephanie cleared her throat. "I saw your face, when you got here. I hope you know that was nothing. Logan and I have been friends for a long time."

"I was surprised, that's all."

"We passed each other on the road and—"

"I'm not giving it a second thought."

"He was telling me how sorry he was about Uncle Henry."

"I'm sorry, too, Steph." Bailey caught her hands and squeezed them. "I miss him. And I'm so, so sorry I haven't called—"

"I'm sorry I haven't called you. Your head, does it hurt bad?"

Bailey instinctively reached up, touched the bandage. Suddenly realizing how much it did hurt, right now. "Not as much as yesterday, but I could use a Tylenol."

She frowned. "They didn't give you anything stronger?"

"They can't because of—"

She stopped. Stephanie's frown deepened. "What?"

She hesitated, then smiled. She couldn't help herself. "I'm pregnant, Steph."

For the blink of an eye, Stephanie just stared at her. As if stunned silent. Then she released a whoop of joy and hugged her. Bailey hugged her back. In moments they were both in tears.

"I'm so happy for you."

"We're keeping it quiet for now—"

"I won't say a word."

"I'm so sorry about Henry—"

"I'm sorry. Your accident . . . I should have called—"

"No, I should have."

Stephanie stepped away, wiping the tears from her cheeks. "I feel like this is all I've been doing. I need to stop."

"You will. Give yourself time."

Whatever Stephanie started to say was cut off by Tony sprinting through the back gate, ears and tongue flying.

"Tony!" Bailey cried, and knelt to greet him. He launched himself at her, knocking her onto her rear. In the next moment he was giving her big, slobbery kisses anywhere he could reach.

Laughing, she managed to get back on her feet, at which point he ran three circles around her, then took off after a butterfly.

"Surprise," Stephanie said.

Bailey laughed again, using her sleeve to wipe her cheeks. "I've missed him."

"I was hoping you'd say that. I wondered if you'd like to keep him."

"You mean, like forever?"

This time, Stephanie laughed. "Abbott Farm is his home. He'll be happier here with you, unless you don't—"

"I do. Yes, definitely." Bailey linked their arms. "I wasn't kidding. I've really missed him."

"Good."

They crossed to the kitchen door, Tony at their heels. Bailey fixed them both a glass of water and they sat at the kitchen table. The sun filtered in from the courtyard, creating bright patches on the weathered cypress tabletop. Bailey trailed her fingers across one, enjoying the warmth.

"I heard you don't remember what happened," Stephanie said.

"From Billy Ray, no doubt."

"I heard it from him first. But it's all over Wholesome now. It's true then?"

Bailey nodded and Stephanie went on. "He told me that you . . . that Uncle Henry's blood was on your jeans."

"He told me the same thing."

Stephanie leaned forward. "Do you think you saw what happened?"

"I don't know."

"But you could have." She reached across the table and caught Bailey's hands. "You could have seen the shooter."

"I could have, Steph, but I don't think so." She looked at their joined hands, then back up at her friend. "That's why I went out there today. To see if I could make myself remember."

"Bailey—" She hesitated, then began again. "I talked to you the day of the accident."

"You did?"

"I called, asked if you could stop by and check on Henry. You said you were on your way to the doctor."

Bailey couldn't hide her excitement. "Did I say what doctor or why I was going?"

She shook her head. "I was working, so we weren't on but a minute or two. You promised to stop by after your appointment, then call me later."

"What time did we speak?"

"Around ten A.M."

A timeline, Bailey thought. Maybe she could piece together what happened that way.

"And we didn't speak again?"

"No." She released Bailey's hands and dropped hers to her lap. "I thought it was odd . . . that maybe you'd had bad news at the doctor's, or maybe that you'd just forgotten about calling. Then I got busy giving riding lessons. Next thing I knew, the sheriff was at my door."

Bailey searched her memory and came up blank.

"The police are releasing the body tomorrow. I'm planning the funeral for Wednesday."

Life. Death. Full circle in one week.

"You'll be there, won't you?"

"Of course." Bailey paused. "Can I ask you something?"

"Sure."

"Raine, just now . . . she was saying some things, awful things, about the family. She said he killed her because she loved him. What did she mean?"

"It wasn't about Logan, if that's what you're worried about."

"Then who, Steph?"

"It's not my story to tell—"

"Is it his dad?"

The look on her face was her answer. Bailey leaned forward, caught her hands. "Tell me."

"Like I said, it's not my story to—"

"There are no pictures of him and Logan, nor anyone else, and he never talks about him."

Steph looked upset, indecisive. Bailey squeezed her hands. "Please."

"Okay." She drew a quick breath and let it out slowly. "I'll leave it to Logan to tell you everything. But the short version is that Logan's dad killed his mother."

Bailey went cold. "But she drowned— Wait, are you saying . . . he pushed her overboard?"

She was, but refused to say more. Within minutes, Bailey was walking her out to her truck. Stephanie climbed in, then looked back at Bailey. "Talk to Logan."

"I will.

"No wonder he didn't tell me. But in a way I'm relieved. Things make sense now, some things anyway. And certainly, Raine's behavior."

"Bailey, can I run something by you?"

"Sure."

"It may sound crazy but I . . . I wondered if Billy Ray could've shot Henry himself."

Bailey's mouth dropped.

"I told you it was out there."

"Why would he do that?"

"A death on Abbott property would bring renewed focus on Logan. An investigation. And a reason for Billy Ray to have access to the farm."

"Abbott Farm, that's where all the bodies are buried."

"Do you think I'm totally nuts?"

She met her gaze. "No. As weird as it might sound, I wouldn't put anything past him."

CHAPTER THIRTY-NINE

Bailey glanced at the kitchen clock. Logan had gone to check on Raine four or five hours ago. She wondered what was happening, if Paul was still with him. If he needed her.

It didn't make sense that he had been gone so long.

Anxious, she started to pace. Again. Over the past hours she had alternated between constant movement and no movement at all. Blank-stare time. Tony sensed her agitation and watched, growling deep in his throat.

"I wondered if Billy Ray could've shot Henry himself."

The thought made her feel sick. The realization that she actually thought it a possibility. He'd said he'd do anything to gain access to Abbott Farm, murder definitely fell into that category.

Bailey stopped pacing. She'd spoken to Stephanie the day of the accident. She'd been on her way to a doctor's appointment. In Covington. Logan hadn't mentioned her being ill, other than her injury and pregnancy—

Of course that's where she must have been going. She must have missed a period and gone to the doctor for a pregnancy test. Or to confirm the results of a drugstore test she'd given herself at home.

She grabbed her cell phone and called up the calendar.

Sure enough, there it was: Dr. Ann Saunders. Wednesday, April sixteenth, at 10:30 A.M. She did an Internet search of the doctor's name, which confirmed her suspicion. Dr. Ann Saunders was an OB/GYN.

She'd known she was pregnant before the accident.

But Logan hadn't.

Even as an uneasy *why* wormed its way into her thoughts, Bailey assured herself she must have meant to tell him after the doctor's confirmation. She had wanted to be absolutely certain before she said anything. To protect Logan. From the loss of it not being true.

She gazed down at that electronic calendar. *Clues to the events of the day leading up to her accident. Right in front of her.*

Of course. Her phone and handbag. Her car. The clothes she'd been wearing.

Why hadn't she thought of this before? Bailey scrolled forward and back in her smartphone calendar. A follow-up appointment with Dr. Saunders.

Not much else. Her friend Marilyn's birthday. A dinner party she and Logan had now missed. Finding nothing else on the calendar, she moved on to the recent images on the camera. Shot after shot of Tony, flowers, the countryside. Why had she taken so many?

Bailey shoved it back into her pocket and went for her purse, dumped the contents out on the kitchen table. She'd never been an organized type. Receipts, notes, grocery lists, all stuffed into a pocket, flap or just tossed into her bag.

With trembling fingers, she started to go through them.

Tony announced Logan's arrival home, and Bailey ran to meet him, excited to share what she'd remembered and what Stephanie had told her. When she saw his face, the words died on her lips. Exhaustion. Despair. As if the weight of the world—and everyone in it—rested squarely on his shoulders. No, she thought, not the world, not everyone. This family. His sister.

Bailey took him in her arms and held him. She couldn't help thinking about his father, what Stephanie had said he'd done. She held him tighter. He rested his head against hers, the tension seeming to seep out of him as the seconds ticked past.

"I got her quieted down," he said finally, softly. "I convinced her to let me take her home." He let out a long, weary-sounding breath. "I gave her a sedative. Waited until she was asleep. Still—"

"What?"

"I was . . . afraid to go. To leave her alone." He slipped his hand into his pocket, brought out the vials of sedatives. "Put these someplace. I didn't want to leave them there."

Afraid Raine would deliberately overdose. She took the vials, slipped them into her own pocket, then tipped her face up to his. "She'll be okay, Logan. Her grief will lessen and she'll work through it."

"I'm not so . . . she threatened it, killing herself. She has before, but this time—" He bit it back and cupped her face in his hands. "I'm sorry that I brought you into this sad family. Got you tangled up in our tragedies."

"I'm not." She searched his gaze and said it again, for emphasis. "I'm not. We're going to bring joy back. You and me." She brought his right hand to her belly. "Our baby."

Tears flooded his eyes. "We used to be happy. Even Raine. She was fun. Funny." He paused. "After Mom died . . . then Roane . . . she changed."

Bailey caught his hand, laced their fingers, led him to the keeping room sofa. He sat heavily, dropping his head into his hands.

She curled up next to him, rhythmically rubbing his back. Giving him time. Loving him as best she could.

"There's something I have to tell you," he said after a couple of minutes. "I didn't before now because it's—"

He was going to tell her about his father. Now, so soon after she and Stephanie talked. She wouldn't have called him, would she?

"It's about my dad. And Mom. It's really bad."

Bailey curled her hand around his. "Nothing you could say will make me stop loving you."

He didn't believe her. She saw it in his eyes. But he went on anyway. "Mom's love was horses, Dad's was sailing. We had a sailboat, a thirty-eight-foot Hunter, docked at South Shore Harbor in New Orleans." He stopped, stood. "I need a drink."

She watched him pour himself a glass of red. He didn't rejoin her on the sofa, but simply stood, gaze fixed on somewhere in the past.

"We'd go for the weekend, sometimes longer. Since I was older, I was allowed to sometimes bring a friend."

"Paul."

"Always. If it was Raine's turn, she'd bring Stephanie. They were wonderful magical times, until—"

He stopped. Seconds ticked past.

Finally, as if having to force the words out of himself, he said, "—that trip. That night."

The night his mother drowned.

"Mom and Dad had been drinking. Something was wrong, we didn't know what, but we felt the tension the whole weekend. We heard them arguing that night. Late. It scared Raine so much she crawled into the fore bunk with us boys. Usually she slept out in the cabin area.

"They took it up to the deck. Shouting. He accused her of having an affair. Of being in love with someone else."

"Who?"

He shook his head and Bailey was uncertain whether because he didn't know or didn't want to say.

"That's the last time we heard our mother's voice."

"I don't understand."

"We awoke the next morning, and she was gone." He cradled the glass between his palms, gingerly, as if afraid he could crush it without a thought. "Dad said he left her alone up on the deck. That he went to bed."

Logan fell silent for a long moment, so long Bailey wondered if he would say more. Finally, he did.

"He radioed the coast guard, they searched."

"Did they find her?" The words came out dry.

"A week later. Along the shore at Fontainebleau State Park in Mandeville."

Bailey laid a hand on her stomach. She felt sick.

"He was questioned by the police. He claimed he was so drunk, he passed out. That he never noticed she didn't come to bed." Logan took a swallow of the wine. "It took six years for charges to be brought against him. Paul and I testified against him at his trial."

"Oh, my God, Logan. I'm so sorry."

He went on as if he hadn't heard her. "The jury deliberated less than an hour. And found him guilty."

"Was he?" she asked. "Did he claim it was an accident or—"

"His story never changed. He insisted he left her there on the deck. The water was calm. We were anchored. He begged us to believe him."

"But you didn't."

"No. All four of us knew he'd done it. Raine blames me. Roane did, as well."

"No." She got to her feet. "How can you—"

"I was the oldest. I should have checked on her. Or broken up their fight. It was my responsibility to step in."

"You were a boy. Parents fight sometimes."

"I was fifteen. Hell, almost sixteen. And no they don't, not like that. At least not our parents."

She suddenly realized what that meant. "Your father's still alive?"

"No. He hung himself in prison. And then a year later, Roane hung himself in the old barn."

Bailey didn't know how to respond, what to say. Just imagining it for him, the man she knew and loved, hurt almost more than she could bear. She could only guess what it must be like for him. And for Raine.

"Now, tonight . . . I never believed what Dad accused her of. Never. Tonight I learned otherwise."

"What do you mean?"

"Mom was having an affair. She was in love with Henry."

"Oh, my God."

"Raine found their love letters to each other. But there's more. Raine and Roane, according to the letters—"

"Were Henry's, not your dad's."

"Yes."

She went to him, cupped his face in her palms. "This doesn't change anything. She's still your sister. Your mother still loved you . . . she was just human. Like the rest of us. Our new life starts now. Me and you and the baby."

He covered her hands with his own, kissed her, then kissed her again. "Thank you."

They gazed stupidly into each other's eyes, their love fest broken by a deep, unmistakable gurgle of her stomach.

"I take it you haven't eaten," he said.

"I was waiting for you."

"How about we grab something at Faye's?"

"Sounds good."

"Mind if I shower first?"

"Not at all."

Bailey followed him upstairs, Tony at her heels. While

Logan showered, she went back to the photos of Tony on her phone. It was a strange feeling, scrolling through pictures she intellectually knew she had taken, but had no memory of.

Bizarre. She cocked her head. Tony, just being Tony. The azaleas. Wildflowers. More azaleas.

And then . . . A red shoe. Nestled in mud. Incongruous among the sticks, soggy earth and shoots of spring growth.

Bailey stared at it, goose bumps roaring up her arms, her spine.

She remembered.

CHAPTER FORTY

As he did most weeknights, Billy Ray had consumed his meal-from-a-box, enjoyed the one beer—Abita Amber, there wasn't any other as far as he was concerned—he allowed himself, and headed into his war room.

He sat there now. Assessing. Questioning. His greatest achievement. And most dismal failure. All the puzzle pieces that he'd found and snapped into place, yet he was the only one who could see the emerging image.

Logan Abbott.

Dixie Jenkins seemed to stare accusingly at him, as if demanding how he could have let this happen to her.

A thumping from his front door dragged him away from his thoughts. He went to it, peering out the side window, right hand hovering over his firearm.

Tucker Law. Local high school football hero and hellraiser. His parents stood behind him, looking anxious.

Billy Ray opened the door. "Tucker," he said, then shifted his gaze. "Martin, Betty, this is a surprise."

"Tucker has something to say to you."

He shifted his gaze to the seventeen-year-old. "That so, Tucker?"

"Yes, sir."

"He has some information about Dixie," Martin said.

"Come on in," Billy Ray said, stepping aside so they could enter. "Have a seat."

They did. Billy Ray grabbed a notepad and pen, then took the chair across from the boy.

"What do you have to say, Tucker?"

He cleared his throat. "I was drivin' past The Landing Friday night. Late. Me and Louis Moore, we'd been out hunting."

He cocked an eyebrow. "At night?"

"Yes, sir. Nutria."

"Gators, you mean?"

Tucker slid a glance toward his father, then nodded. "Yes, sir."

Which was illegal, a fact Billy Ray ignored. Hell, reality television had practically made it open season. "When you say 'late,' what time?"

"Two, three in the morning. Which I suppose made it early Saturday morning. I'd just dropped Louis off."

"Which? Two? Or three?"

He thought a moment. "After two but not three. I remember thinking that. Doing the math, you know. How long I'd have to sleep before getting up for work."

"Go on."

"I saw Dixie, her Mustang. In the Landing parking lot."

Billy Ray fought to take it slow. "You saw her? Or just her Mustang?"

"First, I just noticed her 'stang. It's a sweet set of wheels. Needs some work, but still—"

Billy Ray cut him off, impatient. "Yes, it is. Go on, Tucker."

"Then I noticed Dixie. She was talking to someone in the truck next to her."

"Did you notice what kind of a truck?" Billy Ray asked, unable to hide his excitement.

"A Ford F-150. Real shiny. Black."

Logan Abbott had a black F-150.

"What happened next?"

"She climbed into the truck." He twisted his hands in his lap. "I didn't think anything of it until Mom and Dad—"

"We told him about Dixie being missing," Betty Law said.

Billy Ray fought to keep his excitement from showing. "Have you told anyone else about this?"

"No, sir. Told my folks and we came straight here."

"You did good, Tucker." Billy Ray looked from Tucker to his parents. "Don't repeat this story. Not to anyone. This might just be the break we've been waiting for. And if it is, we don't want the perpetrator to know we're on to him. You get me, Tucker?"

"Yes, sir."

He looked him dead in the eyes. "I mean it. I hear you've blabbed, I'm going to throw your ass in jail."

"Jail," Martin Law said. "What the hell for?"

"Hunting gators out of season. It's breaking the law, no matter what you may think from watching *Swamp People*."

"But we brought you this information! Is this how you pay us back?"

"It's how I ensure you keep your mouths shut. You do that, and I overlook that infraction."

Tucker nodded. "Don't worry, I won't say a thing. But what about Louis?"

"I'll need to talk to him, too. Confirm your story and timeline." He closed his notebook and stood. "Can I count on your silence as well, Martin? Betty? Nothing to no one."

Martin looked at his wife, who nodded, then back at

Billy Ray. "You can count on us. We want this son of a bitch caught, whoever he is."

Not whoever, Billy Ray thought moments later as he watched the three drive off. Logan Abbott.

Finally.

CHAPTER FORTY-ONE

A cry on her lips, Bailey sat straight up in bed. A nightmare, she realized, working to calm herself. Nothing more.

Bailey turned toward Logan, surprised she hadn't awakened him. She hadn't because he wasn't in bed with her. She moved a hand over his spot, finding it cool to the touch.

They'd had dinner at Faye's. She'd eaten some, but mostly moved the food around the plate. And said little. When he'd asked about her change of mood, she'd claimed exhaustion. A headache.

The red shoe. Emerging from its muddy grave.

A snippet of a memory meant nothing. There was a logical explanation, one that she already knew but didn't remember.

She dragged the blankets up to her chin, remembering. Tony barking. The shoe. Being scared half to death by Henry at the edge of the woods. He'd heard Tony and come looking.

"What do you have there, Ms. True?"

She'd told him it was nothing, and asked if he would show her the way back to the path. He had done better than that, he had walked her all the way to the gate.

But not before she had taken a couple of pictures of the shoe.

There, her memory came to a sharp stop.

Stop this, Bailey. Show Logan the picture. Tell him what you remembered. Ask him about it.

Of course that's what she should do. Why was it so hard to focus? To stay calm and clearheaded? The TML? Pregnancy and its runaway hormones? A combination of the two?

She reached for her cell phone, located on the nightstand beside her. Its display glowed reassuringly as she checked the time. Three-fifteen. Late to be up working or anything else. Even for Logan.

Perhaps he'd had to use the bathroom. "Logan," she called softly. "You there?"

Silence. Not even the thump of Tony's tail on the wooden floor. Bailey slipped out of bed. Naked, she grabbed yesterday's jeans and shirt from the floor and slipped them on. "Logan!" she called again as she stepped out into the hall.

Nothing. She flipped on the light and headed down the stairs. She saw that a light burned in the kitchen and from under his office door. Working. No doubt Tony curled up by his feet. She smiled and shook her head. Probably brewed himself a cup of coffee, too. No wonder he couldn't sleep.

Bailey used the bathroom, then headed downstairs. The floor was cool against her bare feet. She tapped on the closed door, then nudged it open. Her greeting died on her lips.

He wasn't there.

Bailey acknowledged the sliver of fear even as she chastised herself for it. She was being ridiculous. "Logan!" she called, starting for the kitchen.

That room proved as empty as the office. So she checked the courtyard, then the remainder of the first floor.

Heart rapping against the wall of her chest, she headed back up to the second floor.

Still no sign of her husband. Where had he gone? Why would he have left her this way?

The way her father had, in the dark of night.

Sudden, complete panic crashed down on her. The garage. His car. It would be there, she told herself. It would.

Bailey ran down the stairs to the mudroom door. She grabbed the flashlight Logan kept there and yanked on her rubber boots. She stepped out into the night. Pitch-black. No moon or stars, both obscured by clouds. A chill wind blew and she shivered, wishing she'd grabbed a jacket as well, but unwilling to go back.

She snapped on the flashlight. The beam sliced through the darkness and she hurried to the garage.

His Porsche was there, she saw. As was her SUV and his truck. So, where was he? Walking on a night like tonight? Dark as pitch? Riding? Would he endanger one of the horses that way—

The horses. The barn. Of course.

She ran around the side of the garage where he parked the golf cart, the vehicle used to get between the various residences on the property and the barns. It wasn't there.

Bailey made a sound, part relief, part embarrassment. The barn. Of course that's where he'd gone. He'd said something about one of the horses being colicky. And he'd taken Tony with him.

She was such an idiot.

Bailey turned to go back to the house, then stopped,

flashlight beam landing on the courtyard gate. A memory snapped into place, filled her head.

She and Logan standing there. She had rushed out to meet him, to tell him what she and Tony had uncovered.

Logan, staring at her as if she had lost her mind. "Tony found what?"

"A shoe. A lady's high-heeled shoe. Bright red."

"Okay."

"By the pond," she said.

"What were you doing out there?"

"I told you, going to see Henry. Tony ran off and I went searching for him."

"Bailey, baby, that wasn't very smart. You could have gotten lost. It gets pretty swampy in places, you could have fallen . . . there are snakes, too. Water moccasins."

The mention of snakes made her queasy. "Except for the snakes, those all crossed my mind. But you're missing the point. When I found Tony, he was digging up something. It turned out to be the shoe."

"Did you bring it back with you?"

"No. But I snapped a picture."

"Seriously?" When she didn't return his smile, he said, "Okay, let's see it."

She showed it to him. He'd gazed at the image for a long moment, then handed her phone back. "Okay."

"Then Henry showed up. He walked me back."

"You're right, it does sound like a big adventure." He opened the gate, started through. "And Tony stayed with him?"

"Yes. Wait—" She touched his arm, stopping him. "What should we do?"

"About Tony?"

"No. The shoe."

"I don't see that we need to do anything about it."

"But . . . how did it get out there?"

"Kids go out there all the time to go swimming. It may seem like the middle of nowhere, but it's actually not that far from the edge of the property and Hay Hollow Road."

"It wasn't a kid's shoe. It belonged to a woman."

"When I say 'kids,' I'm talking about young people. It's a make-out spot. One time somebody couldn't find their shoes, so they left without them."

It sounded logical. "I suppose that could happen."

"I can promise you it has. Come on, let's go inside. I'll pour us a glass of wine."

But she had hung back, Bailey remembered. "How did a woman wearing high-heel shoes get to that spot?"

He looked back. "What?"

"Like you said, it's swampy and uneven. And she wouldn't take them off and go barefoot, because of the snakes."

"Maybe the man she was with carried her?"

An image popped into her head, one of a victim being carried.

Logan returned to her side, took her hands. "They're cold." He rubbed them between his. "This has really upset you."

"Yes, Logan . . . two women from Wholesome have gone missing."

He searched her gaze. "You're being serious?"

"I am."

"You really think Tony may have unearthed one of those women's shoes?"

"It probably isn't. But it could be."

"On our property?"

"Why not? It could happen to anybody. And what if it was and we did nothing?"

"Look, I've lived here all my life and have seen just what I've described to you a hundred times before. Hell,

I've participated before. It's so swampy there because it's spring and we've had so much rain. In the summer, it's dry and lovely. But, if it would make you feel better to take it to the police—"

"It would, Logan. It really would."

"Then that's what we'll do." He rested his forehead against hers. "It's getting too dark now. In the morning, we'll go out there, collect the shoe and bring it to Billy Ray."

Bailey blinked; the memory evaporated. The flashlight in her hand, illuminating the deep of night. The empty drive.

She had told Logan about the shoe. There had been a logical explanation. And they'd dealt with it.

Relief was as heady as a narcotic. Why not join him down there? Show her support. That they were a team and should share everything. Even nurse duty for a sick horse in the middle of the night.

She acted on the thought, staying to the path, keeping the flashlight beam directed at her feet. A strange sensation moved over her as she walked—of being completely alone in some strange world. The towering pine trees and thick underbrush that lined the path seemed to close in on her. The night sounds, the buzz of insects and rustle of some creature in the thicket. Something swooped past her head and her heart leaped to her throat. A bat, she realized, shuddering.

Her every instinct urged her to run. Reason held her back. She couldn't risk falling again. So she kept on, one foot in front of the other, carefully picking her way.

And then the path opened up. Manicured grounds with fenced paddocks. Occasional solar lamps providing a welcome glow to the dark path. The barn ahead. A small, welcoming light at its entrance. The golf cart parked directly under it.

Bailey hurried to it, slipped through the barn doors, then hesitated as the strangest sensation of dread came over her. Something wasn't right here. The barn was dark. The animals sleeping. A lone, lonely light came from the far end, a feeble glow escaping from under a doorway.

Turn around now, Bailey. You don't want to be here.

She thought of the big, warm bed. The locks on the doors. She rubbed at the goose bumps on her arms.

"Logan?" she called.

One of the horses neighed softly in response. Another peered out of its stall as if curious at the commotion.

Bailey switched off the flashlight and started toward the closed door and its feeble glow. She realized she was creeping. Like a mouse—or a thief. She didn't know why, but even as she told herself to stop, she didn't.

She reached the door. Pressed her ear close to listen. Movement. Something being opened and closed. A rhythmic hum. What sounded like a washer or dryer.

The blood pounding in her head, she reached for the knob. Before she could, the door swung open. With a squeak of surprise, Bailey jumped back.

Paul looked as shocked to see her as she was him.

"Bailey?" He held out a hand to steady her. "What are you doing down here?"

Her gaze shifted to the open door behind him. "Looking for Logan."

"Logan?" He reached behind him and closed the door. "It's the middle of the night."

"I know. I woke up and he was gone."

"What made you think he'd be here?"

"He wasn't in the house and the golf cart was gone, so I assumed he came down here."

"I'm using the cart tonight. Catching up on some things."

Her gaze slid over his shoulder again. His office was

at the other end of the barn; what work could he be catching up on here?

"Laundry, feed inventory," he said, as if reading her thoughts. "Not enough hours in the day."

"Logan said one of the horses was colicky. That's another reason I thought he might be here. . . ." At his blank look, her words trailed off. She caught her bottom lip between her teeth. "I feel pretty ridiculous right now."

"Don't." Paul hesitated a moment, then said, "Logan doesn't sleep well. On any given night, he could've wandered down here. But not tonight."

"Will you talk to me, Paul? I want to help him, but I don't know how."

"Help him what? Sleep better?"

She didn't understand the edge in his voice and frowned. "Trust that I won't leave. That I'm safe from whatever boogeyman he expects to pop out and snatch me."

"Sorry, I can't do that."

"Why?" She reached out a hand to touch him; he jerked away. Her cheeks heated. "I see now. You won't help me because you think it's a lie. You think I'll leave him, too. That I'll disappear."

"I didn't say that."

"You didn't need to. If you see Logan, tell him I was looking for him."

"I didn't hear a car."

"I walked."

"Walked?" He frowned. "At this time of night, with your head still bandaged from your last accident?"

She flushed and held up the flashlight. "I was careful. Came prepared."

"There are some things you can't prepare for."

"Like the bat that did a flyby of my head."

He didn't smile. "I'll bring you back up to the house." When she started to protest, he added, "You don't want Logan to return, only to find you missing and freak out."

"A ride it is. Both of us freaking out in one night might be a little much, even for this family."

"Let me turn off the dryer before we go."

He ducked back through the door, once again closing it behind him. Odd, she thought. Almost as if he didn't want her to look inside.

"What is that room?" she asked when he returned.

He looked surprised. "Feed room. Medicine and supplement storage. Laundry room. Why?"

"Just curious."

"Want to see it?"

He started to reopen the door; she stopped him. "Really, just curious."

He nodded and closed the hasp and snapped the padlock tight. "I keep it locked at all times, mostly because of the pharmaceuticals. But the supplements add up, too. Don't need them walking off."

They started toward the front of the barn.

"Bailey?"

He stopped; she looked at him.

"Another woman's gone missing. Did you know that?"

"No." The word came out choked. "When?"

"While you were in the hospital. Her name was Dixie."

"Was?"

"Is," he corrected. "She was last seen at a local bar. I just want you to be . . . It pays to be cautious, that's all."

She swallowed hard. "You're right. Thank you."

A moment later, they were in the cart. It started silently.

"I'm sorry, about earlier," he said. "Refusing to help you with Logan. But I can't encourage him to trust, not after True."

"What . . . what do you believe happened to her?"

"I believe the same thing Logan does." He hit a rut, causing Bailey to come off her seat. She grabbed the dash for support.

"Sorry about that," he muttered. "She was having an affair and left him. It all adds up."

"But it doesn't. Not the way everyone loved her."

"I don't understand."

"No one saw it coming. No one . . . saw that in her."

He hit another rut; it tossed her against him. She scooted away. "It's been since True, hasn't it? That Logan's been unable to sleep."

He glanced at her, then back at the path. "You should ask him, Bailey."

"I know, but he—" She looked down at her hands and absently rubbed away a rusty-looking smudge on her fingers. "It's hard. When I ask things that . . . he shuts me out."

He didn't respond and she reached over and touched his sleeve. "Please. I could really use a friend."

His expression softened and he stopped the cart. "No. His insomnia started when his mother died, it's gotten much worse since True. She was the most . . . wonderful woman. Kind. Funny. Pretty. She was good to me."

Bailey frowned, confused. "True?"

He looked surprised. "What?"

"You're talking about True? She was good to you?"

He shook his head. "Sorry. I was talking about Logan's mother. Elisabeth."

Her name sounded like a prayer on his lips. Obviously, she had been very important to him. "Growing up, I spent more time here than at home. It was she who encouraged my love of horses."

He looked away, then back at her. "Everything was different after she died. Everyone was different."

"When did you suspect that Logan's dad, you know—"

"Killed her? We all knew he did it. The four of us, right away from the moment we learned she wasn't onboard."

"But you didn't . . . say anything? To anyone?"

"Logan did, finally."

"He told me the two of you testified against him."

"We just relayed what we saw and heard that weekend."

"I can't imagine how difficult that must have been."

"No, you can't." He glanced apologetically at her, as if sorry for how sharp that sounded. "Then Roane hung himself. He was so sensitive. So easily . . . influenced. He was despondent the day he did it."

"You talked to him?"

"I did. I was maybe the last. He'd never recovered from his mother's death. The court validating what he knew, what we all knew, only made it worse."

He was silent a moment. "Logan was the one who found him."

"Oh, my God." She paused, hurting for her husband. "He didn't tell me that. Just that he had hung himself in the old barn."

"Not the main barn. The hay barn. We don't use it anymore."

Bailey thought making that distinction was important to Paul, though she didn't get why. "He blames himself," she said. "I wish I could take that away. I don't know how."

"You can't. He was the big brother. He feels like he should have somehow known . . . That's who he is, Bailey."

That's why he blamed himself for his mother, too.

It only made her love him more.

"Thank you, Paul, for telling me."

"You're welcome." He started the cart and they eased forward. "This is a very sad family you've married into."

He rounded the curve and the house's secondary gates came into sight. Moments later, he pulled to a stop at the courtyard gate. She climbed out, then looked back. "What about you, Paul? Why do you stay?"

"Because they're my family, too."

CHAPTER FORTY-TWO

Tuesday, April 22
4:20 A.M.

She watched as Paul turned the cart and headed back the way he had come, then ducked inside. "Logan," she called softly. He didn't reply; but she did a quick search of the downstairs anyway, before heading up.

Where was he? It was almost dawn. She crossed to the balcony doors, opened them and stepped through. The moonlight seemed brighter from above than it had below. She gazed out, past the courtyard wall, to the woods, to where she had seen Henry that day, picturing him.

But as she did, the memory of him there on the path shifted and changed. A memory from another time. Logan. Heading away. Carrying something. A stick . . . No, a shovel.

Her knees went weak. She remembered. The next morning her stomach had been fluttery. Logan had been sweet, felt her head to see if she had a temp.

Then he'd called off their hike out to the pond. He had to go into the city. A problem with a property on the West-bank, Algiers Point.

So she had gone without him. As she had feared, the shoe was gone. The stick she'd dug it out with had been there, the debris from around it. She'd searched the area, thinking maybe an animal had dragged it away.

No shoe, no spot of red anywhere.

She recalled telling herself it didn't mean anything, even as a tingling sensation had moved over her. She'd felt light-headed. Queasy.

He had gone for the shoe. So she couldn't take it to Billy Ray.

"Bailey?"

Startled, she whirled around, nearly slipping on the damp tile. She grabbed the railing for support. Logan, in the doorway.

He started toward her. "What's wrong?"

"Where were you?"

"Bailey?"

"Don't come any closer." She pressed herself back against the rail. "Where were you?"

"My God . . . what's happened—I woke up and was worried about Raine. I went to check on her."

"It's the middle of the night."

"I don't sleep well. And I knew if I didn't check on her, I wouldn't get back to sleep."

"Why didn't you tell me another woman's gone missing?"

"What?" He frowned. "Who told you that?"

"I went looking for you." Her voice broke. "I couldn't find you. Paul hadn't seen you, either."

"You saw Paul? This late?"

"At the barn. Doing laundry."

"I'm sorry I frightened you," he said. "I didn't want to wake you, so I just left."

Henry and Elisabeth had been having an affair. So Logan's dad had killed her. True had been having an affair, so Logan killed her.

Like father like son.

"What happened to the red shoe?"

He frowned, shook his head. "What are you talking about?"

"The shoe. The one I found." She pressed her lips together, although she wasn't sure if she meant to hold back a cry or it was because she was trembling so badly.

"You're hysterical."

"I'm not. What did you do with it?"

"I never saw it. Bailey, you told me about it. We were going to go retrieve it, but I got called away. Next thing I know, you're in the hospital. I'll go now, if you want me to. Or we can go in the morning."

"It's not there."

"How do you—" His expression cleared. "You went alone that morning."

She nodded. "And it was gone."

"Look, babe, there's an explanation for this. An animal carried it off. Or Tony came back for it and has buried it someplace."

An explanation. He always had a logical explanation.

"The shoe was just a shoe," he went on, "forgotten by some drunken lovers. I know it, Bailey. I've lived here all my life."

"I saw you. The night. Heading out into the woods."

"Your memory's come back?" He looked hurt. "Why didn't you tell me?"

"You were carrying a shovel, Logan."

"A shovel? Baby, I don't know what, or who, you thought you saw, but it wasn't me. Stop looking at me that way. Like you don't even know me."

"Do I?"

"Yes." He strode across to the balcony and pulled her into his arms. She tried to pull free, but he held her tight. "You know me."

He kissed her. She tried to turn her head, but he brought

it back, hand in her hair, fingers twisting around the strands.

He kissed her again. And then again. Each time more deeply. Drawing her in. Moving his mouth against hers, his tongue against hers, in a way only he could. Emptying her mind of everything but him, his touch, his breath against her damp skin, his scent.

A hint of turpentine, she realized, arching her neck. It clung to him along with the cool of the night and the pine of the forest.

Turpentine. From Raine's.

Gooseflesh followed his lips. She was on fire. Drunk with passion. He swept her up and carried her to the bed. There, he made love to her, until she arched up against his mouth, hands wound in his hair, his name ripping from her lips.

He entered her then, roughly, ferociously. He thrust deeply, she gripped his shoulders, fingernails digging, holding on. He climaxed with a roar, then rolled off her. No cuddling or whispered love notes.

Retribution, she thought. For cutting him to the quick. Betraying him with unbelief.

The silence stretched between them. Deep and wide. She whispered his name. Instead of responding, he turned onto his side, his back to her.

CHAPTER FORTY-THREE

Tuesday, April 22
9:35 A.M.

The next morning, they hardly spoke. Even Tony seemed subdued. It hurt almost more than she could stand.

Bailey poured herself another glass of juice, more for something to fill the silence than because she really wanted it. Instead of returning to the table, she crossed to the patio doors and looked out at the spring day.

"What's all this?" Logan asked so suddenly she jumped.

She looked over her shoulder. "What?"

He motioned to the pile of receipts she'd dumped out of her purse yesterday.

She had forgotten all about them. "I was looking for something in my purse. Following up on something Stephanie said."

His eyebrows shot up and Bailey went on. "She told me we'd talked the day of the accident. And that I was on my way to the doctor."

"What doctor?"

"An OB/GYN."

"Great. You knew you were pregnant and didn't tell me."

"I didn't say that because I don't know that's true. I probably suspected it. I'm sure my plan was to confirm the news, then tell you. Surprise you with the good news."

He didn't respond and she went on. "Stephanie told me something else. That she asked me to stop at Henry's. I said I would, promised to call her after but didn't. Obviously, I wasn't able to."

"Why didn't you tell me any of this last night?"

"Do you really need to ask? You were exhausted."

"Right." He stood. Didn't look at her. "I'm going to head down to the barn to check on Paramour. Then I have a meeting in Covington."

"Wait!" He paused at the door. She held out a hand. "Logan, please try to understand—"

"Actually, I think I do understand. You think I'm a liar. And worse. Much worse."

She didn't know what to say. She didn't think that, but she didn't not think it. How could that be? How did she explain, when she didn't understand herself?

His expression hardened. "That's what I thought." He patted his leg and Tony trotted after him. He stopped once more. "I didn't hurt True. Or anybody else. But I can't make you believe that. You trust me or you don't, Bailey."

And then he was gone. She sagged against the counter.

Trust him or not.

Love him.

Or not.

She squeezed her eyes shut, confusion hanging over her, dark, suffocating. A cloud of uncertainty. A part of her gave him everything and would stand with him against all odds. But the other part was suspicious. Fearful.

She'd come out of the coma this way. With this terrible sense there was something she knew, something urgent, that she had to share.

Remembering was key. Bailey straightened. Dr. Saunders. The last place she knew she had been—or was supposed to have been—the day of the accident. She retrieved the obstetrician's number and dialed it.

A perky-sounding receptionist answered right away.

"Good morning," she said, "this is Bailey Abbott. I'm a patient of Dr. Saunders."

"Yes, Mrs. Abbott. How can I help you this morning?"

"Could you tell me when I was last in to see the doctor?"

A slight hesitation, as if surprised. "Of course. What's your birthday?"

Bailey told her, and a moment later she was back with the information. "You've only been in once, Mrs. Abbott. Last Wednesday."

The day of the accident.

"Thank you. This may sound odd, but do you have a record of the time I left?"

"Excuse me?"

"When I finished with the doctor and checked out?"

"Are you all right, Mrs. Abbott?"

"Yes, fine. Just . . . retracing my steps."

"According to my records, you checked out at eleven-forty."

Bailey could tell by the woman's voice that she found this call very odd. No doubt it would provide lunch-break laughs later.

She might as well make it a really funny story, as long as she was at it. "And I'm pregnant, right? Around five weeks?"

"Yes, ma'am," the receptionist managed, voice suddenly high and squeaky. "Almost six weeks now."

"Thank you," Bailey said, "for your help and holding back your—"

"Bailey, get off the phone."

At Logan's voice, she whirled around, the device slipping from her fingers. She bent and scooped it up, seeing that either the receptionist or the drop had ended the call.

He looked strange. "What's wrong? I thought you were going—" She looked beyond him. "Where's Tony?"

"At the barn. Bailey—"

She heard the sound of tires on the gravel drive. Her blood went cold. "Who's that?"

"The police— Not Billy Ray. The sheriff's office."

"But how . . ." She shook her head, confused. "Why?"

"A friend of mine called and gave me a heads-up. They want to question me about early Saturday morning."

"Early Saturday morning," she repeated. "I don't understand—"

But then she did. The woman Paul had told her about. Dixie, the one who had gone missing.

CHAPTER FORTY-FOUR

Tuesday, April 22
10:15 A.M.

"It's good to see you again, Mrs. Abbott."

She nodded, numb. She felt Logan's glance and realized their visit with her was another thing she hadn't told him. She felt sick.

"How are you feeling? Better?"

"A little," she managed, the taste of tin in her mouth.

"Have you remembered anything new?"

Again she felt Logan's gaze. He seemed to come alert beside her.

"No." She shook her head. "Nothing."

Rumsfeld's gaze traveled between the two of them. "That's so odd, Mrs. Abbott. Dr. Bauer thought your full memory of events could return within the day."

"Or take as long as a week," she said evenly, surprising herself. "It's only been a couple of days."

The detective cocked an eyebrow. "Clock's ticking."

"I'm not sure what you mean by that, Detective."

He only smiled slightly and shifted his attention to Logan. "And how are you today, Mr. Abbott?"

"Just dandy."

"Glad to hear it. I need to ask you a few questions. About this past Friday." Logan didn't respond and he went on. "Where were you Friday night?"

"At the hospital. With my wife."

"What about early Saturday morning?"

"With my wife."

"The whole time?"

"Pretty much. I didn't want to leave her, in case she came to."

He'd hesitated a fraction of a second. Bailey heard it and she knew the detectives had, too. Why? What didn't he want to say?

"Pretty much. So, you did leave her side?"

"To clear my head, yes. Get some fresh air."

"And that's it?"

"Yes."

"Any idea what time that might have been?"

"No. But it was late."

"I'm sure we can find that out." He glanced down at his notebook, then back up at Logan. "So, you just stepped outside for fresh air?"

"Yes."

"You own several different vehicles, is that correct?"

"That's right."

"Do you recall which one you were driving Friday?"

"The truck. A Ford F-150."

They already knew, Bailey realized. That he'd left her room, the time, what he had been driving. They were testing him. But why?

She decided to ask. "What's this all about, Detective?"

"A missing woman. Dixie Jenkins. Last seen early Saturday morning. Getting into a black pickup truck."

It was all Bailey could do to keep from gasping. Beside her, Logan stiffened.

"You know anything about that, Mr. Abbott?"

"How could I?"

"Did you know Dixie?"

"I do know Dixie. Not well. Over the years, Travis, that's her daddy, has done some work for me."

Rumsfeld stood. Carlson followed. "Thank you for your time," he said, then looked at her. "You still have the card I gave you yesterday?"

"I do, Detectives."

They walked with them to the front door. She couldn't wait to have them out of her house, the door shut behind them.

The detectives started through, then stopped. "When your memory returns, or for any other reason, call me or my partner. You recall promising me you would?"

She nodded. He turned back to Logan. "Your first wife, what was her name?"

"True."

"That's right, True. Did she ever file for divorce?"

"No, I did."

"Gotcha."

"Never heard from her again, huh?" That came from the younger of the two, Carlson.

Logan didn't hide his irritation. "No, I did not."

"I always thought that was strange."

"What's that, Detective Carlson?"

"Most folks, when they want to get out of a marriage, try to get everything they can."

"And?"

"Nothing. It's odd, that's all."

"If you remember, my wife withdrew ten thousand dollars two days before she left."

"Big money to me, a public servant. But for you . . . or the woman you marry, not so much."

"True wasn't like that."

"I guess all she wanted was her freedom."

Bailey'd had enough. "If there's nothing else, I haven't quite recovered yet and need to rest."

"My apologies, Mrs. Abbott. But your husband and I go way back, so we have lots to talk about."

"You went to school together? Grew up in the same neighborhood?"

"Hardly." He smiled slightly. "No, I interviewed him when his first wife disappeared."

"*When his first wife disappeared.*" She felt the words like a blow to her gut, but wasn't about to let this stranger see that.

She coolly cocked an eyebrow and waited.

He cleared his throat. "Like I said, call if you need anything. And be careful. I'd hate to see another accident befall you."

Bailey turned on Logan the moment the detective's vehicle had cleared the gates.

"Where were you Friday night?"

"You know where I was."

"When you left. Where did you go?"

"For a drive." He must have read the horror in her expression, because he quickly added, "I was nowhere near Wholesome or The Landing. I got into the truck, put the windows down and just drove. To clear my head."

"I can't believe you let him treat you that way. Like you're a criminal."

"I've lived with this bullshit most of my life. Maybe now you get why I wanted my lawyer present when they questioned me yesterday. It's not because I'm guilty, it's because they want me to be."

She had a choice, Bailey acknowledged. Believe him or not. Follow her head, or her heart. He'd kept things from her. Deliberately. Important, incriminating things. He'd rushed her into marriage. Into trusting him and coming here. Giving up everything she had to be with him.

Now, she understood why. What he was up against. If

there had been real evidence against him, he would have been charged.

So she went to him, circled her arms around his middle and laid her head on his chest. Beneath her cheek, she felt the steady beat of his heart.

Her heart knew him. She loved him. And he loved her.

He was her happily ever after.

"What are you thinking?" he asked, voice thick.

"We'll figure this out, Logan. You and me. Together."

Just then, Tony came tearing up the walk. Wet and muddy, something red in his mouth. He dropped the object at their feet, obviously very pleased with himself.

Bailey moved her gaze from him to the thing at her feet. Not just anything. A red shoe.

The red shoe.

Her stomach turned over, and its contents rushed to her throat. Hand to her mouth, she turned and ran for the powder room.

She reached it just in time, bent over the commode and heaved.

Logan hadn't gone out to get the shoe, to keep her quiet or to keep it from the hands of the police.

"Baby, are you all right?"

He stood in the doorway, looking anxious.

"Yes," she managed, straightening. She turned to the sink, rinsed her mouth and splashed water on her face. "It's the pregnancy."

He came up behind her and eased her against his chest. He met her gaze in the mirror. "See, just like I told you before. That silly dog came back for it. Buried it like a bone."

"You were right." Her eyes welled with tears. "I'm so sorry, Logan. For doubting you. For—"

"Shh." He turned her in his arms. "It's in the past. From now on we believe in each other, no matter what. Right?"

"Right. No matter what."

"I'll call Billy Ray," he said.

"Wait." She turned in his arms. "I overreacted that day. You're right, somebody was out there necking, couldn't find their shoe and left it behind. Just toss it."

CHAPTER FORTY-FIVE

Tuesday, April 22
12:45 P.M.

Bailey stood at the sink humming as she rinsed her and Logan's lunch plates. The Carrie Underwood song, she realized. The one she had recalled that day in the hospital. Why had it popped back into her head now?

She hummed along, the words tumbling through her head.

Shatter every window 'til it's all blown away . . .

As she did, she recalled the moment she'd realized she had skipped a period and wondered if she was pregnant. The memory burst full bloom in her head, then unfurled like petals of a flower. She had double-checked the calendar on her phone; she always noted "Day One" when she started.

She'd scrolled through. December. January. February. No March.
Late. Nearly five weeks.
"Bailey?"
The sandwich plate slipped from her fingers, hit the tile floor and shattered.

"Don't move!" Logan ordered. "Your feet are bare, let me get it."

He grabbed the broom and dustpan and, in no time at all, dumped the pieces into the trash.

"All clear."

But she didn't move, thoughts tumbling back to that day. Conflicted, she remembered. As if her every dream had come true—in the midst of a nightmare. She'd found an OB/GYN—Dr. Saunders—and made an appointment for the next day.

"Bailey? You've remembered something, haven't you?"

She blinked, looked at him. "Yes. Realizing that I'd missed a period and might be pregnant. Making an appointment with Dr. Saunders. I wanted to know for sure before I said anything to you. To surprise you."

"Mission accomplished, babe."

She laughed. "No joke. You ready to go?" she asked. He'd had to cancel his meeting this morning because of the sheriff's deputies, and had rescheduled it for this afternoon.

"Having second thoughts. Thinking I'll let them meet without me." He lowered his voice. "I'm worried about you."

"I told you, I'm fine."

"An hour ago you were puking your guts up."

"And fifteen minutes ago I was wolfing down a chicken sandwich." She crossed to him. "I'm pregnant, not sick."

"It's not just that. Your memory—"

"Has started to return. Besides, you said it yourself, it's all been pretty anticlimactic."

"They won't all be, Bailey. You know that."

Blood. Everywhere. On her hands and jeans.

"I know. But we can't just sit around waiting for them to drop, like a death sentence. Take your meeting and come back. How long could it be?"

"A couple hours, tops."

"Go. Meet with the developers and I'll bake something."

"Bake something?" He looked confused.

"I have a craving for brownies."

"There's a bakery up by Bridles and Britches, I could—"

"No. Home-baked. My mother's recipe."

A smile touched his mouth. "I do like brownies." He started for the door, then stopped again. "A couple hours. Meet with the developer, gather together some things—"

"Just go!" She pointed at the door.

"Do you have everything you need for the brownies?"

"If I don't, I'll run up to the market."

"You probably shouldn't be driving."

She rolled her eyes. "I'll ask Paul for a ride."

He hesitated a moment, then agreed. "I'll stop at the barn on the way out, let him know. Just in case."

She shook her head. "You worry more than an old woman."

He laughed, then started through the door. "Whatever it takes."

Between the refrigerator and the pantry, she had everything she needed for the brownies, almost as if she had gotten a craving for them before, bought the items, then didn't make them. Maybe that would be her next ho-hum recollection.

Bailey measured, mixed and poured. Logan hadn't lied to her. He hadn't gone back to the pond to get the shoe. How could she have even suspected him of it? Billy Ray's nonsense was getting to her. Bodies buried at Abbott Farm, indeed.

She shook her head, starting to hum again, the words tumbling through her head.

. . . Shatter every window . . .

Tony had gone back for his prize, reburied it, only to bring it to her today.

. . .'til it's all blown away . . .

Bailey poured the batter into the pan, then slid it into the oven and set the timer. She'd need toothpicks, she thought. And oven mitts.

The mitts were easy to find, the drawer directly to the right of the oven. She took the two red mitts from the drawer and tossed them on the counter. One slipped and landed on the floor by her feet.

She bent to retrieve it, then froze.

Two mitts. One for each hand.

Shoes. One for each foot. A right. And a left.

She shook the thought off, snatched up the mitt and laid it on top of the other. So what?

So, which one did Tony dig up? The right? The left? Or both?

Stop it, she scolded herself. She was stealing her own happiness. It was masochistic. Obsessive-compulsive. She trusted Logan.

Bailey let out her breath in a huff. Easy fix. Look at the photo she'd taken the day Tony unearthed it.

She retrieved the phone, called up the photo. And swore.

She couldn't tell. The light, the vegetation around it. She enlarged the image, turned it this way and that. If anything, she became less certain.

One shoe, two shoe, red shoe, blue—

No, only red. Two red shoes. A pair.

. . .'til it's all blown away . . .

Bailey carried the device to the keeping room and sat. She studied the image, mentally going back to that day.

She pictured herself unearthing it. Seeing it come into focus as she dug it free of the mud.

The smell of rain. And new growth.

A right shoe, she thought. Yes. A right shoe.

So, what did Tony bring them this morning? She pursed her lips in thought. She hadn't really looked at it. Not that way.

Go out to the garage and look in the trash.

She acted on the thought. In the garage, Bailey grabbed gardening gloves from the workbench and some newspaper from the recycling bin. She laid the paper on the bench, then crossed to the trash barrel.

Logan had tossed the shoe out here—at least she assumed he had. She flipped up the lid. Her stomach lurched at the sour smell. She wrinkled her nose and prayed she didn't puke again.

Bingo. There it was, lying right on top. Thankful for the gloves, she reached in, grabbed it and carried it to the bench.

But it wasn't a right shoe. It was a left.

She stared at it, light-headed. Her memory was wrong. She pictured that day in her head once more. The shoe. Partially unearthing it, going for the stick, digging it the rest of the way out.

A right shoe.

She could easily be wrong. She'd been wet, out of her element, not looking at it analytically.

Time to remedy that. High heel, maybe two, two and a half inches. Pump with a peekaboo toe. Party shoes. The printing inside the shoe had worn—or eroded—off, but it looked to be about her size, a six. She removed her slip-on and set it beside the red pump. Close, she decided. Give or take a half size. Which meant its owner hadn't been particularly tall.

The leather was cracked and peeling in places, the

brand name unreadable, but for the most part it looked in pretty good shape for having been out in the elements, buried in the muck.

For how long? Five years? Three?

Could this have belonged to True?

"Hey, Bailey, what're you doing?"

She jumped and spun around. "Paul! You scared the life out of me!"

"I'm sorry."

"You're like a cat." She brought a hand to her chest. "How do you do that?"

He smiled. "Years creeping around the barn, I guess. What do you have there?"

"Nothing."

He cocked an eyebrow, amused. "Surely something."

"Something I'm tossing." She quickly rolled the paper around the shoe, then carried it back to the trash bin and dropped it in. If Paul saw the shoe and mentioned it to Logan, she would have to explain—something she wouldn't be able to do without hurting his feelings.

"Why the gloves?"

"I was thinking about cutting some roses." Not a complete lie; she had been—earlier in the day. "What are you doing up here? Logan's not—"

"I know." He slid his hands into his pockets. "He told me you might need some baking supplies, so I thought I'd check before I ran into town."

"That's so— Oh, no! The brownies!" She'd forgotten all about them. She yanked off the gloves, tossed them aside and hurried back to the kitchen. The steady *beep, beep* of the timer greeted her, but she didn't smell burning. A very good sign.

She grabbed the oven mitts, removed the pan from the oven, then went searching for a toothpick to test them.

She felt his gaze on her as she moved clumsily about the kitchen.

"You seem jumpy."

She was, but she wasn't about to admit it to him. Or why. "I haven't done that much cooking in this kitchen yet, and I don't know where anything—Here we go. Toothpicks."

She inserted one; it came out clean and she smiled. "Saved in the nick of time."

"They smell delicious."

"Thanks to you."

"Glad to have helped."

"They're my mom's recipe, triple chocolate. You've got to try one."

"Only if you insist."

He had a disarming smile, she thought. Not sexy and mysterious like Logan's. Paul's oozed charm and likability. He was the quintessential boy-next-door.

"I do insist. Scoop of vanilla ice cream?"

"Or two."

She laughed. "Now you're talking."

She fixed them both the same thing—giant brownie and two scoops of ice cream.

"Logan told me. I hope you don't mind."

"Excuse me?"

"That you're eating for two."

She tried to hide her dismay, but saw by his expression that she'd failed. "Don't be mad. I stopped by the hospital, he had just found out. He . . . was out of his mind with worry. And had no one else to talk to."

"It's okay. I'm glad you were there for him."

"And you," he said. "I'm here for you, too, you know."

Tears pricked her eyes and she blinked against them. "Damn hormones."

He laughed. "How're you feeling?"

"Except for the tears, puking and headaches, I'm great."

"That'll all pass, though. Right?"

"It better." She spooned another big bite of brownie and ice cream into her mouth. "At last," she said around her mouthful, "I can eat like a man."

He shook his head, that charming grin returning. "I've got a confession to make." He looked sheepish. "I knew you were baking brownies, that's why I came up here. I have a particular weakness for them."

She laughed. "Were they worth the subterfuge?"

"Absolutely." He spooned up another bite. "They're amazing. The best I've ever had."

"That would make my mom really happy." She didn't want to linger on that thought and moved quickly on. "Can I ask you something?"

"Sure. But it might cost you a brownie to go."

"You've got it. But only one."

He laughed, nodded and took a bite.

"Why aren't you married?"

He almost choked on the mouthful.

"You must have gotten that question before?"

He cleared his throat. "Only from old ladies at weddings."

"And now, friends' pregnant wives."

He eyed her, amused. "Why do you want to know? You got a friend to fix me up with?"

"Maybe." She arched an eyebrow in question.

"Right girl never came along."

"Never?"

"There was one girl, but it didn't work out."

"Where'd you meet her?"

"LSU."

She scraped the last of the melted cream from her bowl. "Why didn't it work out?"

"Two brownies."

She looked up.

"It'll cost you two."

"Deal."

"She wasn't interested in farm life."

"This isn't exactly a farm."

"She didn't want to live in the country and said she didn't want to come home to a man who smelled like a barn and had dirt under his fingernails."

An ugly edge had crept into his voice, and Bailey realized the woman had hurt him deeply.

He looked away. When he continued, the edge was gone. "I was an Ag student, what did she expect?"

"What was her name?"

"Why? Do you think you might recognize her?"

She had struck a nerve, she realized, and reached across the table and touched his hand. "Forgive me, Paul. I don't know what's come over me, being so nosy."

He grimaced. "No, forgive me. After all these years, you'd think I wouldn't be so sensitive about it."

"She doesn't sound like she was a very nice person."

"She wasn't, I realize that now." He looked at her hand on his, then back up at her. "But you know how young love is."

"Blind?" she said awkwardly, drawing her hand back.

"And hormonal." He stood and carried his bowl to the sink. "I suppose I should get back to the horses."

Silence fell between them. He cleared his throat. "Can I offer you some friendly advice?"

"Sure."

"After True left, Raine packed up everything that had been hers, everything she'd touched that marked this as her home. But all that was left was a shell. Of this place"— he motioned with his hand—"and of Logan. Until you.

Logan's happy again. Fill this house up with the two of you, with your children and theirs."

A lump of tears settled in her throat. She swallowed against them.

"Let everything else go, Bailey. All of it. Questions and doubt. What anybody else thinks. You know what's real. You do."

Yes, she thought as he walked away. Once she'd recovered her lost memories, they would move on. Focus on their marriage, their family. Everything else would take its rightful place as nothing.

Until then, the hole was too big and too dark, filled with nothing but a red shoe.

CHAPTER FORTY-SIX

After Paul left, the quiet thundered down on Bailey. As hard as she tried, she couldn't stop wondering: Had the shoe she and Tony unearthed been a right, not a left?

Her memory could be wrong. It probably was. Considering the events of the past days, why should she trust her memory? It was laughable. Even so, that shoe didn't make sense to her.

She brought her hand to her belly, to their baby, growing there inside her. What were her options, right now?

Think, Bailey. Sort it out. Facts from fears.

Fact. Tony had unearthed a ladies shoe—or a pair— from the swimming hole on Abbott Farm property.

She was afraid it had belonged to True. And if not True, one of the other young women who had gone missing from Wholesome over the years. Why? Because Billy Ray believed Abbott Farm was where all the bodies were buried.

She brought the heels of her hands to her eyes. Because he believed Logan was a killer. The man was obsessed with the notion. Because he'd been in love with True.

And from that tiny seed, her fears had grown, multiplied and spiraled out of control.

Bailey pulled in a deep, steadying breath. Time to take

control back. She could eliminate one of her fears quickly, by learning True's shoe size.

She checked her watch. The way she figured it, she had an hour, tops, before Logan returned home. In that time, she could do a quick search of the bedroom closets and snoop around the attic a bit. Paul said Raine had taken care of True's things for Logan. She could have donated them, as Bailey had her mother's. Or, perhaps, in a symbolic gesture, hauled them to the dump.

But maybe not. Maybe they'd gone no farther than the attic. It was worth a shot.

Bailey hurried upstairs. She would check the guest rooms first. All the spare closets. Then, depending on what she found, she would move on to the attic.

The closets were oddly empty. As if a family didn't live here, she thought. In a way, she supposed one hadn't in a long time. Paul's description of it as a shell was uncomfortably accurate.

Bailey flipped through the meager contents, then moved on. One of the closets held little-girl party and special-occasion dresses. Ruffles and lace, bows and ribbon.

For some reason, gazing at those frilly little outfits brought tears to her eyes. She imagined the joyful little girl who had worn them and wondered what had happened to her.

But she knew. Tragedy. Loss. A broken heart.

I won't leave him, Raine. I promise you that.

Bailey blinked against the tears, cursing her raging hormones. She had made that promise; she hoped to God she could keep it.

The attic was next. It was a walk-in, Logan had pointed to it that first day, on her tour of the house. Light filtered through the one window, falling over the cluttered interior, highlighting some objects and leaving others in shadow. She found the light switch to the right of the door and flipped it up. Fluorescent light spilled evenly over everything.

So many boxes, she thought. Which would they be in?

Recent, so not as dusty. Stacked together. Most probably toward the front, certainly not buried. Marked "True's Things" or nothing at all. Like an unmarked grave.

Stop it, Bailey. Get busy.

She started with the cartons closest to the door and made her way deeper into the space. The farther she got from the door, the dustier it became. She sneezed several times; her throat began to tickle. Near the window, she stopped at the sound of tires on the gravel drive. She tiptoed to it, though she didn't know why, and peered down.

Logan, home already. Pulling into the garage. Climbing out of the Porsche, going around to the passenger side. No. She'd just begun—

But then she realized, she had done this before. With her mind's eye she saw herself. Frantically going through every box, every dresser drawer. Just the way she had today.

The same day she had gone to retrieve the shoe, only to find it gone. The day that had changed everything.

Nothing. She'd found nothing of True's that day, and she would find nothing now.

"Bailey!"

She quickly, quietly closed the attic door and hurried down the hall to the top of the stairs. "Up here!" she called back.

He appeared at the bottom of the stairs, looked up at her. "You're flushed. Are you all right?"

"Fine." She forced a sleepy smile and stretched. "I was napping."

A small part of her died at the lie. She prayed that one

day, when she told him and explained why, he would forgive her.

"It smells delicious down here."

"The brownies. How about I come down and fix you one?"

He smiled. "I'd like that."

"Give me just a minute."

She ran to the bedroom, pulled the coverlet back, then scrunched the pillow. From there, she darted to the bathroom, washed her hands, splashed her face and brushed her hair, trying to clean the dust off her.

That done, she went to meet him in the kitchen. "Everything go all right with your meeting?"

"Fine." He bent and kissed her. "Fears allayed, financing solidly in place."

"Good." She crossed to the pan of brownies, mind racing for an inconspicuous way to ask him True's shoe size even as she acknowledged there wasn't one. "Ice cream?"

"I'll go with your recommendation."

He sounded amused, even lighthearted. As if there were nothing wrong. As if nothing had changed between them.

As far as he was concerned, all had been resolved.

"You're not having one?" he asked as she set the plate in front of him, then took a seat.

"I already did. With Paul."

"Paul?" He took a bite of the ice cream and pastry, then rolled his eyes. "Really good."

"Glad you think so. He came up to see if I needed something from the market, then confessed to being a complete brownie-hound." She glanced up at him. "He was telling me about a girl he dated at LSU."

"How did that come up?"

"I asked him why he wasn't married."

Logan laughed. "Poor Paul."

Bailey ignored that. "She broke his heart. Did you meet her?"

"I did. She seemed nice enough."

"That's not the impression I got."

"Really?"

"She broke it off with him because she didn't want to be married to a guy who smelled like a barn."

"He never told me that, but it makes sense. When they started dating he was in vet school, studying to be a large-animal vet. He was almost done when he chucked it. Said he wanted to work with horses every day and came to run the farm."

She frowned. "I wonder why he didn't tell you? You're his closest friend."

"All that sharing isn't a guy thing. Besides, Paul's extremely private. Always has been. Truthfully, I'm sort of blown away that he revealed as much as he did to you."

. . .'til it's all blown away . . .

"The girl Paul dated, what was her name? Do you remember?"

"If my memory serves, her name was Cassie." He scooped up the last of the brownie. "You seem awfully interested in Paul."

"He's a big part of your life. Our life here." He didn't comment and she went on. "What about his family? He told me a little, but not that much."

"Almost as big a mess as mine." She cocked an eyebrow and he smiled.

"Okay, that was an exaggeration. It was just him and his mom. Don't know much about his dad, never met him. He cut out on them when Paul was really young."

"We have that in common," she said. "I wonder why he never mentioned it?"

"Maybe because the similarity stops there. Unlike your mom, his was angry. And bitter. She took all that out on Paul. I wasn't over there much, but she wasn't . . . kind."

"That's why he loved your mom so much, because she was."

He nodded. "And that's why he took it so hard when she died."

"That's so sad."

"Don't let on I told you all this, he's a proud guy." He stood and carried his bowl to the sink, rinsed it, then looked back at her, expression arch. "I'm beginning to think you're a little too interested in the men around here."

"Men? What are you talking about?"

"Last week it was August?"

She frowned. "I don't understand."

"Asking about his family, if he'd ever been married, where he came from."

"When was that? The day of the accident?"

"It was. That morning." His smile faded. "Up out of the blue, you asked if he dated much, if he'd ever been married."

"I wonder why?"

"Because you're nosy?"

She returned his smile, simultaneously acknowledging it felt like more. Because of the timing.

"Have you talked to Raine today?" she asked, changing the subject.

"No. But I suppose I'd better."

"I thought I might walk over and check on her."

"Really?"

"Yes. Take her a brownie or two. Do you think she'd like that?"

"I do. But you know Raine, she'll behave badly. Maybe I should come along?"

"I can't be scared of her forever. Besides, I'm sure you have things to do."

"I do. Paul wanted to go over the show budget. Make certain you have your cell phone. Just in case."

"Of what? She tries to kill me?"

But he didn't laugh and Bailey wondered if maybe she should be afraid of the unstable Raine.

CHAPTER FORTY-SEVEN

Tuesday, April 22
4:55 P.M.

Raine answered the door in her pajamas. She looked a wreck—face pale, hair sticking out every which way, mascara smudges under her eyes. Bailey's first thought was that the woman was ill.

Then she invited her in, slurring her words. Wobbling as she turned and headed back inside.

She wasn't sick, Bailey realized. She was loaded.

Bailey followed her, shutting the door behind them. It was the first time she'd been inside Raine's home; it was an eclectic and energetic mix of styles and art, country and contemporary.

Here, Bailey saw only a hint of the studio's creative chaos, the pillow and afghan bunched up on the comfy-looking couch, magazines spilled over the coffee table and onto the floor, a few pairs of shoes, a coffee mug and a couple of glasses.

Raine went straight to the couch, plopped down onto it.

"I've brought you a treat."

"More of Logan's good wine?"

"Brownies. I made them this afternoon and thought—"

"Funeral's t'morrow." She dragged the blanket onto her lap.

"Yes," Bailey said, setting the plate on the coffee table.

"Making brownies." Raine peered over at the foil-covered plate. "I wonder what it's like."

"What's that?"

"Being happy."

Bailey laced her fingers together, uncertain what to say. "Is there anything I can do to help you, Raine?"

"I'm so tired."

"I know. I'm sorry for all your loss."

Raine reached for the plate, selected one of the fudgy squares, then changed her mind. "Sorry."

She curled up on her side, head on the pillow. Bailey's heart went out to her. "Can I make you something else? Eggs or some soup?"

"No." She stared straight ahead, eyes curiously blank.

"It will get better."

"No. It won't."

Bailey cleared her throat. She had come hoping for information, she saw now that that wasn't going to happen. Today. Maybe ever. "Are you certain I can't get you anything?"

"A drink."

"I don't think that's a good idea."

"Go away then." Her lids fluttered closed and Bailey thought she might have drifted off.

Then she opened them. "Remember."

Bailey frowned, uncertain what she meant. "I'm sorry, I'm not sure what—"

"You. I need you . . . to . . ."

Her voice lowered, trailed off. Bailey moved closer, squatted in front of her. "What, Raine?"

"To remember."

"What do you need to know?"

"If you"—her lids fluttered, obviously having a difficult time keeping them open—"saw . . . him."

"Who?"

"The . . . who shot—"

Henry.

It suddenly occurred to Bailey that Raine may have in-gested more than alcohol.

"Wait! Raine?" She shook her. Her eyes snapped open. "What did you take? Pills? What?"

"Nothing. Jus' sleepy—" She closed her eyes again.

"No, don't—" Bailey jumped to her feet. If Raine had taken something, there would be evidence of it. Bailey made her way through the single-story cottage. A near-empty vodka bottle on the kitchen counter, the drained orange juice carton beside it. Wine bottles in the trash. No sign of any food being consumed but a box of Triscuit crackers and a package of Oreos.

No medicine vials. Even the bathroom medicine cabinet seemed to have been wiped clean. Advil. Tylenol. Generic sinus medicine. She checked the box and found it with only two doses missing.

Raine's purse. Jacket pockets.

Bailey found her handbag and rifled through it. Nothing. In her coat closet, she found a variety of jackets, checked the pockets and came up with a couple of business cards and tissues.

She turned from the closet to the bed. A pile of clothes on the floor: jeans, T-shirts. As if she had shed them, then left them be. Yesterday's, Bailey thought.

She quickly went through them. Nothing. Where else might Raine have squirreled away some medication?

Her studio.

Bailey checked on the sleeping woman, found her breathing was deep and even, then went to check the studio.

It was just as it had been the other time she had been here. Bailey quickly made her way through the cavernous space, checking workbenches and equipment carts. Nothing.

She stopped and let out a pent-up breath, feeling a bit silly about her panicked search. But Raine obviously wasn't thinking clearly, and people died all the time from mixing prescription medications and booze.

Thinking. Clearly. Neither was she. She'd come here to see what she could uncover about True. See if, by any chance, Raine had stored True's things here.

This was her chance.

In her mad dash through the cottage, she hadn't run across any packing boxes—or places to store them. Bailey did a mental accounting. No garage, attic access from the back hallway, via pull-down ladder, nearly non-existent closet space.

That left here. She did a slow three-sixty, gaze stopping on two doors at the back of the studio. Both closed. Storage closets? Perhaps.

The first one she tried proved to be a washroom, not a closet. Basic head, sink, mirror. Light was burned out. The next door she found locked.

A ring of keys. Hanging off the ear of a small gargoyle, sitting watch near the studio entrance. Car key. What she assumed were house keys. She wondered if Raine had a key to her and Logan's. The thought left her uncomfortable.

She snatched up the ring and crossed to the locked door. Raine had a half-dozen keys on the ring; Bailey tried each one.

The last opened the door. She flipped on the light.

A storage room. Almost a mini gallery. Paintings on the walls, on easels, on racks.

And they were all of True.

Bailey stood in the middle of the room and turned in

a slow circle, taking it all in. Some lovely portraits. True's features glowing, as if from the inside, making True appear an ethereal beauty. An angel come to earth. Others dark. Vile and violent. True with the black heart of a beast. Of a True torn apart by imaginary wolves, screaming in pain. Her fear and despair as palpable in this oil painting as Raine's was in real life.

And in one of these terrible images, True wore red shoes.

Heart thundering, Bailey studied the painting, those small red splashes. Unmistakable, although with them rendered in Raine's expressionistic style, it was impossible to tell what style of shoes they were.

It didn't prove anything. But it could mean everything. It could be the answer she'd come here looking for. Had she painted those shoes from imagination? Or memory?

Only Raine had the answers.

"What the hell are you doing?"

Bailey whirled around. Raine stood behind her, face white with rage.

Bailey held a hand out. "This painting of True, she—"

"Get out."

"The shoes, Raine, the red shoes, I have to know—"

"These are private! This room is private!"

"Please—" She lowered her voice. "I meant no harm, I promise. I have to know, why did you put her in red—"

She curled her hands into fists. "I should kill you."

"What did you say?"

"I could. Right now, with my bare hands. Or I could get my gun—" She took a lopsided step toward Bailey, eyes glittering. "I have one, you know. I grew up hunting with Logan and Roane. And I'm an excellent shot. I could just"—she lifted her hands in a facsimile of a gun—"blow you away."

Shatter every window 'til it's all blown away . . .

"You're talking crazy."

She swayed and grabbed the doorjamb for support. "That's me, poor, crazy Raine."

"I'm leaving."

"No." Raine caught her arm as she moved past, her grip surprisingly strong. "What were you looking for?"

Why not? Bailey wondered, looking her straight in the eyes. What did she have to lose? "True's shoe size."

The other woman looked comically surprised. "What the hell for?"

"You wouldn't tell me anyway." Bailey jerked her arm free. "Forget it. Enjoy the brownies."

"Maybe you're the one who's crazy!" Raine called after her. "Not me."

Bailey reached the door, opened it, started through.

"What does it matter!" Raine's voice turned high-pitched, hysterical. "Same size as mine! Six and a half!"

Bailey didn't turn back or even slow her steps until she reached her own driveway. There, she stopped. Breathing hard. Legs rubbery.

Six and a half. About the size of the red shoe.

The garage door stood open. The big, blue trash bin there to the far left. Mocking her. Taunting her to take a look. *"Come see,"* it seemed to call, *"then you'll know for certain!"*

Even as she tried to reason herself out of it, she started toward it, a sensation rolling over her. Heavy. Almost smothering.

Her head filled with the image of Raine's painting. True, wearing red shoes.

Size six and a half.

What are you doing, Bailey? Just leave it alone. You've already damaged your marriage.

She couldn't leave it alone. It felt as if she was being drawn by some invisible but powerful force. She stepped into the garage. Crossed to the bin. Lifted the lid. Peered inside.

The shoe was gone.

CHAPTER FORTY-EIGHT

All the Wholesome old-timers had turned out for Henry's funeral as well as a smattering of others. Stephanie's friends and coworkers. The staff of Abbott Farm. The curious.

Oddly, Billy Ray was not one of them.

Bailey stopped in front of a table displaying photographs and memorabilia from Henry's life. He'd been movie star handsome before the accident. Dark and dashing. He'd been an accomplished horseman, she saw by the number of show ribbons and medals.

And kind. She saw it in the photos, shining from his eyes.

No wonder Elisabeth Abbott had fallen in love with him.

Faye came up beside her. She had closed the diner so she and the staff could pay their respects. "He was a heartbreaker, that's for sure. Wasn't a woman in the parish who set eyes on him who didn't swoon."

She chuckled, almost to herself. "Him, he hardly noticed. He was just good people. Before the accident and after."

Before Bailey could reply, a collective murmur moved through the room. She turned. Two uniformed officers.

One young and gangly, the other old and portly, both in uniform, sidearms included.

Bailey heard the whispering. The word *"murdered"* breathed from one ear to the next. She saw by Stephanie's expression that she heard, too. It infuriated her. This day was to honor Henry's life, his good spirit, not to gossip about his death.

She cornered the young one. "What's your name, Officer?"

"Earl Stroup, ma'am."

"You should be ashamed," she said softly, so no one but him would hear. "Coming here, armed like that. It's disrespectful."

"I have a job to do, ma'am."

"And what, exactly, is it?"

His face reddened. "Surveillance, ma'am."

"You couldn't do that in a suit?"

He cleared his throat and shuffled from one foot to the other. "I don't mean any disrespect. Henry was a sweet old guy. But me and Bob got our orders."

Just like she figured. "More like, your boss's vendetta to carry out." From across the room, Logan caught her eye, then motioned that the service was about to begin. "Excuse me, Officer Stroup, I need to join my husband."

Bailey returned to Logan's side. He guided her, his hand resting at the small of her back, steadying her. He stood so close she could smell his spicy aftershave, feel the warmth of his body. Yet it felt to her as if miles separated them.

They'd hardly spoken the night before. He'd returned from the barn distant, distracted. She had been grateful not to have to pretend her world wasn't falling apart.

Logan had taken the red shoe. Why?

The viewing room of the tiny funeral home was filled to overflowing. Stephanie had asked Bailey and Logan if they and Raine would sit in the front row with her. Not only because she didn't want to be alone, but because Henry had considered the Abbotts his family.

As she scooted into the pew, Stephanie touched her hand. Bailey bent and hugged her. "I'm so sorry, Steph."

"Thank you for being here."

Bailey nodded and took the seat next to Logan. Paul and August were directly behind them, but Raine was nowhere to be seen. She turned and scanned the rows of faces, but still didn't see her.

She leaned toward Logan. "Where's your sister?"

He, too, scanned the pews, then shook his head. "She was here earlier." He looked over his shoulder at Paul. "You know where Raine is?"

"No clue." He looked at August in question; he, too, indicated he did not know.

"You want me to go look for her?" Bailey asked.

"Don't bother. She'd be here if she thought she could handle it."

Bailey pictured the other woman, curled up somewhere. Falling apart. But still, she knew he was right. Raine wouldn't accept her—or anyone else's—offer of comfort.

She opened her hand in a silent invitation for Logan to clasp it. He did and the minister began. He spoke of life and death. Hope and resurrection. Of a simple man who had loved generously.

The room was warm. Too warm. Bailey breathed deeply through her nose, hoping the oxygen would steady her.

She tried to focus on the preacher, her gaze kept drifting back to the casket.

Could she have done something? Could she have intervened? She'd been close by, so close his blood had soaked her clothes. Coated her hands.

Red. Everywhere.

And now Henry was in a box.

A box.

A small wooden box. Henry beaming at her. A gift. For her.

Bailey brought a hand to her mouth, feeling like she might be sick. No. She had to hold it back. She couldn't, not here. Not now.

She pressed her lips together, gaze fixed on the minister. She began to sweat. Her heart to race.

Henry.

Beaming at her as he lifted the box's lid.

Hand to her mouth, Bailey jumped to her feet. She felt everyone's gaze turn to her, heard the minister stumble over his words.

Logan was saying something. She couldn't stop, couldn't pause to listen. She scooted out of the pew and raced to the ladies' room. She made it safely inside but no farther than a sink. She bent over it and lost her breakfast.

Bailey rinsed her mouth first, then the sink, using paper towels and hand soap to clean it up. Only then did she see that she wasn't alone.

Raine was curled up on the small settee. Staring at her with puffy, bloodshot eyes.

"I'm sorry," Bailey said. "I didn't see you there."

"I have a mint. If you'd like one."

The kindness surprised her. "I would, thanks."

Feeling wobbly, Bailey crossed and sat on the opposite end of the settee. Raine dug an aluminum box out of her purse and held it out.

Another box, Bailey thought.

"They're curiously strong," Raine said.

Bailey smiled weakly at her reference to the brand's campaign line and her sister-in-law's attempt at levity. "I still think I'll need two."

"Keep the box."

"Thanks." She closed her fingers over it. "I appreciate it."

They fell silent. After a moment, Raine broke it with a question. "What's wrong with you?"

"Excuse me?"

"The throwing up. Is it the head injury?"

"No." She hoped Logan didn't mind, but she couldn't not tell the other woman. "I'm pregnant."

Raine went white. The reaction hurt. "You must not be ready to be an aunt," Bailey said.

"It's not that."

Again, nothing. Just that hollow-eyed stare.

"Then what, Raine? Talk to me."

She shook her head and looked away. "Congratulations."

"That's not what I—"

A tap on the restroom door interrupted her. "Bailey? It's me. Are you in there?"

"I'm here, Logan," she said. "With Raine."

He poked his head in. "Are you all right?"

"I'm fine. Just . . . sick to my stomach."

He looked at Raine. "Could you give us a minute?"

She shrugged and stood. "Sure . . . Daddy."

When she'd exited, he came to sit beside her. He gathered her hand in his. "You told her about the baby?"

"She asked why I was throwing up all the time."

"She would." He paused. "I'm glad she knows now."

"She didn't seem all that happy."

"That doesn't surprise me." He angled to fully face her. "I don't want to talk about Raine."

"No?"

"I'm sorry, Bailey," he said. "I've been wrong about everything. How I—I brought you unprepared into this soap opera. How could I expect you to just sit back and act as if everything was fine? It's not fine. It hasn't been in a long time."

"I don't understand."

"There are things . . . I haven't shared. Thoughts and—"

"As long as I have you, everything is fine."

"No." He tightened his fingers on hers. "We have to talk. Everything on the table, Bailey. Everything."

She searched his gaze, suddenly chilled. "What is it, Logan?"

"Not here. Home. Just you and me."

"I love you so much, Logan."

"And I love you."

He kissed her. Raine chose that moment to open the door and peek inside. "You'd better get out here, Logan."

"What's wrong?"

"It's Billy Ray and some sheriff's deputies."

He frowned. "What about them?"

"They're looking for you."

Bailey went cold. He stood to head for the door; she grabbed his hand, stopping him. "Don't go out there. Please."

"Do you believe in me?"

"I do."

"Then have faith. It's going to be okay."

She couldn't return the smile. This moment felt different. Felt coordinated, timed to inflict the most discomfort.

Logan exited the restroom. Bailey followed. Her knees went weak at the sight of Billy Ray and the deputies. At Billy Ray's smug expression. It seemed to shout, "Gotcha!"

Rumsfeld, the sheriff's detective she recognized from the other day, approached Logan. "Logan William Abbott?"

"Yes. What's this about—"

The viewing room doors opened and the pallbearers emerged with the casket, followed by Stephanie, Paul and August. They all looked their way; Stephanie stumbled and Paul steadied her. The townspeople of Wholesome began spilling out behind them, the stunned silence deafening.

"I have a warrant for your arrest."

"On what charges?"

"The abduction of Dixie Jenkins."

"No!" The word slipped involuntarily past Bailey's lips.

Rumsfeld nodded to Billy Ray, who stepped forward with handcuffs.

Logan glanced at her, then back at Billy Ray. "C'mon, Billy Ray. You can't really think cuffs are—"

"Turn around, Abbott."

"—necessary. Seriously?"

"Seriously," he said, yanking one arm behind his back and snapping on the cuff. "You have the right to remain silent." He grabbed Logan's other arm and wrenched it back. "Anything you say can and will be held against you in a court of law—"

He snapped the cuff closed. "You have the right to—"

"You son of a bitch!" Raine pushed past Bailey and lunged at Billy Ray. "This is a lie!"

The two deputies grabbed her and held her back. She fought them, kicking and thrashing. "How can you do this! It's a lie! A lie!"

Billy Ray went on as the deputies escorted her outside, unaffected by her outburst, completing his Miranda recitation. "Do you understand these rights as I have relayed them to you?"

Logan said he did and Billy Ray jerked him forward, with what seemed like all of Wholesome watching. Bailey hurried after them, tears streaming down her cheeks.

"Wait!" she cried. "What do I . . . I don't know what to do!"

"Call my lawyer," Logan said. "Terry King. Tell him what happened."

Billy Ray shoved him into a sheriff's cruiser, then slammed the door. Moments later, Bailey watched it speed away, cherry lights and siren screaming.

CHAPTER FORTY-NINE

Wednesday, April 23
1:25 P.M.

The next few hours passed in a blur. As Logan had instructed, the moment she returned home Bailey called his lawyer. Terry King had explained that Logan would be taken to the parish jail, processed and booked in. He'd warned her that it could be hours before he had an opportunity to speak with him and that she should stay calm.

Easier said than done.

Both Paul and August had offered to stay with her. She had refused. Adamantly. Both had only agreed when she promised to call if she needed anything.

She'd worried their presence might make her feel worse, not better. She couldn't trust August not to say something snarky. And Paul, although staunch and reassuring, she feared would expect her to behave in a similarly stoic manner. She'd wanted to be able to sob, scream or stomp her feet, to throw herself across the bed and howl, or curl up in a ball of silent misery.

All of which she had done since they left. She felt as if her heart had been ripped from her chest.

As if sensing her distress, Tony laid his head across her lap and whimpered. She bent and buried her face in his furry neck.

"What're we going to do?" she whispered. "He didn't do it, Tony. I know he didn't."

Tony responded by licking her hand. She shut her eyes, tears squeezing from the corners.

For all the agonizing over the past weeks and months, over the whispers of others and unanswered questions, over the coincidental and inexplicable, she knew in her heart that Logan had not done this. He couldn't have, not the man she loved.

Ironic that just moments before he had been arrested they'd promised to trust each other. To start anew. To believe in each other and their love.

She straightened, wiped the tears from her cheeks. Wasn't that the essence of faith? Belief beyond doubt? Absolute trust not in what could be examined in the physical world, but in what could only be felt by the heart?

So, had she meant it when she promised him? When she said she loved him?

Tony lifted his head, nose and ears twitching. He growled, low in his throat.

The kitchen door. Softly closing. Footsteps. Bailey's heart leaped with joy. Logan. They'd released him. He had been right, it was all going to be okay.

"Logan!" she cried, leaping to her feet and running that way. "Thank God! I was so afraid—"

She stopped cold. Not Logan.

Raine.

They stood gazing at each other for what seemed to Bailey like forever, but in truth couldn't have been more than a couple of moments. "How'd you get in?"

"I have a key."

Anger washed over Bailey in a white-hot wave. "Have you come to laugh at me?"

"No. God, no. Why would you say that?"

"Why wouldn't I?"

She looked stricken. "I love my brother. More than you can imagine. It's me I'm not so crazy about."

"Or me." Raine didn't comment, so she went on. "Why are you here, Raine? We're not friends. And you've made it more than clear you think I'm a naive fool and beneath your brother."

"Like I said, even I don't like me."

Bailey folded her arms across her chest. "Was it Paul or August who told you to check on me?"

"Neither. This fabulous idea was all mine."

"You'll be relieved to know, I'd rather be alone." She held out her hand. "I'll take the key, then you can run along."

"Sorry, can't do that."

"Please go."

"Sit. I'll make us a cup of tea."

"Raine—"

She cut her off. "I don't blame you for being angry with me. But now's not about what a jerk I've been. It's about Logan." Her voice softened. "This is where he'd want me to be. Making certain you and the baby are fine."

Bailey stared at her a moment, then burst into tears. She brought her hands to her face. "I'm so scared."

Raine held her while she cried, awkwardly patting her back. "I know. I am, too. But it's going to be all right."

When she'd finished crying, Raine led her to the keeping room couch, then instructed her to sit. She squatted in front of her and caught her hands. "Have you heard anything yet?"

"Nothing."

"Which doesn't mean anything. You called the lawyer?" She nodded; Raine went on. "He's very good, so no worries there. Do you know anything about how this process works?"

"No," she whispered.

"First off, arresting is one thing, charging is another. They have to have enough evidence to do that. Billy Ray doesn't make that decision. Neither does the sheriff's office. The district attorney's office does. If the state doesn't think they have enough to move forward, essentially to win the case, they have to release him."

"Really?"

"Yes. People get arrested all the time and aren't charged. If they can't charge him they have to let him go. And they don't have long to make up their minds. Like, seventy-two hours."

"Three days," she whispered, sniffling. "It sounds like forever."

Raine held out a box of tissues. Bailey grabbed several. "How do you know all this?"

"Dad," she said. "Or the person I thought was my dad. And True."

"Logan's been—" The words stuck in her throat. She cleared it, forced them out. "Arrested before?"

"No." She shook her head. "Questioned about True. It was so awful. So unfair. I—"

She bit the last back and stood. "I'll get us that tea."

"Tea?"

"Don't look at me like that. An alien isn't going to pop out of my stomach. Dammit, I'm trying to be a sensitive, caring sister-in-law. You're pregnant, so no alcohol. If you weren't, I'd be opening a second bottle already."

Impossibly, Bailey felt her lips curve into a smile. "My husband's been arrested and my sister-in-law's being nice to me. I've fallen into an alternate universe and can't get out."

Raine laughed. "Life is some screwed-up ride, isn't it?"

A carnival ride, Bailey thought. Spinning out of control. She hugged one of the throw pillows to her chest.

Raine's horrid painting, the one of True wearing red shoes, popped into her head.

That damn shoe. She wished she never found it.

Ask her about it, Bailey.

Raine returned with the tea. She set Bailey's cup on the coffee table in front of her. It smelled like oranges and spice, cinnamon and clove. A comforting combination. She didn't have the energy to reach for it.

She looked at Raine. "I have to ask you a question."

"Okay."

"Did True own a pair of red shoes?"

Raine almost choked on her sip of tea. "Wow, I didn't see that one coming."

"Did she?"

"I don't know. Why?"

"One of those paintings of her, in that room . . . she was wearing red shoes."

"An aesthetic decision. That's all." At Bailey's silence, she added, "That's the difference between realism and expressionism. My artistic choices are emotional ones."

Bailey drew her knees to her chest and rested her chin on them, thoughts racing. "Do you think Logan killed True?"

Raine looked shocked. "No! Of course not. He loved her."

"Love and murder go hand in hand." She blinked against tears. "Isn't that what they say?"

"Logan did not kill True. Despite the heartless monster Billy Ray and others like to make him out to be, he's anything but. He's gentle and kind. He couldn't hurt a flea, let alone another human being."

Bailey's tears spilled over and she pressed her face into the pillow.

Raine came over and tried to comfort her. "Hey, it's okay. I didn't mean to make you cry again."

"I'm just so . . . happy." She looked at Raine, vision blurry with fresh tears. "Because that's the way I feel about him. But no one else . . . everyone else seems to think he's a cold-blooded killer."

"And they're all full of shit."

She laughed, a sound that was more whimper than amusement, then blew her nose. "How did everything get so screwed up?"

"You're asking *me* that?"

Bailey laughed again, then wiped her eyes with the clean tissue. "Thank you."

"For what?"

"Being here."

Raine was silent a moment, then looked back at Bailey. "There's something I need to tell you."

Bailey waited, though a part of her wanted to cover her ears. She didn't know if she could take any more bad news.

"I know Logan didn't kill True."

Her mouth went dry. She tried to swallow but couldn't. "How?" she managed, the word coming out choked.

"Because I know why she left Logan."

"I don't know if I can do this right now, Raine. I don't know if I can handle learning another thing Logan didn't share with me."

"He doesn't know this. Only I do. It's my secret." She brought her hands to her face. Bailey saw that they were shaking.

"My secret," she said again. "Mine and True's."

"Logan didn't know?"

"No. It's been eating me alive. I feel so . . . responsible." She sighed. "I got True, why Logan fell in love with her, why she fell in love with him. What drew them together. But not you."

"Wow. Thanks."

"No, not for the reason you're thinking. They were attracted to each other because of the darkness."

Raine swore and grabbed a Kleenex. Pressed it to her eyes. When she looked up, Bailey saw that her eyes were red. "I promised myself I wouldn't cry."

"I've been promising myself that a lot. You see how well it works."

Raine grimaced. "True and I became friends. Best friends. Her mother was crazy. A total schizo. Heard voices, the whole bit. In and out of hospitals."

"August told me she was bipolar."

"That was the story True told everyone. You know, one mental illness is so much more acceptable than another."

Bailey heard the sarcasm in her voice, but didn't comment.

Raine shredded the tissue. "True was terrified of passing the crazy on."

"I don't understand."

"She was pregnant, Bailey."

"Oh, my God."

"She'd lied to Logan. When they met. Told him she couldn't have children."

"But she didn't use protection?"

"An IUD."

Bailey digested that information. "She wasn't cheating on him."

"No."

"And the credit card charges to that hotel?"

"A doctor over there. Where no one knew her."

"And the money she withdrew?"

"To have the abortion."

Bailey laid a hand protectively on her own belly. "But ten thousand? That's a lot of money."

"I don't know, I can only guess. She had to pay cash for it. And afterward, she meant to have her tubes tied. And Logan would never know."

"But she must have known he'd see the withdrawal."

"No. It was her account. And if he somehow did, she was going to tell him she sent it to her mother."

So many lies. Bailey thought of her own; they turned her stomach. "What happened?"

"I drove her to have it done. The hotel room in Metairie is where she spent the night. She was bleeding. And despondent."

"When she left, why didn't you tell the police the truth? Why didn't you tell Logan?"

"Think about it. It would have made him look more guilty, not less."

"I don't understand."

"A husband finds out his wife aborted their baby, flies into a rage and—"

"Kills her." Bailey released a broken breath. "But to allow him to believe his wife was cheating hurt him so much."

"More than knowing she killed his baby?"

"You were afraid," Bailey said, suddenly understanding more of Raine's motivation. "That you'd lose Logan. That he would hate you for helping her."

Tears welled in Raine's eyes. "I've hated myself ever since, what would make him any different?"

"Didn't you try to talk to her? Convince her not to do it?"

"Of course I did!" She looked away, then back. "I begged her. Logan loved her. He would be so happy about the baby, he'd forgive her lie about being unable to conceive. Anything but . . . that."

"An abortion."

"Yes."

True hadn't been having an affair.

She'd had an abortion. But why leave?

Bailey asked Raine that question and her sister-in-law looked down at her lap, pieces of shredded tissue across it. "I always thought she was so scared he'd find out somehow, that she chickened out and ran away."

Bailey leaned forward. "That doesn't make any sense to me."

"Maybe she felt so guilty, she couldn't face him?"

Bailey shook her head. "None of this makes sense. Run off, like that? Like she'd become a victim, like the other women? Was she that mean?"

"True wasn't mean. She was fragile. Maybe she staged it that way so Logan wouldn't come looking for her? Or she didn't even make the connection, you know. Just left."

"Plus, she would've had to have help."

"What do you mean?"

"Her vehicle. They found it out by the old Miller place. The abandoned barn, middle of nowhere. She couldn't have just walked away."

"I'm thinking she called a friend from her past, arranged for them to pick her up. I know it's weird, but I knew her. Her state of mind was so fragile and she seemed lost and . . . scared."

A headache began at the base of Bailey's skull. She absently massaged the spot. "I think True's dead. Somebody killed her. You know it, too. In your heart."

"Not Logan," Raine whispered, voice cracking.

"No, not Logan. Someone else."

Henry. In a box.

A box.

"Then who?"

A small wooden box. Henry beaming at her. A gift. For her.

"Bailey? What's wrong?"

"At the funeral today, before I got sick . . ." She stopped, the image flooded her mind.

Henry lifting the lid, proudly showing her—

"Oh, my God." She looked at Raine but saw Henry instead.

CHAPTER FIFTY

The memory rushed over her, like the wind that had been whipping through her open SUV windows. Carrie Underwood on the radio, Bailey singing along. Dr. Saunders had confirmed what she had suspected—she and Logan were having a baby!

She couldn't wait to tell Logan. He would be as overjoyed as she was. This made all the worries and concerns of the past days seem small and insignificant.

Everything Logan had told her was the truth. The red shoe had ended up out at the pond for exactly the reason he said. Tony had gone back and retrieved his prize, of course he had. That's what dogs did. Dig up bones, then bury them again.

She couldn't wait to see his joy about the baby, to share hers. They were going to be parents.

Her fairy tale would have a happy ending.

Bailey turned onto Henry's gravel drive, then moments later drew to a stop in front of the cabin. She stepped out, slamming the car door behind her and lifting her face to the sun. It didn't get better than this.

Tony heard her and charged out of the brush, ears flapping, his giant grin giving him the look of a cartoon character. Or one of the creatures in a Dr. Seuss story. He threw himself against her legs, nearly knocking her over. After she'd caught her balance, she bent and petted him. "Happy boy," she said, scratching him behind the ears. "You look how I feel."

He panted and wagged, then turned and charged up the porch steps, barking excitedly to announce her arrival. Shaking her head at his antics, she followed at a more moderate pace, reaching the door just as Henry opened it. He broke into his strange, twisted smile. "Ms. True, you've come to see me."

He always said it in a way that expressed complete surprise and deep gratitude, as if it would never cross his mind that he deserved a friend.

"I have," she said. "And look what I brought you."

She retrieved the Baby Ruth bar from her purse and his eyes lit up. He took the candy bar and ripped away the wrapper. "Have something for you."

He said it around the chocolate and she smiled. "That's so sweet."

"Wait here."

He turned and hurried back inside, then returned a minute later with a wooden box. Beaming proudly, he held it out.

She took it. It was about the size of a man's shoe box, substantial and obviously handmade. The wood was handsome, though nicked up. A hasp held the hinged top closed.

"What is this?"

"For you." He smiled again.

She took a seat in one of the rockers, he sat in the other. "Did you make the box?"

He shook his head, reached across and tapped its bottom. She tipped it up. Initials burned into the bottom. And a date.

L.W.A. May 2, 1988

Logan's initials. She did the mental math and realized he would have been ten. She ran her fingers over the letters, imagining Logan as a boy, proudly "signing" his creation.

A perfect treasure chest for a ten-year-old boy.

Tears stung her eyes. "Thank you, Henry. I love it."

"Open it," he said with childlike eagerness.

Bailey lifted the lid. And caught her breath. The red shoe. Clean and dry and nestled in a kitchen towel.

After he'd walked her home, Henry must have gone back for it. A lump formed in her throat as she recalled the terrible things she had thought about Logan. Awful things.

"I got it for you."

"I see that." She cleared her throat. "Thank you, Henry."

He reached into the box. "Want to try it?"

She didn't, but he looked so hopeful, she couldn't bring herself to say no. She slipped off her mule and into the pump. It fit as if it had been made for her and gooseflesh ran up her leg.

The shoe of a dead woman.

She yanked her foot out, doing her best to hide her shudder.

"True's shoe," he said.

She looked at him. "What did you say?"

But he had already moved on. He reached into the box. "Look."

She frowned. He held up a silver bangle bracelet. Costume jewelry, one of those wide, shiny ones.

She lowered her gaze to the rest of the box's contents. A collection of trinkets. Not new, they looked as if Henry had found them on the ground. She reached in and sifted through them: A sparkly hair clip. An initial necklace, the fancy N hanging from a cheap, dollar-store chain. The bracelet. A tube of lipstick, the color a bold pink. An LSU key fob.

And finally, a girl's class ring. Covington High, class of 2010.

She stared at the ring, the weirdest sensation coming over her. Like that moment when the last of a combination lock's tumblers clicks into place, or when that one puzzle piece fits and you have it. The whole picture.

Bailey closed her fingers around the ring, struggling for calm. She knew what this box was, what the items represented. Even as she tried to talk herself out of it, horror ran over her in an icy wave.

A killer's souvenirs. His box of trophies.

"Bailey!"

Her vision cleared. Raine was staring at her, wide-eyed and worried. "Are you all right?" she asked.

Bailey blinked. "Yes."

"You completely went off grid. Just zoned out."

A killer's souvenirs.

L.W.A. May 2, 1988.

"You're doing it again."

"I remembered—" Bailey stopped. She had no clue how Raine would react if she told her. It could be ugly. The other woman could totally lose it, become violent even.

She needed to think. Take a moment to digest . . . figure it out.

How many objects had there been in that box?

Six. Plus the shoe.

"Talk to me, Bailey. What did you remember?"

True's shoe, he'd called it.

Was it? Could Henry have somehow known that? What had he seen and heard living out there, alone in the woods?

But he thought *she* was True; had found her digging the shoe out of the mud. Then retrieved it for her.

In his damaged mind, it had been *her* shoe.

"Bailey? You're scaring me."

What did she really know about the shoe or the box and its contents? Nothing. In that instant, Bailey decided. "I remembered I saw Henry the day he died. I visited with him."

"My God. He was fine? Nothing wrong or—"

"No, he was fine. He was . . . Henry. Sweet and happy to see—" Her throat closed over the words. "I miss him."

"And that's it?"

Bailey brought a hand to her head. "I don't feel so well."

"Are you going to be sick?"

"No. But I think . . . I need to lie down."

"I'll sit with you."

"No." The word came out more sharply than she intended, and Bailey softened her tone. "I want to be alone, Raine."

"Okay, but I'm not leaving. Tony and I will hang out down here."

Tough, sophisticated Raine suddenly looked like a scared little girl. Bailey squeezed her hand and started for the front of the house. She stopped in the kitchen doorway and looked back: Raine sat on the couch, Tony beside her, her arms around his neck.

In that moment, she realized that her sister-in-law had needed her company in a way Bailey didn't—and never would. Because she was strong. Stronger than she had ever given herself credit for.

Bailey armed herself with her newfound strength as she shut—and locked—the bedroom door behind her. She hurried to her nightstand where she kept a journal.

She uncapped the pen and flipped it open to the first clean page. She jotted:

Six items. All having belonged to a female.

Seven, if she counted the shoe.

No, Bailey decided. Not the shoe. Henry had included it, not the killer.

The killer. It could be anyone. Even Henry. He'd been in possession of the box. The shoe and other items. Wouldn't the police find that suspicious?

She knew better. Sweet, simple Henry was no killer.

Neither was Logan.

She drew in a deep calming breath and carefully noted the six items in the journal.

Hair clip.

Bracelet.

N insignia necklace.

Key fob.

High school ring. She closed her eyes on the last, working to recall every detail of the ring. *Covington High.* Covington, a big city compared to Wholesome, about twenty minutes due south. *Class of 2010.*

What about a name? Or initials? She searched her memory, then made a sound of frustration. If she had looked to see if the band had been engraved, she didn't remember. Yet, anyway.

She wrote: *"Engraved?"*

Bailey then turned her thoughts to the key fob. LSU. The state's flagship university. Boasted a top-ten SEC football team, the Tigers. Bailey hadn't lived in the area long, but it hadn't taken long to understand folks around here were pretty much Tiger-obsessed. Which meant that owning one of these fobs didn't necessarily mean the woman had been a student.

Although it could. Which left her pretty much nowhere.

Bailey tapped the pen on the journal page. What did she know of the women who had gone missing? She recalled that day at Faye's; the newspaper spread out on the table in front of her, headline shouting:

Second Woman Disappears from Wholesome

A brown-haired young woman. Abby something. No, that wasn't right. Amanda. Yes, Amanda LaPier.

She wrote the name down, then searched her memory for the other. It popped into her head. Trista Hook. Four years ago.

Now, Dixie Jenkins. The one Logan was accused of— She couldn't finish the thought and made note of both names.

Bailey studied her notes. Three missing women. Not counting True. Six items in the box. She frowned and wrote: *"Would a killer take more than one souvenir per victim?"*

Amanda, Trista and Dixie. No, not Dixie. She'd been abducted after Bailey's accident and Henry had given her the box *before*.

Bailey made a note and drew a line through the woman's name. That meant, excluding True, only two women had gone missing. Neither with the first initial *N*. Had either of them attended Louisiana State University in Baton Rouge? Bailey wrote a reminder to get online and find out.

Six items in the box. Six trophies.

But only two missing women.

It didn't make sense. Unless she was wrong about the box. Maybe, like the shoe, they were simply items Henry had collected over the years, cleaned up and stored in an old box he'd found in one of the barns or the garage.

They had nothing to do with the missing women or with Logan.

L.W.A. May 2, 1988.

But incredibly damning. If the police had the box, they would think the same thing she had. Of course they would.

Maybe they had. Maybe that was why Logan had been arrested?

She rubbed her arms, chilled. Billy Ray claimed Abbott Farm was where the bodies were buried.

Billy Ray. His display board. Not two women. Not even three or four.

With True, six? Or seven? More?

She pressed the heels of her hands to her head. Why couldn't she remember?

"Bailey?" Raine tapped on the door. "Your phone rang, so I answered for you. It's Logan's lawyer."

CHAPTER FIFTY-ONE

Wednesday, April 23
3:45 P.M.

Billy Ray stood back and let the sheriff's boys do their thing. They'd allowed him a place in viewing, which sat just fine with him. He supposed he could be pissed. It'd started out as his jurisdiction, his case. He'd made nailing Abbott his mission in life.

Precisely the reason he needed to step back. Watch and make notes from the distance of the viewing room. Abbott's lawyer, Terry King, was one of the best and Billy Ray hadn't made a secret about his agenda. Nothing skewed a jury faster than a claim of prejudicial law enforcement.

Billy Ray refocused on the video monitor. King had just arrived; the fun was about to begin. Abbott looked smaller in his jail jumpsuit, not so high-and-mighty. But if he was worried, he didn't show it.

Billy Ray smiled grimly. Before this was over, Abbott would sweat. And Billy Ray couldn't wait to see it.

In the interview room, Rumsfeld began. "Mr. Abbott, you've had adequate time to confer with your attorney?"

"I have."

The attorney stepped in. "My client has assured me you have the wrong man. The Saturday in question, he was nowhere near Wholesome or The Landing."

"Where were you, Mr. Abbott?"

"With my wife at Saint Tammany Hospital. She had a riding accident and was in a coma."

"When Detective Carlson and I questioned you yesterday at your home, you indicated you left the hospital for a short time."

"That's right."

"However, you weren't certain of the time."

"That's correct." He folded his hands on the table in front of him. Nary a tremor, Billy Ray noted.

"You said—" Rumsfeld glanced at his notes, although Billy Ray knew that was simply a ruse. The detective knew exactly the time Abbott claimed to have been out of the hospital. "—really late. Two, maybe three in the morning."

"I said I wasn't certain, but that it'd been very late. That's correct."

"Why, Mr. Abbott? It seems odd to me, to be so unaware of time."

"Have you spent much time in a hospital, Detective?"

"Thankfully, no."

"If you had, you wouldn't ask that question."

"I don't know about that, Abbott. You wear a watch, I see. A very nice one. You have a phone, I assume?" Abbott nodded and Rumsfeld continued. "And every patient room is equipped with a wall clock, for exactly that reason."

Abbott leveled him with an icy stare. "My wife had been in a coma for two and a half days. I'd hardly slept or eaten and was out of my mind with worry. Quite frankly, I wasn't watching the clock."

"And yet, you left the hospital."

"I felt like if I didn't, I was going to explode."

Yes, Billy Ray thought. Spoken like a true psychopath.

Rumsfeld jumped right on it. "Interesting choice of words. 'Explode.' Tension that was going to erupt."

Billy Ray noted that Abbott dropped his hands to his lap.

"I was afraid. For my wife. I needed a moment to center myself."

"A moment. Is that how long you were gone?"

"Of course not."

"How long?"

"I don't know. Again, I wasn't watching the clock."

"What were you doing, Mr. Abbott?"

He blinked, looked away. "Praying."

Billy Ray wanted to shout, "Bullshit!" but contented himself with thinking it.

Rumsfeld pretended to skim the notes again. When he looked back up at Abbott, his gaze was steely. "You weren't worried she would come to while you were gone?"

Abbott flinched slightly, expression stricken. "I did worry about that, yes."

"But you went anyway?"

"I told you, I felt like I had to. Like I was going to go crazy if I didn't."

"Explode, you said."

"You know what I meant. We've all been there at one point or another."

Rumsfeld cocked an eyebrow. "Have we?"

Deliberately aggravating him. Working his way toward that last nerve. Billy Ray smiled grimly. And they'd only just begun.

King stepped in. "Let's get on with it, Detective."

He nodded, then re-pinned Abbott with his gaze. "Would you be surprised to learn you were gone two hours?"

"That's not possible."

"We have time-stamped video of you leaving and reentering the hospital."

"Not possible," Abbott said again.

The attorney leaned over and whispered something in his ear, Abbott nodded. "But as I said twice now, I wasn't watching the clock."

"Two hours is a long time to pray."

"I don't know what to tell you."

Billy Ray snorted. He'd just bet he didn't. Because the truth would get his ass fried.

"Where did you go during that time?"

He pinched the bridge of his nose, then dropped his hand and looked up. "I don't know. I just drove. I was in a fog."

Rumsfeld's eyebrows shot up. "Let's see, you were about to explode, afraid you'd go crazy and in a fog. A man of many emotions."

Color flooded Abbott's face and Billy Ray silently congratulated the sheriff's detective. The man knew his stuff.

"My wife was in a coma. You try it and see how you feel."

"How is your wife, Mr. Abbott? She recover her memory yet?"

"No."

"It's ironic, it seems you're both suffering with amnesia."

"If you're so concerned about my whereabouts, check my cell phone records. Can't you all follow the pings, or something like that?"

"We have, Mr. Abbott. Your cell phone never left the hospital."

"Excuse me?"

"Your cell phone never left the hospital."

Abbott looked at his attorney. Rumsfeld went on. "I find it strange, that a man who professes to be out of his mind with worry over his wife, who hasn't left her bedside in days and wanted to be at her side when she awakened from her coma, would not only leave the hospital for two hours, but would also leave his cell phone behind. If your wife had awakened, how would the hospital have reached you?"

Abbott blanched. "I didn't realize I'd . . . I wasn't thinking clearly."

"Actually, I think you were thinking quite clearly."

"I don't know what you mean."

"You tried to cover your tracks by leaving your cell phone behind."

"That's crazy."

"You knew about our ability to trace your whereabouts tracking your cell pings, so you deliberately left it at the hospital."

Abbott shifted in his seat. *He had begun to sweat.* Billy Ray smiled. They had him. And he knew it.

King stepped in. "You're making an assumption you'll never prove in court. In fact, assumptions are all I've heard so far. If you plan to make this stick, I hope you have more than a concerned husband forgetting his cell phone or being confused about time and place."

"Oh, we do, Mr. King. And we will. I promise you that." He turned back to Abbott with a thin smile. "You own several vehicles, is that correct, Mr. Abbott?"

"It is."

"And which of your vehicles were you driving that night?"

"My pickup truck."

Rumsfeld flipped through his notes. "A black Ford F-150?"

"That's right."

Rumsfeld leaned forward, looking as delighted as Billy Ray felt. His gaze bored into Abbott's. "What would you say if we told you we have a witness who saw Dixie Jenkins getting into your truck that night?"

A desperation Billy Ray had waited all these years to see came into Abbott's eyes. He looked stricken and Billy Ray wanted to stand up and shout it from the rooftops.

It was Abbott's fault True was dead.

And finally, he would pay.

"I'd say that was impossible."

"You have my client's answer. He and I need some time alone."

"I'm sure you do, Mr. King. But don't plan on going anywhere. We have lots more to talk about."

CHAPTER FIFTY-TWO

In Billy Ray's opinion, attorney-client privilege was total bullshit. Just one of the many ways offenders like Abbott went free, time after time. Guilty was guilty. If someone knew that for certain, he should be forced to say so.

Of course, Billy Ray didn't make the laws, but he was forced to abide by them, so he'd played nice with the other detectives, reviewing the video and eating sandwiches all the while knowing Abbott was in the next room plotting with the lawyer on how he was going to wriggle free.

Not this time, Billy Ray promised.

A uniformed deputy tapped on the door. "They're ready."

Billy Ray's mouth went dry. This one was for all the marbles. "You have the information?"

Rumsfeld nodded, although something in his eyes got Billy Ray's back up. Like he felt sorry for him or something. This was his moment, the last thing he needed was anyone's pity.

"Good. Make it count."

He took a seat in front of the monitor, ignoring the feeling of the eyes of the room's other occupants on him. He sent them all a silent F.U. and hunkered down to watch. He didn't want to miss a thing.

Rumsfeld greeted the pair. "I trust you two had the chance to catch up?"

"Absolutely," the lawyer said.

"Good. Is there anything about your client's previous statement he'd like to amend?"

"Not a thing."

Billy Ray snorted. Of course there wasn't. This slippery fish wouldn't go down without a fight.

"We do have a question, however." Rumsfeld nodded and the detective continued. "You say a witness saw Ms. Jenkins getting into my client's truck."

"That's right. A black F-150."

"Did the witness actually lay eyes on Mr. Abbott?" As if knowing the detective wouldn't answer, King went on. "How about a license plate number?"

"No comment on that just yet."

"How many Ford trucks are registered in Saint Tammany Parish? Last I knew, round these parts Ford's the truck of choice. Now, you say it was an F-150 and that it was black, but it was dark and very late. Our eyes can play tricks on us, our minds fill in the blanks. But that, of course, has nothing to do with reality."

Billy Ray wanted to reach through the monitor and throttle the man. Rumsfeld, on the other hand, looked calm, collected and totally in control.

"Whatever you need to tell yourself."

"The night in question, Mr. Abbott was nowhere near The Landing. And that's just the fact."

"We believe a jury will see it differently."

"Wishful thinking, my friend. If that's all you've got, I suggest you release my client now and save yourself—"

Rumsfeld cut him off. "Not happening. Let's move on." He turned his attention to Abbott. "I want to pass a few names by you, Mr. Abbott. Do you remember a young woman named Nicole Grace?"

"Of course I do."

"How do you know her?"

"You're serious?"

"As a judge."

"Her mother worked for my family. She was around the farm a lot as a kid."

"And?"

"She was murdered."

"The case was never solved, was it?"

"Not to my knowledge."

"You two were friends."

"Hardly. She was more than a decade younger than me. I remember her being a sweet kid."

"She had a crush on you, didn't she?"

"What?" He looked at his lawyer. "No. Not that I know of anyway."

"Do you recall what you were doing the day of her murder?"

"I don't even remember what day that was, let alone what I was—"

"June fourteenth. Two thousand and five."

Abbott just stared blankly at him. After several moments, his lawyer leaned over and murmured in his ear. Abbott blinked and shook his head. "No clue."

Billy Ray watched and made notes as the interrogation went on. Questions about the summer Abbott and Trista Hook dated. How serious had it been? Why had they broken up? When was the last time he saw her?

"And what," Rumsfeld asked, "were you doing the night she disappeared?"

"I don't know."

Rumsfeld moved on to Amanda LaPier. "Yeah," Abbott responded, "I gave her a lift one time. She was hitching. Something I don't think is a smart thing to do—"

"Why not, Mr. Abbott?"

"Really?"

He looked at his lawyer, who stepped in. "This is bordering on laughable. Can we move on?"

"Do you have any idea how old she was?"

"None."

"Nineteen. She was nineteen at the time." He paused. "What did you talk about?"

"I don't remember."

"You asked her if she had a boyfriend. Do you remember that?"

Terry King jumped in. "He just said he didn't remember what they talked about. Move on."

"She went missing two years later. Interesting, isn't it?"

Abbott sighed. "I don't follow."

"Come on, Mr. Abbott, you're a smart man. You give a girl a ride—"

"And two years later, she goes missing." King closed his notebook. "This fishing expedition is over."

"Not quite. The night Ms. LaPier went missing, any recollection of your whereabouts?"

"That date?"

"February eighth, this year. Say about three A.M."

"At home in bed with my wife."

"And you're certain of that?"

"We haven't spent a night apart since we married, so yes, I'm certain of that."

"And she'll corroborate?"

"Of course."

Billy Ray narrowed his eyes. He'd hesitated, just a fraction of a second, but that pause, that moment of insecurity, had been there.

He saw the deputy on his right glance his way and realized he'd been talking to himself.

Screw him, Billy Ray thought. What did he know? He hadn't lived this.

Rumsfeld went on. "I want to pass a couple names by you. Ever heard the name Estelle Davis?"

"No. Never."

"Paula Caine?"

"Nope."

"Margaret Martin?"

"Again, never."

"And you'd stake your life on that?"

"Would you, Detective?" Abbott rubbed his forehead, suddenly looking exhausted. "I'll put it this way: To my knowledge, I've never heard of any of those women."

"Nor have I," Terry King said. "What do these women have to do with Dixie Jenkins?"

"That's all for now." Rumsfeld stood. "If you'd like a few minutes with your client—"

"I would."

"A deputy will be posted outside. When you're finished, he'll escort Mr. Abbott back to his cell."

CHAPTER FIFTY-THREE

Wednesday, April 23
7:25 P.M.

Stephanie turned off Hay Hollow Road and onto the gravel drive that led to Henry's cabin. One last, private good-bye. Before she cleaned the place out and packed Henry's things up. To sit by herself and remember the fun they'd had. And what an important person he had been in her life. Before the accident. And after.

She thought of the day he had been trampled. Her dad had forced her to visit him in the hospital. She remembered being so frightened, she'd been unable to look at him. Logan's mother had been there, sitting beside the bed.

She had motioned Stephanie to her side. "Your uncle's a beautiful person," she'd said. "That kind of beauty comes from the inside, not the outside. I still see it. Don't you?"

Stephanie remembered taking a peek at him. His mangled face, the bandages and tubes and something coming over her. An awareness of what Elisabeth Abbott meant. Of the beauty that was her uncle Henry.

She'd never been afraid of him again. And even after it'd become clear that the worst, most permanent damage had occurred to his brain, she had seen that beauty.

All the best had been left. Kindness, childlike acceptance. She'd never seen him get angry or frustrated. He'd always been grateful, even for the small things. Truth was, he hadn't differentiated that way. He'd lost that kind of measuring stick, one that led to dissatisfaction and unhappiness. She wondered if he'd ever had it.

Stephanie flipped on her headlights. The funeral hadn't offered her the chance for reflection. No, it had been an opportunity for everyone else to say good-bye and to share *their* memories of him.

Until Billy Ray had turned what had been beautiful into a circus sideshow.

Just thinking of it caused her blood pressure to rise. She'd been furious with him, she still was. She was hurt.

He cared so little for her. So little for Henry.

It had always been about Billy Ray's agenda.

She released a breath she hadn't realized she'd been holding. She'd heard it said that the line between love and hate was razor thin. This morning it had become a chasm. She would never love Billy Ray again.

Henry's cabin came into view. With a sinking heart, she saw that her desire for privacy had been wishful thinking. Billy Ray, back to her as he set something in the cruiser's trunk. Hearing the crunch of her tires on the gravel, he slammed the trunk and turned to face her.

The silly, self-satisfied smile on his face was the last straw. The fury she had swallowed all day came roaring back. White-hot. Using her uncle's funeral as a way to stick it to Logan. As a way to embarrass him and his family as much, and as deeply, as he could.

For not loving her. For breaking her heart.

It was all she could do not to hit the gas and pin him between her vehicle and his. Instead, she drew to a careful stop and cut the engine. He crossed to the car and opened the door for her. As if nothing had happened.

"Hey Steph. What're you doing—"

"You son of a bitch!" She lunged at him, knocking him backward. She followed, flailing at him. One fist caught the side of his neck. Another his chest, then shoulder. "How dare you!"

"Whoa! Steph . . . What the—"

He caught her hands, so she kicked him instead. "How could you pull that stunt? Uncle Henry was the sweetest man. . . . He couldn't hurt a flea and you show up to his funeral and do *that*?"

"Just listen! Let me—"

"No! I'll never listen to you again! I'll never—"

He dragged her against him, pinning her to his chest, holding her so tightly she couldn't fight. Still, she tried until both the energy and will had drained out of her.

She broke down and he loosened his hold while she cried and clung to him. "How could you? How could you . . . do . . . that?"

"It wasn't my decision, Steph. It was theirs, the sheriff's detectives."

"I don't believe you."

"It's true. I'm just assisting them."

"And you couldn't talk them out of arresting him at Henry's funeral? He wasn't going anywhere!"

"Abbott's got friends at the sheriff's office. Someone who has fed him information before. They were afraid someone would tip him and he'd flee."

"Flee?" Stephanie stepped away from him, her legs wobbly. "And go where? This is his home."

Billy Ray shook his head. "People with means can make a new home anywhere."

In that moment, she realized that Billy Ray—who had lived here in Wholesome all his life—didn't know the real meaning of home.

Thank God he hadn't loved her. Thank God she'd let him go.

As if sensing a change in her, he frowned. "Logan's a bad guy, Stephanie. Worse than a bad guy. A killer. A serial killer."

She laughed. It slipped unbidden past her lips. "Seriously, Billy Ray? A serial killer? Logan Abbott?"

"This isn't only about True. Who do you think took Trista Hook, Amanda LaPier and now Dixie Jenkins? Who do you think killed Nicole Grace, all those years ago? Who knows, maybe he killed his mother, too."

"My God, you're serious."

"Damn right, I am."

"His dad was convicted of pushing her overboard."

"And who testified against him? That family, Steph, think about it. So much death. Too much to be a coincidence."

Logan's father and mother. His brother and wife. Now, Uncle Henry. "So, you've got him now."

"Yes."

"How? What do you have on him?"

"Enough." He hesitated. "A witness saw Dixie getting into his truck the night she disappeared."

Stephanie hadn't expected that. Something so . . . damning. "Oh, my God. Poor Bailey."

"No." He shook his head. "Bailey's lucky. She could've ended up like True. Or the others."

Stephanie couldn't wrap her mind around it. Logan, whom she had known all her life. Who had never been anything but kind to her.

What did she believe?

Not that. Maybe later, but not now.

"We'll have a search warrant for the property in the morning. All ninety acres."

"And your dreams will finally have come true."

"Don't be that way."

"And what way is that? Honest?"

"The bodies are here, Steph. You'll see."

She passed a hand over her face, suddenly exhausted. "What are you doing out here, Billy Ray?"

"Pardon?"

"Why are you here? At Henry's place?"

He slipped his hands into his pockets. "To take down the crime scene tape."

"I thought the sheriff's office put it up?"

"I offered to take it down. Scene was cleared. Days ago."

"And you've done that?"

"Yes."

"Then I want you to go."

"Steph—"

"I came out here to be alone with my memories of Uncle Henry. I won't allow you to take that away from me."

He had already taken so much.

His face puckered with regret. "Sure. Sorry, I—I hope we can be friends."

"Friends? You're not serious?" She laughed at his earnest expression, the sound hard. "No, we can't be friends. Not ever."

"At least now . . . I hope you see. That you understand."

"Understand what, Billy Ray? That you never loved me? I got that a long time ago."

"I did love you. Just not—"

"The way you loved True."

"Enough," he finished. "But it was still real."

He reached out a hand; she jerked away and he dropped it. "Please leave."

He complied, walking to his vehicle, opening the door.

"I just want you to understand why I couldn't let this go. I knew I was right, Steph."

He drove off and she headed into the cabin. It took all her energy to keep moving. To not give in to exhaustion and grief. Henry wouldn't have. He didn't when Elisabeth Abbott drowned or when Roane hung himself. And she wouldn't now.

Stephanie switched on the table lamp. A circle of warm light fell over the living room and she crossed to Henry's favorite chair, a battered recliner, and sank into it.

It smelled of him. She burrowed deeper into it and pulled his afghan over her. It, too, smelled of him.

The cabin had been Henry's for life, now it reverted back to the Abbott family. Some folks might've been pissed about that; she got it. This was Abbott family land, a piece offered to her uncle out of goodwill mixed with guilt.

She didn't want it anyway.

She moved her gaze over the room. Things never changed here. Just became more worn. The same old afghan and throw pillows, the same photographs, all arranged in exactly the same way. His simple mind had seemed to find comfort in the familiar.

Stephanie's gaze landed on some photographs on the mantel and she frowned. One was missing. As long as she could remember, it had sat in the very same spot. True, standing on Henry's front porch, smiling at the camera.

She stood and crossed to the mantel. Her imagination wasn't playing tricks on her; the photograph was gone. Recently, judging by the frame's silhouette left in the dust.

Billy Ray. That's why he'd been here. The lying son of a bitch, he'd had no right.

What else had he taken? She spun away from the mantel and made her way through the three-room cabin.

Another photograph had been lifted, but more troubling, the closet door stood open. She crossed to it, took a quick inventory, then shut the door. She turned. Her gaze landed on the dresser. Several of the drawers hadn't been pushed all the way in. She strode over, pulled one after another out. They had been rummaged through.

What had he been looking for?

She closed the drawers and returned to the living room. Maybe she was losing it. Imagining it all? Any one of the Abbotts could have been through, maybe even the sheriff's office had conducted a search.

But the missing photos of True had Billy Ray written all over them.

She brought the heels of her hands to her eyes. When she drove up, he'd been slamming the trunk. He'd put something in it. A couple of framed photos? Crime scene tape? Or something more?

She dropped her hands, any thought of reliving fond memories long gone. Frustrated, she turned off the lamp and headed out into the evening, careful to lock the door behind her. She didn't know if Billy Ray had been up to something, telling the truth or lying, and she didn't care. His craziness was no longer part of her life.

But as she drove away, she couldn't help but wonder what Billy Ray—or someone else—had been searching for.

CHAPTER FIFTY-FOUR

Bailey sat at the kitchen table. She'd fixed herself a bowl of chicken soup. The last thing she felt like doing was eating, but she had to. For the baby's health. And her own.

She brought a spoonful of soup to her mouth, then another and another. Forcing herself. She'd spoken to the lawyer three times. The first, he'd simply been reporting in. He'd arrived at the parish jail and had spoken with Logan, who he said was doing as well as could be expected. The second had been troubling. They had a witness who claimed that, early Saturday morning, during the time Logan had left the hospital, he had seen Dixie Jenkins climb into a black Ford F-150 truck.

It'd made her sick to her stomach, that they could even think he would leave her side to go do . . . that.

The third had been illuminating. The lawyer shared that the detectives had grilled Logan about True and the other missing women. About where he had been and what he had been doing, all those years ago when they'd disappeared. If he had known them. Surprisingly, Billy Ray had not been one of the interrogating officers.

Bailey got what they were up to. They figured they had an ironclad connection to Dixie Jenkins, now they were going for a link to the other women.

Terry King hadn't been impressed with their "evidence." It wouldn't hold up, he'd promised her. If they had nothing else, her husband might even be coming home.

If they had nothing else. She had the feeling they did. And she knew what it was.

The box of trophies.

Bailey finished her soup and carried the bowl to the sink. She hadn't mentioned the box or its contents to the lawyer. Not yet. She wanted to make certain of something first.

She pictured the cabin, the crime tape stretched across its front. The police would have searched the place. If they had, they would have found the box.

With Logan's initials burned into it. Damning him.

Bailey wiped her palms on her thighs. Worthless items Henry had found in his travels. Treasures to him. That he'd offered to her.

She closed her eyes. *Please, God, let it be so.*

"I can't believe you're so calm."

Raine. Standing in the doorway. After the second call, Raine had opened a bottle of wine and retreated with it and a glass up to her old bedroom.

From what Bailey could see, there was still wine in the bottle. A good sign.

"Me either," she said.

Raine walked into the kitchen. "I heard the phone ring."

"Terry King. Again."

"And?"

"Not good. They grilled him about True and the other women."

"What other women?"

"The ones who went missing."

"What the hell for?"

Bailey looked at her. "What do you think?"

"I swear to God, I'm gonna—" She bit back what she was about to say. "This is Billy Ray's doing."

"I agree. I think we should do something."

"What?"

"I need to go out to Henry's."

"Now?"

"Yes."

"You're looking for something."

It wasn't a question, but she answered anyway. "Yes."

Raine swept her gaze suspiciously over her. "What?"

"I'll tell you if I find it."

"That makes no sense." She narrowed her eyes. "This has to do with what you remembered earlier. When you said you talked to Henry the day he died."

"It does."

"And whatever it is could help my brother."

"Or hurt him." She paused. "Or mean nothing at all."

She thought a moment, then nodded. "Totally ambiguous and clearly messed up, just the way I like it. But you're driving."

Bailey agreed but drove slowly, carefully navigating the unfamiliar roads. She'd never driven to the cabin at night, and the winding gravel drive could be particularly tricky.

Raine grew more and more quiet as they neared the cabin. Once inside, she fell apart. She wandered from room to room, touching things, and ended up in Henry's armchair, knees to chest and staring blankly ahead.

Bailey didn't have time to console or coddle her. She, too, went from room to room, but meticulously searching. Under the bed and through the closets. Not a perfunctory glance, but thoroughly checking every corner or crawl space.

Forty-five minutes later, Bailey gave up. She walked out to the porch and sank onto one of the rockers. The box wasn't here. She had checked everywhere, even the tool-shed out back. She dropped her head into her hands. The law had it, whether Billy Ray or the sheriff's office didn't matter. They had it and would use it against Logan.

He was innocent. After all the back-and-forth and agonizing doubt, she knew—to the very core of her being—that her husband was as much a victim in this as anyone.

All it had taken was his being arrested for her to realize this. It didn't get more ironic than that.

Raine came out and sat beside her. "I take it you didn't find what you were looking for."

Bailey dropped her hands and looked at the other woman. "No, I didn't."

"What does that mean?"

"I think the sheriff's office has it. And are going to use it against Logan."

"What do we do now?"

"I don't know." Her cell phone went off. "August," she muttered, and silenced the phone.

"You're not going to take it?"

"I'm sure he's calling to check on me and find out what I've heard and frankly, I don't have the energy right now."

Raine sighed. "There was a time I thought he would save me."

"From what?"

"Myself. My life."

Her phone pinged the arrival of a voice mail. "You've got to fix you first, Raine," she said gently. "Nobody can do that for you."

"Spoken like somebody who has their act together. Sickening."

Bailey thought of the intellectual and emotional acro-batics she'd been performing the past week. "Not so much. It's just a lot easier to tell other people how to get their acts together than to do it yourself."

"You gonna listen to that message?"

"Do I have to?"

She'd only been half kidding. Raine knew it and pressed her. "What if he heard something? In this little burg, August knows pretty much everybody and their everything. You never know."

Bailey sighed and accessed the message. For a moment, she thought he hadn't left one, then she heard his voice.

"Need . . . talk . . . you. Something import . . . Sorry, so . . ." His words drifted off into a silence broken by slow, labored breathing. "Henr . . . I saw—"

The message ended.

"What's wrong?"

"I don't know, August sounded— You listen."

Raine did, expression growing alarmed. "He's totally out of it," she said.

"Drunk?"

"Maybe, but . . . maybe something else. He's a recovering addict and has been to some pretty dark places. Which is why we got along so well. Kindred spirits."

The blood began to thrum in her head. "Dial him back."

Raine did; Bailey could faintly hear the signal. "He's not answering!"

"Maybe we should call 9-1-1?"

"No! It's probably nothing and this is such a small town—"

"Do you know where he lives?"

"Of course."

Bailey stood. "Call Paul. Make certain August's not at the farm, then tell him what's going on and that we're on our way to check on him. Then try August again."

CHAPTER FIFTY-FIVE

Wednesday, April 23
11:25 P.M.

August rented the guesthouse of a neighboring horse farm. Raine directed Bailey to the property's delivery entrance, which curled around a pond and led to the tiny glass and cypress structure.

Even with the wall of windows, he would have complete privacy, Bailey thought as she braked behind his SUV. And a beautiful view of the pond and rolling pastures.

She and Raine leaped out and ran for the door. It was open and they burst inside.

"August!" they called simultaneously. "It's Bailey!"

"And Raine!"

He didn't reply and Raine ran through the living area to the circular stairs that led to the loft. "August, I'm coming up!"

The metal stairs creaked as she raced up them. "He's not up here!"

The back porch. That faced the pond. What looked like a figure in a chair.

"He's outside, Raine. I see him!" She ran to the sliding glass door and slid it open. At the same moment she cleared the door, the back light snapped on.

"August, you scared the life out—"

She stopped. He sat slumped in a chair, head cocked back at an unnatural angle, eyes rolled back in his head. The color had drained from his face, leaving it pasty white, his lips blue. A thin line of drying blood ran from his nose to his upper lip.

Bailey took a step back. She'd seen her mother dead. Had held her hand as she'd taken her last breath, refused to leave her side until her hand had grown cold and stiff.

It had been heartbreaking. But this was different. Unnatural and horrifying.

She shifted her gaze. A vial and syringe lay on the patio at his feet. A belt, half across his lap, hanging over the side of the chair.

At a sound behind her, she spun around.

Raine. A shotgun in her hands.

A gunshot, exploding in the quiet.

Blood. On her hands. Her jeans.

Bailey blinked and her vision cleared. "What are you doing with that, Raine?"

She looked down at her hands, then back up at Bailey. "I think he meant to—" She frowned, took a step forward, then stopped, blood draining from her face.

Bailey held a hand out. "I'm so sorry, Raine."

For a long moment, Raine simply stared at him, then she turned expressionless eyes on Bailey. "Maybe I should join him?"

"No." She shook her head. "Raine—"

"Maybe it's all my fault. Like a curse. So if I die, everyone else lives."

"Put down the gun." Bailey held out a hand. "Please."

"I know how to use this. I'm a pretty good shot. Better than Logan. Or Roane."

Her voice shook. "I don't think I want to live. Not with all this death."

"Don't say that, Raine. Logan needs—"

Bailey caught a movement inside the house. In the next instant Paul appeared at the sliding glass door behind Raine. He held a finger to his lips and slipped through the door.

"He needs you. So do I."

In the next instant, Paul plucked the gun from Raine's hands and drew her into his arms. She began to weep.

"Take this," he said, indicating the weapon. "And call 9-1-1."

The ambulance arrived first, followed by Billy Ray. Bailey couldn't bring herself to look at him. She was so angry, she shook.

He had won. He had Logan in custody and even more tragedy had befallen this family.

The paramedics left as quickly as they had come. Once they cleared the scene, Billy Ray went straight to Paul. "What happened?"

"August called Bailey. He sounded strange, so they called me. We came to check on him. Obviously, we were too late." The sound of Raine's sobs increased. "Excuse me, I'm going to take her inside."

Billy Ray turned to her. This time, Bailey stiffened her spine and met his gaze. "I'm not talking to you."

"Don't be angry at me. I'm just doing my job."

She laughed, the sound low and furious. "No you're not. This is your personal vendetta. This whole family is."

"You're upset, I get that. But—"

"There's no 'but' to this situation, Billy Ray. There never will be."

For a moment, it seemed as if he wanted to argue, but he didn't. "Tell me what happened."

"I'm not talking to you."

"You have to, I'm the law."

"You're not the law. You're a bully, Billy Ray. A bully with a badge."

She expected him to threaten her, to do what he did best—throw his weight around, intimidate.

Instead, he seemed to freeze. He stood for long moments, his gaze on hers, then nodded. "Fine. Make yourself comfortable inside with Paul and Raine."

CHAPTER FIFTY-SIX

Thursday, April 24
1:10 A.M.

Billy Ray waited in the guesthouse doorway, Bailey Abbott's voice resounding in his head.

"You're nothing but a bully, Billy Ray. A bully with a badge."

He shook his head, trying to force it out. No. His father had been a bully. Abbott was a bully. Not him. He had spent his life making certain that he didn't become what he most loathed.

Billy Ray started to sweat. He felt it on his upper lip and he wiped it away, then tugged on his collar. He couldn't breathe. Couldn't think clearly. He opened the door and stepped outside. The cool, early morning air struck his damp skin and he shuddered. It rippled over him and he sucked in a shaky breath. Better. Cooler. In control of himself and his thoughts.

Rumsfeld and Carlson rolled up. Another STPSO cruiser behind them. He forced an easy smile and put one foot in front of the other to meet them at their vehicle.

"Sorry about the timing," he said. "Considering the circumstances, I figured you two should be the ones to do this."

"Timing's a bitch, but good call. What do we have?"

"O.D. August Perez, one of Abbott's trainers."

"Interesting. In terms of timing."

"That's what I thought. Abbott's wife, sister and his stable manager found him."

Rumsfeld frowned and looked at Carlson. "A curious assortment. How'd that come about?"

"Apparently, Perez left Abbott's wife a weird-sounding message. They came to check on him. That's all I know. Vic's on the back deck."

Rumsfeld nodded and looked at the assisting deputy. "Babysit the witnesses while we check out the vic. Nobody leaves until we've questioned all three."

The deputy headed into the house and they circled around back. They reached the deck and the safety light snapped on. Rumsfeld crossed to stand in front of the victim.

"Yup. He's dead."

"No wonder," Carlson said, squatting down to get a look at the vial. "Ketamine."

Billy Ray whistled. "We've had some recent break-ins at vet clinics. Drugs stolen, including ket. I wouldn't have taken Perez for being that dumb."

"We're gonna need the techs."

"I got it," Carlson said, dialing.

While he called, Rumsfeld turned in a slow circle. Billy Ray had the sense that he missed nothing, not even a speck. It made him feel small town.

"Private back here," he murmured.

Rumsfeld grunted.

"What're you thinking? Accidental or—"

"What the hell?"

Billy Ray turned to Rumsfeld striding toward the windows. And then he saw it. A rifle. Propped against the window. He'd missed that, first go-around. Rookie move. The worst.

Rumsfeld looked at him. "Son of a bitch, Williams. They could've blown our heads off."

Heat climbed Billy Ray's cheeks. "They didn't." It sounded lame, even to his own ears, and he felt like a fool.

"Techs are on their way," Carlson said. He crossed to stand beside his partner. "Big miss, Williams. Sucker's loaded."

"I messed up. Won't happen again."

Rumsfeld examined the gun. "A Remington 700. Shoots a .308, among others."

"Rodriquez was shot with a .308."

"And Perez worked at Abbott Farm."

Rumsfeld nodded. "I think it's time to have a little chat with our friends inside." Rumsfeld looked at him. "You want to take notes?"

"Hell, yes. I say we start with Abbott's wife. She's the one Perez called."

But Rumsfeld disagreed and interviewed the other two first. Raine Abbott was distraught to the point of unintelligible. They did manage to learn that Perez had drug issues in the past, but as far as she knew he hadn't used in a long time. They also discovered she'd found the rifle on his bed and she'd brought it down.

Paul Banner had even less information. Raine and Bailey had called him. When he'd arrived the women had been on the back deck and Raine had been hysterical.

Which left Bailey.

"Are you feeling all right?" Rumsfeld asked. "Need a glass of water or—"

"No. I'm okay."

But Billy Ray saw that she wasn't. Her hands were shaking and she was white as a sheet.

Obviously, Rumsfeld saw it, too. "You don't look so good, Mrs. Abbott."

"All right then, a glass of water please."

Billy Ray set it in front of her. She took it but didn't acknowledge him, even with a glance.

"I need to ask you some questions, Mrs. Abbott. About the sequence of events that led you to be here. Your answers will help determine Mr. Perez's manner of death."

She frowned. "But I . . . it looked like a drug overdose."

"That's the way it appears, yes. But 'manner of death' refers to how the coroner's office will classify his death. Was it an accident? Suicide? Or even murder?"

Her eyes widened as if the thought of the last had never crossed her mind. Billy Ray noted it.

"I understand he called you?" Rumsfeld said.

"He called me. I didn't pick up."

"Why not?"

"I didn't feel up to it. I was sure he was just checking on me and—"

"What?"

"August could be . . . difficult. He left a message."

"How long passed before you checked it?"

"Not long. Five minutes. Less, even. Raine urged me to."

"Raine Abbott?" She nodded and he went on. "So she was with you?"

"Yes. Keeping me company because my husband . . ." Her voice trailed off.

Was in custody.

"Why did she urge you to check it?"

"She thought he might have some information."

"About?"

She met his eyes, the expression in hers defiant. "My husband. August was well-connected in the community."

"On the message, what did Mr. Perez say?"

"Not much. He sounded . . . out of it. He couldn't seem to form his thoughts. I had Raine listen to it and she was . . . alarmed."

"Think, Mrs. Abbott, can you recall anything he said?"

"That he was sorry. He mentioned Henry—"

"Rodriquez."

"Yes."

"What did he say about Mr. Rodriquez?"

She hugged herself, rubbed her arms. "I don't remember . . . just that he said his name."

"Is the message still on your phone?"

"Yes."

"May we listen to it?"

She retrieved the message and handed the device over. Rumsfeld and Carlson both listened several times, then handed it to Billy Ray.

"Need . . . talk . . . you. Something import . . . Sorry, so . . . Henr . . . I saw—"

Billy Ray frowned and listened again. An apology? For what? Henry? Or something else he'd known but hadn't shared with her?

"Did you have any idea Mr. Perez was shooting up ketamine?"

"I don't even know what that is."

"It's a horse tranquilizer. Affects the central nervous system. You may have heard of it called K, Special-K or Vitamin K?"

"No, I'm not . . . drug savvy." She brought her hands to her face. "I had no idea he did . . . that." She dropped her hands. "Can I go now?"

"Just a couple of more questions. Did you know him well?"

She shook her head. "He was helping me overcome my fear of horses."

The evidence collection team arrived, as did the coroner's investigator. She watched them go past, her expression lost. A lump formed in Billy Ray's throat and he quickly averted his gaze.

"Thank you for your help, Mrs. Abbott. We may need to speak with you again, so please don't leave the area."

She nodded. "Could I have my phone, please?"

"I'm sorry, but we're going to have to keep it for now."

"What? But I—I don't understand."

"For Mr. Perez's call. It could prove to be evidence."

"Evidence?" Her voice rose. "Of what?"

"We'll get it back to you, I promise. In the meantime, you might consider acquiring another for temporary use."

CHAPTER FIFTY-SEVEN

The news that August Perez was dead of an overdose of ketamine had spread through Faye's like a California wildfire. It'd been all anyone talked about and as the hours of her shift passed Stephanie had grown more weary of it.

And sadder, as well. She hadn't known August very well, but he had been a brilliant horseman and a member of their little community.

More loss. Another friend gone. Not an event to salivate over, the way a dog did a juicy bone.

Several times she'd had to stop herself from reprimanding a particularly animated gossip. Faye would've been pissed. And she'd have been right. It wasn't her job to correct her customers' manners or reset their moral compasses.

Serve pancakes, deliver eggs and smile. That summed up her job.

It didn't help that she hadn't slept well and was to-the-bone tired. Faye had offered her the week off; like an idiot she'd refused. She'd laid Uncle Henry to rest, she'd wanted to move forward. That didn't happen by taking time off work, no matter how kind the offer.

However, she hadn't anticipated her little run-in with

Billy Ray. Something wasn't right about his having been there. She didn't buy his stated reason—taking down the crime scene tape—or his assertion that the sheriff's office detectives were the bad guys. Poor Billy Ray had to do what they said. What a crock.

When he'd talked about Logan she'd seen a kind of glee in his eyes. He loved this. He loved that finally his wild accusations were being taken seriously. A serial killer? Logan? And to blame him for his mother's death as well? The man had lost his grip on reality.

"Y'all come back," Stephanie said, delivering the check to her second-to-last table. She refilled coffee for the other, then started collecting sugar caddies from the tables to re-fill them in anticipation of the lunch rush.

Her thoughts returned to her encounter with Billy Ray the previous evening. He'd been inside Henry's cabin. She hadn't seen him, but she didn't need to. The missing pictures of True were all the evidence she needed. What else had he been looking for? She trusted him about as far as she could throw him.

Her last table stood to leave. She called out thanks, collected her tip and cleared it.

"Faye, you mind if I take a break? I'm beat."

"You do that, sugar. Me and Rayanne got this."

Stephanie grabbed an apple, her phone and water bottle and headed outside. She saw she had missed a call from the sheriff's office. Detective Rumsfeld, asking her to call.

She took a bite of the apple and dialed him back. He answered immediately. "Rumsfeld."

"Detective, this is Stephanie Rodriquez, returning your call."

"Ms. Rodriquez, I have some good news. We have a strong suspect in your uncle's murder."

"Oh, my God, who is it?"

"I'm sorry I'm unable to tell you that yet. But I anticipate it won't be long."

"Thank you." She blinked against tears. "I can't tell you how much this means to me. Really."

"It means a lot to us, too, Ms. Rodriquez. I'll be in touch soon."

She thought of Billy Ray. "Wait! There's one more thing, I was wondering if it would be okay for me to remove the crime scene tape from my uncle's cabin?"

"We've taken care of that, Ms. Rodriquez."

"Are you certain? The last time I was there, it was still up."

"Let me just glance at my calendar." He returned a moment later. "Deputies removed it Tuesday afternoon."

More than twenty-four hours before she'd run into Billy Ray out there.

Stephanie thanked the detective and ended the call. She'd been right to be suspicious. Lying snake. He'd been putting something in his trunk when she drove up. What? More than a couple of framed photos of True. And not crime tape.

What could he have wanted from her uncle's so much that he had lied to her about it?

At the toot of a horn, Stephanie turned around. Bailey, turning into the parking lot.

Stephanie met her at her car and gave her a hug. "How're you holding up?"

"About as well as you'd expect."

"Have you . . . heard about August?"

"I was the one who found him. It was awful."

"Oh, my God."

"He'd called me—" She bit the last back. "I need your help, Steph. It has to do with Logan."

"What have you heard? Is it . . . bad?"

"It's not good. That's why I need your help."

"Name it."

"Remember that room at Billy Ray's house that you told me about, the one with the board and diagrams?"

"Sure."

"You were right about what it was."

"How do you know?"

"He showed it to me."

Stephanie frowned, obviously confused. "When? Why?"

"He thought seeing it would convince me that Logan killed True. And abducted Amanda LaPier and Trista Hook."

"But it didn't convince you?"

Bailey shook her head. "It actually had the opposite effect. It proved to me how personal it all is to Billy Ray. He . . . On the board he had other women's names, women I'd never heard of. He even suggested Logan might have had something to do with—"

"His mother's drowning."

"Yes. How did you know?"

"He said the same thing to me last night."

Tears flooded Bailey's eyes. "I'm so afraid."

Stephanie's heart went out to her. "It's bullshit, Bailey. I've known Logan all my life, and he didn't do what they're saying he did."

"I know." She stuffed her hands into her jacket pockets. "He couldn't."

"How can I help?"

"I need to get into Billy Ray's house. I need to look at the board again."

"Why?"

"I have questions I need answered."

"Why not just ask him?"

"I don't want him to know what I'm thinking. I don't want him to see how scared I am."

Stephanie understood. A guy like Billy Ray was dangerous when he knew he had the upper hand. As she knew from experience, he wouldn't hesitate to use it.

Stephanie glanced at her watch. Any minute Faye was going to bellow for her, so she would have to be quick.

"I have to tell you something. Last night, I went out to Henry's, I can't really explain why, but—"

"I know why, Steph."

Stephanie squeezed her hand in gratitude and went on. "Billy Ray was there. I caught him putting something in his trunk."

Bailey paled. "What?"

"He lied to me. He told me he'd taken down the crime scene tape. He seemed really weird, like he was up to something. So when I talked to the sheriff's detective right before you got here, I asked about it. He said his deputies had taken it down Tuesday afternoon."

"Why'd he lie?"

"I don't know, but when I went inside, I could tell he'd been looking for something."

"I think he found it, Steph."

"What?"

"Stephanie! For the love of God, girl, you taking a break? Or a vacation?"

"Sorry, Faye!" she called over her shoulder. "I'm coming!"

"Wait." Bailey caught her hand. "Will you help me?"

"If I can. I'll call you when I get home, after I've taken care of the horses. But we'll have to pick the exact, right moment to do it."

"We?"

Stephanie smiled. "You honestly think I'd let you go alone?"

CHAPTER FIFTY-EIGHT

Billy Ray entered the sheriff's office complex, juggling a coffee caddy and bag of pastries from Faye's. He nodded at the woman manning the information desk; she waved him through. Just like he belonged.

He whistled under his breath. He felt good. Better than he had in years. Too bad about Perez, but you mess with shit like K, and sometimes you paid the ultimate price.

He climbed the stairs. Today was the day. They expected the judge to grant the search warrant for Abbott Farm: house, garage, barns and all ninety-plus acres.

And there they would find all the proof they needed to put Abbott away for life.

Billy Ray entered the Investigation Division. Rumsfeld and Carlson were huddled in front of the computer monitor.

"Morning," Billy Ray said, setting the coffee and bag on Rumsfeld's desk.

Rumsfeld looked up. "It's almost noon, Williams."

"Rough night last night. Figured you might be ready for another round."

"Try round four. I'm caffeinated-out, man."

Carlson agreed but reached for the pastry bag and

peered inside. "But I can always eat." He selected a cheese Danish. "Thanks, man."

"Grab a chair," Rumsfeld said. "There've been developments."

Billy Ray did and waited, concentrating on playing it one hundred percent cool. Nothing could go wrong. Not now. Not when he was so close.

"We've got a ballistics match in the Rodriquez homicide."

"The 700 from the Perez scene."

"Yes."

"That's good news." Billy Ray moved his gaze between the two detectives. Something was up, something they hadn't shared yet. "Although I never would've figured fancy-pants Perez to own a rifle let alone be the shooter. But then shooting up Special-K didn't much seem his style, either."

"That's just it, Williams. We're not closing this one quite yet. We'd like another link between Perez and the gun."

Louisiana sported some of the most tolerant gun laws in the country, requiring neither registration nor permit to buy or carry a rifle or shotgun. "The weapon was in his possession."

"Say our witnesses. Mr. Perez wasn't in the position to confirm or deny."

"You don't trust them."

"Trust isn't part of the equation. It's my job to doubt everything."

"You think one, or all, of them planted it?"

"Could have. But why?"

Billy Ray shook his head, growing frustrated. "What about prints? That'd tie him to it."

"Interestingly, Perez's aren't on it."

"Not one?"

"Not a single one."

"Okay," Billy Ray said, "he wiped it after he killed Rodriquez."

"That's one theory."

"You have another?"

"He always does," Carlson said, wiping his mouth with a paper napkin. "It's all part of livin' the dream."

Rumsfeld sent him an annoyed glance. "Let's take this at face value. Perez was in possession of the gun used to kill Rodriquez. Witness said she found it on his bed. Bed made, gun lying across it."

"Right."

"Why?"

"I don't follow," Billy Ray said.

"Why wipe your prints from a weapon and leave it lying across your bed?"

"He meant to shoot himself with it. Or he wants us to find the gun, figure it out."

Rumsfeld cocked an eyebrow. "Again, why wipe it beforehand?"

He had a point, Billy Ray silently admitted. "So, maybe he plans to get rid of it, but decides to have himself a little party first and overdoses. Or he means to get himself good and relaxed and then shoot himself."

"An experienced drug abuser knows he shoots up, the last thing he's going to be able to do is pull the trigger. Which brings us back to the question of what really happened. Did Perez accidentally overdose? Or was it suicide?"

Billy Ray thought a moment. "I'm leaning toward accidental overdose."

"Why?"

"From what I knew of Perez," Billy Ray began, "he had a very favorable opinion of himself. Hard to see him ending it all. Plus, in my opinion, he wasn't the attack-of-conscience type of guy, and taking his own life and leaving the weapon he used to kill Rodriquez for us to find smacks of that. Finally, no note."

Carlson spoke up. "What about his call to Bailey Abbott? He's gonna confess, but she doesn't pick up. So he leaves a message apologizing and asking forgiveness. Even mentions Henry by name."

"That travels into the attack-of-conscience category. Not buyin' it."

Carlson shook his head. "He does it the same day his victim is buried and his friend Abbott is arrested. It all crashed down on him at once."

"But Abbott's arrested for Jenkins, not Rodriquez." Billy Ray's phone went off. "Excuse me a moment." He stepped out of the cubicle. "Williams."

"Billy Ray—Chief, it's Earl."

"I'm in a meeting, Officer Stroup."

"Travis Jenkins just called."

"And?"

"I don't . . . it's good news. He—"

"Spit it out, Stroup."

"He heard from Dixie. She's fine."

Billy Ray reached a hand out to steady himself. It felt as if his world was rocking. "No."

"She ran off and got hitched."

Billy Ray strode out to the hallway, away from prying eyes and ears. "Bullshit."

"He said it was her. She's in San Antonio."

"I don't believe it."

"Some guy she used to date. She—"

Billy Ray cut him off. "You tell Travis not to speak to anyone else about this."

"But Chief—"

"Until I have a visual on her myself, she's missing and Abbott stays in jail." *And the search warrant proceeded as planned.* "You hear me, Officer Stroup? Your job depends on this."

"Yessir."

Billy Ray ended the call. He took a deep breath and let it out real slow. Pulling himself together, wiping the emotion from his face, the panic from his eyes. He took another breath, released it the same way. Carlson might be a bit of a boob, but Rumsfeld missed little. He couldn't afford questions right now.

He had been here before. He'd managed it then, he would this time as well.

He ambled back into the Investigation Division. Rumsfeld looked up. "Everything okay, Williams?"

"Perfect," he said, smiling easily. "Everything's just . . . perfect."

CHAPTER FIFTY-NINE

Bailey glanced at her watch. Stephanie had called twenty minutes ago and said that she was on her way to pick her up. If she still wanted into Billy Ray's house, now was their moment. Bailey had used the time to pull her thoughts together. She'd stuffed a small notebook in her purse, made certain she had a pen and her cell phone, then filled Tony's bowl with water.

From outside came the toot of a car horn. The dog didn't look happy about her leaving, and she wagged her finger at him. "You be a good boy while I'm gone."

The truth was, she could leave him to roam the farm while she was away. He knew where he lived and the property was fenced, but she couldn't stand the thought of his not being here when she returned.

She slipped out the front door, locking it behind her, then hurried to Stephanie's truck. She climbed in.

"Ready?"

"As I'll ever be." Bailey fastened her safety belt. "What was the rush?"

"Billy Ray stopped at Faye's for coffee and pastries. He was meeting Detectives Rumsfeld and Carlson in Slidell. At the sheriff's complex."

"He told you that?"

"Nope. Eavesdropped. He told Earl he'd be gone for a while."

Stephanie's truck rumbled past the barn. There was no one in sight. "What do you think that means?"

"You're not going to like it."

"What else is new?"

"You still have a sense of humor. That's good."

"It's either that or fall apart."

Stephanie reached across and squeezed her hand. "When I saw Billy Ray last night he said they'd have a search warrant today. For the farm."

She curled her hands into fists. "All his dreams are coming true."

"I'm sorry."

"Logan didn't do it."

"I know."

The simple reply, the confidence in it, brought tears of relief to Bailey's eyes. She wasn't alone. "How are we getting in?"

"A key I have from when we were dating."

"He didn't ask for it back?"

"It's a long story." Her lips lifted slightly. "Well, maybe not that long, but it doesn't paint me in a very good light. He never officially gave it to me."

"Sneaky."

"Pretty much." She was quiet a moment. "Billy Ray is too paranoid and suspicious to ever give someone a key to his place." She looked away, then back. "I'm not proud of this. In fact, it's embarrassing. A dozen times I told myself to toss it, but I didn't. I kept it out of spite. After the way he hurt me—"

"You don't have to explain."

"But I do. For me, not you."

Bailey got that. Didn't make it right or even healthy, but she got it.

"I've never used it, I promise. Just having it gave me this . . . irrational, I don't know . . . like this small measure of control . . ." She let the words trail off. "After this, I'll get rid of it."

"Is it wrong of me to be really, really thankful you have it?"

Stephanie laughed weakly. "That's me, always thinking of others."

"We know how we get into the house, the question is, how do we get in the super-secret chamber?"

Stephanie grinned at her sarcasm. "Kick down the door?"

"If I have to."

"Just so you know, whatever he took from Uncle Henry, I'm taking it back."

Bailey nodded. She understood how it felt to be cheated by someone you love. In her case it had been her father. At one point she longed to take back what he'd stolen when he left: her trust and security. The piece of her heart that only he had been able to fill.

Stephanie wasn't going to be able to take that back. Only time could.

They fell silent. Stephanie drove past Faye's, then took the first left after. As they rolled past the P.D., they both glanced that way. No cruiser. Only Robin's red VW Beetle.

Stephanie parked just up the block from Billy Ray's. Bailey's heart pounded, the realization that they were breaking and entering fully hitting her.

"What if one of the neighbors notices us?" she asked.

"Can't control that. Act natural. Wave. They've seen me here before."

They headed up the walkway to his door. "Prepare yourself, the key might not work. He might have changed the lock, just because."

"It will. It has to."

Bailey said a silent prayer as Stephanie fitted the key into the lock. She twisted; the lock didn't budge. She tried again, then looked at Bailey. "It's not working."

"Let me try."

Stephanie stepped aside. Bailey pulled the key, then pushed it back in, jiggled a bit; it caught and the dead bolt slid back.

Bailey realized she'd been holding her breath and let it out in a rush. "The first gate of hell," she muttered.

They stepped into the house. It crossed her mind to wonder if Billy Ray was crazy enough to have the place under electronic surveillance. Or booby-trapped.

In the next moment, she saw that they wouldn't have to worry about kicking in a door. The door in question stood open.

She looked at Stephanie in surprise. "Prayers answered."

But they hadn't been, she realized, stepping into the room. The display board was blank. Billy Ray had removed everything.

Gone. It was all gone.

"No." She blinked and shook her head, as if by her doing so everything would reappear. "He couldn't have. Not yet."

"I'm so sorry, Bailey."

She wanted to cry. "He got his man," she said. "That's it, isn't it? He didn't need it anymore."

His man.

Logan. Her husband. She brought a hand to her belly. *The father of her child.*

"Check the closet," Stephanie suggested. "You never know."

Bailey did. Two cardboard boxes. "Bingo. Let's get to it so we can get out of here."

One box was full, the other nearly empty. Bailey started with the full one. Photos. Newspaper clippings. Notes.

The victims in neatly organized and labeled folders. The first was Nicole Grace. The fifteen-year-old girl found strangled.

Nicole. The letter *N*.

The image of the initial necklace, its lightweight chain draped across her fingers, popped into Bailey's mind.

With the image, Henry's voice. And her own. Asking where he had found the box.

"Where did you get these things, Henry?"

"Found 'em."

"Where?"

"Aren't they pretty?" He looked hurt. "I thought you'd think they were pretty."

"I do, Henry. Please . . . I just—" She cleared her throat. "Were they all together like this? In the box?"

He nodded. "Did you see? Logan's box. Roane had one, too." He frowned. "Don't know where his went. With him, maybe."

Bailey's stomach went sour. She struggled past the feeling. "So, all the pretty things were in the box. Where, Henry? Where did you find the box?"

"I shouldn't have taken it. I'm sorry."

"It's okay. I'm not mad." She made her voice as gentle as possible. "I just need to know where you got this."

"The bad place. I'm not supposed to go there. No one is."

"The bad place?" She frowned. "What do you mean?"

"Bad things—" His eyes filled with tears. "Roane."

The hay barn. Where Roane hung himself.

Located far from the house. No longer used, left to deteriorate. What better place for a killer to set up shop? Obviously, he stored his treasures there. Did he bury his victims there, as well? Did he bring them there to die?

She reined in her imagination. She couldn't let it run away with her, not now.

Her hands shook. She tried to hide it from Henry. "I need to go there. You have to tell me how to get there."

"Miss True, you can't go out there."

"You could take me, Henry. Show me the way."

"Can't drive." He peered out the window. "Too far to walk now."

The golf cart, she thought, then rejected the idea. She would have to explain why she needed it.

And she wasn't ready for that. Not yet.

This might be her only chance. She had to know. Before she took this to Logan. Or the police.

"How can we get there, Henry?"

"Ride."

She started to shake her head, then stopped. August had told her she was ready. Tea Biscuit was as gentle a horse as one could be.

She was up to it, she promised herself. She could do it. Not just for her marriage, but now, for her child as well.

"Yes, Henry, that's a good idea." He smiled happily and she stood. "I'll go change clothes and come back on Tea Biscuit. Then we'll go together."

CHAPTER SIXTY

Bailey lifted her gaze. Stephanie in the doorway. Looking at her, the oddest expression on her face.

Bailey blinked. "What's wrong?"

"Just checking on you. What have you found?"

Not what she'd found, what she'd remembered. But she didn't have time to share that now. She shook her head. "It's pretty much all here. How about you?"

She slid her hands into her pockets. "The photos he lifted from Uncle Henry's. Some others. I don't want to be here much longer. I have this feeling he'll be back soon."

Bailey nodded and got back to the material in front of her. She took the spiral notebook and pen from her purse.

She carefully wrote Nicole Grace's name and placed a number one beside it. The teenager had been strangled. The initial necklace must have been hers. Her killer had taken it from around her neck.

Trista Hook. Long, wavy hair. In one of the pictures, she had it pulled away from her face. Could the sparkly hair clip have been hers? She noted her question and moved on.

Amanda LaPier. Number three. She flipped through news clippings, stopping on a brief bio. Graduated from

Covington High in 2010. *The class ring had belonged to her.*

In her mind, that clinched it. The class ring, the initial pendant . . . A killer's souvenirs. His box of trophies.

No doubt that's what it had been.

Billy Ray had begun a file on Dixie. Bailey saw nothing in it she didn't already know.

True's file. Logan's. Then . . . nothing.

She frowned. The other three women, where were they? She pictured the whiteboard, the diagram. Remembered standing in front of it . . . the names.

Why had Billy Ray excluded them from the box? What did it mean?

Something. Something important.

"Ready when you are."

Bailey glanced up at Stephanie. "One last look through."

She took her time, knowing this would be her last opportunity to peek into Billy Ray's mind. She made a few more notes, reviewed them quickly, then stood.

"Leave the top off the box and the closet door open."

Bailey frowned. "Why?"

"It'll totally mess with his head."

In another situation, where the stakes weren't nearly so high, she would have smiled—even laughed—at the suggestion. But the stakes today were about as high as they could get. "Are you sure you want to do that? He could figure it out."

"Let him. I'm itching for a confrontation."

She was, Bailey realized as they drove away from Billy Ray's. She could see it in the way she clenched and unclenched her hands on the steering wheel, the muscle that jumped in her tight jaw.

"What's wrong?" Bailey asked.

"Too many memories. That's all."

But it wasn't. Obviously. "What did you do in there?"

"Looked around."

"Find True's head in the freezer?"

"What! No."

"Someone else's head?"

"No, God, no. Bad joke, Bailey."

"I was only half joking."

They fell silent. Bailey tried one more time. "You found something, didn't you?"

Stephanie glanced at her, then back at the road. "I'm not ready to talk about it."

"Okay, I get that."

"What about you?" She flexed her fingers on the wheel again. "You said you had questions you needed answered. Did you get what you went for?"

Names. Confirmation.

"I did."

"Anything you're ready to talk about?"

She hesitated, then nodded. Stephanie was the only real friend she had. "Pull over, Steph. There's something I have to tell you."

Stephanie turned into an empty church parking lot, cut the engine and turned to face her. "You've got my full attention."

"I've remembered the day of the accident. Most of it, anyway."

Stephanie had gone very still. Instinctively, Bailey thought. As if afraid any movement would cause Bailey to change her mind or her memory to evaporate again.

"I visited Henry that day. I talked to him."

"How was he?"

Her question came out choked. Yearning.

"He was good, Steph. He was . . . Henry."

Stephanie's eyes flooded with tears. She blinked to chase them away, but several escaped and rolled down her cheeks. She swiped at them as if irritated with herself. "If only I'd gone out there myself. I would have seen him one last time. Maybe he would be alive. Inside with me, safe. That hunter—"

"He wasn't killed by a hunter."

"How do you—" Her eyes widened. "You remembered—"

"Hear me out, then you decide. When I got there that day, Henry had something for me. A . . . box. A handmade box that—" She cleared her throat. "Logan's initials were on it. And a date. May 2, 1988."

"What was—"

"Inside? An assortment of things. A necklace and hair clip, a girl's class ring. A lipstick. A couple others."

"Uncle Henry was always finding stuff in the woods. Trash, lost items."

"He told me when he found the box, the items were already in it."

"Okay."

She didn't get it. "I wanted to look at Billy Ray's notes on the missing women. To see if I could link any of the items to them."

Stephanie was staring blankly at her. Bailey went on. "The necklace was an initial pendant. The letter *N*. The girl who was strangled back in 2005 was named—"

"Nicole. Oh, my God."

"And the class ring was from Covington High, class of 2010. The year Amanda LaPier—"

"Graduated."

She'd gone white. "Yes."

"Uncle Henry thought he'd found a treasure chest. But he'd found a little box of horrors."

Stephanie was silent a moment. When she spoke again, Bailey heard hope in her voice. "Do you think, maybe . . . it's nothing. Just what Uncle Henry thought? Innocent?"

"Innocent." Such a beautiful word. "Until today I thought maybe . . . I'd hoped that, too. But the coincidence of the necklace and ring . . . I don't have any doubt, not anymore."

"Did Uncle Henry say where he'd found it?"

"The hay barn."

"The—" She stopped, the look of horror coming over her face again. "Where Roane— The perfect spot. No one goes out there anymore."

"Right. In fact, nobody was *supposed* to go out there. That's what Henry said. He thought I was mad about it."

Stephanie frowned. "Who told him that?"

"I don't know. He didn't say, but I would assume Logan or Paul."

"Or Raine. Oh, my God, Billy Ray. He was looking for the box."

"Maybe."

"Otherwise, what happened to it?"

"The sheriff's deputies may have collected it, when they searched Henry's after his murder."

Stephanie drummed her fingers on the steering wheel. "One problem. It seems to me, if they'd found that they would have been all over Logan. They would have questioned me. Henry would've been considered a suspect."

"You're right, I hadn't thought of that." She pursed her lips. "Billy Ray was out there, you were certain he'd been inside the cabin. You saw him putting something in his trunk."

Stephanie nodded. "That was it, the box."

It made sense. "So where is it now? In the hands of the deputies? Or still in his trunk?"

"The deputies have to have it," Stephanie said. "It's a surefire way to fry Logan."

"No," Bailey said, realizing something she hadn't before. "It would muddy the water."

"What do you mean?"

"Billy Ray has to tell him where he found it. Like you said, if he took it from Henry's, it casts suspicion on Henry."

"So, he plants it wherever it's most likely to damage Logan." Stephanie met Bailey's eyes. "The search warrant, Billy Ray was certain they'd be granted one. He was practically giggling about it."

"He's stashed the box on Abbott Farm. Of course he did." Bailey's heart sank and she curved her arms around her middle. "What do we do? It could be anywhere."

"You go to the police. Tell them the story. Tell them about your memory returning."

"They won't believe me. They'll think I'm trying to save my husband. Because of the baby. Or because I'm blinded by love. They'll think that I somehow found out about him, what he is and . . . Women do that. You hear about it all the time."

"Are you one of those women, Bailey? One who can be blinded by love?"

"No." The word spilled forcefully past her lips and she felt as if a giant weight had been lifted from her shoulders. "No, I'm not. And Logan isn't a killer."

"Hold off on the sheriff for a few hours. I'm paying Billy Ray a visit. I'm going to get him to talk."

"How?"

"I think I have something on him. Something big."

Stephanie didn't want to say what it was; they rode the rest of the way to the farm in silence.

Paul was waiting for her. When Stephanie stopped the truck, he strode over and yanked open her door. "What the hell, Bailey! Where were you?"

"Obviously," Stephanie answered for her, hopping out, "she was with me. What's up?"

"It's Logan."

"Oh, my God—" Bailey slid out of the truck. "What's happened, Paul? Is he all right—"

"Yes. It's good news, Bailey." His voice shook slightly. "Dixie Jenkins is alive."

It took a moment for his words to sink in. When they did, her knees went weak with relief. She grabbed the car door for support. "Please tell me this isn't a joke."

"Not a joke. She ran off and got married."

"But her car . . . the way she left it—"

"Pretty crazy, right." He searched her gaze. "You know what this means, Bailey? They're releasing Logan. Within the hour, his lawyer said."

With a whoop of joy, Bailey threw her arms around him. He hugged her back just as tightly. She turned to Stephanie and hugged her. "He's coming home, Steph! I knew he didn't do that. I knew he couldn't!"

Stephanie hugged her back. "Go. You'll want to be there when he walks out."

Bailey looked at Paul. "Will you drive?"

"Of course."

"Steph, you want to come along?"

She smiled. "Nope, there's something I have to do. But give Logan a congratulatory hug from me."

CHAPTER SIXTY-ONE

Bailey made it to the parish jail just in time to see Logan walk out of the facility, a free man.

"Logan!" she cried, and ran to him. He took her in his arms and held her, his face buried in her hair. Hers in the crook of his neck. They stood like that for a long time, aware of people passing them, of the lawyer and Paul's stilted conversation. Of Paul's not so subtle clearing of his throat.

They drew apart, though only inches. Bailey drank in his face. He looked like he had aged five years in the past twenty-four hours. She wondered if she did as well, although by the way he was looking at her—as if she was the most beautiful thing he had ever seen—she thought not.

Paul clapped him on the back. "Glad you're coming home, man."

"I'm not there yet. Let's get out of here before they change their minds."

Logan and the attorney spoke briefly before they parted ways. Paul drove while she and Logan sat in the backseat, holding hands. Bailey had so much to tell him, but the thoughts wouldn't form on her tongue. And she was glad.

They would have time for talking, but for now she was content with the warmth of him next to her, the feel of her hand encased in his.

Paul glanced at them in the rearview. "They told you about August?"

Beside her, Logan stiffened. "Oh, yeah. With pleasure. They asked me if I knew he was an addict. I didn't. You have any idea?"

"None."

Bailey jumped in. "Raine knew. She said he'd struggled with drug dependency in the past. But that he was over it."

Logan looked at her, frowning. "She never mentioned it to me."

Paul spoke up. "Makes sense, that of us all she would have known. Birds of a feather and all that."

Something about the way he said it felt small and unnecessary. Bailey laid her head on her husband's shoulder.

"They asked me a lot of questions about the gun," Logan said.

"Really?" Paul sounded surprised. "Why?"

"I don't know. They were curious why he had it, if he was a hunter. As far as I knew the man had never hunted in his life. It didn't seem his style at all."

Paul agreed. "Funny how you can be friends with someone, work with them for years and not really know them at all."

"They asked about his relationship with Henry."

"Henry?" Paul repeated, obviously surprised. "Why?"

"Think about it. They say Henry was shot by a hunter—"

"And a hunter uses a rifle. Maybe the same kind found at August's place?"

"No," Bailey said. "August couldn't hurt anyone."

"There was something about their questioning— Never mind."

Paul met his eyes in the rearview once more. "No, what?"

"I had the feeling they knew, or suspected, something they weren't telling me but were wanting me to confirm."

"Like what?"

"No clue, man." He made a sound, part weariness, part disgust. "But that's what cops do, try to get you to confirm their accusations, no matter how far-fetched."

She knew he was thinking of Billy Ray and curled her fingers more tightly around his. "It's over now."

"For now," he corrected. "He's not going to stop."

"So, let's stop him," she said, tipping her face up to his. "It's an abuse of power, a personal vendetta."

Paul agreed. "This could be the ammunition you need."

Logan sighed, leaned his head back against the seat. "All I want to think about right now is being home and in the arms of my beautiful wife."

At that, they fell silent. They rode the rest of the way without speaking, arriving at the farm to find Raine waiting for them.

She ran to her brother and embraced him. "Thank God . . . thank God . . . I was so afraid I'd lost you, too!"

"I'm home, Raine." He stroked her hair while she held him and sobbed. "It's okay. Everything's going to be okay."

"No . . . no, maybe not. I—" She struggled to pull herself together. "There's something I have to tell you, something I should have told you a long time ago. You might . . . hate me after. But I have to do it anyway. Alone. Okay?"

She meant to tell about True's baby, Bailey realized. The abortion.

He looked over at her in question; even though her heart hurt for him and she wished she could keep it from happening, she nodded.

"We'll be in the study," he said.

A moment later, he and Raine disappeared into the house.

She turned to Paul. "You don't have to stay."

"Do you know what's going on?"

"I think so."

She didn't share and he looked hurt. "They may need me. I'll hang around."

"Raine might. Logan has me."

"Right." He shoved his hands into his pockets. "Old habits."

"Let's go in, the mosquitoes are starting to bite."

It was nearly an hour before Logan and Raine emerged from the study. It was obvious they'd both been crying. Wordlessly, Paul took Raine's hand to escort her home. She let him with a murmur of thanks and a glance back.

Bailey held her own hand out. Logan took it and she led him upstairs, to their bed.

Silently, she undressed him, telling him with hands and mouth how much she loved and needed him. That she understood, that she was here for him.

She drew him down with her, into her. They'd only been apart a day, but it felt like weeks. Months even. Bailey realized it had been the emotional distance between them, her suspicion separating them.

She trusted him completely now. She felt it in her body's response to him. Not just physical but somehow spiritual as well. Wild, free. She held not one part of herself back, not one thought or feeling. It hadn't been like this since before the accident, before the red shoe and Billy Ray's outlandish theories.

Afterward, they nestled together under the covers.

"We have to talk," he said.

"Yes."

"No more secrets."

"No. God, no."

He rested his forehead against hers. "What I said in the car, it's true. It's not over, Bailey."

"What do you—"

His stomach growled loudly. In response hers did, too. She laughed. "What a pair."

"Jail grub leaves something to be desired. What's your excuse?"

Laughing, she jumped out of the bed, taking a pillow with her. As he started after her, she swung it at him. Surprised, he stumbled backward, then grabbed a pillow of his own.

A raucous pillow fight ensued, complete with chasing each other around the room, jumping on the bed and feathers raining over them as her pillow burst with her last blow.

They tumbled to the bed and made love again, this time slowly and tenderly. An exquisite expression of their love.

When it was over, he collapsed beside her. "I'm done. Completely spent."

"No round three?" she teased, playfully nipping his chest.

"Not until you feed me. I'm weak with hunger."

She laughed. "You? I'm the one who's supposed to be eating for two."

His smile turned tender. He splayed his fingers on her belly. "How is she?"

"She?"

"I just have a feeling."

Bailey smiled. "She's fine. Growing."

"I see that." He looked up at her, eyes misty. "In jail, thinking about you two was all that kept me sane. You gave me something to hope for."

CHAPTER SIXTY-TWO

They raided the refrigerator and pantry. Ate chunky-style peanut butter from the jar, cereal from the box and left-over pizza cold. Bailey drank milk, Logan Abita beer.

And they spoke of nothing of consequence. The weather and the farm, of baby names and of their dreams. Their future together.

The way newlyweds did. The way they should. Bailey held tightly to those moments, memorizing each word and thought, each glance exchanged and smile shared.

The calm before the storm, she thought. And as if her own thoughts had conjured it, his mood changed, became serious. Almost brooding.

"We have to talk," he said.

She wanted to argue. To beg him for a few more minutes of bliss. But it was too late, he'd already moved on.

"Yes," she said. "We do."

They positioned themselves across the kitchen table from one another, interview style. Face-to-face, she thought. Eye-to-eye.

He began. "I've made a mess of everything, I know that. From the beginning, by not telling you about everything. My family, True, the investigations. I wanted to keep us, what we had, in a bubble." He laughed, the sound sharp and unforgiving, directed at himself. "I was a fool.

"Now, tonight I learn I was even more a fool than I—"

He choked on the words, emotion seeming to overcome him. He looked away, a muscle jumping in his clenched jaw.

"Don't," she said. "It's not your fault."

"How can it not be my fault? I was her husband. How could I have not known?"

"Because she didn't want you to."

He didn't accept that; she read it in his eyes.

"True and I, the fight we had before I went to Jackson, I accused her of having an affair, Bailey. She'd been distant. Secretive and moody. She denied it, but I knew she was hiding something from me. But instead of coaxing her, I stormed out. Left her alone and heartbroken."

Bailey held her hand out. He took it. "That's why it was so easy to convince myself that she'd run off with someone else. I don't believe that anymore. I think she's dead. I think the bastard who took Amanda and Trista, whoever he is, killed her."

"I do, too."

His eyes turned glassy, and he looked quickly away. After a moment, he cleared his throat, met her gaze once more. "I let her down, Bailey. Someone hurt her, but instead of moving heaven and earth to find out who, I chose to vilify her. How do I . . . forgive myself for that?"

The words came out tight. She leaned forward, her own eyes teary. "We find out who," she said. "We make it as right as we can."

He seemed to digest that, then went on. "I didn't just start believing that tonight. It began the night you and I argued. I was angry and hurt. I couldn't sleep. I kept thinking about True, about Billy Ray telling you that those women were buried here on the farm. The thought was repugnant. It infuriated me. But I wondered, what if he was right? Could he be right?"

He paused, met her eyes. "That's why I went online. Looking for something, anything that would free us from all this suspicion."

"I saw it, the search, on your computer."

"I knew you had because you changed. We changed."

She swallowed hard. "I should have asked you about it. I should have trusted you, but—"

"I wasn't trustworthy."

"No—"

"Yes. I imagined how it must look to you. Saw it through your eyes. And how messed up it all was. That it could ruin what we had. But I was so afraid of losing you. And then you and Tony found that shoe. I tried to play it cool, but it totally freaked me out."

Her mouth went dry; her heart began to pound. "Did you recognize . . . was it True's?"

"I knew it wasn't hers. I'd never seen them before and she wasn't a red-shoe kind of person."

"So why'd you take it out of the garbage?"

He looked almost comically surprised. "You went into the trash for it?"

"I couldn't stop thinking about the damn thing."

"I don't blame you. I didn't just look guilty, I acted guilty, too."

"No more doubts," she said. "That's behind us."

"We're a pair, aren't we?"

They smiled simultaneously, and in the instant Bailey could almost believe they were any other couple in love, that there wasn't the specter of murder hanging over them.

Almost, but not quite.

She screwed up her courage. "There's something I have

to tell you. Upstairs you said it wasn't over, but you didn't know what they could have. I do."

She met his questioning gaze evenly. "I've remembered the day of the accident. Everything but finding Henry dead." He nodded and she went on. "I went to check on Henry, the way Stephanie had asked me to. He had something for me. Something he found."

She went on to describe the box and the items inside.

"Okay. So Henry was always treasure hunting. He picked up stuff he found and he put it all in a box. What's the big deal?"

"Not stuff he'd collected here and there, Logan. He found the box with all of the items in it. It was someone's special collection."

"I get that. But what does that have to do with the missing women—"

She saw the moment he got it, connected all the pieces. "You think the items belonged to them?"

"I know they did."

"You have . . . proof?"

"Circumstantial. The class ring was from Covington High, class of 2010, the year Amanda LaPier graduated.

"There's one more thing about the box, Logan. Your initials are on it. Burned onto the bottom."

Something horrible and sad crossed his features. He stood and went to the sink. For long moments he stood there, hands braced on the counter, head bowed. "I made that box when I was ten," he said finally, voice thick. He cleared his throat. "Dad helped me. It's one of the good memories I have of him. . . . I remember being so proud of it. And now—"

Violated, she thought. The memory. All of it.

"I'm sorry."

"I hadn't thought about it in years. I figured it'd been tossed out long ago."

"When was the last time you saw it?"

He thought a moment. "In the barn or garage . . . some-time after Dad died."

"The hay barn, maybe?"

He seemed to freeze. "Why would you think it'd be—"

"That's where Henry said he found it."

"The hay barn," he repeated. "I haven't set foot in there since Roane. Nobody has."

"Someone has," she corrected. "Besides Henry."

They fell silent. Seconds ticked past, becoming min-utes. "What are you thinking?" she asked.

He looked over at her. "How lucky I am, that after all of this, you're still here."

She stood and crossed to him. "I love you." She slipped her arms around him from behind and rested her cheek against his back.

"Why?" The word came out broken.

"You're worth loving, Logan. I believe in you."

He turned in her arms and rested his forehead against hers. "Now we have to work on everyone else."

"Rumsfeld's the only one I'm worried about. Let the rest of them think what they want."

He smiled and held her at arm's length. "Why do you suspect the police have the box?"

She explained about looking for it and about Stepha-nie catching Billy Ray at Henry's, putting something in his trunk.

"That son of a bitch. If the police have it, I'm screwed."

"Then why'd they let you go?"

"Not enough to charge? Or they figure I'm not going anywhere, so they let me go, maybe lead them to evidence. I don't know." He dragged a hand through his hair. "It doesn't really make sense. Unless there's more we don't know."

"I have another theory. Billy Ray had the box, but

expecting a search warrant for the farm, he planted it here. To frame you."

For a long moment, Logan was silent. "Billy Ray really might have been right. Otherwise, why is the killer's collection here?" As if thinking out loud, he began to pace. "It's someone who knows the area well. Knows our family history, about Roane and that we abandoned that barn. The layout of the farm. But that could be almost anyone who's lived in the area for a while."

"At least since 2005."

He stopped, looked at her. "Because of Nicole."

"Yes." He started to pace once more. "He lures them here . . . how? Drugs? Sex? I don't know . . . something. Or does he restrain them? Lure them into his car, then—"

He suddenly stopped, obviously exhausted. Expression: beaten. "I don't know where to start. When the law's against you, where do you turn?"

"To me," she said softly. "We'll do this together." She held out her hand. "Tomorrow. You need rest, Logan."

"There's no time. Rumsfeld, Billy Ray, they—"

"I need rest. For me. And for our baby." She reached out again. "I'm not going without you."

When he hesitated, she added, "We'll be able to think clearly. We'll know what to do, Logan."

He took her hand. She led him upstairs to bed. Within moments of his head hitting the pillow, his breathing became deep, even and rhythmic.

Tonight it was she who wouldn't sleep. She who would stand guard, worrying about keeping him safe, protecting him from those who would destroy them.

CHAPTER SIXTY-THREE

Billy Ray sat at his kitchen table, three fingers of Kentucky whiskey untouched in front of him, gaze straight ahead. Abbott was gone. Released, charges dropped. No warrant was coming. No search of the property.

Everything, all his hard work, shot to hell.

By some substance-addled, bleach-blond bimbo.

Abbott had won again. The bully always won. On the playground. In the war room.

Behind closed doors.

"Hello, Billy Ray."

He shifted his gaze. Stephanie stood in the kitchen doorway. He blinked, wondering if he was hallucinating, though he knew he wasn't. "How did you get in here?"

"You left the door open."

He frowned. Had he? He didn't even recall arriving home.

"I heard about Logan being released."

"Come to gloat?"

"Is that what you think?"

"You hate me," he said. "You've made that clear."

"You're wrong about that. You hurt me. But I don't hate you."

"If not to gloat, then why are you here, Steph?"

"I have a question. I want to know where you got this." She crossed to the table, held out her hand. Lying in her palm was a simple gold wedding band.

His mouth went dry, his head light. "Where did you get that?"

"You know where."

Tucked into his bureau drawer, wrapped in one of his dad's old handkerchiefs.

He stared at it. Heat washed over him, then clammy cold. "I could arrest you for breaking and entering."

"You won't."

"And why's that?"

"You'll have to explain how you came to have True Abbott's wedding ring in your possession."

He forced a laugh. "That was my mother's ring."

"Really?" Stephanie held it up and read the inscription. " 'My True Love.' "

"So?"

"I find it odd that your mother had the same inscription on her wedding band as True Abbott."

He couldn't take his eyes off the ring. It caught the light as she held it up between her forefinger and thumb. Winking at him.

Taunting him. Calling him a fool. A blind fool.

"What do you want from me?" he asked, the words coming out a croak.

"The truth."

His right eye began to twitch. His head filled with an image.

True's hand. Still and pale. Her fourth finger. The ring, winking at him.

Winking at him. In the light.

My True Love.

She'd called him, he remembered. Used the card he'd given her that very first day, when he'd rescued her from the side of the road. Asked him to meet her. Logan was out of town, gone to Jackson on business.

"Billy Ray, I need to talk to you."

His heart soared. Finally, the moment he had waited for. She was reaching out, turning to him. "When?" he asked, barely able to form the words. "Where?"

"The sooner the better. Someplace no one will see us."

Something in her voice. Something desperate. "Do you know where Miller Road is?"

"Yes."

"At the very end is an abandoned farm. The barn is right there. Meet me there in an hour."

Stephanie snapped her fingers. "The truth, Billy Ray. What's so hard about that?"

He blinked, disoriented. "True was afraid of him, of Logan. Controlling her every thought, her every move. She couldn't breathe when he was around. Always tiptoeing. Afraid something she said or did would set him off."

"I know all your theories, Billy Ray. I've heard them a million times. And I know this is True's ring because she showed me the inscription. How'd you get it?"

"She gave it to me, before she left him."

"I thought you said he killed her? All these years, isn't that what you said?"

"He did."

"After she gave you the ring and left?"

He met Stephanie's eyes, but saw True's blue ones instead. Bright with tears.

"Thank you for calling me, True. You did the right thing. You won't regret it."

"Billy Ray—"

"No, please. Let me talk."

He reached for her hands, she slid them into her pockets. It hurt, felt like a slap in the face, but he pushed

*the hurt aside. The same as he had every time his father
had struck as he stepped between him and his mother.*

He hadn't been able to protect his mother.

He would protect True, no matter the cost.

*"I see what he is, True. I know. I'm the law, I can pro-
tect you."*

"No, you're wrong. I'm here because—"

*"I'm not wrong." He shook his head. He had to con-
vince her. He had to make her see. "I have a gun. And a
badge. My uncle is the chief of police. He won't be able
to touch you—"*

"You need help, Billy Ray."

"No. I need you, True. I love you."

"You don't even know me."

*"I know you're sweet and kind. You're beautiful, inside
and out. I'll take care of you—"*

*"I love him, Billy Ray. That's not going to change, not
ever."*

*"We can go anywhere. We'll leave Wholesome. Go
where he won't find us—"*

*"Look—" She dug into her purse. "I have money. Ten
thousand dollars. You can have it, Billy Ray."*

She held out the stack of bills. "See? You can have it."

*He frowned. Money. A lot of money. Her wedding ring
winking at him. "I don't understand—"*

*"It's for you. To leave Wholesome, start a new life. To
get the help you need—"*

"You're sweating, Billy Ray."

His vision cleared. Stephanie. The ring in her hand.
"She was so afraid of him, of what he would do. That's
why she gave me the money. I didn't want it. Only her."

"What money?"

"The ten thousand." He rubbed his palms together.
They were wet, sweating. The way they had been that

day. "She was too afraid to leave him. The same as my mother was too afraid."

She was staring at him, revulsion in her eyes. He wiped his brow. His upper lip. "Stop looking at me like that."

"You killed her." She took a step backward. "Oh, my God, you did it."

"No." He shook his head. "He did. With his jealousy. His . . . rage."

"But she didn't see it that way, did she?"

"Now, he's free again. And Bailey's in danger. Don't you see?"

Sweat, dripping in his eyes. Soaking his shirt.

"What happened?" Stephanie asked. "She didn't love you and wouldn't leave him so you . . . strangled her? Like Nicole Grace was strangled? And maybe the others, too. And you kept her ring. As a souvenir."

Nicole Grace? The others? "What are you talking about?"

"True's dead. You've known it all along because you killed her."

"I didn't kill her! She slipped and fell."

"And what? Hit her head? C'mon, Billy Ray."

"I was trying to make her see. Make her understand! It was an accident!"

"True, sweetheart—"

"Don't call me that."

"Baby, please—" He caught her by the shoulders. "I love you. We'll use that money to start our new life together."

"Let me go!"

"Not until you say yes. Until you—"

"You're hurting me!"

"Stop fighting me! Just listen—"

She broke away from him and ran toward her car. He

caught up to her, grabbed her arm. She spun around, swung at him, hitting him in the side of the neck.

Surprised, he released her. She lost her balance, fell forward. As if in slow motion he saw her head hit the ground with a horrible crack.

Billy Ray realized he was crying. Blubbering like a baby. "I loved her. I'd never hurt her. Never lay a hand on her!"

"But you did hurt her. You did lay a hand on her."

"I didn't want to. I didn't know what to do! You have to understand! She was acting crazy. Irrational. All I wanted to do is stop her, make her listen to me. To understand."

"This ring is the proof. Just like the other trophies are. The ones you wanted the sheriff's detectives to find. It's why you were so desperate to get a search warrant."

Understand. She had to understand.

"It's how you've always known the bodies were all buried at Abbott Farm. Because you buried them there."

He blinked again. The tears mixed with his sweat, stinging. He swiped at them. *What was she talking about? It was Abbott. It'd always been Abbott.*

"This ring is proof of what you did, Billy Ray. You took it as a trophy, didn't you?"

"A trophy?" He shook his head. "She wasn't his anymore. So I took it and put mine on her finger."

She took a step backward. "You're insane."

"Give me the ring."

"No." She took another step back. "I'm going to the sheriff's office with it. And you're going to jail. Where you belong."

"I can't let you do that, Stephanie." He got to his feet, reaching for his sidearm.

It wasn't there.

He'd removed his holster, he remembered. When he'd

gotten home. Dropped it onto the couch, then stopped, gaze on the loaded Glock, picturing himself slipping the gun from its holster, pressing the barrel to his temple and pulling the trigger.

Stephanie had seen the gun, when she'd come in.

He saw it in her expression.

She turned and ran at the exact moment he lunged. He knocked the table sideways, the whiskey flew, splashing like amber-colored tears on the floor and wall.

She reached the living room before he did. She had her hands on the gun, around the grip. Pointed at him.

"Don't make me do this, Billy Ray!"

He charged. The sound of the shot rang in his head. The blast reverberated through his body.

He stopped. Brought a hand to his chest. "Give . . . me . . . the—" His knees gave. He grabbed the chair for support. It went over, him with it. He stared up at the ceiling, feeling the blood pulsing, gushing from the wound in his chest. His vision dimmed.

True smiled and beckoned him.

CHAPTER SIXTY-FOUR

Stephanie sat across from the two sheriff's detectives. True's wedding band lay on the table between them. She'd called 9-1-1 and calmly told the operator that she had shot Wholesome Police Chief Billy Ray Williams in self-defense. He was alive and needed medical attention, and requested Detectives Rumsfeld and Carlson by name.

The ambulance had come, as had the detectives. They had taken her into custody. And now, here she sat.

She folded her hands in front of her, surprised with how steady they were.

"Start at the beginning, Ms. Rodriquez."

"The beginning," she repeated.

"How you came to be at Chief Williams's home this evening."

"Because of the ring. I confronted him about it."

"You told us it belonged to True Abbott."

"Yes. I knew because of the inscription. Did you read it?"

" 'My True Love.' "

"Yes." She lowered her gaze to her folded hands, then returned it to Rumsfeld's, then Carlson's. "He had it. So I knew he killed her."

"True Abbott?"

"Yes."

Rumsfeld looked at his notes, then back at her. "You say 'he had it.' How did you know that?"

"I found it. In his bedroom."

The two detectives exchanged glances. "You were romantically involved?"

"Once upon a time. I still had a key. I used it this afternoon, to get in."

"Were you alone?"

"No. Bailey Abbott was with me."

"To look for the ring?"

She shook her head again. "The box of trophies."

The detective frowned slightly. "What kind of trophies, Ms. Rodriquez?"

"You know. A killer's trophies."

The energy in the room changed. She felt tension. The heightened electricity.

"Maybe you need to back up a little more. I'm confused."

"I'm sorry." She swallowed hard. "How is Billy Ray? Have you heard?"

"In surgery. You're a very good shot, Ms. Rodriquez. He's lucky to be alive."

"I couldn't let him get the ring. He wanted to keep me from telling you about it. About what he did."

"We expect Billy Ray to live, Ms. Rodriquez."

"Good." She nodded for emphasis. "He needs to pay for what he's done. The women he hurt."

"Women? More than True?"

"All of them."

"Let's talk about the box of trophies you mentioned. What made you think he had such a thing?"

"Bailey Abbott told me about it. The day of the accident, my uncle showed it to her."

Again the exchanged glances. "She's recovered her memory?"

"Yes. She asked my help getting into Billy Ray's."

"She thought the box was there?"

"No. She was certain Billy Ray had planted it, to frame Logan."

"Why would she think that? Your uncle had the box. It seems to me that would make him look guilty?"

"Because—" She stopped. "It was gone. She looked for it."

"Anyone could have taken it. Logan, for starters."

"I caught Billy Ray at my uncle's. When I arrived he was putting something in his trunk. He told me it was the crime scene tape. He said you'd asked him to take it down. Or he offered." She brought a hand to her head, bone-numbing fatigue crashing down on her. "But you confirmed he lied about that."

"What would you say if I told you August Perez killed your uncle?"

"August?" She frowned. "He couldn't have."

"Why do you say that, Ms. Rodriquez?"

"He didn't hunt. He told me once. Told me he didn't believe in it." She shrugged. "He wasn't from around here."

"Maybe it wasn't an accident?"

"Why would he want my uncle dead?"

"I can only speculate at this point, but the rifle we found at his place was a ballistics match with the weapon used to kill your uncle."

That didn't sound right. "August had a rifle?"

"He did. Perhaps Mr. Perez killed him to retrieve that box of trophies."

"No."

"What makes you so certain of that?"

She rubbed her temple, trying to remember. Something . . . something, just beyond her reach. "I'm so tired. I can't think."

"I could have Carlson get you some coffee?"

"Yes, please. And water."

Carlson exited the room and she folded her arms and rested her head on them.

"Would you like a mint?"

She lifted her head. Rumsfeld held out a Starlight peppermint.

"Thank you." She took it. "Horses love these, did you know that?"

"No, I didn't."

She unwrapped it and popped it into her mouth. The peppermint stung her tongue and cleared her head.

And she remembered the why. "The box couldn't have been August's."

"Why not?"

"The initial necklace in it. An *N*. For 'Nicole.' Nicole Grace."

She'd caught him by surprise. She saw him struggle to place the name. "The fifteen-year-old girl from Wholesome," she said, "who was strangled to death."

He nodded. "Back in 2005."

"Yes."

"So why does that eliminate Mr. Perez?"

"Because he didn't live here then. He moved to Louisiana in 2009."

CHAPTER SIXTY-FIVE

Friday, April 25
6:35 A.M.

"Hello, Williams."

Billy Ray looked up at Rumsfeld through half-shut eyes. He stood beside the hospital bed, Carlson hovered just behind him. Over twenty years on the force and he'd never been shot. Until now.

With his own gun. By a woman he'd thought he could control.

She'd turned out to be smarter than he. They all had.

He closed his eyes. It hurt to breathe. To swallow. To move his head.

It hurt to be alive.

"You feel strong enough to chat a moment?"

He reopened his eyes and nodded, wincing at the slight movement.

Rumsfeld pulled over a chair and sat. "You know why we're here."

"Yes," he managed, voice thick and raw. "Stephanie Rodriquez."

"Yes. She shot you last night. We need to take your statement."

The gig was up. Over and done. He closed his eyes again. "I'm so tired. So . . . damn . . . tired."

"I know, man."

He heard the squeak of the chair on the linoleum floor as Rumsfeld inched it closer to the bed.

"A couple minutes. Enough for us to move on, then we'll leave you be."

"No." He shook his head, looked at him. "You won't."

The detective frowned slightly. "Rodriquez claims she shot you in self-defense."

"Yes."

"Yes, it was self-defense?"

"Yes."

"She came to us with a wild story, Williams. One about you having killed True Abbott."

"No."

"You did not kill True Abbott?"

Carlson, he saw, took notes. "No."

"Rodriquez had in her possession a wedding band. One she says belonged to the former Mrs. Abbott. One she says she recovered from your bedroom."

"Yes."

"Excuse me?"

"That's the . . . truth."

Rumsfeld cleared his throat. "Is True Abbott dead?"

"Yes."

"And you know this to be a fact?"

"I do."

Rumsfeld leaned closer. "And how do you know this to be a fact?"

"Because"—tears leaked from the corners of his eyes—"I buried her near the pond at Abbott Farm."

Rumsfeld and Carlson both seemed to freeze. Their faces took on expressions of comic disbelief. "Bring me paper"—Billy Ray cleared his throat—"I'll write my . . . statement."

Rumsfeld looked over his shoulder at Carlson. "Paper and pen, something for him to write on. Now."

Rumsfeld turned back around. "So, you confess to killing True Abbott?"

"No. It was an . . . accident. She fell. I panicked. . . ." He bit back a sob. "Shouldn't have covered it up."

"What about Nicole Grace? Did you accidentally strangle her?"

"No. Abbott—"

"What about Trista Hook? Do you know where she's buried?"

He shook his head. "Abbott."

"And Amanda LaPier?"

"Abbott. Logan Abbott."

Carlson returned with the paper, pen and a clipboard. Rumsfeld motioned him to hold off. "Are you telling me you admit to being responsible for True Abbott's death, but none of the other women's deaths or disappearances?"

"Not . . . me." Billy Ray motioned Carlson over. "Abbott. He's the one."

CHAPTER SIXTY-SIX

Bailey awakened early. Beside her, Logan still slept. They had talked on and off all night. Sleeping, then waking simultaneously, as if they were so connected they were one being. Funny thing was, they hadn't whispered of what this morning might bring, or what their next step should be, but they'd talked of the future. Their future. Children they would have and love, places they would go. Of holidays and anniversaries, weddings and the grandchildren they might have someday.

As if they had used those precious hours to live out the rest of their lives together.

Bailey watched him as he slept. So peaceful. Totally relaxed. She hadn't seen him this way since the island. So beautiful, she thought. She reached out and trailed a finger along his cheek.

His eyes snapped open, the expression in them feral. Like an animal awakened in the wild, instantly alert and ready to attack.

With a squeak of surprise, she snatched her hand back.

His eyes cleared and he smiled sleepily. "Morning, love."

"I woke you up. I'm sorry."

"I'm not." He pulled her into his arms. "You're trembling, sweetheart. Are you cold?"

She forced the shadows away. "Not anymore."

"What time is it?"

"After eight."

His lips twitched. "How much after?"

"Just. Why?"

"There's something I need to do."

"What? I'll come with."

"No, you stay. I need to talk to Raine again, then I'm going to pass something by Paul."

"You're shutting me out again, aren't you?"

"Absolutely not." He kissed the tip of her nose. "I can't do this without you. Right now, we only have each other."

"You're going to tell Raine and Paul everything."

"That's the plan."

Something about the way he answered left it open for a change of plans. Why? She started to ask him; he stopped her with a deep, lingering kiss. A moment later, he was up and stretching. She followed him out of bed, toward the bathroom. Tony opened an eye, as if wondering why his humans were acting so strangely, then shut it again and burrowed back into his feather-dusted bed.

She slipped into her robe and brushed her teeth while Logan dressed. Neither spoke. They exited the bedroom and descended the stairs in silence, as well.

"I'll make you a cup of coffee," she said as they reached the landing.

"Don't worry about it. I'll get some at Raine's." He kissed her. "I won't be gone long."

He started for the front door; she caught his arm, stopping him. "Remember, no secrets."

"No secrets." He searched her gaze. "This is something only I can do. I promise."

He crossed his heart, then kissed her again. She watched him go, the strangest sensation rolling over her. Of finality. Of good-bye.

Tears stung her eyes and Bailey blinked against them. Damn hormones, she thought, heading into the kitchen.

She made herself a decaf latte, carried it to the table and sat. But before she sipped, Tony started to bark.

Bailey set down her mug and went to check on him. As she reached the front hall, the doorbell rang. She peered out the side window; her stomach sank. Detectives Rumsfeld and Carlson had come calling.

She wished she could pretend she wasn't home, but they had seen her. "Tony! Quiet."

She swung open the door. Her greeting died on her lips as Tony charged down the stairs.

The detective's hand went to his gun. "Restrain your animal, Mrs. Abbott!"

"Tony, no!" She grabbed his collar; he nearly yanked her off her feet.

The fur of his ruff stood up and he growled, deep in his throat. "I'm so sorry. I've never seen him act like—"

Rumsfeld cut her off. "For the dog's safety and your own, you need to confine him. I don't want to be forced to take him down."

"Of course," she said, as shocked by the deputy's threat as she was by Tony's behavior. "Excuse me." She dragged him to the study, then locked him inside. He immediately started clawing at the door.

"I don't know what's gotten into him," she said, returning to the detectives. "How can I help you?"

"Is your husband home?"

Her mouth went dry. "No, he just left for his sister's. I expect him back shortly."

"May we come in?"

She hesitated. "Why? If you're looking for Logan—"

"We need to ask you a few questions."

No reassuring smile this morning, he was all business. "I suppose. Come on in."

They stepped inside. Tony, who had quieted, started pawing at the door again.

"Would you like coffee?"

"No, thank you. You might like to sit."

For a moment, she couldn't breathe, let alone speak. She nodded and led them to the kitchen. Her latte sat cooling on the table; she took the chair by it and automatically curled her hands around the mug.

Clinging to it like a lifeline.

Waiting.

Rumsfeld sat in the chair directly across from hers; his partner stood behind him. "It's come to our attention that Henry Rodriquez was in possession of a box of women's items, a box he presented to you the day of his death."

"Yes," she managed.

"Do you know what that box contained?"

"I think so."

"And what is that, Mrs. Abbott?"

She couldn't form the words. This was it, what she and Logan had feared. It's why she'd been overcome with sadness as he'd walked away. Why they had lived their lives and their children's lives last night.

Their last night together.

Her fairy tale was ending.

"He didn't do it," she whispered.

"I'm sorry, what did you say?"

"My husband, he didn't do anything wrong. He's innocent."

"What was in the box, Mrs. Abbott?"

She shook her head.

He ticked the items off for her. "An initial necklace that belonged to Nicole Grace. A hair ornament that belonged to Trista Hook. Amanda LaPier's class ring. And a brace-let, lipstick and key fob we haven't placed yet. Is that an accurate description of the box's contents?"

When she didn't reply, he asked again. "Is that what was in the box, Mrs. Abbott?"

"Yes."

"The box with your husband's initials burned into the wood?"

Tears spilled down her cheeks. "Yes."

"And you kept this information from us to protect your husband?"

She met the detective's eyes. "Because he didn't do anything."

"Yes or no, Mrs. Abbott?"

"Yes."

"Interfering with an investigation is a crime, did you know that?"

"I guess so."

"Concealing evidence is also a crime, Mrs. Abbott. Are you aware of that?"

"I wasn't! I didn't! I only just remembered."

"When?"

"Yesterday . . . no, the day before. Wednesday some-time. And not everything yet. Not finding Henry, or even being on Tea Biscuit. It's been coming back in segments."

"What's going on here?"

"Logan!" She jumped up and ran to him. "They know about the box! They think it's yours, that you murdered those women—"

"It's okay, baby. I haven't done anything wrong."

"Mr. Abbott, you'll need to come with us."

"Am I under arrest?"

"Not yet."

"May I call my lawyer?"

"Of course."

"No!" she cried. "He didn't do anything! Please, you have to listen to me!"

"It's okay," he said again, freeing himself from her arms. He kissed her. "I'll be home soon."

Bailey followed them to the door and out of the house, then watched helplessly as they helped Logan into the cruiser, slamming the door behind him.

She jerked at the sound. It was followed by a second, as the two detectives slammed theirs in unison. The sounds reverberated through her. Like shots.

Bailey's legs went weak and she grabbed the door frame for support. Henry on his front porch, smiling his strange smile. The box in his hands. Her, hurrying to her vehicle. Reaching it, looking over her shoulder.

"I'll be back, Henry. With Tea Biscuit."

She climbed in and waved, doing her best to not act like she was freaking out.

Because she was. Big time. Like can't-think-beyond-absolute-terror freaking out.

Get it together, Bailey. You can do this.

She reached the asphalt road in record time, and turned toward Abbott Farm. Her thoughts raced. Her heart pounded. She gripped the steering wheel so tightly, her knuckles turned white.

Was she doing the right thing? She couldn't go to Billy Ray or the sheriff yet. Then when? The box, Logan's initials on it, the items inside.

Damning evidence. Incriminating him.

No. She flexed her fingers on the wheel. There had to be a simple, logical explanation for the items in that box.

And maybe she would find it at the hay barn.

A white Mercedes SUV whizzed past, going in the opposite direction. Raine, she realized, glancing in her rearview. Was she on her way to visit Henry? Or heading somewhere else?

If Henry's, would he show her the box? The items inside? What would she think?

Bailey reached Abbott Farm, passed the barn. It looked deserted. The morning chores had all been completed and the ones associated with sundown were several hours away. She didn't see August's SUV, which was odd because he typically had training sessions during this time.

Bailey arrived at the house and ran in. She stripped out of her navy trousers and white blouse and into blue jeans and a T-shirt. After pulling her hair into a ponytail, she ran back out to the car.

Within a couple of minutes, she was in the barn. As she hoped, it was deserted. Even Paul's blue pickup was gone. She was grateful. She didn't want to have to explain any of this.

She'd never tacked up Tea Biscuit on her own, but she knew she could do it. She set to work. Bit. Bridle. Blanket. Saddle pad, then saddle. Cinch it tight. Adjust the stirrups. Double-check everything.

She let out a breath she hadn't realized she'd been holding, aware of time passing. The mare snorted softly, as if mimicking her.

"Good girl," she said, leading her out to the mounting platform. "We can do this, right? We'll do it together."

She mounted the mare and guided her toward the trail. Tea Biscuit seemed skittish, and Bailey wondered if she was picking up on her rider's nerves or if she simply wasn't in the mood.

You're in control, Bailey reminded herself. She couldn't give the mare an opportunity to think otherwise.

You can do this Bailey. You can.

She took it slow, even though her every instinct screamed to dig her heels in and urge Tea Biscuit to a gallop. She had never ridden the path between the barn and Henry's and the few extra minutes wouldn't make a difference. Especially since she was pregnant. Henry wasn't going anywhere, neither was the hay barn.

As they took the final curve that would bring them to Henry's, a sharp crack broke the quiet. She didn't have time to wonder what it was before a second reverberated through the forest.

Tea Biscuit whinnied and reared up. For a split second, Bailey was fifteen again, hanging on to the stallion's mane, crying out in terror as her boyfriend and his buddies had a good laugh at her expense.

But she wasn't a teenager anymore, she reminded herself. Bailey fought the panic, concentrating on every instruction August had ever shouted at her.

Within moments, she had the mare quieted and back under her control. Even though her hands were shaking, a feeling of power surged through her. Bailey laughed, momentarily forgetting Henry, the box with Logan's initials on it, the items inside, the hay barn and what she might find there. She had faced the very thing she had feared all these years—and beaten it.

"Good girl," she said, and dug her heels into the horse's side, increasing her pace to a trot.

The back of Henry's place came into view. His paddock. His old gelding, saddled and ready.

She trotted Tea Biscuit over to the other horse. There, she swiveled in the saddle, scanning the area. "Henry!" she called.

A thrashing came from the woods just beyond the property line. "Henry! Is that you?"

He didn't respond and she swung off Tea Biscuit, then led her into the paddock.

"Henry! Where are you?"

She stopped to listen. Instead of Henry's response, she heard the rumble of an engine, the sound of tires on the drive, kicking up gravel.

Fear sent her scrambling toward the thicket, shouting Henry's name. She found him on the ground, faceup, a gaping, bloody wound in his chest. His eyes were open. Unblinking.

"No!" The one word ripped from her lips and she ran blindly forward. She tripped on some exposed roots, landed on her knees and crawled the rest of the way to his body. She pressed her fingers to his neck, didn't pick up a pulse and bent close to his mouth. He wasn't breathing.

CPR. She had taken a course. She went to press her hands against his chest and stimulate his heart; they sank into the wound.

She yanked them back. Looked down at them. Blood. Everywhere. On her hands. Her shirt. Sobbing, she wiped her dripping hands on her jeans.

Bailey whimpered. She had to get help . . . Logan. Paul. Someone. She stumbled to her feet and raced back to the paddock, the waiting mare. In moments, she was on the trail, fear pounding in her veins, pushing the horse faster, harder.

Tears streamed down her cheeks. The sounds she'd heard earlier, gunshots, she realized. One. Then another. The sound of a vehicle in the drive. Spitting up gravel.

Who . . . why . . . sweet Henry. He'd never hurt a—

The box. A killer's trophies.

Not an accident.

The thought popped into her head. She looked over her shoulder, back toward the cabin. What if—

Pain ricocheted through her skull. Bailey felt herself flying through the air. In the next moment, she felt nothing at all.

CHAPTER SIXTY-SEVEN

Friday, April 25
9:45 A.M.

A buzzing jolted her back to the moment. Her phone, vibrating. She checked the display.

Raine.

She started to answer it, then stopped. She stared at the display, the name, heart thundering. Remembering. Raine passing her on the road, going toward Henry's.

"I should kill you. . . . I'm an excellent shot."

Raine had grown up on a farm. Hunting with her brothers. She'd said so.

Bailey brought a hand to her mouth. Henry had found Raine's box of trophies. She'd stopped to see him; he'd shown it to her. Told Raine about their talk. That they were going out to the hay barn.

Tears flooded her eyes. For Henry. Sweet, trusting Henry, who'd loved Raine, the daughter he had never been able to claim. She wouldn't have wanted to kill him, but must have felt she didn't have a choice.

Bailey thought back. She would have had time, traveling by car. To get her rifle, go back, kill Henry and take the box.

Bailey dialed Logan, then hung up when he didn't answer. Of course he hadn't, she thought. Besides, what did she think she was going to tell him? "And by the way, your sister's a serial killer"?

Her hands were shaking. Her head light. She sat on the front step and dropped her head into her hands.

Breathe, Bailey. In and out. Deep, and even.

She did, her heart slowed, but not her thoughts. Raine had killed Henry because he'd found her trophies and she'd had to keep him quiet. She'd probably planted the rifle at August's—and helped him overdose as well.

And what of True? Had she killed her? Out of jealousy? In a rage? Had all those things she told her about a pregnancy and a crazy mother been a lie?

No. Raine loved True. She loved her brother. She wouldn't, couldn't have done that.

"Bailey! Are you all right?"

She lifted her head. Paul hurrying toward her. Face puckered in concern.

"I saw the detectives leave, with Logan. What's going on?"

She jumped to her feet and ran to him. She threw her arms around him and held him tightly.

"My God, you're shaking like a leaf—"

"I've remembered what happened that day! I know who killed Henry, who killed those other women. I know!"

"Okay, slow down. I can hardly understand what you're—"

"She'll kill us, too, if she has to!"

"She? Who—"

"Raine. I saw her, on the road to Henry's . . . heard her leaving after. And the box was gone."

"Box? What box?"

"Her souvenirs, from each of the women. From killing them. Henry found it at the hay barn—"

"Bailey, do you realize what you're saying? It's crazy. How could Raine do all that?"

"I don't know how she did it . . . how she convinced the women to go with her or how she killed them, but—"

"Get ahold of yourself!" He gripped her shoulders, shook her. "Raine wouldn't hurt anyone, least of all Henry."

"But she did. You've got to believe me." She searched his gaze. "To protect her secret she did. Why do you think she was curled up in his bed, sobbing? It took hours and a sedative to get her calmed down. Not grief at having lost him. Guilt at having killed him!"

"Where were the police taking Logan? Was he arrested again?"

"No. Not yet. They were taking him in for more questioning. That's where we need to go."

He nodded. "I agree. I may think all this sounds farfetched, but I'm a little biased. Maybe you want to change? Don't want to sound crazy and look crazy."

She looked down. She was still in her drawstring pajama bottoms, T-shirt and robe, but didn't laugh at his attempt at humor. She wondered if she would ever laugh again.

"Where's Tony?" he asked.

"Locked up. In the study. The detectives threatened to shoot him."

"To shoot Tony?" He shook his head. "I'll get him."

Once upstairs, she rinsed her face, then went to her closet. She grabbed the first pair of trousers her gaze landed on. She yanked them off the hanger and pulled them on. They wouldn't zip.

The fact startled her still. Bailey looked at the button closure. A good half inch between the button and loop.

The baby. Growing so fast, she thought. Thriving despite all the chaos in her life. She'd just worn these—

She thought back. Recalled the day. At Billy Ray's. Looking at his "proof."

The three women from outside Wholesome.

She had scribbled their names on a scrap of paper. Tucked it into her pants' pocket.

She slipped her hand into the right trouser pocket. A slip of paper. The one from that day, at Billy Ray's.

She closed her fingers around it, drew it out.

Three names. The first on the list, Margaret Cassandra Martin.

Bailey shifted her gaze to her bedside table, her iPad on it. She hurried over, snatched it up. Googled Margaret Cassandra Martin. Her picture came up. The same picture that had been posted on Billy Ray's board. Along with a news story about her going missing. She skimmed the piece, finding what she had been looking for almost immediately.

Everyone called her Cassie.

"The girl Paul dated, what was her name?"

"Cassie, I think."

Fear settled on her chest like a sack of bricks. Paul. Not Raine. Paul, who had lived in Wholesome all his life, who was part of the very fabric of this family and life on the farm. No one would notice his truck coming or going, or his being in the barn or woods late at night.

What was she going to do?

Her phone. Where was— On the entryway table, she realized. She'd set it there after trying Logan.

She looked around for a way out. Jumping from the balcony would leave her incapacitated; screaming for help would reach no one's ears but Paul's.

Paul. He would be up any moment, wondering what was taking her so long. She tossed the tablet on the bed, then stopped. Looked at it.

Her iPad. An e-mail. Logan had set it all up for her,

though she'd yet to use it. She snatched it back up, fumbling, fingers tripping over themselves as she accessed the program.

"Bailey?" Paul, from the bottom of the stairs. "You almost ready?"

"Almost!" she called back. "Just a minute!"

She found Logan's address, clicked on it. He wouldn't get the e-mail in time. Not to save her or the baby. She fought back a sob. But Paul wouldn't get away with this. Never again.

Quickly, she typed *"Paul's the—"*

"What are you doing?"

"—one."

Before she could hit send, he was across the room, wrenching the tablet out of her hands. "No!" she cried, and lunged for it.

He swatted her aside, easily, as if she were no more than an insect. She fell against the dresser, the photos of her and her mother tumbled.

He turned on her. "Bitch! You couldn't mind your own business? You couldn't just leave everything the fuck alone? Now what am I going to do?"

"Just leave. Go away. I won't tell anyone about you."

He shook his head, lips curling in disgust. "Fat chance, sweetheart. Besides, this is *my* home."

Her vision blurred with tears. She took another small step backward. "Don't hurt my baby. Please. For Logan's sake."

"Don't you call his name to me. This is your fault." He all but spit the last at her. Gone was any resemblance to the charming boy-next-door she'd thought him to be. "You brought this all on yourself."

"I'm sorry. It won't happen again." Tears squeezed from the corners of her eyes.

"You're right about that."

Bailey spun around and darted for the door. "Tony!" she screamed. "Come, boy! Come!"

Paul caught her, dragged her back, one arm at her middle, the other at her throat. She clawed at the latter, struggling to breathe.

"Tony's taking a little nap right now," he whispered against her ear. "But don't worry, he'll be fine."

She fought bursting into tears. She had figured Tony was her only chance. Now she had nothing.

Paul half dragged, half carried her to the walk-in closet. "This is my family, Bailey. Mine. I protect them."

He suddenly released her and she nearly fell, stumbling into the hanging clothes, grabbing at them for support, gasping for air.

No sooner was it filling her lungs than he had her on her knees, wrenching her arms behind her back. Securing her wrists with one of Logan's ties. A basic blue, one Logan wouldn't notice was missing. Especially when all he'd be able to think about was where she might be. Tears stung her eyes and she blinked against them.

No. She had to concentrate on the moment and finding a way out of this.

With another tie, he secured her ankles, cinching it so tightly her feet immediately began to tingle.

"How does killing innocent women help this family?" she asked, voice shaking.

"That's me. It doesn't have anything to do with this family." He laughed softly, the sound affecting her like nails on a chalkboard. "Plus, you presume those women were innocent. I can assure you they were not."

"Nothing to do with them? Then why's Logan being questioned in connection to those murders right now?"

"They've got nothing."

"Your box of trophies."

"I'd wondered if Henry showed it to you." He straightened, looked down at her, his hands on his hips. "Police don't have it. I do."

His words rocked her. "But how? Henry—"

"Idiot told me he'd been out there, to the hay barn. I immediately went to check on them and found they were gone. They were mine, Bailey. He had no right to take them."

"He was just a sweet, simple old man. Why'd you kill him? He didn't know what it was."

"I couldn't take the chance he'd tell anyone. But apparently, the damage had already been done." He looked at his watch, then back down at her.

"The police know about the box. They'll keep looking—"

He cut her off. "They do know. Stephanie told them all about it." He laughed at her expression. "I have a friend in the sheriff's office. Anything even remotely associated with Abbott Farm, she passes along.

"I should have planted them at August's when I killed him, but I didn't want to give them up. I earned them."

She felt sick. She fought the wave of nausea back. "You killed August, too. Why?"

"He saw the rifle in the back of my truck and was stupid enough to ask me about it. I made something up, but I couldn't take the chance he'd mention it to the wrong person."

"But now that the sheriff's office knows about the box they'll be looking for it. They'll—"

"They'll nothing. Stephanie repeated what you told her. And you'll be long gone. Big deal. You lied. Women lie."

He said it with such disdain, as if women were the lowest form of life.

He pursed his lips. "The question is," he said, "what

to do with you?" He looked around, made a sound of exasperation. "I didn't expect this to happen today. But when you went off about your memory returning and all that nonsense about Raine being a killer, you forced my hand."

He sent her a look that communicated complete loathing.

"Why do you hate me, Paul?"

"I don't. I liked you, Bailey. Until you got nosy. In the garage that day, I saw it."

"It?"

"The red shoe. You tried to hide it from me, but you were acting so guilty." As he talked, his gaze moved over the room, as if it might provide him with an answer of what to do with her. "You're the worst liar ever."

"And you're the best."

"Thank you."

"I didn't mean it as a compliment."

"Your mistake. One of many."

While he talked, she worked to free her hands. Subtle movements, straining against the silk fabric, twisting. She began to sweat. Her hands and wrists became slippery.

"I knew what you were thinking, that the shoe might have been True's. You were wondering if Logan killed her." He made a sound of disgust. "Another faithless woman. I don't know why I'm always surprised. They're all the same, whether they're your mother or lover—"

"Or best friend's wife."

"Stop talking. I need to think."

Which meant that was the last thing she needed to do. *He wouldn't kill her in the house.*

But he didn't know where to take her. Or how to do it.

"Whose shoe was it?"

"Trista's. She liked to dress trashy. It was such a pretty night that night. The pond seemed the perfect spot."

The matter-of-fact way he relayed it, like a pleasant trip down memory lane, sent a chill up her spine. "Let me go, Paul. I'll disappear, you'll never hear from me again."

He laughed. "I believe that. The moment you're out of my sight, you're squealing like a stuck pig."

"I only care about the baby," she pleaded. "Me and the baby, we disappear. We—"

"Not happening. I won't let you hurt Logan."

"But this will hurt him!" Her wrists burned, each movement agony. "You love him, Paul. So turn yourself in—"

"And be tried for murder one? Be executed? You're out of your mind."

"You plead guilty, tell them everything, give the girls' families closure in exchange for—"

"Life in prison? No, thank you."

"This is over. You've got to see that."

"Where are your suitcases?"

He snapped his fingers in front of her face. "Your suitcases."

"In the attic."

"Which ones are yours? What color and brand? And don't bullshit me."

"Why do you want to know? Please," she begged. "Just tell me that."

"You're going to disappear, Bailey. Just like you wanted."

But not the way she had meant. She really wouldn't see anyone ever again.

"But I'm going to do it right. Unlike Billy Ray. The idiot."

"What do you mean, unlike Billy Ray?"

"He killed True." At her obvious surprise, he laughed. "The boy who cried wolf. My friend at the sheriff's passed that one along as well. He confessed this morning."

He shook his head in disgust. "Of course, Billy Ray

swears it was an accident. I'm sure it was, he was infatu-
ated with her. It was pathetic.

"Tried to pin her death on my meticulous work. It was
all staged—the car, her phone." He shook his head. "But
he hadn't known about the hotel room or money."

Bailey struggled to come to grips with what he was
telling her. He hadn't killed True. Her disappearance was
linked to the others, but not in the way anyone would
have guessed. "All along, you really did think she'd left
Logan?"

He nodded. "I was so angry at her. I feel kind of bad
about that now. Anyway, *I'm* going to do it right. Nobody's
going to wonder what happened. You left Logan. Took all
your stuff. You suspected him of murder. His family was
crazy. Guilty or innocent, you'd had enough."

"Nobody will believe it."

He laughed. "Everyone will believe it. Suitcases, what
color?"

"I'm not going to tell you."

"Whatever, it's not going to matter."

He started out of the closet, she stopped him. "Wait!
How'd you do it? The missing women?"

"Easy. Asked them if they wanted to party."

And they said yes.

"Then I incapacitated them with my own little cock-
tail of horse tranqs. See, all that schooling didn't go to
waste."

"But you quit. Because you couldn't hack it."

Angry color flooded his face and she realized she had
pushed a very dangerous button. "Who told you that?
Raine? Stephanie? That's what Cassie said, too. Before she
broke up with me. But she paid. They all did."

Women. He hated them. Starting with his mother.
Bailey took a stab. "Even Logan's mother, right? How did
she betray you, Paul?"

It was his turn to look surprised. "How do you know that?"

"You were on the boat that night. You pushed her off, didn't you?"

"I wanted to comfort her, that's all. I loved her, but she"—his voice hardened—"rejected me. Told me to go away. Leave her alone. The same as mine always had. Another whore."

The tie seemed to be loosening. Just a little more and she might be able to slip a hand out.

Bailey worked to steady her voice. "That's a big stretch, don't you think? She was a whore because she wanted to be alone after a fight with her husband?"

"She was having an affair! Cheating on Logan's dad with Henry. A groom, for God's sake! I heard them. In the barn. Whispering together. Doing . . . things. It was vile."

Henry and Elisabeth.

"I saw my opportunity. And I took it."

"That night on the boat?"

"No, in the barn that day. The stallion. He was already agitated. I was so angry at her, all it took was a well-aimed pebble."

He'd orchestrated the accident that had disfigured Henry.

"You son of a bitch!"

They both looked toward the doorway. Raine stood in it, face pinched white with rage.

She held a gun, had pointed it at Paul's head. "You killed my mother."

The blood drained from his face. "Where did you come from?"

"Everything that's happened since she died . . . Daddy and Roane, everything . . . it's your fault. You destroyed my family."

"You need me, Raine. Logan needs me. I'm the glue that holds us together."

"I'm going to kill you, Paul. For what you did."

"C'mon, Raine. You know you can't do this. You're not strong enough."

Bailey thought otherwise. The woman's hands were steady as a rock.

"Logan was on to you," she said. "After talking to Bailey last night, he came to the conclusion that those trophies had belonged to someone very familiar with Abbott Farm. Someone who had twenty-four-hour access. Someone who had been here all along. That left two people. Me. And you."

"You're lying."

"He told me he was going in to talk to Rumsfeld this morning and asked me to watch out for Bailey. When she didn't answer the phone, I came over. Prepared. Which is more than I can say for you."

With a howl of rage, he charged. Raine pulled the trigger. The shot reverberated through the room.

Paul stopped, looking confused.

"That's for my mom," she said. She pulled the trigger again. "And that's for my dad. Both of them."

Still he didn't go down. Raine took a step toward him, pulled the trigger again. "And that one's for Roane, you son of a bitch."

He went down. Bailey heard the scream of sirens. Raine must have, too, but she crossed to stand directly over him. His eyes were open. Each shallow breath he took made a gurgling sound.

"Stop, Raine," Bailey said. "He can't hurt us now. Please just put the gun down. Please."

Raine shook her head, adjusted her aim. "He's a monster. He deserves to die."

"Raine—"

"And that's for August," she said, squeezing the trigger. "And these . . . are for me."

She fired again and again, emptying the chamber, then let the gun slip from her fingers. It hit the floor with a thud just as Rumsfeld, Carlson and a half-dozen other sheriff's deputies burst into the room.

EPILOGUE

Bailey came awake to a tiny, insistent whimpering. She cracked open her eyes. The bright light stung them and she blinked, moving her gaze. Taking in the bed with its stainless steel rails and scratchy sheets. The hospital, she remembered. She'd come in last night.

"Merry Christmas, sweetheart."

Logan in the chair by the bed. A pink bundle in his arms.

"Merry Christmas." She smiled. "How is she?"

"They just brought her in. Hungry, I think. Rooting around for something I can't help with."

Bailey raised the bed and held out her arms. A moment later he carefully laid Lizzie in her arms, then bent and kissed her. "Best Christmas present ever."

She was. Pink and perfect. They'd named her Elisabeth after his mother; if she'd been a boy, they'd have chosen his father's name.

Bailey gazed at her as she nursed, only able to drag her gaze away to look at her husband. To drink in his joy.

In the months since Paul's death, there had been some dark days. Days so deep and black Bailey had worried he might not emerge.

As the bodies had been unearthed. When they had

realized most of their questions would never be answered: Why those young women? How had Paul killed them? Had Paul strangled them, the way he had Nicole Grace? Had they fought for their lives, or had the tranquilizers he'd administered stolen their ability? Had Abbott Farm been the scene of the crimes or simply a place for Paul to bury his dead?

The sheriff's office had found traces of blood, revealed by Luminol, in the washtub and dryer in the barn; and in the medicine closet every equine sedative available. And ketamine. Bailey had wondered, that late night she went looking for Logan at the barn, when Paul had acted so strange about that room, had Paul been disposing of evidence?

Another thing they would never know.

The darkest day had come with True's remains being identified. Then, her funeral, which all of Wholesome had turned out for. When Billy Ray had given his statement in court, never apologizing, still blaming Logan in his own twisted mind.

Ironic that Billy Ray had been right about so much. Everything but the guilty party. The victims, Logan's mother's death, the location of the bodies. Everything but the guilty party. His hatred of Logan—and his own troubled past—had blinded him to the real destroyer.

Then Logan had cried out to her, heart stripped bare, begging to know how to forgive, how to move on and start over. Her reply had been simple: one day at a time.

So that's what they all had concentrated on. Not on Paul, who had been a dark force destroying their lives from within, but on the moment. The song of birds and rustle of leaves, burgeoning baby bumps and the smell of cookies baking. Silly dog antics and long, drugging kisses.

Every so often the darkness still descended, though the times between such episodes grew longer.

At the tap on the door they both looked up. Raine with a huge teddy bear and Stephanie with flowers. Both beaming with happiness.

"Can we come in?"

In the next minute, the room was filled with exclamations of joy. While the two women cooed over Lizzie, Bailey met Logan's eyes. In them she no longer saw shadows of the past. Instead, she saw the future. Their future, bright and beautiful.